Maggie Furey was born in north-east England. She is a qualified teacher but has also reviewed books on BBC Radio Newcastle, been an adviser in the Durham Reading Resources Centre and organised children's book fairs. Her debut fantasy series, The Artefacts of Power, rapidly established her as one of the most exciting new fantasy writers to emerge in recent years. She lives in County Wicklow with her husband and two cats.

Find out more about Maggie Furey and other Orbit authors by registering for the free monthly newsletter at
www.orbitbooks.co.uk

D0041232

MAGGIE FUREY
THE HEART OF MYRIAL

BOOK ONE OF THE SHADOWLEAGUE

www.orbitbooks.co.uk

ORBIT

First published in Great Britain by Orbit 1999
This edition published by Orbit 2000
Reprinted 2004, 2006

Copyright © Maggie Furey 1999

The moral right of the author has been asserted.

Map by Neil Hyslop

A CIP catalogue record for this book
is available from the British Library.

ISBN-13: 978-1-85723-971-3
ISBN-10: 1- 85723-971-7

Typeset by Palimpsest Book Production Limited,
Polmont, Stirlingshire
Printed and bound in Great Britain by
Mackays of Chatham plc, Chatham, Kent

Orbit
An imprint of
Little, Brown Book Group
Brettenham House
Lancaster Place
London WC2E 7EN

A member of the Hachette Livre Group of Companies

www.orbitbooks.co.uk

This book is dedicated, with love, to my parents,
Jim and Margaret Armstrong,
who never let me run short of books to read.

SEA OF ICE

LAND OF WINTERTHRONE

*Labyrinth

GHARIAD
(Land of the
Ak'Zahar)

LIATRIS

Tiarond

Valley of
Two Lakes

CALLISIORA

GENDIVAL

CLOUD
MOUNTAINS
(Home of
the Angels)

KAHIKATEA
(Land of the Gaeorn)

ISLAND OF ISSHERA
(Land of the Centaurs
and the Wind-Sprites)

NEMERIS
(Land of the Otterfolk
and the Selkie)

FEL KARIVIT
(Land of the Alvai)

FOREST OF RAKHA

ZALTAIGLA
(Land of the Dragonfolk)

DESERT

FIRELANDS

Curtain walls

ONE

WITHOUT A MIRACLE . . .

L eather was dreadful stuff to wear in the rain. It stiffened, it smelled, it mildewed. It took *forever* to dry out and, worst of all, it clung to the body in a clammy, chill embrace, like the clasp of a long-drowned corpse. Veldan shuddered at the revolting image. An overactive imagination had always been her curse. With a shake of her head, the Loremaster took herself to task and thrust the disgusting notion from her mind. I'm letting these bleak and sombre mountains get to me, she thought, not to mention the bedamned weather. Rain, rain, and still more rain – it had never let up once during this clandestine crossing of the land of Callisiora.

Although she could do nothing about her leather clothing – all the garments in her pack were equally soaked by now – Veldan could at least take off the mask. There was no one to see her up in this forsaken spot. She reached behind her head, pushing her short black hair aside, and fumbled for the silver clasps securing the black silk concealing her face. It peeled away like a second skin. She sighed with relief as the fresh air cooled her brow and cheeks.

'About time, too,' her partner grumbled. 'Just wait – one day you'll leave that cursed contraption where I can get at it,

1

and I'll *eat* the wretched thing.' Kazairl turned his head all the way round on his long sinuous neck and looked back at his rider. Veldan could see a sharp red gleam of irritation within the fire-opal depths of his eyes.

'Leave me alone, Kaz,' Veldan sighed. 'You don't understand – it's a human thing. People don't want to look at my disfigured face, and I don't want them to see it. I don't want their disgust – or their pity.'

'Tchaaaa!' the firedrake snorted. 'Anybody dares pity you, and I'll eat *them*. You don't need that ridiculous thing on your face, Boss. Your scar is healing all the time – or it would if you'd let the air get to it. You don't look near as bad as you think. Besides, every time I see that damnable mask it makes me feel guilty – and it takes a lot to make a firedrake guilty. If I had only been there that day, you'd have been all right.'

'Kaz – don't,' Veldan told him hastily. They had shared this old pain too many times. 'We Loremasters understand the risks of our work, and I only have myself to blame. If *I* had moved faster that day, it never would have happened. Anyway, it's over now. We should be concentrating on this journey, not the last one that ended so badly.'

'That would all be very well,' Kazairl muttered sourly, 'if this mission was going any better than the last.'

'You're right,' Veldan sighed. 'Our bad luck's proving harder to shake off than a dockside tavern's fleas.' Along with Kaz and Aethon, the Seer of the Dragonfolk, she had penetrated the Curtain Walls – the barriers of magical force that separated realm from realm – over a month ago, and had been crossing rainy Callisiora ever since. 'Sometimes I wonder if we're ever going to make it home.'

'We'd damn well better!' Kaz snorted. 'I'm not staying in this miserable excuse for a country a moment longer than I have to. I'm sick to death of avoiding a bunch of ignorant, superstitious primitives who don't know that anything exists beyond the Curtain Walls, and who have no better sense than to confuse our world of Myrial with some sort of all-powerful god they've invented. Yet half the stupid idiots don't believe that I exist, despite the evidence of their own eyes. *They* think I'm a figment of imagination, while the other half are sure I'm just a ravenous monster.'

'You *are* a ravenous monster,' the Loremaster reminded him drily.

'I am now,' the firedrake agreed glumly. 'Between the rain and the floods, there's been precious little here to eat for any of us.'

At his words, Veldan glanced across at her other travelling companion, the Seer whom she had sworn to guard, nurture and protect. It seemed increasingly doubtful that he would survive this journey.

Aethon looked ghastly. He trudged along as though he barely had the strength to put one foot before the other on the steep and stony mountain track. It must be a dreadful strain on the dragon, she thought, to support and propel such a massive body, almost as long as a village street. His scaly form, once the brilliant, glittering gold of the ring that Veldan wore on a chain around her neck, was now the dull, pallid yellow-white of wheatstraw.

The Loremaster's heart was filled with dread and anguish at the thought of losing the dragon, and not simply because of the urgency of her mission. During this long, hard journey, Aethon had become very dear to her. Because he was the Seer of the Dragonfolk, she had been expecting a venerable creature: formal, imposing and staid. Instead she had found a dragon who was still fairly young as his species reckoned

3

their span. He had been delightful company for most of the journey, despite the heavy burdens of his calling, and his humour, intelligence and joy in life had shortened the long hard miles. Once they had entered Callisiora, however, the weather had deteriorated to this dank and dismal chill. Because they were forced to keep to the wilderness to avoid the humans, the going became cruelly and unremittingly hard. Each day Aethon's verve and spirit had been drained a little more, and the Loremaster, her heart breaking, had been unable to do anything but witness his long, slow demise. Now the Seer had reached the end of his endurance. He had not spoken a word all day, either in the telepathic mode used by Loremasters or in normal Dragon speech, which consisted of complex interwoven patterns of coloured, moving light mingling with mellifluous and plangent sound. Veldan knew Aethon was conserving his energy, just to keep going.

'He don't look too promising, does he, Boss? I doubt, myself, he'll make it.'

'Shhhh, Kaz,' Veldan chided, even though she knew her partner was thinking in their private mode and there was no way that Aethon should be able to 'overhear' them.

'What for? Poor deeg's so far gone he wouldn't notice if you let off a plasma cluster in his ear.' The slumbrous glow of Kaz's eyes took on a wicked glitter. 'Now, there's an idea . . .'

'It's a better idea than you realise.' Veldan had the pleasure of seeing the firedrake's jaw drop in astonishment. As usual, he had been out to shock her – and he didn't fail that often. 'Poor Aethon feeds on the sun's energy, as well you know,' the Loremaster went on. 'A plasma cluster in his ear might be a little too close for comfort, but if you let one off in his vicinity, it might be just the tonic he needs. I would

4

have thought,' she added reprovingly, 'that you'd have more sympathy, considering.'

'Just because we come from the same branch of the evolutionary tree,' Kaz chanted, every tilt of his long, elegant head expressive of his mockery. 'Tchaaaa!' His snort of disgust came out as an explosive hiss, like escaping steam. 'The Dragonfolk decided they were too damned cerebral and highly evolved to eat meat, and so they developed in a different way – then had the gall to look down their snouts at *my* primitive, lowly race! Well, see where their ridiculous snobbery has got them now!'

Veldan bit back the blistering scold that sprang to mind. It wouldn't discourage him in the least. Besides, she and Kaz had been partners for almost a decade. She understood why he was so jealous of the Seer of the Dragonfolk, and surprisingly, it had nothing to do with Aethon's unique ability to send his mind wandering through the pathless mists of time to catch tantalising glimpses of the future – sometimes vague, but sometimes cruelly clear. Kaz understood that to be so loosely anchored in time could prove more of a bane than a blessing. Aethon had scant control over what he saw. Sometimes the mists that hid the future would part to reveal the information he sought, but more often the visions were unconnected, or so obscure as to be indecipherable. Also, the dragon's talent isolated him from others. No one wanted to get close to a creature who might have intimate knowledge of their future – bad deeds as well as good – not to mention the time and circumstances of their death. The converse was also true: Aethon had learned the hard way to avoid close friendships. The sure but secret knowledge of the time remaining to a loved one was too much to bear. Truly, the Seer had paid dearly for his gift. In all their travels, the

Loremasters had never seen such a profoundly lonely creature as the dragon.

Though the firedrake had no urge to share the Seer's gifts, and knew better than to be jealous, Veldan was aware that he was slightly irked by her fondness for the dragon, for while they had travelled together, she had come closer to Aethon than most. She also knew that Kaz could not help but envy the dragon's splendour. For one thing, Aethon was three times the size of Kazairl, who measured only about eighteen feet from nose to tail. For another, the dragon, at least in better times, shone a lustrous gold, whereas Kaz's scales held a medley of softly gleaming metallic hues that could be altered at will to blend in with any surroundings. In truth, Veldan thought her friend's subtle, ever changing coloration far more beautiful, but she had no more luck convincing Kaz of that than he had in trying to persuade her to get rid of her mask.

Most important of all, Kaz bitterly envied the dragon his wings, those vast, translucent golden sails, ribbed like bat-wings and spangled with darker, gleaming scales connected by a network of slender silver veining. It was a tragedy that those same wings would probably be the indirect cause of the dragon's death, Veldan thought sadly. Lacking the energy of sunlight that the broad surfaces needed to absorb, Aethon was slowly starving. Because of the climatic upheavals in the last few months, his people were close to suffering the same fate. The Seer was on his way to Gendival, the Loremaster headquarters, to confer with Cergorn, Senior Loremaster of the Shadowleague. It was Veldan's duty to ensure that he got there safely.

During the previous night they had used the cover of darkness to sneak undetected past Tiarond, Callisiora's capital. Veldan was glad she'd been unable to see the place this time around. She doubted that the current climatic conditions had been kind to the city or its inhabitants. She preferred to remember it as she had known it last: austerely beautiful, with sloping streets zigzagging between steep terraces carved into the mountainside, the enclosing walls, the towers and the greater buildings all crafted with care and skill from the warm golden stone so common in this area.

She sighed. They were so close to success now, but still so far away. If we can just make it over the Snaketail Pass, Veldan thought, we'll only have another day and night's travel – and we'll be home. Aethon can confer with my masters, as he came all this way to do. Maybe the climate in Gendival will be better . . .

'Veldan, can we rest a while?' The dragon's mental tones sounded faint and faded.

Damn, thought Veldan. It was hard to guess the hour because of the heavy overcast, but she knew the sun must be at least an hour or two past the zenith. They *had* to make it over the top of the pass and into shelter on the other side before night set in! In framing a reply, she tried to soften the brutal truth – that if they let him stop now, he would never move again. 'I'm sorry, Aethon, but you must try to go a little further. We've come so far now – it's only another mile or two. Once we make the head of the pass, we'll rest, I promise.'

'Very well – I'll try. I bow to your experience.' The dragon's thought was accompanied by a weary sigh, and Veldan felt her heart clench with pity.

They had almost reached the treeline now, and were passing into the heavy layer of cloud that smothered the high peaks. Veldan shivered again. The Snaketail Pass was never the most wholesome of spots, but this time it seemed positively eerie. Great jagged cliffs reared up on either side, and the track, climbing more steeply than ever, had narrowed to a winding thread between two dark, unyielding walls. Because of the steeper gradient, Veldan slid off Kaz's back and went ahead on foot, with the Seer following behind her. The firedrake brought up the rear, for the larger dragon was having difficulty squeezing through the narrow places in the track. If he became trapped, he would need Kaz's help to free himself.

An icy gale rushed down the narrow gap, bringing with it rain squalls hard as hailstones, as though water and air had been compressed between two giant hands. The wind moaned and screamed as it tore through the constricted space, and the hideous lament was echoed and re-echoed by the cliffs above, the wailing of all the lost souls who had lost their lives in this harsh and hazardous place . . .

'Bat crap!' Kaz's sharp thought made her flinch. 'Forget about lost souls, Boss – unless you want to join them, that is. Worry about the water instead. Can't you hear it?'

Only then did the Loremaster realise that the sounds she'd been hearing did not all come from the restless wind. Below the shriek of the gale was a deeper, hollow roar. Veldan muttered a savage curse. Somewhere up ahead, a deluge of floodwater was racing down the narrow trail. At any moment, a great wall of water would come thundering down the track and sweep them all away.

'Tchaaaa!' Kaz's scornful snort almost made her jump out of her skin. 'Honest – you and your imagination! Your brain is rusting in this rain. We won't be swept anywhere, sweetie. If a flash flood comes down here, our big friend will stick like a cork in a bottle. You'll get nothing worse than a bruise or two and a soaking, and me – well, I doubt I'll even get my toes wet!'

The firedrake snickered, and Veldan sighed. The dragon was between them, so Kaz was too far away to be hit. In any case, she knew from bitter experience and a vast collection of bruised toes and skinned knuckles that her blows had no effect on his scaly hide, just as her threats and protests made no impression on his scathing tongue and wicked sense of humour. Though he often called her 'Boss', their partnership was founded on equality and mutual respect; he only used the word as a kind of pet name, to boost her confidence when she was feeling low. Exasperating as he was, she loved him dearly.

They had reached a part of the pass where the crags to the right of the cutting sloped back from the road less steeply. Far above the trail, the last of the pinewoods clung precariously to the precipitous gradient. Even now, some of them were leaning at odd angles, as the soil was gradually washed away from between their roots by the incessant rain . . . Veldan shuddered. This place was a deathtrap. How long would it be before the landslides started? *How long?*

Another turn of the trail brought them to the source of the roaring sound. Veldan gasped with dismay. Even Kaz was without a glib-tongued comment. On the left-hand side, where the track curved sharply, a break in the escarpment led down into a narrow gorge that sloped, steep and straight, to the bottom of the ridge. That gap was the luckiest thing that had happened to her in a long time, Veldan thought wryly. The torrent, cascading from the watershed above, took the straightest route down, and left the trail to form a new river that filled the bottom of the gully with churning brown floodwater. Veldan stepped back, swallowing to clear the ringing in her ears. This near, the roar was close to deafening.

'Well, the good news is that we weren't swept away,' Kaz said laconically. 'But the bad news is that we have to wade through this deluge from here on up . . .'

'Pox on it! Will this bad luck *never* leave us?' To her horror,

Veldan found her sight of the flooded track obscured by a misty haze as her eyes filled with tears of angry frustration. To make matters worse, she knew that her old self – the one who had existed before her recent brush with death – would have taken these difficulties in her stride. Maybe Cergorn was right after all, she thought. I'm not ready yet. I shouldn't have taken this mission. Her reasoning – that she must get back into action as soon as possible, or she would lose her nerve – seemed feeble and futile now.

'Come on, sweetie . . .' Kaz's voice was surprisingly gentle and Veldan realised, with a guilty pang, that he was concerned about her – and had probably been worried ever since she had volunteered them for this assignment, so soon after their last disastrous journey. The firedrake's words, as always, braced her. 'We Loremasters spit in the eye of bad luck,' he reminded her. 'The fates won't shit on us forever. So long as we don't let this string of calamities beat us, our fortunes are bound to change in the end.'

Dear Kaz. What would I do without him? Veldan kept her thought strictly to herself. Their odd relationship was strong enough to prosper and endure without such overt displays of sentiment. 'Very philosophical,' she told him. 'Now I know we're *really* in trouble.'

Kaz flicked his forked tongue lazily across his jaws, his firedrake version of a leering grin. 'Your call, Boss – you want to try for it, or shall we go back down?'

Veldan shrugged. 'We try.' In truth, they had no choice. There was no other way across these mountains and if they retreated, they had automatically failed. The Seer would die of starvation in these barbaric, hostile lands. There remained a slim chance that dragon and drake would be strong enough to breast the floods and somehow gain the crest of the ridge before Aethon's strength gave out completely.

Pull yourself together, Veldan. We can do this. The Loremaster wiped rain out of her eyes, and made a careful assessment of the situation. About twenty yards ahead, the cliffs closed in and the trail narrowed again. The pent-up floodwater poured through this constricted space with considerable force, and she knew that Aethon would find it difficult to combat the pressure of the icy cascade. Where she currently stood, however, the trail was wide enough to allow some room for manoeuvre . . .

'Kaz – you squeeze around the Seer and get in front. I'll need you to break trail, and take the brunt of the current . . .'

'No problem.' The firedrake began to inch past Aethon's recumbent bulk. 'I'll take you too, Boss – and don't give me a hard time. You might put a good face on it, but I know you're not fit yet. You couldn't fight the force of that torrent any more than Aethon.'

Instinctively, Veldan wanted to protest, but there was no point. He was right. She turned to the dragon. 'Aethon? Aethon! Can you hear me?' If he was this far gone already . . .

'I . . . I hear you, Veldan . . .' The thought was no more than a whisper. 'Do not fear. I can continue . . .'

'It's not far now,' Veldan tried to encourage him. 'Just this one last stretch. Follow Kaz – and let me know if you get into difficulties.'

'Fear not. I will.'

By this time, Kaz was in position. The firedrake's long, slender, low-slung body was humped in a half-crouch by the edge of the torrent where the floodwater ran across the angle of the trail and plummeted down into the gorge. Though his face was expressionless, his tail switched jerkily back and forth to emphasise his distaste. Despite his reptilian appearance, Kaz was a warm-blooded creature and felt the cold as acutely as his human partner. He turned to regard her, and dipped his head in the firedrake equivalent of a shrug. 'Wet feet from here, sweetie – but not for you. Hop aboard.'

Veldan placed her booted foot just above the angled elbow of Kaz's foreleg and clasped the final spine of his neck crest as she clambered up to perch herself on his shoulders. As she swung herself up, a white-hot stab of pain seared through her left shoulder and arm. Would these wounds never heal properly? Though the scars seemed to be knitting well on the surface, the Ak'Zahar had used poisoned weapons, and the far-reaching effects of the venom had lasted an unnervingly long time.

'Ready, Boss?' Again, there was that dark shade of worry in Kaz's thoughts. Veldan knew he had sensed her pain, but knew better than to mention it.

'Let's go.' The Loremaster held tightly to Kaz's neck crest as his undulating stride swung her forward, and they set out up the final, flooded stretch of the track. Veldan heard Kaz hiss as he entered the swirling, freezing water, then the sound was drowned by a low, ominous rumble that seemed to emanate from the very rocks all around them.

There was barely time to look around. From the corner of her eye, Veldan glimpsed the sloping earth of the mountainside above her sliding forward in a huge rolling wave like a shaken quilt, then the surging wall of mud, water and trees was upon them. She tightened her grip on Kaz's neck as the firedrake tried to leap forward out of danger, then a massive concussion knocked the breath from her body. She felt herself being torn away from her partner, fighting in vain for breath as her mouth and nose clogged with wet, sticky mud. A vast roaring darkness swept Veldan away, hurling and tumbling her like a rag doll as though a giant hand had cast her aside. Instinctively, she tried to curl herself up tightly to reduce the risk of broken limbs, and tried vainly to protect her head with her arms. There was nothing else she could do – apart from one final, desperate gamble.

Through the midst of the pain and panic, Veldan arrowed a single, concentrated ray of thought towards her home: Gendival, the Valley of Two Lakes, the heart of the Shadow-league. It was all she could hope to project at such a tremendous distance, a single, desperate cry for help. It was the only thing she could do – and the last. Unconsciousness, when it came, was almost a blessing.

About a league back down the mountain trail from the Snaketail Pass, the faint vibration of the earthslide passed unnoticed in the city of Tiarond. People there had far too many problems of their own to care about nature's vagaries in the world outside.

Tiarond was nestled within a loop of the river, between two protective spurs of Mount Chaikar, or the Throne, in local parlance. The city clung to the mountain's face, forming a roughly triangular shape that followed the natural lie of the concavity between the two converging spurs. At the apex, high up where the spurs converged, was a narrow cleft, not much wider than Kazairl was long, that formed a tunnel into a secret, sequestered gorge embraced by towering cliffs. This heart-shaped canyon was the core of Tiarond, and housed the Temple of Myrial and the Holy City of the God.

Within the Temple of Myrial, shadows stalked the immense and lofty chamber, gathering between the pools of lamplight that played on gold and glittering gems torn from the heart of the surrounding mountains. Zavahl crept forward down the long, pillared aisle, feeling dwarfed, for the first time in his life, by the size and splendour of the building that was rightfully his home. He despised himself for his weakness. At no time in his life had he ever been afraid of his God. After all, what had *he* to fear? He had been born into the role of Hierarch, Priest-King of Callisiora, and had put on his powers and responsibilities with his swaddling clothes. He was Myrial's representative on earth, the most powerful man in the realm, but now, as he approached the heart of the Temple and the Holy of Holies, he found himself quaking, as weak-kneed as the most primitive and superstitious of peasants as he paused for a moment before the great screen of silver lattice that concealed the Sanctorium of the Eye.

Through the intricate lacework, Zavahl could see the shadowed entrance to the Holy of Holies, where the great Eye of Myrial communicated the God's wishes to his Hierarch. Once, by looking into it, the Priest-King could have seen everything that was happening in his land. Now it remained dark and dead to him, another guilty secret of his heart. Only the Hierarch himself was permitted to enter the mystical presence of the Eye. So far, no one else was aware that it would no longer awake to his touch. But how much longer could he keep his failure hidden?

Zavahl was at his wits' end, and becoming increasingly afraid. For more than half a year, the sun had failed to penetrate the heavy layer of dark cloud that shrouded the dying city and the lands beyond. For months it had rained without ceasing. Rivers had burst their banks, and most low-lying areas of Callisiora were lost beneath floodwaters that had swept away crops, houses and people alike.

In Tiarond, food and fabrics were rotting, houses coated inside and out with fungus and foul mould. Crops had remained unplanted and unharvested in the morass that had once been fair and fertile townlands in the valley. Farmbeasts and their young were drowning where they fell or dying of starvation or disease, as were an increasing number of the townsfolk. Sickness was spreading like wildfire. Violence and terror stalked the streets like predator and prey, while grief and hardship overhung the city in a pall as dark as the lowering clouds. All over the city of Tiarond, all over the realm of Callisiora, the suffering people were looking to Zavahl for help. It was up to him to intercede for them with the God – but he could not. Clearly, Myrial was displeased with His servant. This calamity is my fault, Zavahl thought bleakly. Somehow, I have failed.

Would he fail again today? The Hierarch stooped to take off his shoes, and removed from his brow the slender diadem with the single crimson stone denoting his rank. Barefoot and bareheaded, he took a deep breath, slid the silver filigree panel aside, and stepped through the dark, forbidding portal.

Even after thirty years, the immense black vault, larger even than the temple itself, still came as a surprise. The first time Zavahl had been forced to venture beyond the doorway, he had been a little boy of five scant years. He remembered his dread, knowing he must go alone, as the Hierarch always was alone, into that dreadful, mysterious place, forbidden to all save himself, to confront his God face to face. Even at that age, he had been too proud to cry, but he remembered shaking so hard that he could barely stand. The priests – some hard-faced and harsh, like old Malacht who had reared him, others firm but sympathetic – had opened the silver panels and pushed him through. Awed as always by the vast, echoing grandeur of the Temple, he had somehow expected the Holy of Holies, hidden behind its delicate silver screens, to be a small and secret place. The initial shock and reverence of his first step into Myrial's dark core had remained with him throughout his life.

His feet now sure from many years of walking this path, Zavahl stepped out into the dark emptiness beyond the portal. The silence was so profound that it roared in his ears, like the murmur of the blood in his veins, or the sound of the sea caught in a shell. Even the soft whispering shuffle of his footsteps was lost, swallowed up in the immensity of the void. Putting one foot before the other with profound concentration, the Hierarch walked carefully forward. Darkness or no, he knew he was crossing a bridge, a slender shallow arch without kerbstone or rail that sprang out over nothingness, an abyss whose depths went far beyond all human knowledge.

Zavahl crept forward, cowed and insignificant as that child of so many years ago. In this infinite darkness, all the power and panoply of a Priest-King vanished away to nothing. And that was as it should be, for what was a mere man, no matter how puissant, compared to the might of One who was both World and World's Creator?

All the while, the Hierarch was carefully counting his footsteps, trying to retain some notion of how far he had come; preternaturally aware, every moment, of the measureless, lethal drop that waited scant inches either side of his unseen feet. He was weary from distance and strain and suspense when he finally became aware – perhaps through some subtle change in the surface beneath his feet, perhaps through instinct alone – that he had reached his goal at last.

Confidently, without groping, he reached his hand out into the darkness and encountered a plinth of a smooth, unknown material whose curves felt neither warm nor cold to his touch. Running his fingers over the slanted top, Zavahl found the recessed oval he had been seeking, and placed his hand flat against the sleek surface. There was a loud click as the Hierarch's ring of office – traditionally worn with the red stone, a twin of the larger gem on his diadem, inward on the palm instead of outward on the back of the hand – clicked, like a key in a lock, into the small hollow that had clearly been crafted to accommodate the gem.

A low, thrumming vibration broke the silence, like the sough of some gigantic indrawn breath. A soft, almost imperceptible glow awakened with the sound, the kindling of a deep red light that formed the shape of a gigantic circle, set on its edge and suspended high in the darkness in front of the hopeful priest. The centre of the circle, ringed by the low red light, remained as dark as the surrounding void – a hole into eternity, the pupil of the Eye.

The deep, rushing sound expanded to fill the immensity of the chamber, sounding like all the winds in the world exhaling in one deep, vast sigh. The waxing ring of smoke-red light changed colour, brightening to crimson then scarlet, copper to gleaming gold to the fierce white glare of a blacksmith's forge. Then the sound changed, throbbing with a slow, majestic rhythm like a giant's heartbeat. With each beat, the ring of white flame pulsed and flared like a living thing, so that Zavahl, half blinded by the splendour, found himself pinned like an insect beneath the fierce stare of the God.

As the ferocious glare died away, the fiery circle splintered and sparked, dissolving into a ring of rainbow flashes like the many-hued glitter of a diamond in the sun. Silence fell, an expectant hush. Zavahl held his breath, hoping, praying . . .

This was the moment when the darkness in the centre of the Eye should lift and break apart to show him wonders: images of the past and present, the state of his realm and the mundane lives of the people in his sway. The mighty Voice of Myrial should speak to his servant; answering queries, handing down advice, instruction or orders, and informing the Hierarch of his will. In a quaking voice, Zavahl implored his God. 'O Great One – hear thy servant's plea!'

O Myrial, help me now.

Zavahl waited, not breathing, so tense that his whole body vibrated like the taut string of a bow. His heart sank as the ring of light that rimmed the Eye began to flicker fitfully, some sections flaring with a lurid yellow light while others went dark entirely. Despite his frantic, fervent prayers, the pupil of the Eye remained blank, dark and dead. The Voice of Myrial became a snarling buzz that rose to a discordant shriek, forcing Zavahl to clamp his hands over his agonised ears.

As soon as he ceased to touch the smooth plate on the surface of the plinth, the sound and light cut off with shocking abruptness. The darkness of the void dropped down around the Hierarch like a smothering cloak. Sick with disappointment and despair, aching with the aftermath of tension, as though every inch of his body had been beaten, Zavahl shuffled back along the perilous bridge like an old, old man.

Back in the Temple, he shielded his eyes from the blaze of gold and jewels, their glittering magnificence made cheap and tawdry by the unearthly splendour of Myrial's mysterious Eye. Zavahl put on his shoes and took up the diadem of the Hierarch. He hesitated, his hands arrested in the very motion of placing the circlet upon his brow. *What right have I to wear this?* he thought. *It's more than clear by now that Myrial has turned his back on me. Somehow I have erred, and the whole of Callisiora is paying the price of my mistakes – but not for much longer.*

Zavahl's hands shook as he put on the diadem of the Hierarch. In two days it would be the Autumn Hallows, one of the four great turning points of the wheel of Callisiora's year, the start of winter's rule – and the feast-night of the Dead. In the realm's barbaric past, a sacrifice had been made on each Eve of the Dead, a messenger to intercede with Myrial on behalf of the living, so that the God would protect his people, and see them safely through the long, hard winter ahead.

A chill struck through the Hierarch, cold fingers reaching out from an open grave. This year, blood must be shed again, to save the land from ruin. If Myrial failed to intercede in three short days, Zavahl, as Hierarch, must become the Great Sacrifice on the Eve of the Dead – both Victim and Saviour, to restore the life of the land . . .

'Ah, Hierarch.' The dry voice came from behind Zavahl, making him start violently. 'So that's where you've been hiding. Are your pleas to the god still falling on deaf ears?'

'You are a warrior, Lord Blade,' Zavahl responded coldly. He glared at the tall newcomer whose gleaming insignia, cropped grey hair and stern, upright bearing proclaimed him as the commander of Myrial's Holy Warriors, the Godswords. 'You may fancy yourself as a scholar, but perhaps you should leave the matters of the God to those best qualified to deal with them.'

Blade's mouth quirked in cold amusement. 'Ah, I stand corrected, Lord Hierarch. And that would be you, I take it, judging from your spectacular success in gaining Myrial's ear over the last few months?'

Zavahl ground his teeth. There was no possible answer – and Blade knew it. Though he had never seen the weatherbeaten, hard-faced Commander break into a genuine smile, he detected a spark of triumph in the warrior's glacial grey eyes. Blade was no fool. He had a mind like a steel trap. He had already deduced that Zavahl must soon die. His next, barbed comment only served to confirm the fact. 'Excuse me, Hierarch, I won't take up any more of your precious time.' With that, he turned on his heel and left the Temple, the brisk beat of his footsteps echoing in that vast vaulted space.

Zavahl watched him go, praying, in a burst of spiteful rage, that Myrial would strike the bastard dead. That prayer, however, brought the same result as all the others he had made over the last few months. Nothing. And time was running out fast. Two more days. That was all he had. Without a miracle, the Hierarch was marked as a dead man.

In the doorway of the Temple, Lord Blade paused to glance back at Zavahl. The Hierarch stood in the shadows, unmoving, his shoulders slumped in weary defeat. You poor, pathetic fool, the Godsword Commander thought. And the worst of it is, you'll never know why your world has fallen apart. From his pocket, he brought out a golden ring with a large, red stone that glittered and glowed even in the dull half-light of this rainy day. It looked to be an exact duplicate of the Hierarch's ring – but it was not. The replica was on Zavahl's finger at this very minute. You won't get an answer from your god without this, my friend, Blade thought. If you really want to know why you've fallen from Myrial's favour, you only have to look this way. He dropped the precious ring – the trigger for Myrial's Eye – back into his pocket, and, smiling to himself, went on his way.

Two

Gendival

The broad lower reaches of the Valley of Two Lakes were steeped in peace, basking in the clear early morning sunlight. Near the clustered grey stone buildings and the high, round spire of the Tower of Tidings like a warning finger pointing to the sky, the Lower Lake glimmered bright and joyous as a newborn soul, spangled with ripples from leaping trout and sparked with the bright plumage of the waterfowl thronging the reedy brink. Shimmering dragonflies hovered and darted on the warm breeze that whispered through the groves of ancient oak and venerable beech cloaking the broad sweep of hills on either side. The folk of the nearby village – built long ago to serve and support the Shadowleague – were busy on the water and about the shores: fishing, fowling or laundering, making the most of this fine day in a long period of unsettled weather. Their merry voices, gossiping, singing and calling salutations, mingled with a cascade of cheerful birdsong.

Far out on the lake, unnoticed by the busy folk close to the shore, the tranquil surface erupted in a fountaining starburst of foam. A sleek, blunt-nosed head emerged from the turbulent froth, followed by length upon length of slender neck. The dark hump of a massive body was a distorted shadow beneath the waves, and a long, smooth tail lashed the surface, far behind. The monster swept swiftly towards the shore, its neck cutting a silvery V-shaped wake across the rippled water. It was heading directly for the cluster of helpless women washing clothes at the edge of the lake.

The bow wave from the approaching creature pushed a surge of water into the shallows and across the lakeside shingle, immersing the laundresses past their knees. One heavily built woman, clearly the leader of the group, raised a brawny arm and shook her fist at the approaching nightmare. 'Plague on you, Afanc! Get away out of here, you clumsy creature – stirring up the mud like that! A whole morning's hard work, gone to waste – all the sheets will be to wash again, and who's to do it, I would like to know? Not you, that's for sure, you great lummox!'

In the face of her challenge, the monster let out a hoot of dismay and stopped dead in a great swirl of water, eliciting another raucous chorus of protest from the formidable crones on the bank. Looking abashed, it sank its head below the surface and glided away, in a far more circumspect manner, along the edge of the lake. Well away from the fuming laundresses, there was a curving inlet where the lake's stony brink dropped sheer into deep water. Here, on the gently sloping lawn that edged the little bay, an odd collection of individuals had begun to assemble. It was not unusual for these meetings to be held by the lakeside, rather than in the great hall of the Shadowleague headquarters, because the Afanc, who was Chief Loremaster for all water-dwellers, could not leave his watery habitat.

Cergorn, Archimandrite of the Shadowleague, had watched the encounter between matron and monster – especially the subsequent rout of the latter – with a smile on his face. As the Afanc approached, hanging its head in embarrassment, he schooled his features to sobriety and nodded in greeting to the gigantic lake-dweller. 'Welcome, Loremaster Bastiar. With your presence, our council is now complete.'

The Afanc craned its long, black, green-sheened neck and peered closely at the foregathered council members, who backed hastily away from the blast of its foetid breath.

'Have mercy!' Cergorn gasped. 'Not so close. You smell like a rotting swamp!'

'But then I can't see you all,' the monster complained, its telepathic 'voice' strangely high-pitched for a creature of such vast size. 'You know how poor my eyesight is, Cergorn.' Cocking its head to one side, it peered again at its fellow Loremasters. Cergorn knew what an odd sight they must all make – even a centaur like himself, with his human torso surmounting the dappled, cloud-grey body of a powerful warhorse.

Towering over Cergorn on his left was Skreeva, the Shadowleague representative of the Alvai, the intelligent insectoid race that ruled the land of Fel Karivit. Her glistening, translucent wings spread like a rustling cloak over the silvery chitin armour of her body. Her triangular head was dominated by two glittering compound eyes as intricate and beautiful as the finest diamonds – and, like diamonds, their beauty was soulless, inhuman and cold. Her long, hinged forearms were armed with saw-edged blades to hold and pierce, and each foot was tipped with a razored claw. With her fearsome set of intricate double mandibles and the rigid, expressionless mask of her chitinous face, the Alva looked exactly what she was – a perfect killing machine – but next to the Gaeorn who fidgeted on Cergorn's other side, Skreeva looked as harmless and innocent as a newborn lamb.

Maskulu looked like a creature born of darkest nightmare.

Gaeorn were subterranean dwellers, and though Cergorn
knew that beauty was a matter of custom and expectation
and tried not to let his own prejudices affect his judgement,
he privately considered it a mercy that such abominations
did not normally emerge to tarnish the clean light of day.
Its slender form was low to the ground but stretched for
some five or six yards, ending in a malignant-looking forked
tail. All along its black, segmented body ran a multitude
of legs, each one ending in a pair of barbed and poisoned
claws, and clusters of long, bristling hairs could be seen
where each segment joined the next. Dark scales glistened
slimily, iridescing faintly in the sunshine and distorting the
pure golden light into the sickly, greenish luminescence of
decay. Small, bright eyes glittered redly, with a restless, feral
hunger. Bizarre feathered antennae jutted out from above
Maskulu's flattened face, which was adorned with a set of
spiked compound mandibles even more fearsome than those
of the Alvai. It was a good thing, Cergorn reflected, that
humans, with their grasping, acquisitive natures, had been
kept apart from the Gaeorn – for the ghastly, glittering jaws
of the earth-dwellers were formed of pure diamond. Though
it was extremely difficult to kill one of these fearsomely
armed and armoured horrors, many humans were stupid
and greedy enough to consider the rewards well worth
the risk.

Neither the Gaeorn nor the Alvai had jaws that would adapt
to human speech. Though the Gaeorn made a vocal sound like
the harsh grinding rattle of sliding gravel, they communicated
through a series of clicks and pauses of varying length that
formed a complex code. In their natural habitat underground,
the sounds were produced by striking a stone surface with their
mandibles. The message would carry a long way through the

strata of rock, to be detected by the sensitive bristles along the Gaeorn's sides.

Instead of voices, the Alvai used a language of rasping vibrations, created either by rapid agitations of their wings or by rubbing together their saw-toothed limbs. Cergorn could understand the speech of both races, and could reproduce the Gaeorn language with a fair amount of fluency, but there was really no need. As Maskulu and Skreeva were Lore-masters, agents of the Shadowleague, both were accomplished telepaths.

'*Is* our council now complete?' Maskulu demanded. 'I under-stood that the dragon would be here. Why has he not come? Has something happened to him? Has Veldan botched this mission too?' His mental voice sharpened with overtones of accusation. 'It seems that the great Archimandrite has erred in his judgement. I told you it was a mistake to entrust such a delicate mission to a human – *and* one who had so recently and spectacularly failed.'

The Gaeorn had started to fidget, always a bad sign. His race were notorious for their short tempers, and their patience ran out quicker than a sailor's pay. It was best not to irritate them. Those diamond mandibles, made to chew through rock, could bite the head off a human – or a centaur – in a flash. None the less, Cergorn, not Maskulu, was Archimandrite of the Shadowleague. Occasionally, some of the bigger, more aggressive beings needed reminding. Insurrection was the last thing the Shadowleague needed at this difficult time. Some twenty years or more had passed since there had last been a true renegade Loremaster, but in some ways, the Loremasters of Gendival were still picking up the pieces from that unfortunate episode. The Archimandrite didn't want a repetition. With a mental voice as cold and implacable as iron, he rebuked his subordinate. 'That decision was mine to make, Maskulu. Remember that you are merely a Loremaster. Should *you* ever become Archimandrite, the responsibility will be yours – but not one moment before.'

The Gaeorn reared up, hissing, his mandibles stretched wide to rend and snap. His red eyes flared in fierce rebellion, but Cergorn's cold gaze, fixed on the hideous face of the subterranean creature, did not falter. Their locked stares were the only outward manifestation of their battle of wills; the true struggle for supremacy took place within the realm of thought. The Archimandrite, mentally the stronger of the two by far, was bringing the full force of his disciplined mind down like a hammer of ice and iron on the blazing core of the Gaeorn's defiance.

Presently, Maskulu's glittering mandibles relaxed. His eyes dimmed to a sulky, smoky crimson as he lowered his body from its fighting stance. 'Archimandrite, I beg your pardon. I am a Gaeorn – belligerence is in my blood. Sometimes I forget . . .'

'You weren't recruited into the Shadowleague to forget.' Deliberately, Cergorn let his eyes fall on others, one by one. 'That applies to all of you. The world is in desperate straits, and we are all that stands in the way of complete destruction. If *we* start to bicker among ourselves, everything will be lost.' Sensing their acknowledgement of his words, he stretched his arms out towards his subordinates, drawing them all into the warm embrace of his approval. The Shadowleague was a family – their *true* family, no matter what their species. It never hurt to point that out every now and again.

Loremasters were, of necessity, fiercely independent individuals, used to making their own way (and half the time, their own rules) in the world. Recruited from almost every realm, they came from races who were often at deadly odds with one another, yet they themselves, as agents of the Shadowleague, had to live together in the neutral realm of Gendival, and work in close co-operation with colleagues who would otherwise have been their foes. Loremasters were knowledgeable, highly trained, often highly strung, and accustomed to shouldering tremendous responsibilities. During these meetings, the Archimandrite found it wise to let them have their heads for a little while at first. After a spark or two had flown, it was easier to rein them in.

A light, tinkling laugh broke the tension, like the chiming of tiny silver bells. The fifth participant in the meeting, who so far had remained watchful and silent, had wisely chosen that moment to dispel the lingering shadows of conflict. Cergorn smiled. There were those who complained that wind-sprites were feckless and fickle. Cheerful, mischievous and irreverent they certainly were. To the uninitiated, it seemed as though they couldn't hold a sensible thought in their minds longer than an eyeblink. The centaur knew better, for his people shared Isshera, a tranquil, golden isle far out in the warm Southern ocean, with the Zephyri.

The wind-sprites were masters of deception and illusion. To normal sight they were practically invisible, their position only betrayed by a sliver of shimmering distortion in the air, a whirl of dust, a swirl of leaves, or a sudden draught that caused curtains to billow and candle flames to flicker and flare. Few people were aware of how powerful they were – or how perilous. Imagine the destructive fury of a whirlwind, Cergorn thought, or the force of a hurricane. Think of uprooted trees, roofless buildings, deluges, blizzards, and shipwrecks in stormy seas. Oh yes, the Zephyri were deceptive all right – but he loved them. And this particular sprite, Thirishri, Chief Loremaster of the air-dwellers, he loved best of all.

The near invisible twist of shimmer that was the wind-sprite whirled out for a moment across the surface of the lake, water purling up behind her to mark her passage. She snatched up a glittering plume of spindrift and flung it in an arc of spray across the assembled Loremasters. Once again, they heard the chiming tinkle of its laugh as the Alva, who hated to get her wings wet, leaped hastily to one side, cursing in her own rasping tongue.

Friends – let us settle. Let tempers cool. The Zephyr's telepathic 'voice' was the silvery sigh of a soft summer breeze. From the others came a subvocal murmur of assent. A brief flash and sparkle in the air showed the Zephyr returning to the land, and taking up her former place in the semicircle by the lakeside.

'Indeed,' said Cergorn. 'We must attend to business. There is a great deal to discuss. You'll have noticed that quite a few people are missing today,' he began. 'Some have sent messages, but I have no idea what has happened to delay the others – Aethon, for example, with Kaz and Veldan. Without Aethon we have no representation from the Dragonfolk, and that's another indication of how bad things have become. The systems seem to be breaking down everywhere.'

No good word has reached me from any of the air-dwellers, Thirishri put in. *In the lands to the north, the Skyfolk have been all but annihilated by the Ak'Zahar. We have heard nothing from the Angels for some time . . .* Her tones held a slight edge of accusation.

The Gaeorn reared up, bristling and hissing. 'It has nothing to do with usssss – we have too many problems of our own, to make war upon our ancient foes. Since the Curtain Walls that form the boundaries to our lands have started to weaken, our realm, like Callisiora, is suffering from unremitting rain. Our tunnels are flooded, and many have perished. Though our prey live on the surface, a great number of animals have drowned or died of starvation or disease, and food is becoming increasingly scarce. If we of the Shadowleague do not find the remedy soon for what ails our poor world, then I fear all will be lost.'

'Drought is the curse of Fel Karivit,' the Alva put in. 'The Curtain Walls on our eastern borders have been failing for some time – mostly in the area where we adjoin the desert lands of the Dragonfolk. The two weather systems, once kept apart by the Walls, have merged with terrible consequences for both lands. The dragons starve because their skies are clouding and their lands are wreathed in mists as our precious moisture seeps into their air. Our homes are crumbling in the hot, dry atmosphere from their desert, and the Dierkan can no longer grow their crops to feed us.' She was referring to the lowly insect slave-race, bred by the lordly and powerful Alvai to serve them. 'Already, it is whispered that some of our people are eating their Dierkan slaves. Our race is sinking back into barbarism. Who knows where it will end if this is permitted to continue?'

'The Curtain Walls continue to deteriorate,' the Afanc said. 'In the seas, they have already broken down. Kyrre of the Dobarchu came upriver yestereve with grave tidings from the Leviathan and the Delfini . . .'

'What?' Cergorn said sharply. 'Why was I not told at once? I have been expecting her tidings long enough – why did she not come straight to me?' The otter-like Dobarchu were swift and accomplished travellers, and were normally extremely dependable couriers. 'Where is she now, Bastiar? Why isn't she here?'

The Afanc shook its head gravely. 'The delay is my fault, Archimandrite. I found her by the lake shore last night, barely conscious through exhaustion. Cergorn, she has been wounded in many places, and her thick pelt was all that saved her from being seriously burned. She was too fatigued and distraught to do more than sketch the bare details, and I took her to the Healers. This morning, they decided to let her rest a little longer before she came to you. I suspect that lately she has witnessed unspeakable atrocities.'

Cergorn gritted his teeth and reminded himself that the Afanc, with a lifespan of several centuries, possessed far more patience than his shorter-lived colleagues. 'Can you give us the bones of her news?'

Bastiar bobbed its head in assent. 'In some places, the world is beginning to stir uneasily in its sleep. In the Antaean Sea a new volcano is forming, wiping out most marine life for miles around.'

The monster blew out its breath in an enormous sigh. 'The Curtain Walls were never completely effective underwater, where they were designed to allow free movement of ocean currents while inhibiting the passage of living creatures. But now they have ceased to function as an effective barrier. The inhabitants of different areas are mingling, with disastrous results. Sharks and other predators swarm into new areas, where the inhabitants have no defence against them. The Dobarchu themselves are besieged, their numbers decimated, the survivors trapped in one small sea-loch, where they will starve before much longer. Medusa and Blackstars proliferate, and starfish and sea-snails consume acres of living reef. Alas for our poor oceans! But what can we do?'

Cergorn sighed. 'I wish I had an answer for you. Though Iskander created the Shadowleague long ago to preserve the wisdom of the Ancients, it was established all too late. Too much information concerning our world's origins and creation had already been lost, and our written and cited records have failed us.' He looked at the assembled Loremasters. 'Though we all arrived upon this unique and lovely world of Myrial at more or less the same time, I spoke particularly to those with the oldest and most mature civilisations – the Dragonfolk and the Leviathan. I begged everyone to search their legends and folk tales, their sagas and their myths. Our last frail hope is that, buried in the morass of superstition and half-forgotten lore, we might find some clue to the knowledge we have lost.'

'Knowledge we have *lost?*' snapped the Gaeorn. 'Knowledge that was stolen, more like. When the Ancients, whoever they may have been, dumped us all here, the last thing they wanted was for *us* to remember our own origins, it seems.'

Our origins are probably less important than those of the Ancients themselves, said the Wind Sprite. *We do know that their powers were so great as to be inconceivable to us. We are aware that they created this world as a sanctuary for species who were threatened or endangered on their own worlds of origin. We know they made a haven for each race, with lands and climate suited to our various needs, then they created the Curtain Walls to keep those climates from mingling with the same disastrous results that we are seeing now.*

'*And* to keep our races apart from one another, lest those of a more *war-like* and *carnivorous* inclination molest the rest of us civilised beings,' added the Afanc, looking pointedly at the Gaeorn and the Alva.

'Which was just as well for a few *weak* and *inadequate* races I could mention,' Maskulu sneered.

'Not to mention *tasty*,' muttered Skreeva. She looked thoughtfully at the herbivorous Afanc, her mandibles twitching.

Cergorn cast his eyes skywards. Truly, this lot were more

like a bunch of unruly children sometimes, not reputable and respected Senior Loremasters. 'That's quite enough!' he snapped. 'Let's get back to the situation in hand – *if* you can manage to stop squabbling for a few minutes.'

We know the Ancients brought our ancestors here, Thirishri, the peacemaker, brought the discussion back to business, *but that's more or less all we *do* know about them, or their remarkable abilities.'

'It would be of inestimable benefit to know more about *them*,' Skreeva agreed. 'Ancients indeed – why, we don't even know what they looked like! They created this world, then left us here and vanished without trace. It has taken us generations of study, digging our way – sometimes literally – through the annals, records and legends of every race we can reach to piece together even that much. Why did they have to go away and leave us with so few clues?'

'We know it was they who made the Curtain Walls to separate our realms and our races,' said the Gaeorn, 'but what use is that information, if we don't know how the Walls are created?'

You are right, Maskulu. The Zephyr's reply was like the patter of wind-driven rain. *If we have no notion of how the walls are made, how can we learn why they are failing? And, more importantly, how to put them right?*

'And why are they failing now, in our time, when they have endured intact for aeons?' The Afanc's mental tones held a shrill edge of indignation, as though, Cergorn thought, the lake monster considered the disintegration of the world to be a personal insult.

He was about to reply when his thoughts were scattered by a strident shriek for help. Pain lanced through the Archimandrite's head as the telepathic matrices between the Loremasters shattered and fragmented, recombining to form a pitiful, plaintive howl, part grief, part entreaty, part warning. The Loremasters were reeling, stunned, their wits scattered by the violence of the cry. Cergorn acted with instinctive speed. 'Track it!' he bellowed, using both the vocal and telepathic modes. 'Identity! Location!'

There was a feeling of *west* – a stylised image of a sunset. Flashes of mountains, falling rocks, a zigzag trail. Panic. Pain. Dire need. Then, abruptly, the matrix was clear again. The sending was gone.

'Plague!' Cergorn muttered. 'Pestilence, poison and pox! All right, everyone – heads together. Let's see what we picked up between us.'

The Upper Lake, separated by half a mile of reedy water meadow from the lower waters where the Loremasters were gathered, might as well have been in another world, so different was its atmosphere. Long ago, it was said, the place had been cursed, and the landscape seemed to bear out the legend. The surroundings were wild and sullen, the dull, leaden waters enclosed by sombre evergreens and barren crags. Even when the sun shone bright over the tranquil lake in the lower part of the valley, this sinister, bleak tarn in the shadow of the looming hills wore a perpetual veil of cloud, as though in mourning. Not a creature stirred along the lakeside. Not a bird sang to break the brooding silence. The cheerless landscape was devoid of life, save for one lone figure, a dark-haired, bearded young man who sat slumped on a lichen-covered boulder on the tree-fringed shore.

The gloomy Upper Lake was the perfect backdrop for Elion's state of mind. He gazed into the distance with unseeing eyes, the dismal tarn lost in the darkness of memory. Melnyth, once his partner-in-errantry, filled his mind, her face bright with merry laughter, her red hair blowing like a banner in the breeze. Melnyth in that tavern brawl in some nameless seaport, stopping a gang of fighting longshoremen by throwing the horrified landlord's entire stock of rare spirits, still in their bottles, into the midst of the fray. Melnyth the archer, her face taut with concentration, shooting a distant foe from a galloping horse. Melnyth the battling fury, with bright sword or sturdy staff in her hands and enemies falling around her like wheat at harvest-time.

Melnyth, senior in their partnership, some ten years his elder: his mentor, teacher, guide and friend. Melnyth, her tanned face drawn with weariness in the light of a midnight campfire, hands clasped around her hunched-up knees and her hair brighter than the flames, her eyes shadowed with sadness as she turned to him with the wry, sidelong look that acknowledged his helpless passion for her, and her own inability to return his love as he would have wished . . .

And Melnyth at the finish: fighting for her life in the dark, foetid labyrinth; citadel of the Ak'Zahar. Melnyth at bay, bleeding from a dozen wounds, the dark, winged shapes surrounding her, reaching out for her, shrieking like demons for her blood and trying to pass the lethal circle of her flashing sword, which had started to falter in a tiring hand. Melnyth beset; torn to pieces by fang and talon, crying out to him with her last breath to flee, to save himself, to carry home the vital information that they had come here to find.

Melnyth, who died so that Elion might live to mourn her. Four moons ago she had been alive. All the time between then and now was a black abyss of pain that went on forever . . .

Elion buried his face in his hands. It was no good. His grief was unbearable, and staying in this place, so full of memories, was too hard. Sorrow had brought him to the point where there were only two choices left. All he needed to do now was decide. He could always leave Gendival and the Shadowleague, and ask one of the healer-telepaths to expunge the memories of his past few years as a Loremaster from his mind, replacing them with the recollections of an invented, happier, past. But, until Melnyth's death, all his Shadowleague memories had been happy ones. He had already lost her – could he bear to lose the memory of her too? However much it hurt, it was all he had left of her.

His other choice was oblivion. The lake was deep here. If he were to plunge into the water, weighed down with his boots, his sword and other accoutrements, he could be reunited with Melnyth – and if, as he suspected, there was no afterlife, at least he would be free of all this pain . . .

'Elion? Elion!'

As the hand touched his shoulder the pensive Loremaster started violently. From the testiness of the voice, it sounded as though Cergorn must have been calling him for some time. Red-faced and guilty, he scrambled to his feet, hoping that none of his thoughts had leaked around the basic shielding that was the first thing every telepath learned. 'Sir?' There was no getting out of it – he had been caught moping in solitude against the Archimandrite's express advice.

Cergorn looked down at the Loremaster and shook his head. 'Here again, Elion?' he sighed. 'Though you have all my sympathy in your loss, you're just not helping yourself by brooding alone like this. No one would ever ask or expect you to forget Melnyth – we all loved her – but raking over and over her death does her no honour and you no good.'

Elion scowled. 'Melnyth was my partner. I have a right to mourn her death.'

'And no one would question that right! But you didn't die

with her, Elion, much as you think you should have done. You belong to the living, not the dead. For your own sake you must let yourself come to terms with her loss.' Cergorn gave his subordinate a shrewd and penetrating look. 'Melnyth was a woman who embraced life to the full. I think she would be deeply saddened to see you throw your heart into her grave like this.'

Elion's raw temper snapped. 'Damn you – how dare you! Melnyth never even had a grave! She ended her life as carrion! Fodder for the accursed Ak'Zahar!'

'So? It happens.'

Elion was so shocked at the brutality of the Archimandrite's words that he failed to see the sympathy on Cergorn's face.

'A Loremaster's life is brutal, quick and nasty – as their death, more often than not. You knew that very well when you volunteered. How many partners do you think I've lost in my lifetime? How many do you think *you* will lose – if you survive? You had better get used to the idea now, boy – or get out of here and take up potato farming for a living!'

'Maybe I should!' Elion flared. 'It's better than turning into an unfeeling monster . . .'

Cergorn's mouth narrowed to a stern line, and Elion knew he had pushed his luck too far. He shut his mouth quickly, and took a backward step.

'Do you remember when you were nothing but another snot-nosed village urchin?' the Archimandrite asked him in a soft voice. 'You were an endless nuisance, following me around day after day, nagging and plaguing and pleading with me to make you a member of the Shadowleague. And do you remember what I told you?'

Elion nodded, writhing a little at the memory of the small pest he once had been. 'You said that to make me a member of the League was not in your power. You said I would have to earn it.'

Cergorn nodded. 'That's right. And eventually you *did* earn your membership. And with it, as you should have expected had you been listening to me all those years, came the honour and the hardship – and the pain. Sooner or later, every one of us loses friends, comrades, partners. We learn to get through as best we can. We mourn them and honour them, and we never forget them – but we don't let them dominate our lives. We can't, Elion. We daren't. How could we stay sane? Instead we learn to go on with our lives and our work, so at least their memory will count for something.'

He paused for the space of a breath, his penetrating gaze never leaving Elion's face. 'Bearing all this in mind, I'm sending you on a new mission, Elion. Now. Today. How soon can you be ready to leave?'

Ice sheeted down Elion's spine. 'But you *can't*! I was injured – I'm not ready for active duty! I've lost my partner – you can't send me out *alone*!' Protectively, he clenched the fingers of his right hand, where the breaks had almost healed now. Throughout his protests, he had been backing steadily away from Cergorn, unconsciously distancing himself from the centaur's orders. Suddenly, the bank was crumbling away beneath his heels; without realising it, he had come to the brink of the lake.

A brawny arm flashed out, grabbed his flailing arm and hauled him back to safety. Once more, he found himself eye to eye with the implacable centaur. 'Now, listen to me,' said the Archimandrite bluntly, 'in the normal course of events, I would not be sending you anywhere, let alone on a mission as fraught with difficulty as this. But the truth is that the world is falling apart around us and all my other human agents are up to their ears in trouble elsewhere. Elion, this is a grave emergency. Kazairl and Veldan, along with the Dragonfolk Seer, are in serious danger.'

Elion's blood turned to ice. 'Cergorn, no! I can't work with *them*! Not after everything that happened in the lair of the Ak'Zahar!'

The Archimandrite cut ruthlessly across his protest. 'I'm sorry, but you're all I have to send. Besides, it's high time this bad blood between you and Veldan was resolved once and for all. I've let you act like a pair of damned idiots for long enough. Now, you'll be glad to hear that I'm not sending you out alone.'

Elion felt his distress lightened by a small spark of hope. 'Thank providence! But who . . . ?'

'You can count yourself most honoured.' For the first time, Cergorn smiled. 'A Senior Loremaster has volunteered to join you. In truth,' he added ruefully, 'I couldn't talk her out of it – and don't think I didn't try. I won't be very happy here, doing without my partner for a while, but she seems to feel that you people need someone to keep an eye on you.'

Elion gasped. 'What? You mean Thirishri? But, sir . . .'

Cergorn held up a hand. 'Whatever you're about to say, you should say it to *her* not to me – but don't think it'll do any good. I've been trying to get the best of an argument with her for over a hundred years, and I haven't succeeded yet.' He clapped Elion on the shoulder. 'You and Veldan owe each other more than you realise, my friend. It's up to you to help her now. Just do the best you can – and let's hope against hope that it isn't already too late.'

THREE

WAYFARERS

'Myrial save us! Would you look at *that*!' Kanella had clambered up on to the wagon's high seat to peer as best she could through the dense grey haze of the downpour. On the far side of the mountain pass the route ran through a long, narrow cutting between precipitous crags. Months of ceaseless rain had turned it from a stony track to a rushing torrent.

Tormon looked up, at the humped, cloud-draped shoulders of the mountains, and at the pinewoods, with their precarious toehold on the dizzying slopes above the road. He shook his head. 'That's asking for landslides. If the road isn't blocked further down, I'll eat Rutska's bridle.'

Absently, the trader patted the damp, arching neck of the great black horse while he weighed up the situation. Animals and humans alike were very weary, for they had been climbing for hours, making slow, painful progress up the south-eastern flank of the mountain by the zigzag road that had earned the name of the Snaketail Pass. As always, they had been looking forward to this sweet moment of conquest, when the summit of the ridge had been reached and they could rest awhile on level ground before taking the easier downhill route back to civilisation. Now, however, their plans were in ruins. Already they would be too late to reach Tiarond before the gates closed for the night. Should they retreat, and lose the year's profit – or go on to risk their wagon, their cargo and their lives on that lethal-looking road? As it was, they would be lucky to break even this year. The appalling weather had been playing havoc with their regular route, and by this time they were almost a month overdue on their usual schedule. If they didn't reach the capital soon, there would be no getting there this winter.

Tormon shook his head doubtfully. These were bad times for nomadic traders such as himself, his lifemate Kanella and their five-year-old daughter, Annas. The perpetual rainstorms had blighted their wandering existence. The gaily painted wooden wagon was home as well as livelihood, and in happier times, they made an annual circuit around the varied regions of Callisiora, only spending the worst of the winter in the capital city of Tiarond, high in the northern mountains.

The impending winter brought the close of the traders' year. Spring marked its true beginning. From Tiarond they would leave the high country with the spring thaw, and move south-west to the fertile plains, bringing luxuries from the city as well as tools, implements and weapons wrought of metal mined in these northern mountains to the farmers in the rich arable lands. They would wander here for two or three months, earning extra coppers and trade goods by helping out with the planting and later the early hay harvest, before heading south to spend a leisurely summer travelling along the warm, hilly coast of the southern ocean. Here they would sell their cargo of flax, cereals, legumes and hides, and fill the wagon with trade goods from the coastal area – woven cotton garments; attractive pottery; dried smoked fish; olives, grapes and figs; herbs and garlic; and cheese from the sheep and goats that grazed the rounded hills that overlooked the sea.

As the season turned to autumn, the traders would head back towards Tiarond by the eastern route, taking in apple-picking on the way, and returning to the northern mountains with a cargo that included oil, wine, spices, pearls and other expensive but easily portable items from the south, as well as fruit, rough cider, and fleeces from the hardy sheep of the wild, bleak moorland that skirted the north-eastern boundaries of the mountain range.

For most of the time, it was a pleasant life, full, rich and endlessly varied. Each stop along the way was brightened by friends old and new. Of course, there were hardships. Occasionally bandits could be encountered in the more remote areas. Bad weather could produce conditions that varied from rough to unpleasant to downright hazardous – and for months now, the weather had been the worst in living memory.

'Here, lovey – you hold the horses for me.' Kanella put the reins into her little daughter's hands. Annas sat up straight on her wagon-seat perch, clutching the leather straps tightly. Her dark eyes, so like her father's, shone with pride, but the expression on her little face, under its fringe of straight, dark hair, was very serious.

Kanella hid a smile. The two great horses, either one of whom could blow little Annas away with a single snort, needed no one to hold their reins. They had been trained to stand at a word. But the responsibility was good for the little girl, and it meant a great deal that her mother should trust her with the precious horses. Even though she was only five years old, Annas took her duties very seriously.

Thanking her daughter gravely, Kanella scrambled down and sloshed through the mud to join her lifemate. Her shoulder-length hair, a warm golden brown like dark honey, was dripping where the wind had blown her hood back from her face. She peered down through the murk at the flooded track, then looked up worriedly at the sky. 'What do you think?' she asked him. 'There's not much more than a couple of hours left before dark. Do you want to camp here and try in the morning, or should we risk it now and camp lower down, in case things get worse overnight?' Half a lifetime younger and a good deal shorter than the trader, she tucked herself into the circle of his arm and looked up at him, her freckled, pointed little face grave and her brown eyes shadowed with worry.

Because of her almost child-like lack of height, Tormon was always filled with an irrational urge to cherish and protect her – irrational, because Kanella's tiny stature concealed muscles like wire rope and a constitution as tough as nails, and behind that sweet, impish face lurked a brain that was clever, quick, intuitive and wise beyond its years. They made a good team, drawing on and respecting each other's particular strengths. His bargaining skills and travelling experience, gleaned from almost four decades of wandering, complemented her shrewdness, her insight – and her special skills as a horsewoman.

Tormon hugged her to his side. 'I was going to ask *you*. Should we risk it at all? Do you think the horses could make it down there? We can't abandon the wagon, but I don't want to put your babies at risk.'

Kanella turned to consider her 'babies' – two massive, muscular black beasts, each of them over eighteen hands high. Her father was a noted breeder of these Sefrian Moonshine horses, so called because of the silvery play of light on their sleek black coats. He had given her the stallion Rutska and Avrio, the gelding, as a dowry, along with a black mare who was back on the family farm carrying Rutska's foal.

'I'm not sure . . .' Kanella said. 'They would probably be all right – but if one of them should fall, we'd never get him up again in these conditions.'

'I could wade as far as the first turn, to check the road,' Tormon suggested.

Kanella shook her head. 'You'd never make it back against the force of that torrent. Let me think . . .' she frowned. Tormon knew that scowl. She was working on the problem, considering all possibilities. With a half-smile on his face, he waited.

'Got it!' Kanella's frown vanished. 'Take Esmeralda. She's sure-footed, and easily strong enough to pull you back up the slope.'

Despite his worries, Tormon laughed. 'The runt comes to the rescue again!'

Kanella thumped his arm with mock ferocity. 'Runt indeed! She may be small but she earns her keep.' She disappeared behind the wagon, and emerged a moment later leading a small, soaked, disgruntled brown and white donkey.

Esmeralda, though small, was a hard-working member of the team. During summer, the traders took her as a pack animal on their forays into the more inaccessible parts of the southern hills, where there were no roads to accommodate the wagon. When they camped they would use her to carry wood and water and, at the end of their annual trip, when they were packing a full load, she pulled a light two-wheeled cart to share the burden with the horses on the long, hard drag up into the mountains.

The donkey was a long-standing member of the family, having joined the traders on their first trip after they had become lifemates. During their summer travels, they had found a peasant beating an emaciated beast who had clearly collapsed beneath the weight of its load. Kanella, uttering a word that came as a considerable shock to her new partner, had leaped down from the wagon with a howl of rage, snatched the stick from the astounded peasant's hand, and proceeded to give him a taste of his own medicine, though in her anger she'd forgotten her own diminutive size, and things might have gone badly had not Tormon, also enraged by the man's cruelty, come to assist her. The wretch ran off screaming curses, and Kanella knelt beside the poor animal, with tears of anger and bitter sorrow streaming down her face, for they had come too late to save the donkey's life. Only when Kanella stood up, did she discover the terrified foal hidden behind its mother's bulging load.

The pathetic creature, like a dishrag draped over a bundle of sticks, as Tormon had described her, had come under Kanella's care, and the trader had watched with amazement and increasing respect as a new aspect of his partner's personality unfolded. She nursed the foal day and night, refusing to give in, though its hold on life was tenuous, until (as Tormon told the story afterwards) Esmeralda had admitted defeat and decided to live after all, and had ruled the traders and their assorted livestock with an iron will ever since.

Kanella had unhitched the cart, but left the donkey's harness in place. Tormon took some rope from the wagon, tied one end round his waist, and attached the other tightly to the sturdy leather straps. Inside, his belly was tight with apprehension. This might not be such a good idea – but what was the alternative?

There was a small, tight frown of anxiety on Kanella's face. 'Be careful,' she told him. 'If it gets too difficult, don't take chances. We can always turn back and winter in Breasel. I'd rather lose the year's profit than risk you and Esmeralda.'

'Don't worry, sweetheart. I'll take care.' Tormon stood by the bend at the top of the path, where water from the peaks cascaded through a crevice high in the cliffs on the western side of the trail, spraying down in a slender waterfall to turn the winding pass into the bed of a new river. Esmeralda laid back her long brown ears and glanced at him sidelong beneath the shaggy fringe of her forelock, rolling her eyes to show the whites. Tormon knew he must get her started right now, before she had a chance to think about it, or she would plant her feet and become as immovable as a small brown and white rock. 'Come on, you!' He flicked her hindquarters with the end of her reins, and Esmeralda, with an outraged expression, set off down the flooded trail.

Tormon stepped into the flow with a shudder as a stream of icy water trickled into his boots. At first, the going was not as bad as he had expected. The roar and boom of the torrent was alarming in the constricted space between the cliffs, but on the upper reaches, at least, the water barely came to his knees. Though the current tugged him strongly, he could keep his balance well enough with the support of the sure-footed little donkey. It helped that the flood had scoured the usual layer of mud and moss from the track so that it was firm and fairly even beneath his feet. If he and Kanella were careful, they should be able to get the wagon and horses down here without too much difficulty . . .

Tormon was so preoccupied with trying to work out the safest, easiest way to manoeuvre the horses and the clumsy vehicle down the twisting trail that he barely noticed the swirling water getting deeper. His head was full of plans until he scrambled round the next curve of the track – then his heart turned to lead.

The landslide they'd been dreading had already happened. The trader delivered a blistering oath as he gazed in sinking dismay at the jackstraw heap of mud and trees that blocked the trail and then fell silent, his attention focused on the problem ahead.

On closer examination, the obstruction was not as bad as he had feared. Luckily, it had happened above the widest part of the pass, where a stony gully branched away from the main trail. A comparatively small section of the slope had torn itself loose, and most of the rubble had thundered straight across the trail and down into the ravine. The track itself was chiefly blocked by a tangle of broken pine trunks and boughs, for the floodwaters had already washed away much of the earth and mud that had blocked the spaces between them. A couple of hours hard work with shovel and axe, Tormon thought, and the trail could be made passable again, especially as he had the horses and Esmeralda to haul the shattered timber out of the way. The only risk lay in the possibility of further landslides – a danger not to be taken lightly – but at least the mountain had already been swept bare above the area where they would be working. Why, with a little luck they could be safe in Tiarond before nightfall, settling down for another peaceful and hopefully profitable winter!

Tormon patted the neck of the donkey, who was fidgeting at his side. 'Come on, girl. Give me a pull back up the hill to fetch my axe, and then we can get started!'

It was hard work getting the balky horses and heavy wagon, not to mention Esmeralda's cart, down the flooded track, and Kanella worked up quite a sweat. As soon as they reached the area where the landslide blocked the trail, she pitched in with axe and shovel to help Tormon clear the track, for she wanted to do whatever she could to speed their departure from this dangerous, godforsaken spot. She might be tough, however, but she was nowhere near as strong as her lifemate, and in her zeal to escape this sinister place she started too fast, laboured too hard, and exhausted herself in next to no time.

Finally, weariness forced Kanella to stop and rest her aching limbs. She climbed up and opened the low door in the front of the wagon to check on Annas. Much to the little girl's disgust, she had been ordered to stay inside: the area of the landslip was far too dangerous for a child to be wandering about. Risky situations cropped up frequently in the travellers' lives, and Annas had learned the value of obedience at an early age and knew better than to argue. Besides, the miserable, unrelenting rain took much of the charm out of exploration.

Kanella peeped into the wagon, comforted by the familiar, homely sights. The warm, lamplit interior of the vehicle was tightly crammed with boxes, bags and bales. The harsh pungency of fleeces mingled with the summer scent of herbs and the tangy spice of cloves and autumn fruit. Space was at a premium. Wax-stoppered jars of rough-glazed clay crowded the shelves that lined one wall, each deep shelf edged with a raised lip of wood to protect its contents from falling off during an unexpected jolt of the wagon. A table top was cunningly hinged so that it folded back against the wall when not in use and two wooden chairs, similarly designed to fold and stack flat, were propped beside it. Hammocks, rolled and tied, hung from sturdy ceiling hooks to free the recessed space of the bunk at the rear of the wagon. Most of the goods that had been squeezed into that nook were now piled and roped on to the donkey-cart outside. Annas was curled up on a pile of fleeces at the back of the cramped, spice-scented alcove, fast asleep, her picture book – a rare treasure – still open at her side.

Not wanting to risk waking the child, Kanella closed the door gently and climbed down. She stood huddled out of the wind in the lee of the wagon, wishing fervently that *she* could also sleep. Preferably somewhere – anywhere – else. Tormon, of course, had pointed out with typical masculine logic that the loose parts of the upper slope had already come down in this area, so they were on the safest part of the trail, but the idea of being trapped in this constricted space, with half the mountain (whatever Tormon claimed) poised to rain down on them from above, made Kanella's scalp crawl. To take her mind off her disquiet, and also because she was freezing to death standing around, she set off to investigate the mud-choked ravine to her right.

'Be careful,' Tormon called after her. 'Don't go too far. It's safe enough out here, but some of that stuff in the gorge still looks a bit unstable to me.'

Kanella smiled to herself. There was no way she'd go too far into the gully, not unless her good sense had deserted her entirely. Besides, there was no way she *could* go very far, unless she wanted to clamber over slippery, unstable slopes of slick mud and the lethal spikes of splintered tree trunks. Yet she would have said exactly the same thing to him, under similar circumstances. It was completely unnecessary – and impossible to resist.

The grim devastation in the ravine took the smile from Kanella's face as she scanned the site of the landslide. It could have been a scene from the end of the world: grey, misty drizzle, churned-up earth, the only brightness that pale gleam of gold around the side of a mound of mud and broken branches . . . Kanella frowned. *Gold?* What in the world could it be? Her curiosity got the better of her. She had to take a closer look.

Moving slowly and with great caution, Kanella inched her way up the nearer side of the mound. It was a precarious business. She was forced to test the ground before committing her weight to each footstep, but even so her forward progress was halted every now and again by a cracking branch or the slither of stones rolling under her feet, forcing her to flail her arms for balance or dive forward and grab at the nearest support. Going down the other side of the hummock was even worse, but she succeeded at last, scrambling down to where the slip of gold gleamed faintly in the dim grey light. Kneeling, she poked experimentally at her find. On close examination it looked like part of a triangular sail from one of the little boats belonging to the fishermen of the warm southern ocean, or maybe the edge of a bat's wing – if sails or bat's wings had been made from leathery, spangled cloth-of-gold.

Kanella knotted her brows in puzzlement. Now she was close to the strange object, she was still no wiser – then suddenly, as she rubbed the edge of the cold, leathery stuff between her fingers, an image clicked into her mind. She recognised it as an illustration from her daughter's picture book – a picture of a golden, fire-breathing monster . . .

Kanella leaped to her feet. 'Tormon!' she shrieked. 'Come quick!'

Wiping rain out of his eyes, Tormon straightened, leaned on his shovel and tried to catch his breath. Despite his strenuous efforts, it was proving difficult to uncover the peculiar creature that Kanella had discovered, a great deal tougher than it had been to clear the trail, which he had completed as his chief priority. All the while, Kanella had hovered at his shoulder, seething with impatience to return to her find, but he had been adamant. Their safety came first. Now, he was glad he had taken the precaution to ensure their onward progress, for it was becoming increasingly clear that they would never free this creature tonight. So far they had only found the wing edge and part of an alarmingly huge leg. The tangle of boughs that formed the hummock kept catching the spade and hampering his digging, and haste was needed, for night would be falling soon, and they must be safely clear of this perilous mountain path before darkness fell.

'Hurry, Tormon.' Kanella was on her knees in the mud, tearing at the rubble and branches with her bare hands. 'It's freezing! We'll lose it if we aren't quick.'

'That's supposing it isn't dead already. I don't see how it could have survived being buried like this.' Tormon hated himself for putting such a look of disappointment on his lifemate's face, but one of them had to be sensible. 'Listen, love,' he told her firmly. 'We can't stay here any longer – it just isn't safe. I know your heart goes out to all poor hurt creatures – but what about Annas? Do you want to risk her being buried under another landslide? Because that's exactly what we'll be doing if we stay here any longer. Besides,' he put an arm around her shoulder, 'what will happen if we *do* dig it out and it's not dead? The beast must be colossal! We can't very well put it in the wagon and bring it with us, now, can we?'

Kanella bit her lip and nodded slowly, reluctantly accepting the wisdom of his words. 'But isn't there *anything* we can do, Tormon? What if it isn't dead? It's such a wondrous creature – why, it's a *miracle*! I hate to think of just leaving it here.'

Shouldering the spade, Tormon took her hand and led her

firmly away from the trapped monster. 'The best thing we can do is get ourselves down the mountain and make camp where it's safe for Annas. Then we'll head into Tiarond first thing in the morning and go straight to the temple. It's our duty to report this creature to the Hierarch himself.'

'Tormon! Dare we?'

'Of course.' Tormon pulled her close to him in a one-armed hug. 'For one thing, he'll be able to organise the manpower to come up here and dig the creature out – and for another . . .' he grinned at her, 'miracles are definitely *his* province, not ours.'

He tied the muddy spade to the outside of the wagon and Kanella scrambled up into the high seat and took up the reins, much to the clear approval of the tired, wet and irritable horses. Tormon was relieved that they were finally moving. Already his practical mind had shelved all notions of miraculous creatures and was thinking ahead to where they would camp, and how soon they would get there. Not once did it occur to him that he and Kanella had never bothered to search for any further victims of the landslide.

fOUR

LOST AND fOUND

At first there was nothing. He could hear nothing, see nothing, feel nothing. It was as if his body no longer existed, as if all that remained of him was this confused, unfocused spark of consciousness. What was he? Was this death? The feeling of lassitude was overwhelming. The inner fires that gave him his name smouldered so low that he could no longer feel them. His limbs were wrapped in gelid cold . . . Limbs – he remembered limbs! I can't feel them now, he thought. Surely I must be dead . . .

It was difficult to concentrate, hard to remember . . . What happened? Where was I? Have they buried me? Why else would I be alone in the dark, with cold clay all around . . .

Clay? Mud! A roaring, rumbling, churning, battering wave of suffocating darkness. Crashing down. The choking, the sliding and rolling, the fighting and clawing, the fear and the losing . . .

Veldan! Kazairl let out a bellow of anguish that cracked the drying clay around him and shook a slither of stones from the rocks near by. That initial explosion of shock, that first jolt of panic, impelled him from the shallow layer of mud and rubble in which he had almost been entombed. Such rash movement, such quick and profligate expenditure of strength was injudicious. Inevitably, there was a price. White pain flared through his limbs like lightning, but at least he was free.

Shaking his head in an ineffectual attempt to clear the clouds of pain and confusion, Kaz reeled and staggered on unsteady legs. A tender area on the firedrake's head, between his horns, throbbed with blinding pain. The injury seemed to be affecting his balance, too, because every time he moved his head, the world blurred and tilted and spun around him in a most unsettling way. He had probably been unconscious for many hours, and was lucky to be alive at all. The firedrake, scale-armoured, fanged and clawed, with a spined tail that could whip around to deal a devastating blow, had one vulnerable area, on top of his head. This was why his skull was protected by two sets of horns: the bony triangle above each eye that gave the rakish wedge shape to his skull, and the longer backswept curving horns that arced gracefully out behind the first pair.

Desperately, Kaz tried to concentrate on his surroundings. How long had he been lying here, when his partner needed him? Several hours, at any rate. It was night now, and blacker than a vampire's heart beneath the layers of lowering clouds. Though he possessed tolerably good night vision, the firedrake could see little in the shadowed gully. The only sounds were the liquid trickle of running water, the rasp of his own hoarse breathing, the click and scrape of his claws against the rocks underfoot, and the soft, whispering patter of the endless rain.

Where was Veldan? How deeply had she been buried? In addition to night vision, the firedrake possessed other abilities that would aid him. He could sense the heat of other living creatures as an incandescent glow in his mind's eye, whether or not they were in direct line of sight. His sense of smell was also very powerful. Whether she was dead or alive, he could locate his partner from scent alone. Grimly, on unsteady legs, Kazairl began to quarter the bleak morass of mud and rubble in search of his lost companion.

Veldan wasn't easy to find. The gully was choked with mud, rocks and a hideous tangle of broken trees from the slope above, their branches ensnarled and enmired into an almost immovable barrier. The landslide had hurled Kaz far down the narrow ravine, and he was forced to be careful and methodical, combing every inch of the slope as he worked his slow, painstaking way uphill. Each branch that he broke off or hauled aside must first be carefully checked – as far as this was possible in the darkness – to ensure that its removal would not bring about a collapse of its neighbours, crushing his partner underneath.

The search seemed to drag on forever, until Kaz wanted to raise his muzzle to the weeping skies and howl his loss and frustration. In the end, when he had almost run out of gully to search, he found his partner at the top of the slope, close to the road. It was a very near thing. He had already looked in that place twice and missed her. She was buried, completely hidden, under a tangle of branches, and was so desperately cold that he'd failed completely to sense her body heat.

Using teeth and claws, Kazairl tore frantically at the barrier that separated him from his partner. When at last he broke through to her, he was relieved to find her heart still beating, but horrified by how faint and slow it sounded. Yet he could appreciate that Veldan was lucky to be alive at all. She had been shielded by the springy upper branches of a pine tree that had formed a protective cage around her body, preventing her from being crushed and providing the vital air pocket that had saved her from suffocating in the slough of mud.

Veldan had been found – but that was only half the battle. Kaz knew they needed assistance. He had to find human help and soon, or his partner would die after all. And then he remembered the Seer, with a sudden pang of guilt. What of the dragon? Was he alive or dead?

Kazairl shook his head, wincing as a streak of pain from the injudicious movement shot through his skull. It was no good – he couldn't save them both. In the amount of time it would take even to find Aethon, Veldan might lose her life. And the dragon had almost certainly perished in the landslide. He had already been half-dead from cold and starvation before the catastrophe.

Oh, Veldan, it looks as though we've made a shambles of this mission too. The firedrake's head drooped in defeat. It didn't help that his tongue and jaws were not articulated for human vocal speech. He would find it extremely difficult to communicate with any humans who might help his partner. Shadowleague agents might possess telepathic abilities – it was one of the chief criteria for selection – but the ability was rare among these ordinary, primitive members of the human species.

Kaz made his way to the edge of the waters that still streamed down the twisting trail. First he drank deeply and gratefully, clearing the last residues of grit out of his throat and from between his teeth. He then submerged his head completely in the icy flow, hoping to dull the agony in his throbbing skull and clear his thoughts, if only for a little while. Just long enough to let him do what he must.

It was a nightmare, trying to hoist Veldan up on his back. Kaz grabbed the front of her shirt in his teeth with utmost delicacy, so as not to tear the material and drop her, then lifted her carefully. She dangled limply from his jaws like a broken doll, and he couldn't suppress a muffled whimper of agony to see her in such dreadful straits. Taking all the strain of his partner's dead weight on his long, flexible neck, he turned his head carefully and draped her across his back. He knew that if she had sustained internal injuries or broken bones he might be doing permanent or lethal damage, but what choice had he? Leave her there in the cold and the mud to die? Moving carefully, he tried a slow step or two, keeping his gait as smooth as possible so as not to dislodge his precious burden. It seemed as though she might stay in place. He hoped she would.

With dogged determination the firedrake turned and set off back down the trail he had climbed – when? Yesterday? The day before? Following his frenzied efforts to find his partner, the veils of pain and confusion were returning to his mind, and he felt faint and shaky from hunger and the deep, damp chill of the mountain air. There was only one thought in his mind. Help Veldan. Save her life at any cost. But he dared not enter the city. Who could he find to assist him, out here in this bleak wilderness?

There was no doubt about it – old bones never stopped aching on this cold, damp mountain. These days Toulac definitely needed a little extra something to keep her going. 'Whoa, boy!' She stopped pulling on Mazal's bridle, and the big grey horse stopped instantly, letting the chains that hauled the log go slack. Toulac chuckled as he began to nose at the pockets of her sheepskin coat. As wily an old campaigner as his mistress, Mazal knew better than to pass up any chance of a rest from work – especially this late in the day. Tugging

56

off a glove, Toulac fished a shrivelled carrot out of her pocket and slipped it to the horse, then dipped deeply once more to produce a small, flat metal flask. With a swift, surreptitious glance up and down the hillside to make sure that she was unobserved, she tilted it to her lips and took two or three swift swigs, feeling the warmth of the spirits seep through her. Then, with a sigh, she dropped the flask back into her pocket, put on her glove and resumed her hold on the bridle. 'Come up, lad.'

With a snort that was suspiciously close to an echo of his mistress's sigh, the horse threw his weight into the harness and began to pull. Once more the chains took up the slack, and the heavy log, part of a fallen giant whose roots had worked loose in the waterlogged ground, began to slide across the bleak, rainswept hillside, down towards the sawmill at the river's edge. At least only one tree had come down here, Toulac thought. It could have been a damn sight worse. She had heard the landslide several hours before, and the resulting tremor had finally felled the tree she was dragging now. She wondered what devastation had been wrought further up the mountain.

It had been one of those weary-sky days, when the rainclouds, instead of staying in their rightful place above, drooped down to lie heavily across the mountain slopes in a dark and drizzling mist. To Toulac the grey evening was full of ghosts, though that was hardly surprising. After nigh on six decades of life, almost everyone who meant anything to her had gone now, and left her behind. Comrades, lovers – even brave, respected foes: they all stalked her today, thronging around her in the mists of memory. Faces, places, battles lost and won; celebrations and wakes in the warm company of her fellows, all of them drunk, not only on beer and moonshine, but on sweet relief at having survived another fight and lived another day. Until, one by one, they had dropped away and left her all alone, too damned old to make her living as a warrior and too damned stubborn to join the company of her fellows in death's great army. The tide of Toulac's life had ebbed, casting her up on this lonely mountainside to fill in the time as best she could until she died.

It was odd, the way things came back around, Toulac reflected. She had been born in this sawmill on the outskirts of the Tiarond townlands, but she had never, ever thought she would end her days stuck back here in the same wretched place. Encouraged by a father who treated her as the son he never had, she had always wanted to be a warrior. She'd started her military life among the Godswords, the Temple warriors who fought in Myrial's name, and it was soon discovered that, in addition to an aptitude for both strategy and swordplay, she possessed a singular gift for taming and training horses. In consequence, she was often called upon to deal with young or fractious beasts, and her senior officers soon began to find her indispensable.

A steady climb through the ranks was halted abruptly when the old Commander retired, for Lord Blade, his replacement – a formidable young upstart who had appeared out of the blue one day and had taken a route to power that was swift, straight and deadly as an arrow's flight – had strong ideas about the unsuitability of female warriors, and had purged them from the ranks. Since then her sword had been for hire, as a guard to merchants or travellers or in the small warrior bands maintained by the continually feuding clans who skirmished back and forth among the north-eastern region's wild craggy hills.

'And that's where we should have stayed, you and I. Eh, old

lad?' Toulac patted the warm neck of the warhorse. 'I'd rather we'd gone in battle, in our prime, than be brought so low as stiff joints, aching bones and this miserable bloody drudgery day after day.'

Just as Toulac reached the sawmill, Robal came ducking out of the dark doorway and stooped to help her unhook the chains. He was a big, heavyset young man, with wispy fair hair and a round, beardless face. 'Is this the last one, Mistress Toulac?' he asked.

'Unless there are more deadfalls. There won't be more from the loggers until the floods subside enough to float the timber down safely.' She had already explained this to him about a hundred times today, and had told him not to call her 'Mistress' about ten thousand. Same old routine. Toulac gritted her teeth and tried not to let her impatience sound in her voice. It wasn't Robal's fault if she was out of sorts with the world, and he couldn't help it if he wasn't bright. 'Strong in't arm and thick in't head,' they used to say in the northern hills, and the description fitted her assistant perfectly. Still, without his strength she'd be hard pressed to run the sawmill at all, so she supposed she could put up with his other limitations.

Except one.

'Mistress Toulac! You've been drinking again!' Robal accused her. 'I can smell the vile brew on your breath.'

Robal was one of Myrial's most devout followers. Unfortunately for Toulac, the interpretation of the God's will rested, at any given time, with the incumbent Hierarch, Callisiora's ruler in matters both spiritual and temporal. Doubly unfortunate, to the warrior's way of thinking, was the fact that this particular Hierarch's version of Myrial's will seemed to condemn anything that had the slightest chance of being fun. It hadn't always been this way, Toulac thought grimly.

She remembered the previous Hierarch, Istella, who had been the grandmother of Gilarra, the current Suffragan, second in power to the Hierarch himself. Istella! Toulac sighed nostalgically. Now *there* was a woman who'd believed in enjoying life! And her granddaughter fared fit to follow in her footsteps. If only she had been born first, instead of that pious, pompous, po-faced pri—

'Mistress, why do you keep doing this! No wonder we have this endless rain. Myrial is punishing us all for the sins of such as you—'

'Oh, bollocks!' Toulac snorted. The day, her depression, the monotony of her life – all came crashing down on her. This musclebound idiot's piety was the final straw. She cast off the final chain from the log and hurled it aside. 'Robal, you're dismissed. You just preached yourself out of a job.' Rummaging in the opposite pocket from the one in which she kept the flask, she drew out a handful of copper and silver coins. 'Here – I can't be bothered to count it. Take the lot and get out of my sight.'

Toulac almost relented at the horrified expression on his face. Myrial only knew, the opportunities for employment in Tiarond for one such as Robal were few and far between. Then she hardened her heart. If the sawmill was striving to bore her into her grave, then Robal was nagging the nails into her coffin. Whatever had happened to the old survival instincts? It's him or you, Toulac old girl, she thought to herself. Take your pick. She turned back to the stricken man, who was still standing there, slack-jawed, with the rain running in rivulets down his face. 'Go on,' she told him. 'What are you waiting for? The sawmill is closed as of now. I just went out of business.'

Turning her back on him, she took hold of Mazal's bridle

and led the impatient warhorse away. 'Come on, old lad,' she murmured. 'Let's go and get drunk.'

Toulac's home, built by her grandfather, was near the mill, on a hand-levelled plateau safely above the flood level of the river. A sturdy building of quarried stone had replaced the small timber dwelling of previous generations, and the place had been constructed with a growing family in mind. Nowadays, however, Toulac was the only survivor, and most of the rooms lay unused: dusty, dank and dark. The spacious kitchen was the one exception. In her childhood memories it had always been the heart of the home, the starting-point from which the family set out into the day, and the place where they gathered in the evening to talk, eat and rest. It was a cosy room, dominated by its great cooking range that boasted a large fireplace, with a bake oven at one side and a copper for hot water on the other.

When Ailse, Toulac's mother, had been alive, this house had been her empire and she its tyrant. The menfolk were expected always to take off their hats and wipe their feet before entering, or woe betide them. Within Ailse's shining, neat domain, politeness and good manners were expected at all times, and strong drink and coarse language were absolutely taboo. Nowadays, Ailse wouldn't have recognised the place as her own, with its grimy windows, mud-smeared floor and cobwebs in every corner. The table was covered with dirty crockery and all manner of congealed and sticky food spills, liberally dusted with a scattering of crumbs. A line of much-mended washing was hung from one side of the room to the other, above the fireplace. The only pristine object in the room, Toulac realised with a flash of amusement, was the gleaming sword that stood in the corner of the chimney-breast.

Mother must be spinning in her grave to see this, thought

Toulac as she led the wet, muddy warhorse over the threshold and into the warm kitchen. She chuckled to see Mazal looking around appreciatively at this strange place, his nostrils flaring at the scents of apples, grain, and doubtless all manner of other equine delights. This was a far cry from the dark and lonely stable that was his usual home!

Toulac shrugged as they shut the door. It's a good thing those busybodies from the city couldn't see her now. A horse in the kitchen would convince them once and for all that the mean old bitch up on the mountain had turned senile at last. But she'd had Mazal since he was a foal, and had trained him herself. Tonight, when her mood was so bleak, his presence somehow seemed appropriate. He was the last of her old companions – why the blazes *should* he have to stay outside in his miserable cold shed? Maybe some company would help to keep the ghosts away . . .

Toulac lit the lantern on the table, and saw the dusk outside deepen instantly into darkness. She poked vigorously at the dim embers that were all that remained of that morning's carefully banked fire, and piled small kindling on top to begin their revival. Just like all of us, she reflected, watching the tiny buds of flame blossom on the ends of the twigs and hearing the cheerful crackle as the fire began to awaken. Both fires and people needed air and food to survive, as well as the occasional bit of kind attention. Toulac grimaced with disgust as she realised the self-pitying direction in which her thoughts were turning – again. Further along this path lay self-destruction, that much she knew for certain. So far she had managed to turn back each time, but one day – who knew? One day, if she wasn't careful, she might follow the road right to the inevitable bitter end.

Toulac leaped up from the fireside as if she had been burned.

It was better to occupy herself than to brood. She arranged some small logs on top of the kindling to build the fire up to a hearty blaze, then, shedding her coat at last as the atmosphere warmed, she rubbed down the weary Mazal and settled him in his own corner with a bowl of grain and chopped carrots, his special treat. For herself, she simply hacked a chunk off a cold roast of beef – with beasts dying piecemeal in the farmlands, it was still possible to get hold of meat if you had the right contacts – and ate it with some bread. Cooking had never been one of her favourite pastimes, and she tended not to bother unless it was really necessary.

Some instinct of self-preservation warned Toulac that getting drunk tonight would be a bad idea. Her mood was already close to maudlin self-pity, without giving it any further assistance. None the less, she went to her whiskey jug, poured herself a stiff measure, and warned herself sternly that this was her ration. Settling herself in her rocking chair by the fire, she took her sword across her lap and began to clean the already shining blade, occupying her hands while she gave some serious thought to her future.

Had she really meant it when she'd told that pious idiot that she was closing the sawmill? Why, she must have been insane! *You old fool*, her sensible self chided the reckless adventurer within her who had somehow never grown old with the passing years. *What in Myrial's name were you thinking of? Face facts, Toulac – wearisome burden though it may be, without this mill we starve. No one wants a sixty-year-old soldier, or bodyguard, or mercenary!* And yet, though she knew the only sensible – in fact the only possible – option was to continue to operate the sawmill, a stubborn core of steel inside her simply refused to waste whatever years remained to her in this pointless drudgery. *What shall I do? What can I do? Where could I go?* The words ran round and round inside her head like a litany. *There must be something. There* must *be!*

The rocking chair creaked softly while the fire purred and crackled in the grate. From Mazal's corner came the sound of steady munching. Occasionally the peaceful domestic sounds were drowned by a sharp rattle as the capricious, rising wind hurled a spatter of raindrops against the shutters. But Toulac's ears were attuned, after so many years of night-watches in the wilderness, to the slightest change in the pattern of noise. During a lull between the restless gusts of wind she heard it distinctly – the soft thud and squelch of heavy footfalls in the mud. Toulac set her cup down on the hearthstones with a sharp click and sat up rigid in her chair. Something was moving around outside – and whatever it might be was bloody big!

A crash of broken crockery came from the corner as Mazal plunged in panic. His hindquarters had caught the old dresser and sent an avalanche of plates sliding to the floor. Pottery crunched beneath his great hooves as he backed into the defensive position of the corner, ears back, teeth bared ready to fight and eyes rolling wildly. In all their years together, Toulac had never seen him look so terrified, but there was no time to reassure him. Taking a firm grip on the hilt of her sword, she slid stealthily to her feet and crept towards the window. If she squinted through the crack between the shutters, maybe she could get a glimpse of what she was up against . . .

She was halfway to the window when a sharp crack of splintering wood halted her in her tracks. The beast, whatever it was, had blundered into one of the stout support posts of the porch and snapped it like a piece of kindling. Toulac felt her heart thudding in her chest. What in the seven pits of perdition was out there? Maybe Myrial does exist after all, and has sent this thing to answer my complaint that I'm sick of life, she thought wryly. Wouldn't *that* be a joke on me? Her attention was jerked back to the situation in hand by a harsh grating noise: the sound of heavy claws biting into the sturdy wooden floor of the porch. Toulac took a deep breath. So. This was it. The intruder wasn't about to go away. If she wanted to survive beyond the next few minutes, it was no damned good trying to hide.

At that moment, life seemed far sweeter to the veteran warrior than it had done for many months. She darted across to the fire and thrust a long branch from her wood box into the heart of the flames, letting it kindle into a blazing torch. Sword in one hand and firebrand in the other, she moved towards the door, expecting it to be smashed open at any moment in a burst of shattered timber. She was wrong, however. Instead, there came a series of soft, heavy thuds, for all the world as though some giant, aware of his destructive strength, were trying to knock carefully on her door.

Toulac swallowed hard to clear her dry throat. 'Whoever you are, I don't open my door after dark! Go on – bugger off! Get out of here!' Though she felt pretty foolish, at least the shouting helped to bolster her courage.

A long moment of silence followed. Mazal trembled in his corner, his grey coat streaked dark with the sweat of terror. For the same reason, Toulac found her hand growing slick on the hilt of her sword.

Something hit the door with terrific force. With a loud crack the latch broke and the bolts tore loose with the tearing sound of splintering wood. Toulac jumped backwards as the door flew open so hard that it rebounded with a crash against the wall.

It was all too much for Mazal. Before the former warrior could stop him he broke out of his corner and bolted through the open doorway into the darkness. As the sound of hoofbeats dwindled away into the distance, Toulac heard him give one last shrill, terrified scream.

'No!' Toulac cried. She could see no sign of danger – nothing stood within the rectangle of inky night framed within the doorway. The predator must have followed poor Mazal . . . Her eyes blurred with tears. Angrily, she scrubbed them away with the back of her left hand, only to find them replaced by a new supply. 'Don't be a sentimental old fool,' she muttered angrily. 'Stupid creature probably saved your life – don't waste this chance . . .'

Quickly she scuttled across to the damaged door, hoping there was some way it could be secured again. When she drew close, she noticed a dark red smear down the outside surface. Blood? How strange! Then Toulac stopped in her tracks, a stifled oath dropping from her lips. The soft yellow lamplight from the doorway spilled out across the raised wooden floor of the covered porch that ran along the front of the building. A body was sprawled at the top of the steps, with another smear of blood beside it. It looked like a woman, covered in mud, blood, and Myrial knew what else. She was dead or unconscious, it was impossible to tell. Just in front of the sprawling figure it looked as though someone had been gouging the planks with a blunt dagger. The slashes might have been the marks of a giant claw, except for one detail: they formed four, big, straggling letters, clumsily executed, but their meaning quite clear: *HELP*.

'Well, I'll be damned,' Toulac murmured, stooping for a closer look, until a soft sound, half-growl, half-sniffle, made her lift her head with a jerk. There, waiting politely beyond the edge of the porch, was the weirdest creature outside of a nightmare that Toulac had ever encountered – a fecking huge great lizardy thing with eyes that glowed like multi-coloured moonlight. Toulac started to laugh. The fearsome creature should have looked like Death incarnate, except that it was trying to use a great clawed foot to mop up the blood streaming from its battered nose.

fIVE

Close to
The Edge

Sleeplessness, in the long, dark hours, could be a dreadful burden, especially for a leader with a whole collection of worries on his mind. It was impossible for a centaur to toss and turn as a human could – their bodies weren't built for it – but Cergorn had spent the whole night fidgeting restlessly on his double-level, shelving bed. The broad base, its deep, springy padding of fragrant bracken usually so restful to a horse's limbs, seemed less comfortable than usual, while the upper area, where he rested his human torso, felt hard beneath its generous pile of pillows and cosy furs.

Though he had been lying as quietly as he could, clearly he had not been still enough. Cergorn muttered a curse under his breath as his partner sighed and rolled over. Her elbow poked him in the face as she rubbed her sleepy eyes. 'Whasmatter?' Syvilda muttered, sounding far from pleased. In the darkness, he heard her yawning hugely. 'You've been all over the bed tonight. It's like sleeping next to a spring hare.'

'Sorry, Syvilda,' Cergorn replied sheepishly. 'I was trying my hardest not to disturb you.'

'Huh. You only *think* you were. I know you, Cergorn – I ought to, after all these years. When you fidget like that, it only means one thing – you want to unburden yourself of all those middle-of-the-night problems, and put them on *my* shoulders instead.' Syvilda scrabbled around on the table beside the bed and lit the oil lamp – her preferred means of lighting in the bedroom because of its soft, warm glow.

Though his lifemate had sounded grouchy in the darkness, one glance told Cergorn that she didn't really mind being awakened *too* much. Though she looked rumpled and sleepy, a twinkle in her shrewd, dark eyes assured him of her sympathy and understanding. She would be ready to sit up all night if necessary, and let him talk his worries through until his mind was clear.

How lovely my lifemate looks tonight, Cergorn thought. The black pelt of her lower body, with a veritable starfield of dazzling white spots sprinkled across her back and quarters, was gleaming with good health and assiduous care, while her silver human hair, normally so immaculate, was all tousled from sleeping. The mellow glow of the sparkling crystal lamp beside the bed smoothed the myriad minute lines of age from her skin, creating an imaginary bloom of youth that would last until daylight. The true, deep beauty of Syvilda's face was no illusion, though. Her high cheekbones, slender neck and the strong, clean modelling of her jaw and brow would always prevent the destructive hands of age from taking too rough a hold. Cergorn had loved that face for over a century now, and he knew he would continue to do so for the rest of his life.

At that moment, his beloved poked him hard in the ribs. 'Well?' she demanded in ironic tones. 'You woke me so I could listen, and now you sit there as dumb as an oyster. You'd better start talking soon, because if I'm losing my beauty sleep for nothing . . .' She let the threat hang, unfinished, in the air.

Cergorn threw up his hands in not altogether mock dismay. 'Where would you like me to start? We've only got half the night.'

Syvilda shook her head reprovingly. 'Now don't start exaggerating, Cer – you've problems enough these days without making them any bigger than they need be. Anyway I know all about the Curtain Walls failing – we've been living with the repercussions for several seasons now. No, my dear – you have something else on your mind entirely. What's wrong? Are you worrying about that absent partner of yours? You must be missing her.'

'I am,' Cergorn admitted, blessing his lifemate's generous, understanding heart. Though Syvilda was a member of the Shadowleague, she was not a roving Loremaster but a skilled and respected master-artificer, one of the special handful of folk who researched and studied the incredible implements and contrivances of the Ancients. Most of the mysterious relics that had been discovered thus far were so advanced and complex in concept and design that they would appear to the more primitive denizens of Myrial as miracles or magic. Syvilda was an expert in the various uses of crystals – as far as anyone could claim to be an authority on anything the Ancients had wrought. It was an old complaint with Cergorn, not to mention every other member of the Shadowleague.

'If you're going to go off into a dream whenever I mention that dratted wind-sprite, then it's a good thing that she's incorporeal and I'm not the jealous kind,' Syvilda muttered.

'Actually, I was thinking about the Ancients.' Cergorn put an arm around her shoulders. 'I wonder why they left us in such woeful ignorance. Why, almost every scrap of knowledge the Loremasters possess has been gleaned in spite of the Ancients, not because of them. All those years of hardship, all the long journeys and endless quests – all the wasted hours of study and experimentation to find out what little we know – and we've barely scratched the surface!'

'My dearest Cer, what *are* you thinking of?' Syvilda raised her eyebrows. 'Don't you have enough on your plate as it is without wasting time on that endless old complaint? The Shadowleague has been bewailing its ignorance since the day it was formed, and we'll doubtless go on doing so until this wretched world falls apart around us – which could be any day now, the way things are going! If you ask me, the sooner Shree comes back, the better. Between us, we can usually contrive to keep you on track!'

'I'll second that,' Cergorn agreed. Already, Gendival was proving a lonely place without Thirishri. Though he still had his family to comfort, counsel and support him, he missed his Shadowleague partner. A profound and consummate bond was inevitably forged within Loremaster pairings, a singular closeness, tempered in the fires of hardship, adversity and crisis. 'You know,' he said, 'Shree's absence has come as a salutary lesson. Maybe I was a little harsh, after all, in the way I handled Elion.'

'I'm not so sure,' Syvilda said thoughtfully. 'He was sunk too deeply in his grief, Cergorn – he was in danger of becoming obsessed with Melnyth's memory. I think you may have jolted him just in time; he should have too much on his plate now to be thinking constantly of his dead partner. I'm certain, how-ever, that Elion's grief for Melnyth will continue, unhealed, for a long time, and we must take that into account. It will affect his judgement and his relationships with other Loremasters, especially Veldan and Kazairl.'

'You're absolutely right. This won't be easy for any of them.' In reuniting the three survivors of the perilous Ak'Zahar spy mission, Cergorn knew he had taken a fearful gamble, but, with the Curtain Walls collapsing, these were desperate times indeed, and there had been no choice. Lying beside his wise lifemate, he evaluated the strengths and weaknesses of his three Loremasters.

Veldan should have been the perfect Loremaster. She had courage and a hard-headed, gritty determination that could be counted on to see her through the toughest ordeal. In addition, she possessed keen intelligence and was a deadly fighter with a wiry strength that belied her slender build. Unfortunately, following her wounding by the poisoned weapons of the Ak'Zahar, she was out of training and sadly lacking in stamina. 'You know, my original mistake was sending Veldan out to escort the Seer,' Cergorn said thoughtfully.

Syvilda nodded gravely. 'You're right. It was too soon. She was so insistent, though, about getting back into action before she lost her nerve. It was her choice, Cer. You can't blame yourself for everything.'

'Who else should I blame?' he castigated himself. 'I trusted her judgement – the judgement of a girl who had been shocked, terrified and seriously wounded in a dreadful ordeal – before my own. What kind of leader does that make me?'

'All right – so you made a mistake. Hopefully you'll know better next time, but it can't be helped at this stage. Veldan's chief flaw was always a lack of confidence in her own abilities.'

'Sadly, it's all too true, but before the Ak'Zahar mission, she could more than compensate for that. Now, in addition to her physical injuries, her self-belief has been deeply dented by her ordeal. Kazairl's problem, of course, is the depth of his attachment to his partner.' The Archimandrite shook his head. 'I'm afraid that Kaz wouldn't hesitate to kill Elion, if he should get too nasty with Veldan over Melnyth's death. As for Elion himself – he's a fine young man, but he's fiendishly proud, and as stubborn as a stone once he gets an idea into his head. And talk about unforgiving – he's the sort who'll carry a grudge to the far ends of creation, at no matter what cost to himself, if he thinks he's right.'

Syvilda nodded again. 'You've placed them in an explosive situation, Cergorn – there's no doubt about it. It's a great relief to have Thirishri there to keep an eye on them. That was a wise decision on your part.'

'It was a wise decision on *her* part, you mean,' Cergorn confessed. 'I didn't even get that right. Plague on it!' he cursed. 'Originally, I'd hoped that sending Veldan to escort the Seer would have been just the sort of easy little trip she needed to regain her self-assurance. I should have guessed that, with conditions so unpredictable, she might run into difficulties.'

'Well, the strongest steel goes through the hottest fire,' Syvilda told him wryly. 'This will make or break them, Cergorn, and maybe that's what they need. I can't see the enmity between them being resolved any other way. They'll come through this mission either healed or destroyed, but there's no path in between.' She yawned again. 'Sorry.'

'Look – let's put the light out, and you go back to sleep for an hour or two,' Cergorn said. 'You have a long, hard day ahead of you, too, and it isn't fair of me to keep you awake like this. There's no point in this endless worrying over Elion, Kaz and Veldan. The time for that is long past, and now events must fall out as they will. At least they have Thirishri there to help them.'

Syvilda hesitated. 'Cer . . . I wasn't going to mention this – in fact I was determined not to add to your load of worry –

but, since we're sharing midnight confidences, I think I must. There's something you ought to know.' She looked so grave that Cergorn's heart sank. Syvilda had always possessed an unerring nose for trouble, a talent that had been of inestimable use to him in the past. This time, however, more trouble was the last thing he needed. Oh, no, he thought. Now what?

With the ease of long practice, his lifemate picked up his thought. 'There's trouble brewing among the artisans,' she told him. 'Some of them, particularly those from races like the Gaeorn and the Dobarchu, whose folk are suffering very badly from this climatic imbalance, are suggesting – very strongly – that the Shadowleague should abandon its secret identity and start to teach and disseminate the knowledge of the Ancients.'

'What?' Cergorn was up on his feet before he realised he had moved. 'Not Amaurn's damned heresy again! When will they understand that it's against everything we stand for? Most of the races who ended up here had destroyed their own worlds or had their environments destroyed around them through misuse of powers similar to those the Ancients used to create this one! The Shadowleague was formed to act as guardian of such knowledge, to keep it out of the hands of ordinary folk. It's for their own protection!'

'It's nothing but talk at the moment,' Syvilda hastened to reassure him. 'Just hot air, from a bunch of hotheads. It was different with Amaurn. He was intelligent, charismatic, ambitious – and on top of that, a visionary. He truly believed that the only way forward for all the races of Myrial was for them to interact and evolve. And to be honest, Cergorn, it's a problem we're going to have to address.' Again she hesitated, not meeting his eyes. 'It's their world too, you know, the inhabitants of all the realms. Do you think it's really fair to keep them in such ignorance? Of course we needn't tell them everything, but surely we could release enough to allow them to help themselves. Advanced mining tools, for example, would have saved literally thousands of lives in that tunnel flooding the Gaeorn suffered.'

He stared at her aghast. 'The advanced mining tools that depend on the use of explosives, you mean? And where would *that* lead? Once they started to develop along that track, there's no way we could stop them. Can you imagine the knowledge of explosive weapons in the hands of a belligerent race like the Gaeorn?'

Syvilda grimaced. 'I suppose not. But the dilemma is more complicated than it seems on the face of it. If *I'm* having doubts in the dark watches of the night, imagine the feelings of the Artificers and Loremasters who are losing dozens of their people every day. Be warned, Cergorn. This question won't go away.'

The Archimandrite looked down at her, frowning, unable to believe that she could not be in complete accord with him over this matter. 'The question will have to go away,' he said flatly, 'because the answer is *no* – and no matter what happens, it will never change. As Archimandrite, I took a sacred oath to keep that information secret and safe – and as long as I'm Archimandrite, that's the way it will stay.'

As long as I'm Archimandrite ... A shiver ran through Cergorn as the bold words echoed mockingly in his mind. It felt as though he had somehow mocked the Fates. Firmly he told himself not to be so stupid. His lifemate, however, was not to be deterred so easily.

'Cergorn, you're making a big mistake in trying to run away from this issue. It'll only lead to worse trouble in the long run.' Syvilda sighed, then smiled at him winningly, in a way he'd come to know only too well over the years they had been together. She intended to get round him, one way or the other. 'Why don't you sleep on it?' she suggested. 'Maybe there's some way we could compromise, and try to find some harmless items that could still help the folk who are in trouble. Think it over, my dear, and then we'll talk again.' She turned over and snuggled into the pillows, clearly determined to get some rest.

Not surprisingly, sleep continued to elude the Archimandrite. For two decades he had felt secure in the knowledge that he had killed the heresy perpetrated by the renegade Amaurn, the charismatic stranger who had come to Gendival and had been adopted into the Shadowleague, only to attempt to overthrow the very precepts on which it had been founded. When Amaurn fled Gendival, I thought his insane notions had gone with him, Cergorn thought. If only the wretch had been executed, as I intended! If only he had not escaped that night! Yet in all reason, how could Amaurn be to blame? In almost twenty years, there had been no sight nor sign of him. It was as though he had vanished from the face of the world. The charismatic stranger with the steel-grey eyes, the burning ambition, and the seditious ideas was nothing more than a cautionary tale to the younger Loremasters, and a fading memory to their elders. Who could fear him now? Only me, Cergorn thought. Because I am the only living person in the whole of Gendival who knew who Amaurn was, and whence he came. I'm the only one who understands the chaos he would have unleashed upon the world had he been allowed to have his way.

Eventually Cergorn gave up on sleeping and stole out of bed with exaggerated care, so as not to awaken his sleeping lifemate. Quietly, he crept out of the house. Gendival was still shadow-sunk, the valley bottom steeped in deep pools of indigo and charcoal grey. A dull pewter gleam came from the unrippled lake. To Cergorn's left, the scattered dwellings, workshops and gathering places of the Shadowleague formed darker shadows, some clustering more thickly along the valley floor, others scattered further apart, towards the sloping, tree-cloaked sides. The buildings were mostly low and sprawling, built from the local grey stone to blend in with the valley's spectacular natural beauty. Though it was impossible to make out details in this dim light, the settlement had been constructed in a whole variety of shapes and sizes, not only to suit a myriad of different uses, but to accommodate as many as possible of Myrial's disparate races. Only the soaring, phallic shape of the Tower of Tidings, down near the shore of the lake, stood tall above the others, pointing a solitary finger at the heavens.

The tower, high and isolated, was manned constantly by a team of Loremasters known as Listeners, chosen for their strong telepathic abilities. They were especially trained to work together, augmenting one another's power. Their task was to maintain a constant scan for any messages from agents in the field, no matter how distant, no matter how faint. The sight of the building, silent and waiting, was enough to start Cergorn worrying again about Elion. It was too early yet for messages from Thirishri – they wouldn't even be crossing into Callisiora until tomorrow – and who knew what would await when they got there. The Archimandrite hoped that Elion would be strong enough to deal with the crisis.

Elion gazed around the vast cavern formed from a volcanic bubble deep within the mountain's core. The place was dark as a demon's innards, and suffocatingly hot. The only illumination was a

77

dim, copper-tinged light from the lake of glowing lava that lay an immeasurable distance below. Acrid fumes rose from the scorching depths, scalding Elion's throat and filling his eyes with stinging tears.

The three Loremasters, Veldan, Melnyth and himself, crept along a ledge that was little more than a crack in the expanse of the cavern wall. The trail was so narrow that they could only move forward in single file, and they had been forced to leave Kazairl behind, guarding their backs at the cavern entrance. The firedrake had protested vehemently against his partner going on without him, and the muted rumble of his unhappy thoughts formed a constant background in Elion's mind, an unwelcome addition to the tension of a desperately perilous situation.

Melnyth was in front. As the most experienced of the warriors she had insisted on taking the most hazardous position. Elion followed, with Veldan bringing up the rear. He could hear her breathing, harsh and fast, behind him, and understood just how vulnerable she must be feeling right now, without her partner at her side.

When the attack came, it was blindingly swift. In one breath they were alone on the ledge, in the next a trio of Ak'Zahar had dropped noiselessly from the shadows of the unseen roof on their leathery wings. They came hurtling across the void towards the Loremasters, borne up by the hot thermals that rose above the lava. Before Elion could fit an arrow to his bow, one of the winged abominations had peeled off and vanished into the heart of the mountain to raise the alarm. The secrecy that had been their only chance was gone now. 'Retreat!' Melnyth yelled. 'We've mucked it!'

The eyes of the Ak'Zahar burned with a smoky crimson light and their stinking breath hissed through their pointed teeth as they swooped down on the Loremasters. There was only time for a glimpse of their faces: skin like cracked grey leather stretched over elongated, sharp-boned skulls. Even as Elion fitted an arrow to his bow a bola – two weighted stone balls tied together with a long leather thong – came whistling through the air, and whipped around the bow, snatching it from his hands and hurling it into the glowing depths. Elion made a desperate lunge for it, and one of the whirling balls smashed into his fingers. He heard the crack of snapped bone an instant before the pain hit him like a club. In helpless agony he doubled up over the edge of the abyss.

Veldan's shot went wide as she dropped her bow to snatch him back to safety. A strident shriek pierced the air as Melnyth's arrow found its mark. One of the winged vampires dropped like a stone. Melnyth ducked reflexively as a second bola whirred over her head, hit the wall behind her and clattered to the ground. The vampire came fast behind its missile, wielding a long, black, jagged blade. There was no time to nock another arrow. The Loremaster drew her own sword, sidestepped the vampire's thrust and brought her blade up to block.

By now Elion had the agony of his broken hand under control, but he was still unable to use a weapon. Worse, the ledge was too narrow for anyone to pass, and he was blocking Veldan from going to Melnyth's aid. His partner, however, seemed to be handling the fight in her usual inimitable style. Already her assailant was floundering in the air and bleeding freely. Then, for a split-second, Melnyth hesitated, recovering herself swiftly before her foe gained ground from her lapse. 'Run!' she yelled. 'Get out! I'll follow!'

At first it made sense to Elion. They had been discovered. Escape must now be their chief concern. Melnyth could finish the vampire without help, but they would all get out far quicker if he and Veldan got clear of the precipice. It was only when he had reached the end of the ledge and looked back to see if she was following that he saw what Melnyth must have seen. An entire host of Ak'Zahar, approaching from the far side of the canyon and hurtling rapidly towards his helpless partner.

'No!' he screamed. He started to run back the way he had come, only to be brought up short by Veldan's iron grip on his arm. Tears streaked the woman's face, and Elion knew with a sudden cold certainty that Veldan had also seen the attacking horde and had taken the chance to run, abandoning Melnyth to her fate. 'You bitch,' he shouted, wrenching his arm from her grasp.

Setting her teeth, Veldan grabbed him again. 'Come back,' she yelled. 'She's buying us time! It's her decision – you can't help her. Don't waste her sacrifice!'

Elion lunged back towards the ledge, pulling her with him. 'I love her. I can't leave her!'

Veldan planted her feet, slowing his progress. 'She loved you, you fool!' Already she was talking of Melnyth as of one dead. 'That's why she's doing this! If you get killed you'll mock her dying wish!'

It was all happening too fast – there was no time— Already Melnyth was surrounded. The Ak'Zahar, in their mindless lust for blood, were attracted to the nearest, most accessible victim. While they were occupied with Melnyth, there would easily be time to run . . . except that he couldn't leave her.

Elion started forward again, only to see Melnyth fall and vanish amid a throng of foes. His wits deserted him completely. Vengeance was the one thought in his mind. With a throat-tearing howl of grief, he charged towards his partner's killers, with Veldan still clinging like a burr to his arm. Grief lent him a crazed strength and he pulled her along in his wake. Stubbornly she refused to let go. Behind them, Kaz was scrabbling frantically in the restricted space of the cavern mouth, trying to dig his way through solid rock to come to the aid of his threatened partner.

Too late. Elion had attracted the attention of the Ak'Zahar. As one their heads snapped round towards him. As one they took flight, leaving Melnyth's body in a dark, crumpled heap on the ledge. Too late, the grief-crazed Loremaster came to his senses. Even as he let Veldan pull him back towards the relative safety of the cave mouth and the maze of defensible tunnels beyond, the vampires were upon them.

Near the cavern entrance the ledge was just wide enough for two to pass. Unexpectedly Veldan yanked him off balance, and Elion went spinning towards the cave mouth, where he hit the ground hard. From the tail of his eye he saw the foremost vampire fall on Veldan, wielding its sword in a downsweeping arc. She moved so fast that Elion barely saw her sword move as she managed a desperate, partial block of the stroke – enough, at least, to prevent it cleaving her skull. The momentum of the attack was just too great, however, and the creature's sword sheered across and caught the side of her face, her shoulder and her arm. Veldan screamed as the jagged edges of the blade tore into her flesh. She fell to the ground, bleeding, as the vampire closed in for another killing stroke.

Suddenly there was a loud crack and a crash of falling rock. Kazairl had broken out of the tunnel. He ran straight over the top of Elion, his formidable claws missing the Loremaster by a hair's breadth. The firedrake stood protectively over his fallen partner and opened his great jaws wide. A stream of fire shot forth, and the air was filled with the stench of burning flesh as the Ak'Zahar ignited, one by one, and fell like fiery meteors, down into the chasm's depths . . .

Elion sat up, shuddering like a man with a fever. He let the present seep slowly back into his mind. He had stopped to rest in the last of the Gendival wayshelters, a simple refuge carved, cave-like, into the bedrock of the hillside by some Gaeorn of long ago. The huge subterranean creatures with their bristling bodies and fearsome diamond mandibles might be repulsive to his human eyes, but they certainly knew everything there was to know about stone.

The shelter was simple enough inside: around the walls, various odd-shaped shelves and hollows had been carved into the stone as couches to accommodate the sleeping forms of many different species of Loremaster. A spring trickled down one wall into a stone basin and a fireplace vented out through an ingeniously concealed chimney in the rock. To the right of the entrance, in an annexe, was space for two horses, though only one – his own – was housed there now. Two large iron chests stood against the opposite wall. These contained emergency food supplies and grain for the horses, spare weapons, harness and blankets, and other miscellaneous equipment. A passage with two sharp bends led outside, so that the chamber itself was well protected from the elements. A door of metal grillework, cunningly crafted to fit the interior of the passage, could be bolted into place for defence.

The shelter was cosy but very dark. The fire had burned down to a scattering of embers that smouldered with a rich slumbrous glow like a handful of rubies. With his dream still fresh in his mind, the dim red light reminded Elion once again of the Ak'Zahar caverns. He shook his head and rubbed his eyes, trying to disperse the clinging shreds of the nightmare. The Loremaster felt close to despair. Would the memory of that terrible day never leave him? Each night he relived it, over and over again, until he thought he must go mad.

It is because you will not stop fighting the past. The light in the cavern brightened a little as the wind-sprite came to rest among the embers and fanned them to a brighter glow.

Elion grimaced. He must have been dreaming loudly if

Thirishri – or Shree, as she had insisted he call her – had picked up the details of his nightmare so clearly. He scowled. 'Everybody's too damn full of advice these days.'

Thirishri's sigh was like the wind in distant trees. *Maybe. But think: when you battle an enemy, you must stay close to him, yes?*

'Not if I have my bow with me.' Elion was determined to be awkward. He didn't want another sermon or lesson or lecture from anyone else. It seemed as though he'd heard one from every blasted Loremaster in Gendival by now.

The wind-sprite was not to be deterred. *Still, you must stay close enough to strike, whether it be with sword or arrow, spear or stone. But what happens if you refuse the fight and walk away?*

'He'll come up behind me, probably, and stab me in the back. Why don't you just mind your own business and leave me alone?'

This time, Shree's sigh blew a puff of hot ash into Elion's face. The Loremaster swore and rubbed his stinging eyes. He knew perfectly well she'd done it on purpose.

*Listen to me, Elion. You will never be free of your nightmares until you stop fighting the past and accept it. Accept that all of you made mistakes that day. If Melnyth had not tried to play the hero one time too many and had run with you, if you had not detained Veldan long enough for her to be attacked, if *she* had not prevented you from dying with your partner, as you chose and wished to do—*

'What?' Elion shouted, aloud as well as within his mind. 'Just what are you trying to say?'

That you feel you have failed Melnyth, because she died and you did not. It is yourself you fight, Elion, and yourself you hate.

The wind-sprite's words shocked Elion as though she had given him a physical blow. Before he could gather himself to form any kind of reply, a breeze ruffled through his hair. *I am going outside to scout now. It is time we were on our way.* Then Shree's presence was no longer in the cave. Just as well, too, Elion thought. He was sick and tired of listening to her advice. Of course he hated himself – he had failed his partner. How could he ever forgive himself? But the fault was not entirely his own. Veldan had forced him to abandon Melnyth, and he hated her still more.

When Elion finally stepped outside the wayshelter he was relieved to discover that it was morning. In the darkness of the cavern it was easily possible to lose track of time. The Loremaster straightened his shoulders and breathed deeply of the cool, sparkling air, glad to be leaving the dark place of his nightmares behind. It was one of those brisk, bright, breezy days when sunshine and showers played tag across the skies. The high moorland was balm for an abraded spirit. The vast sweeps of fell made human troubles seem petty and far away, and the air was clean and sharp as a whetted knife. The shrill whistling of the wind only served to accentuate the depths of silence in these boundless hills.

Then the windsong took on a different, flute-like note, and the Loremaster knew that Shree had returned. *Are you ready to leave?* she asked. The time had come to pass through the Curtain Walls. There was no putting it off any longer. Elion sighed. In truth he was afraid to leave the safety of Gendival, and he dreaded the unknown days ahead.

Come on, the wind-sprite urged. *The sooner we start, the sooner it will all be over.*

Elion glared. Why did she have to sound so damned *cheerful* all the time? 'One way or another,' he growled.

A spatter of windborne grit hit the back of his head. *If you really want to scowl at me, I'm over here,* Shree laughed.

Under his breath, Elion cursed. Some partner the Archimandrite had wished on him, and the worst of it was, he couldn't even get his hands on her! His mood was not helped by the behaviour of his horse, a snap-tempered brute with white-rimmed eyes and teeth like axe blades that Cergorn had assured him was the fastest mount in the Gendival stables. Elion's own beast, a sturdy, gentle mare who'd been endlessly tolerant of his shortcomings as a horseman, had perished on the way back from the ill-fated mission to the Ak'Zahar lair, and he missed her greatly, though in general he regarded the stupid creatures as nothing but a useful means of getting from place to place. Unlike this chestnut fiend, that mare had been obedient and quiet. She'd never kicked and plunged, rolled on the ground in an attempt to crush him, or tried to scrape him off under low branches. *She* had never craned her head around to take a chunk out of his backside every time he tried to mount! By the time he'd tightened his girth and scrambled aboard the sidestepping chestnut, he felt as though he'd done a day's hard work already, and the fact that he was actually on his way with his skin intact – if, indeed, that was the case – always came as a surprise.

The path, little more than a faint sheep track, led away from the last wayshelter and curved around the broad green shoulder of the fell before dropping in a gentle gradient into a deep, grassy valley that threaded, arrow-straight, between two hills, then suddenly vanished into nothingness behind the Curtain Walls.

Despite almost a decade as a Loremaster, Elion had never really become accustomed to the sheer immensity of the Curtain Walls. The sight of the great magical boundaries that rose in a vast network all over Myrial, separating realm from realm, still filled him with a superstitious awe, half tinged with fear. The barrier of magical force stretched endlessly across the landscape, cutting off all view of what lay beyond. It was like a colossal waterfall of light, with its flow reversed, so that it sprang up out of the ground and streamed up into the skies until lost from sight. Today the light was different: a pale, milky bluish-white, streaked here and there with flashes of darker colour: sapphire, emerald, ruby and amber. The sound that boomed from the Walls was also like the roar of the waterfall, magnified a thousand times. The roar was interspersed with crackles like snapping sparks in a campfire, and with a high-pitched buzz that was almost a whine.

Elion frowned. 'The colours are wrong. What happened to the clarity? I've never seen that revolting, milky-looking light before.'

The sounds, too, the wind-sprite agreed. *All that new crackling and hiss. This is bad, Elion – much worse than we expected. It looks as though the walls are beginning to fail even here, on the very borders of Gendival.*

As man and wind-sprite drew closer to the Curtain Walls, Elion's skin began to prickle uncomfortably, as though insects were crawling all over his body with sharp, pointed little feet. He could feel the hair stir on his head and arms, and even his short beard began to bristle. Forcing himself to concentrate despite the discomfort, the Loremaster reached out with his mind to access the telepathic matrix, and besought the powerful, complex intelligence that lay at Myrial's very core. It only took an instant to give the command that allowed him to pass through the Curtain Walls, but in that flash the Loremaster's ordinary senses shut down completely. For a dizzying instant his sense of self expanded, to become the entire world. He spun through an infinity of space in an eternity of time – and in another flash he was Elion again, giddy and trembling, but safely back in his own world.

The buzzing of the Curtain Walls had changed in pitch. The barrier parted like a vast curtain, and, knowing that the time of its opening would be brief, the Loremasters hurried through into the gloomy lands beyond.

As the walls closed behind him, a deluge of sleety rain hit Elion in the face. The valley continued where it had left off on the other side of the barrier, except that its lower reaches were now a morass of mud. The fells closed in at the end of the vale, and though the view beyond was lost in mist, the Loremaster knew that in the leagues beyond the hills became a range of high, forbidding mountains, their tops lost in swathes of thick, dark cloud. Squinting his eyes, he gazed into the distance, trying, with eyes and mind, to penetrate the shifting murk. Were Veldan and Kaz still alive up there, or had they perished, along with the Dragon Seer, in the treacherous passes of the heights?

Elion shivered, and belatedly raised the hood of his cloak as a trickle of icy water ran down the back of his neck. 'Come on,' he said to the wind-sprite. 'Let's get up there and find out what's happened to the others.'

There was no reply.

'Shree? Where are you?'

High above you, Elion. High and far. Looking at the patterns in the clouds and the shifts in the wind. You'd better get a move on, Loremaster. There must be a rupture in the Curtain Walls to the far north. A cold front is coming down on us fast. If you don't get over the pass in the next few hours before the snow comes, you won't reach Tiarond this side of spring.

Six

The Servant of Myrial

'This situation is intolerable!' Lady Seriema, head of both the powerful Miners Consortium and the Mercantile Assembly, and the richest trader in Callisiora, planted her hands on her hips and glared at the Hierarch. 'Just what do you propose to do about it?'

Thank you, Myrial, Zavahl thought wearily. This is all I needed – and before breakfast, too. He remained seated, hands steepled, maintaining a neutral expression of polite attention while quietly, inside, he seethed. At least, to be thankful for small mercies, the harridan's tirade was going on long enough to give him plenty of time to think up an answer.

'You are Myrial's representative! With whom does the responsibility rest, if not with you?' Seriema was well into her stride now. She paced the room with jerky steps, while still managing to pinion the Hierarch with her cold, pale eyes. It's a good thing for her that she inherited all that wealth and power, Zavahl thought spitefully. At least it compensates for her total lack of charms in other directions. By Myrial, but she's plain! Had she not been such a thorn in his side, he would have felt sorry for her, an old maid at twenty-nine, with her straight sandy hair and those glacial eyes the colour of ice water in a broad, square-jawed face. Her body was clumsy and shapeless, with a bosom as flat as a board and a thick waist that melded into her hips in a straight, almost masculine line.

Zavahl gritted his teeth as her shrewish, strident voice broke into his thoughts. 'When can we expect to see an end to this interminable rain? The Consortium demands to know. Already we are teetering on the brink of ruin! If this accursed rain goes on much longer, the entire trade network of Callisiora will collapse!'

And I hope it takes you with it . . . bitch. Finally, Zavahl stood. 'Lady Seriema, I am honoured by your confidence in me . . .' he paused long enough to let the sarcastic barb strike home 'but I must remind you that I am merely the Hierarch, not great Myrial himself, who doubtless has his own ineffable purpose in sending down this rain upon his people. Who are we to judge what is so far beyond us? If he is testing our faith and endurance . . .'

Seriema's face mottled with anger. '*You* are testing *my* faith and endurance!' she snapped.

'Madam, how dare you!' Zavahl finally lost control of his temper. 'I demand that you moderate your tone, lest I summon the Godswords and have you cool your temper in a cell! You forget that you address the ruler of Callisiora . . .'

'And *you* forget who keeps you and your precious Godswords in power with the riches we tear from these mountains!' Seriema's lip curled in scorn. Walking right up to Zavahl, holding his eyes every step of the way, she pointed her finger in his face. 'The Miners Consortium has voted. We expect you to rectify these insupportable circumstances in which we find ourselves. As all other means have apparently failed, we expect you to do your duty by your subjects, and undergo the Great Sacrifice on the Eve of the Dead, to appease the God.'

Zavahl's blood turned to ice. Though he had been expecting this, the brutal reality still stunned him. 'And if I do not?' he asked quietly.

'First, we shall use our networks to spread the word throughout the land that Zavahl the Hierarch is a snivelling coward who has failed his subjects. Then the people of Callisiora will come here to the sacred precincts. Remember – this is a defensible place, but you are also vulnerable. I doubt the Godswords would continue to protect you at that point, but if they did, we would simply starve you out. We will drag you out of the Basilica, like a snail from its shell, and offer your life to the God.' Before he could speak, she was gone, almost colliding, on her way out, with the hapless serving-man who had brought the Hierarch's breakfast and had been politely waiting outside – doubtless listening to every word – until the altercation was finished.

Outside the Temple the night's heavy drizzle had changed into a downpour. Trapped between the high cliffs of the canyon that housed the Holy City, the wind swirled and gusted, whining and tugging at Blade's cloak. The Basilica, the Scriptorium and all the other buildings within the Sacred Precincts seemed dark and deserted this morning, and the Godsword Citadel, headquarters of Myrial's holy warriors, possessed a similar appearance of abandonment. All the better, thought Blade as he lingered in the shadows of the draughty archway of the Citadel entrance. Few would be out and about on a morning like this to witness his deeds. Affecting a casual air, as if he had just come out for a breath of air and a glimpse of the sky, the Godsword Commander kept his eyes fixed avidly on the imposing doorway of the Temple.

Lady Seriema stepped out of the Basilica, her heavy features distorted by a scowl and her mouth screwed up tight with displeasure and distaste. Blade smiled to himself. The Hierarch had done half his work for him already. He emerged from the shadows, strolling across the courtyard to intercept her at the bottom of the steps. 'My Lady – what a pleasure it is to see you again.' He took her hand, and bent his head to kiss it, glancing up sidelong to see her reaction.

'Lord Blade,' she returned his greeting flatly, but he saw the faint flush of confusion that darkened her cheeks.

Relinquishing her hand, Blade straightened with a smile. 'You are out and about commendably early, my Lady. You've been visiting the Hierarch?' Her mouth tightened in irritation, and Blade continued quickly before she had a chance to tell him to mind his own damned business. 'Ah, come now, Lady Seriema,' he said smoothly. 'There's only one man within the Sacred Precincts who could put such a frown on your face.'

She laughed, and he knew he had won her over. Blade allowed his features to relax into the smile the Hierarch had never seen. 'May I offer some small recompense for your trials, my Lady? I have come across a rare new tea, a delicate and delectable blend of flowers from the south.' Again, the calculated, charming smile. 'What do you say, Lady Seriema? We deserve a reminder of the summer sunshine on this dreary, rainy day.'

The ill-tempered scowl had lifted from the woman's face. 'Why, thank you, Lord Blade. Some tea would be most welcome.'

Placing a courteous hand beneath her elbow, Blade escorted the most powerful woman in Callisiora back to his lair within the Citadel. I have you now, he thought. By all that's sacred, you've been a difficult woman to charm, probably because no man has ever dared try it before, or no one has considered the benefits to be worth the hard work, despite your wealth and power.

Over the years Seriema's reputation had gone ahead of her, and the truculent, mistrustful, ill-favoured virgin had proved too much of a challenge for most men. Blade, however, was not most men. Gaining Seriema's trust had required a skilful and delicate touch, for she was too astute and intelligent to be gulled by simple flattery, but at last he was making progress. This was the first time she had consented to visit him in his quarters within the Citadel. As they walked across the wet square he entertained her with polite trivialities, knowing all the while that within the next half hour he would have extracted from her every detail of her interview with the Hierarch, though he knew already that she must have demanded that Zavahl make the great Sacrifice. Blade certainly hoped so, after all the hard work it had taken to put the idea into her head.

'Leave me.' Brusque as always, Zavahl dismissed his servant. The man scuttled away and fled the chamber, all too evidently relieved to escape the oppressive presence of his master. Zavahl left the food to congeal on his plate and turned back to the window. As he gazed out across the roofs of the Sacred Precinct, he felt dwarfed by the towering walls of the shadowy canyon, which had once seemed such a secure protection. For the first time since his childhood, he knew how it felt to be truly afraid. The God he lived to serve had turned away from him, and the land that he ruled was dying by inches. Now it seemed he, too, must die – but how could he find the courage? Full well he knew that if he did not volunteer himself as the Great Sacrifice, the decision would be made for him by the people he ruled.

'*O Great One, have you abandoned me?*'

He tried to pray, but the words would not come. How could he commune with Myrial when the God remained deaf to his pleas? He slumped against the sill of the high tower window and looked out through the sweeping curtains of rain. Beyond the high canyon walls, the city he ruled was falling into decline and decay. The ceaseless rattle of the downpour, hour after hour, day after day, was shredding his nerves and eroding his courage. With that relentless drumming in the background, how could a man be expected to think, to plan – to pray?

O God, why have you cursed us? Soon, there will be no one left to worship you . . . And not much time remains to me, now that the Tiarondians have lost their respect for Myrial's useless representative. They blame me for the destruction of their world, and will destroy me in turn.

The Miners Consortium were not the only ones to be disaffected. Seriema, he thought wryly, had been the only one with balls enough to come right out and say what everyone else was thinking. Already there was an ugly mood in the city, a tension, a sense of desperation in the air. So far the murder and looting had remained on a manageable scale, but already the size and number of the guard patrols had been increased. The frustration and anger of the starving, bereaved Tiarondians was gradually mounting, and now it would be contained no longer. The dam of tradition and respect for authority was crumbling a little more each day. On the Eve of the Dead, the barriers would finally burst, and Seriema's work would be done for her. The anger of the people would flood down upon one man. Zavahl, the Hierarch who had failed.

With an abrupt jerk of his arm, Zavahl swept the covered dishes from the table. Food splattered across the carpet in an explosion of porcelain. He looked down in disbelief at the mess, alarmed and sickened by the swift, unexpected violence on his part, he who always kept his emotions so tightly under control.

What's happening to me? Am I losing my mind?

The Hierarch's thoughts swerved away from such a dread eventuality. From the days of his earliest recollection, Zavahl, always aloof and self-contained, had put on loneliness with the Hierarch's robes of office, but never in all the thirty-five years of his life had he felt so alone, so isolated and so vulnerable. The walls of his austerely furnished chamber had closed around him like a prison, a thick barrier of stone that isolated him from all the other human life in the land he ruled. His self-control was dangerously close to breaking-point.

It was all his fault.

Only once in his life, on a black night three years ago, Zavahl's will, normally so strong, had faltered, and betrayed him into temptation. And this was the result. Myrial was punishing the whole of Callisiora for his weakness. How could a man bear such guilt and survive?

He was Hierarch, the Priest-King who ruled in Myrial's name. What if Myrial was displeased not with the common folk but with himself alone? This was his greatest fear. It was no light responsibility to be the living representative of the God – and clearly he had failed his people. Even the food on the table compounded Zavahl's guilt. As Hierarch, he was always served with the best of whatever scant provisions remained in the beleaguered city, while down in the streets below his people were starving.

Zavahl curled his lip, despising his own weakness, he, who had vowed so many years ago to transmute his carnal appetites into a pure, transfigured love for his God. Despite this resolution he had been let down by the needs of his unruly body. Only once had he assuaged his physical lusts, but once had been enough.

Driven to action by his restless thoughts, he pushed past the heavy curtain in the doorway and dashed up the short flight of stairs that led to his bedchamber. The walls of the corridor were not protected by hangings, and the chill that came off the naked stone took his breath away. In his bedchamber the air was mercifully warmer, and Zavahl was glad to see that the servants had made up the fire. Fortunately the mineral-rich mountains that were the source of the city's formidable wealth also provided abundant coal, and in these days of endless rainfall, the fires in the Hierarch's quarters were kept constantly ablaze. The mighty Basilica, both Temple of Myrial and Hierarch's Palace, had been carved directly out of the living rock of the Sacred Peak. As Zavahl had discovered long ago, dwelling inside a mountain had its fair share of inconveniences.

Zavahl passed the fireplace, ignoring its invitation to stay and bask for a few minutes in the heat of the cheerful flames. Unlocking a polished wooden cabinet that stood against the wall in the corner, he pulled out a mask of soft black leather which, when he put it on, concealed the upper half of his face. He looked at his reflection in the mirror. Only his hair, straight, shoulder length, a mix of brown shades from dark to light, remained the same. The harsh, ascetic planes and angles of his face had vanished, their severity blurred and softened by the disguise. His eyes, dark, watchful and expressionless as always, regarded him with their customary cool appraisal through the openings in the mask. Only his mouth betrayed the secret sensuality locked away within him.

At the sight of the mysterious figure on the other side of the glass, Zavahl felt the usual frisson of half-guilty delight. The

Hierarch of Callisiora had vanished, replaced by this enigmatic stranger, an anonymous cypher who could perform such deeds and experience such pleasures as the Hierarch dared not contemplate. When he donned the mask, it seemed as though he shed the conscience that had plagued him all his life, dogging his every footstep with the exasperating persistence of a whining child. Zavahl the Hierarch became Zavahl the man . . .

Zavahl's lips twisted in a sneer of self-contempt. Wearing this mask, he had once broken his self-imposed strictures and betrayed his God. In this disguise he had gone to the lower town to pass a night of black debauchery among the taverns and the whores. At the time he had known he would be punished for his failings, and now, at last, retribution had come. Tomorrow night he would be bound to a stake and burned in a great fire until his screams ceased, his flesh blackened on his bones, and his soul rode up on the smoke and flames to intercede with Myrial and save the future of those same damned harlots and others like them. Zavahl clenched his fists, digging his fingernails hard into his palms to stop his hands from shaking. *Oh God, I'm so afraid. I don't want to die* . . .

He was jerked from his reverie by the sound of footsteps ascending the tower stairs and a loud, brisk knock at the outer door of his chambers. Zavahl started violently and snatched the mask off as though it burned him, cramming it hastily into his pocket. Guilt and startlement flared into anger. This suite of high chambers was supposed to be his eyrie, his sanctuary away from the pressures of his exalted role. No servant, unless specifically summoned, dared disturb him here, so the intruder could only be one person – his assistant and deputy, the Suffragan Gilarra. 'Zavahl? Are you there?'

He could hear her rich voice, constrained with breathlessness from climbing the tower stairs, calling from the outer room.

Zavahl the Hierarch took over, pushing Zavahl the man into the background. He straightened his shoulders and smoothed the crumpled folds of his long, black robes. With an effort he schooled his features into an impassive mask to conceal the doubts and fears that tormented him and the guilt that clung to him always, like the smell of bonfire smoke. Walking swiftly, as if, by hastening, he could leave his conscience behind, he returned through the chilly corridor to the main room and threw the connecting door open with a bang. 'I hope your tidings are worth this interruption,' he growled.

Gilarra, short, plump, and plainly dressed, her richest garment the thick cloak of shining, silver-streaked dark brown hair that flowed all the way down her back, raised her eyes to the ceiling in a look of pure disgust. 'They would have to be worth it, to drag me all the way up those accursed stairs,' she snapped. 'Why can't you do your sulking on the ground floor, like the rest of us?'

'Because *I* am Hierarch.'

Anyone else would have been silenced by the steel in his voice, but Gilarra, as always, struck back. 'You're a pain in the backside, if you ask me. You forget that your rank is simply an accident of birth, Zavahl. If you had been born just ten breaths later . . .'

'*You* would have been Hierarch instead,' Zavahl finished. 'And you never forget it for a single instant, do you?'

Gilarra glared at him, her dark eyes sparking with anger. 'Things would have been different, that's certain . . .'

'You're implying that all this –' Zavahl gestured jerkily out of the window '– is *my* fault? I knew it! It's what you've wanted all along – that I should become the Great Sacrifice. Well, now you have your wish. Once you've got rid of me, then *you* will be Hierarch in name at least, until my successor grows old enough to rule.'

Gilarra sighed, pushing her long hair back from her pretty face in a weary, exasperated gesture. 'For Myrial's sake, don't be so stupid. We're in enough trouble without you inventing more. Do you really think I'd *want* to inherit this unholy mess?' she added wryly. 'I have far too much sense . . .' Her eyes widened as the import of his words hit home to her. 'The Great Sacrifice? Zavahl, no! You can't mean it!'

Despite her protests, Zavahl doubted her sincerity. She would love to have him out of the way, of that he was certain, even though she dared not admit it, even to herself. He gave her a long, hard look. 'If this situation continues until the Eve of the Dead, there won't be any choice. You know that, Gilarra, so why don't we stop pretending? If we hesitate, our beloved subjects will make the decision for us – I've already had an interview with Lady Seriema of the Miners Consortium on that very subject – and how much damage would be done, how many more lives would be lost in the riots that would ensue?' He shook his head. 'Don't lie to me, please, not even through some misplaced sense of kindness. You aren't the only one who has reached the conclusion that Myrial requires a new Hierarch, you know that. No one, neither in this world nor the next, wants me to rule any longer. Everyone seems to concur that I'd be more use dead.'

'I don't know how you can be so calm,' Gilarra whispered.

Zavahl shrugged. 'I have no choice,' he said lightly, but he could not meet her eye, lest he give himself away. Turning away from her, he looked out of the window as he spoke. 'I want you to start arranging the ceremony now – the Eve of the Dead is tomorrow, so we don't have too much time.' His own fear made him cruel. 'I'm afraid you'll have to conduct the Sacrifice yourself. Still, think of the power that will be in your hands when I'm gone. That should be worth a few unpleasant memories.'

As the silence stretched between them, he realised how deeply he had distressed her. Gilarra had always been too soft-hearted for her own good. He dared not turn around to face her, however. How could he let anyone see the extent of his doubt, his fears, his cowardice? His duty was plain before him. Surely any Hierarch worthy of the name should go unflinching to his fate, not knotted up inside with terror like Zavahl? No wonder Myrial had abandoned him! It was a matter of pride to him that no one must realise how vulnerable he was feeling, not even she who knew him best. Though they had been born a mere ten breaths apart and brought up together in the Sacred Precincts, close as brother and sister, he was none the less convinced that she coveted the position of Hierarch, and that she wished their roles had been reversed.

The selection of the Priest-Kings was a tradition dating back beyond Callisiora's recorded history. Following the death of an Incumbent Hierarch, the successor was the first child to be born within the temple precincts, whether the offspring of a priestess, a scribe, or even a servant. If the child was male, then the first female born afterwards would be Suffragan. If the firstborn was a girl, then the Hierarch would be a woman, and throughout her reign the feminine aspects of the god would predominate, and Myrial would be referred to as 'She'. If, as at present, the Hierarch was male, then Myrial's masculine aspects would take over.

'Zavahl? Are you listening?'

The Hierarch, in control once more, turned to see Gilarra's dark brows drawn together in concern. 'Look, you can't just give up like this,' she insisted. 'It's ridiculous – you're over-wrought.' She looked hard at the broken dishes and spilled food smeared across the rich carpet. 'How long is it since you've slept or eaten? You've got to get some rest – then maybe you'll think of some way out of this.'

The Hierarch shook his head 'I can't sleep. The sound of that accursed rain gets into my dreams.'

Gilarra shook her head in exasperation. 'You're too much alone, you fool. It's bad for you. There's no hard and fast law of celibacy for the Hierarch, and for the life of me, I can't see why you find it necessary or even appropriate. If you only had someone that you could turn to – a lover, or a lifemate – it would help you through this crisis.'

'Like *you*, you mean?' Zavahl sneered. 'The most honoured and exalted woman in Callisiora, living in the artisans' quarters and breeding like the commonest peasant?'

Gilarra stepped forward, eyes blazing. For an instant, Zavahl was sure she meant to strike him. Then she mastered herself and drew a deep, hissing breath between her teeth. 'Zavahl, you are a cold-blooded, contemptible fool. Bevron is my life-mate, and we had little Aukil because we wanted him. Our son is an expression of the love we bear one another, and this soulless, cold-hearted stone tomb might suit Myrial and *you*, but it's no place to bring up a child.'

At her words, Zavahl felt the bite of jealousy – a swift pang, easily mastered. What nonsense, he told himself. Why, Gilarra is more like your sister. Of course we perform the Great Rite each Winter Solstice, to bring Myrial's gift of life back to Callisiora, but that's just a ritual when all's said and done. Nothing more. I don't need anyone, he thought. Holy, All-Powerful Myrial should be the sole concern of any Hierarch. But why, when I have made such sacrifices, has Myrial turned his back on me for one brief night's transgression?

With an effort, Zavahl dragged himself back from the dark abyss of his thoughts. He had no desire to quarrel with Gilarra, but he disagreed strongly with her need for a life outside this temple. An apology would be out of the question. 'What was your news?' he asked brusquely, choosing to change the subject instead.

'What? My *news*? After what *you* just told *me*, how can it possibly matter?'

'Tell me,' Zavahl insisted. 'I'm still Hierarch – at least until tomorrow night.'

'If you insist.' Gilarra shrugged. 'Guess what the peasants are up to now?' Her shrug bespoke her opinion of the rustics who lived beyond the city that was her entire world. 'A message just came up from the gates of the Precincts. Apparently some superstitious yokels – traders or something – found a weird creature in the Snaketail Pass – the God only knows what.' She grinned at Zavahl. 'They've only decided it must be a dragon – a *dragon*, can you imagine? Anyway, they concluded that mystical, mythical beasts must be *our* province, so they've brought their happy tidings all the way here to you. What do you want to do? Shall I give them some gold or something, and send them away?'

Zavahl stopped breathing. A *dragon*? Could it be true? Had Myrial given him a miracle after all? A magical beast, straight out of legend, would surely be the perfect sacrifice to placate an angry God, much better than one failed Hierarch. Zavahl tried to sound decisive, though he knew in his heart that he was clutching desperately at any straw. 'Come with me, Gilarra. We must look into this.'

'*What?*' The Suffragan's expression was thoroughly scandalised. 'Are you seriously planning to trail all the way up to the Snaketail Pass on the word of some superstitious thick-wit who probably found an odd-shaped tree trunk? Zavahl, have you lost your *mind?*'

'Does it hurt to hope?' For once Zavahl spoke so softly that it took the wind right out of her sails. As he turned to leave the tower he could almost feel her shaking her head in dismay behind him, but at least she came.

SEVEN

The Dispossessed

⁶'What do you mean, get out?' Viora demanded. 'This is our home! You can't throw us out into the street!'

'Think again, mistress.' The larger of the two hulking men, built like an ill-thatched barn, took a menacing step forward across Viora's threshold, slapping his cudgel into his palm for emphasis. 'This place belongs to Lady Seriema – same as every other house in this yard. None of you scum have paid any rent for months, and now she wants you out.'

'But please . . .' Already knowing it was hopeless, Viora played for time. 'This isn't our house – we're only staying here with our daughter and her lifemate for the time being. If only you could wait until *he* comes home – it's his place, really . . .'

The other bully – the one with the broken teeth and the scarred, lumpy face of the inveterate fistfighter – cursed under his breath. 'You bloody Lower Town riff-raff have no idea of the realities of life, do you? It's Lady Seriema's place, *really* – and she wants you stinking, idle rabble off her property!'

'But what will we do?' Viora pleaded. 'The famine isn't our fault! No one can put any food on the table, let alone pay rent! Why, half the folk who live in this yard are already ill

with the blacklung fever through wet and cold and hunger!
If you throw us out in this wretched weather, most of them
won't last the night!'

Why am I doing this? she thought. She knew perfectly
well that begging would have no effect whatsoever on Lady
Seriema's pack of hired thugs, who were known as 'Seriema's
bullies' to the Lady's tenants. These days, all of the merchants
– in fact anyone in Callisiora who could afford the high cost
– employed a similar gang of swords-for-hire to protect their
property and enforce their interests, usually at the expense of
the defenceless poor.

Somehow, though, Viora just couldn't go tamely, saying
no word of protest, but she knew better than to try anything
more aggressive than pleas. She could hear other bullies in
action as they fanned out among the ramshackle wooden
houses of Goat Yard, and thought of the other occupants:
Leh and Keda, the two widows of indeterminate years who
shared a home and made candles to scrape a living; Lewal,
the night-soil collector, with Thalle his spouse and their brood
of children; and Sobel the tanner, who dutifully supported the
mean-spirited, vile-tempered mother of his dead lifemate, a
pretty, empty-headed, cheerful little creature who had perished in childbirth two months before.

We didn't need this, Viora thought in despair. Didn't we
all have troubles enough to begin with? Already she could
hear pleading and cries, curses and blows. She tried to crane
past the bullies to catch a glimpse of what was happening,
but her view was blocked by the broad-shouldered bulk of
the two men in her own doorway, and she had too many
troubles of her own at that moment to worry about those of
her neighbours.

'Where you go is your problem, none of ours,' snarled the

hulking brute with the cudgel. '*You* are our problem – but not for long!'

Viora let out a squeal of terror and stumbled backwards as he lunged at her with club upraised. She fell against the wall, giving her elbow a crack that brought tears to her eyes. To her astonishment, the ugly bully with the battered face stepped up and grabbed his companion's arm. 'There's no need for that, Gurtus. This lot won't give us trouble.' He gave Viora a reassuring nod. 'You and yours go quiet, mistress, and I'll see no one harms you. If you behave, see, I'll give you a moment or two to pack up what you can carry.'

There was no point in arguing. At least the man was trying, as far as he could, to be decent. Viora knew that this was the closest to compassion he would come, and she was lucky at that.

'What are you doing there? Let me through, damn you!' Felyss, Viora's daughter, came out of the house next door, where she had been helping to care for a sick child. The two bullies drew aside to let her past, though Viora, with a flash of panic, saw their eyes slide over the young woman's shapely form. She pulled her daughter inside quickly, and bundled her back into the narrow little kitchen. There was no need to explain in any detail. As Felyss passed between the two houses, she must have seen what was happening all over Goat Yard.

'Where's Ivar, and your father?' Viora demanded. 'Quick – we don't have much time.' Even as she spoke she was rummaging in cupboards and pulling items down from shelves, stacking everything on the table.

Felyss, looking dazed, watched her mother in bemusement as the older woman whirled around the kitchen. 'They went into the Upper Town to see if anything had been thrown away behind the big houses. They should be back soon.'

Empty-handed, as usual, Viora thought. In these hard days, even the rich couldn't afford to throw anything away. 'Don't just stand there gaping – help me!' She handed the girl an old flour sack. Felyss seemed to come back to her senses. Her hands flew quickly across the table as she packed items into the sack: bowls, spoons, knives; two cooking pots stacked inside one another; a few onions and wizened potatoes and the dried-up end of a haunch of bacon. Viora handed her a small bag of flour and a smear of dripping, wrapped carefully in paper. A crock half full of honey, a bag of dried ingredients for tea and the precious wooden box of herbs that Viora used for her simple, homely cures went into Felyss's sack, along with a handful of candles. As an afterthought, Viora added the long, sharp carving knife. At a pinch it could be used as a weapon as well as a tool.

Viora made sure she had a spare flint and striker and a small wad of tinder in her belt pouch, and that her daughter was similarly equipped. Then she raced up the creaky wooden staircase, Felyss at her heels, her heart hammering fit to burst. On the way they had to pass the lumpen-faced bully, still on guard in the doorway. 'Get a move on!' he bawled after them. 'I'll not give you much longer!'

Upstairs, in the two cramped bedrooms squeezed beneath the eaves, the women worked feverishly, piling blankets and warm clothing together and tying into four unwieldy bundles. All the while, Viora was struggling with a dreadful sense of unreality. How could this be happening? How could her family be cast adrift in this way? They had always been decent, thrifty, hard-working folk; respectable and respected in their little community. What had gone wrong that they should be thrown aside like so much garbage? At least Scall is safe, she thought. That's one comfort. For several months her son had been apprenticed to her sister, Agella, the blacksmith in the Sacred Precincts.

Felyss came staggering out of her room, half dragging the heavy, clanking bag that contained the tools of her lifemate's trade: the long knives for skinning and gutting, slicing and boning, and the blunt, heavy slaughterman's hammer that could strike out an animal's life or be used to break up bones and crack them for the marrow. The girl was having a difficult struggle with the bag, which was almost too heavy for her to lift, but Viora understood. The tools of a man's trade were vital to his self-respect, even in times when there was no work available for him. For the same reason, she had packed the slim leather case belonging to her lifemate, Ulias. It still contained his precious needles and thimbles, threads and shears, even though his hands had been crippled for several years now by painful, swollen joints of knotbone disease, and his tailoring shop, once so successful, was long gone, leaving them thrown upon the mercy of their daughter and her mate, who now had also lost *their* home. It's as if we're cursed, Viora thought bitterly. What have we done to deserve this?

Even as she reached the top of the stairs on her final trip, she heard the commotion outside. Felyss clutched her arm convulsively, her brown eyes wide with fear. 'Mother! It's Father and Ivar!'

Viora prayed, with little confidence, that her menfolk would do nothing stupid to antagonise the bullies. It seemed unlikely that Ivar would stand tamely by while his home was taken from him. For haste, she kicked the bundles down the stairs and, with a strength she hadn't known she possessed, heaved

Ivar's heavy tools after them. She rushed downstairs, Felyss just behind.

The doorway was clear now, the bullies were otherwise occupied. The two women emerged to see Ivar down on the ground, curled into a groaning knot as the thugs kicked him with their heavy boots. Clearly he had made the mistake of protesting the eviction. Ulias was kneeling, slouched against the wall, mopping ineffectually at the blood streaming down from a cut in his scalp. His clothes were dusty and his poor, knotted hands scraped raw. Viora could imagine the scene quite clearly: he had rushed to help the younger man and had been hurled aside as carelessly and effortlessly as though he had been a three-year-old child. His injuries may have been slight, but his pride and self-esteem had been wounded far more deeply. She rushed towards him, but was drawn back by a dreadful cry. Felyss was rushing at her lifemate's assailants, one of Ivar's long, sharp knives flashing in her hand.

'Felyss – no!' Viora screamed. The bullies turned at the sound of her voice and saw the girl charging towards them, the ugly blade wavering in her inexperienced fist. The larger of them – the hulking brute – laughed. He left his companion to continue Ivar's beating and moved so swiftly that Viora saw nothing but a blur. Then his great, meaty hand was around Felyss's wrist as he twisted her arm to make her drop the knife.

Felyss howled in agony, and the blade clattered to the ground. The brute continued to hold her wrist while his other hand came up to slap her, each cracking impact hard enough to knock her head back and forth. Suddenly he released her wrist and pushed her hard in the chest. Felyss went down, and he was on her almost before she hit the ground. Her struggles stilled abruptly as he picked up Ivar's knife and flashed the blade in front of her face. The threat was clear. Ivar, who had been trying desperately to struggle to his knees beneath the onslaught of his assailant's blows, stopped as if he had been turned to stone.

Felyss whimpered as the bully used the knife to slit her dress away from her body. His companion, the one Viora had considered almost to be a decent man, watched avidly, his tongue running over his teeth as he waited his turn. 'Don't be all day, Gurtus,' he snickered. 'And don't be wearin' her out, neither, before I get my chance.'

As her pale skin was exposed, Felyss shook violently, but her bruised and bleeding face was set as still as stone. With her heart breaking, Viora watched her daughter close her eyes, and understood that she was trying to shut herself away from the horrors to come. Unable to help herself, she tried to get to her feet, wanting to beg, to plead, to do *something* to aid her child, but she was pulled back by the clasp of her husband's twisted hand around her wrist. Ulias's eyes met hers, and she saw the tears streaming down his face. 'Run,' he whispered. 'Now – while they are occupied. *Get away!*'

'I can't! Felyss . . .' It was hard to get the words out between her clenched teeth.

'*Do you want to be next?* Run, damn you! Save yourself! We can't help Felyss!'

Viora understood that the admission of his helplessness had been enough to tear the heart out of Ulias. Maybe he was right, maybe if she ran, she could find help . . . But deep inside she knew it was too late. None the less, she nodded her submission and felt the grip on her wrist relax. She had no memory of springing to her feet, but suddenly she was running, as fast as she could, down towards the alleyway that led out of the yard. Even as she ran, she heard her daughter start to scream.

Gasping for breath between her sobs, Viora ran blindly down the alley and into the wider thoroughfare of the Shambles. She had no idea what to do next, her anguished mind too shocked to function. There was no help from the passers-by. Everyone in the neighbourhood knew that the bullies were in Goat Yard, and one look at Viora told the rest of the tale. As she ran down the street, she might as well have been invisible, the road clearing before her with miraculous speed as people slunk out of her way. No one in the Lower Town could afford the kind of trouble she brought with her.

Then Viora's fortunes altered. Turning the corner by the slaughtering pens at the bottom of the street, she collided headlong with a tall, blond young man in a black cloak. Because of his mail shirt, he came off considerably better in the encounter, and he reached out a steadying hand to Viora as she reeled away, preventing what would have been a certain fall.

'Here now – what's this?' Blue eyes, steady and concerned, looked down from under the brim of a blindingly polished steel helm. 'What's wrong, mistress? Why were you running, and in such distress?'

With a sense of relief that brought her close to fainting, Viora realised that she had run right into a Godsword patrol. Afterwards she could never remember what she had said, but before she had gasped out a dozen words of her story, she saw the officer's face begin to darken. He held up his hand to stop the torrent of words and tears that threatened to spill from her. 'Show me where,' he said bleakly.

As she ran back through the shadowy alley that led into Goat Yard, Viora saw smoke pouring from the windows of several of the ramshackle wooden houses, and glimpsed a man with a flaming brand going from one house to another, spreading destruction in his wake. She heard her daughter screaming still – a shrill, anguished keening that went on and on without pause, like the cries of some wild creature in the steel jaws of a trap. As she burst out into the yard itself, she glimpsed Felyss struggling beneath the second of the bullies. The first man stood by watching, as he fastened up his clothes. Too late, Viora realised that her Ivar no longer lay huddled on the ground. Slowly, painfully, he had crawled over to the doorway of the house where his bag of knives lay on the ground. There was no trace of Felyss's hesitation as he took out a long, keen blade and rose up behind the watching bully, slitting his throat from ear to ear.

As the spray of hot blood drenched the other bully, he rose up from Felyss with an oath, groping for his sword. It would have gone badly for Ivar had Viora not brought help. The running soldiers burst past her, moving very fast. By the time she reached the scene, the surviving bully had been disarmed, though not before he had turned on the Godsword officer, spewing out a mouthful of blustering protests. That drew the attention of the other four thugs who had been busy burning and wrecking the houses of Goat Yard so that Seriema's displaced tenants could never return. As one, the Godswords encircled the bully and his victims. A dozen blades swept hissing from their sheaths.

The hirelings came to an abrupt halt, suddenly less confident. The two groups stood for a moment in silent, hostile confrontation, then one man, seemingly what passed for a leader, stepped out in front of the other bullies. 'What the bloody blazes do you think you're doing?' he demanded truculently. 'Why don't you just bugger off, the lot of you? We're on official business for Lady Seriema, and we don't need you Godsword girlies with your shiny armour and your stupid black cloaks sticking your noses in where they don't belong!'

The officer's cold, implacable expression did not alter one iota. Wordlessly he signalled to one of his men, who gave his cloak to Felyss, now weeping in her lifemate's arms, her hair matted and her body painted crimson with the blood of the man he had killed. Ivar, his battered face swollen almost beyond all recognition, glanced up at the soldier and nodded gratefully, but his shoulders were slumped in hopeless defeat. He had been caught by the Godswords in a red-handed murder, and so had just sealed the warrant for his own execution.

In the long moment of chill silence that followed, the snick of a crossbow bolt slotting into place sounded loud. Wordlessly, the Godsword sergeant raised the bow, and sighted along it at the thug, who, by this time, had turned white and begun to squirm and fidget. The young Commander of the Godsword troop finally deigned to reply, in a voice that was biting and cold with contempt. 'I'm aware that Lady Seriema wanted to clear these plague-infested slums in the Lower Town. I'm also aware that she has provided temporary accommodation in her warehouses down by the river for the folk who were made homeless as a result. What, exactly, were her orders to you?'

The thug took one step backwards. 'Well – to clear these houses so they can be knocked down – ah – sir. We was to get these rabble out, and see that they gave no trouble, and make sure they couldn't come creeping back here when our backs was turned.'

The officer stared at him unblinking. 'I see. Correct me if I'm wrong, but I heard nothing in those instructions about assault and rape.'

Briefly the bully floundered, finding himself on very shaky ground, but suddenly he rallied. 'What about him?' He pointed to his fallen colleague. 'That was murder, that was! I demand you arrest this riff-raff! The other stuff what we did was just self-defence!'

The Godsword officer stirred the blood-drained body with his toe. '*We* didn't see any murder,' he replied in an offhand tone. 'Looks like he met with an accident to me. Fell on this knife, probably – wouldn't you say so, Sergeant Ewald?'

The burly, balding man with the crossbow spared a glance from his quarry. 'Definitely, sir. As you say, sir, he fell on his knife I expect. Nasty-looking blade, sir, if you ask me. He should have been more careful.'

'There you are,' the officer said pleasantly. 'It was just an accident, as you see. And to avoid any further mishaps among you, I suggest you take your men elsewhere – right now.'

The thug's jaw dropped. 'But sir – Lady Seriema said—'

'You may refer Lady Seriema to me if she has any problems. Lieutenant Galveron. Second-in-Command to Lord Blade. She can always find me at the Citadel.' Though the officer's voice remained level, a tightening of his jaw and a cold glint in his eye made the bully and his colleagues group closer together for support.

'Ah – right you are, sir. We'll just be going then,' the leader stammered.

'If I were you, I'd put those fires out first,' Lieutenant Galveron prompted. 'Oh – and one more thing. When you go back to your Lady, tell her from me that I won't tolerate assault and rape among her hirelings. If this ever happens again, I will hold her personally responsible. Is that clear?'

The man gulped. 'You want *me* to tell her that?'

The sergeant's crossbow rose a fraction.

'Yes, sir!' the bully gasped. 'I'll tell her! You can count on me, sir!' Gathering his followers, he hurried back to the houses, whose wood was so waterlogged that they had done little more, so far, than smoulder. Nevertheless, Viora thought, they would not be habitable now. Seriema's men had done their work well.

Felyss's other assailant tried to edge away surreptitiously in pursuit of his fellows, only to be brought up short by the point of Galveron's blade. 'Not you. There are laws in this city against what you've done today.'

Looking on, Viora sighed. That's all very well, she thought, but what's the point? Even if the Hierarch does bring this man to trial, none of us will dare to bear witness against him. If we do, his fellows will seek us out for revenge.

Lieutenant Galveron gestured away across the yard towards the alley. 'Run,' he told the thug. The bully cast a longing glance towards the route to freedom, then looked back at the unmoving sergeant with his crossbow poised. He gulped and licked his lips. 'No,' he whined. 'I'm not running. You'll shoot me in the back! I'd be better off with a trial!'

'Suit yourself.' The Godsword officer shrugged. 'But you should know that the Hierarch tends to delegate this sort of case to the Suffragan Gilarra. She told me once that she holds a very strong opinion that rapists should be castrated.' He half turned to his men. 'Take him along, lads.'

With a sense almost of disappointment, Viora saw the black-cloaked soldiers close in around their prisoner and march him away, with only the Sergeant staying back beside his officer. She scarcely knew what she wanted – her feelings were such a mix of wrath and anguish – but somehow, it seemed wrong to let this man go, even into the hands of the Godswords, without exacting some kind of terrible revenge. Lieutenant Galveron caught her eye. 'Wait,' he said softly.

Why? Viora wondered, then suddenly, her question was answered. As the soldiers neared the mouth of the alley, there was a disturbance in the black-cloaked ranks, a yell and the sound of a scuffle. The soldiers drew aside to reveal that the prisoner had taken to his heels, and was running headlong towards the narrow exit to the yard. Almost unhurriedly, the Sergeant took aim. With a buzzing whine the bolt hurtled through the air and buried itself in the back of the running man's neck.

'Nice shot, Sergeant Ewald. The usual report, please. Shot while trying to escape.' Galveron turned to Viora with a wintry smile. 'Mention castration and they always run sooner or later. I'm sorry we couldn't manage a slower, more painful death for him, but the Sergeant here is just too good a shot.' He extended a hand to help Ulias, but Viora's lifemate had already scrambled to his feet.

'Sir – my family owe you a great debt,' he told the young officer.

'I'm just doing my job, sir.' Galveron inclined his head respectfully to the older man. Viora could have hugged the young officer as she saw how that one small gesture was balm to Ulias's shattered self-esteem. The Lieutenant regarded the house behind them with a frown. Though no flames were to be seen, wisps of smoke still drifted from the windows and doorway. 'I'm sorry, but the rest of those thugs are still around here, and I wouldn't advise you to stay here once we've left – not after you did such a good job on their mate there.' He looked at the bully with his throat cut, then at Ivar, and laid a finger alongside his nose. 'Unofficially, my compliments, by the way. You've just made the world a better place. But your house is uninhabitable, and it won't do you any good to linger here. Is there anyone who can take you in? Can my men escort you somewhere safe?'

Ivar was standing with his arms protectively around Felyss, who buried her head in his shoulder as if to hide from the whole world. He shook his head. 'My family are all dead. All our neighbours are in the same fix. There's no one else.'

Viora hesitated. 'There's my sister, the blacksmith in the Sacred Precincts,' she admitted reluctantly. She and Agella, so very different in character, rarely saw eye to eye over anything. Earlier this year, Viora had swallowed her pride for the sake of her son Scall, and begged the smith to take the feckless dreamer of a boy as an apprentice. Even in this dreadful crisis, she hated to be beholden to Agella a second time.

'You're Mistress Agella's sister?' said Galveron in surprise. 'I know her well. I'm afraid she won't be allowed to take you in, however. No outsiders are permitted to stay in the Precincts. It's one of our strictest laws. I know that must seem very hard to you, and I'm sorry, but there can be no exceptions.'

Viora's heart sank as she turned away. She knew about the rule, of course. She had hoped that under the circumstances this kind young officer might turn a blind eye, but he was too upright a character for that. But maybe the guards on the Tunnel Gate would be more flexible. If she could only get word to her sister, surely Agella would find a way to take them in.

Spurred on by the pitiful state of her daughter, Viora decided to try. First, however, Galveron would have to be deceived. Were he to gain the slightest inkling of her plans, he'd make sure she was kept out of the Sacred Precincts. On the other hand, if he thought the family were leaving the city, he would leave them alone. She turned back to him, deploring the lies that came to her so easily. 'I hate to ask you when you've helped us so much already, but do you know of anywhere that might shelter us?'

Galveron sighed. 'I'm sorry, mistress. Clearly you have no money, so an inn is out of the question. Everyone else seems to have troubles of their own these days. There seems no place in Tiarond these days for the dispossessed, apart from Lady Seriema's warehouses. You should go there. The buildings in which she stores her merchandise are in far better condition than the home you lost, and at least you would be warm, dry and sheltered.'

Ivar held the trembling body of his lifemate more tightly to his chest. His voice came out as a low, animal growl. 'Felyss's folks can go there if they will, but me and my lass will have no more to do with that flint-hearted bitch, nor anything that belongs to her. Not after what she's done to us today. Not supposing we die out on the streets this very night.' He lifted his head in stubborn pride, but there was an ugly light in his eyes.

'I understand your feelings,' the Godsword officer said with a frown. 'But the weather is changing. There's a storm coming, and we'll have snow before tonight. Think about it, man. You might get away with it, but your lifemate is in no condition to stay out on the streets in a blizzard. Nor are her parents. They'll never survive the night.'

Ivar muttered something indecipherable, the words coming out again as a low, animal sound. Viora shivered. Lieutenant Galveron glanced at her, his face mirroring her concern, before he turned back to Ivar. 'Then if I were you, I would leave the city altogether, and travel south to the lowlands before the worst of the winter weather sets in. Things aren't easy there, either, because of the flooding, but at least the lands are more fertile and the climate will be warmer for a homeless family. I know a lot of folk have been doing just that lately, but it's up to you.'

'Whatever happens, Ivar, we'll all stick together. As the officer says, it's up to you.' Ulias looked at Ivar, waiting for a decision. The younger man had been the head of the house that had been destroyed, and he had slain his lifemate's attacker. Clearly, the choice would rest with him. Viora was relieved. Right now, her daughter needed all the support a loving family could give. Clearly, Ivar himself was in no fit state to take care of her.

After a moment, the slaughterman nodded. 'Let's try it,' he said decisively. 'There's nothing left for us here in this accursed place. I want to take Felyss away from here, and find somewhere safe where she can heal and put this terrible day behind her – if she ever can.'

'I packed what I could,' Viora put in. 'So long as it wasn't damaged by the fire . . .' She darted into the doorway of the house. It was safe now. The bullies had doused the flames, then slunk away, trying not to attract the further attention of the Godsword troops. She came out backwards, dragging her precious bundles. They were smoke-smeared and spark-singed here and there, but otherwise seemed intact.

'I wish you and your family good fortune,' Galveron said softly. 'I'll escort you to the gates. My advice is that you find a place to camp outside for the night and continue on your way at first light.' He took a deep breath. 'May Myrial protect you all.'

Viora found clothing for Felyss in one of the bundles and dressed her, wrapping her as warmly as she could manage. The girl remained listless and unresponsive, letting her mother move her flaccid limbs as necessary, her eyes gazing far away into some deep, dark pit of unendurable horror. If Ivar helped and supported her, she would walk, blind and stumbling, allowing herself to be led. Galveron distributed the pitiful bundles among his men, to carry until they parted from Ivar's family at the city gates. It seemed no time at all before they were leaving. Viora looked behind her one last time at the smouldering remains of Goat Yard. Until today it had been her home, and a happy place. Though no one who lived there had material goods to spare, they had all looked out for one another, and the squalid little yard had held an abundance of laughter and love. That's all gone now, Viora thought bitterly. After what had happened here today, she was glad she would never have to set eyes on the place again.

Once he had taken the shattered family as far as the city gates, Galveron headed back towards the Citadel with his patrol, still seething with rage at the atrocities he had witnessed. Sergeant Ewald walked alongside him. 'You won't half catch it if Lady Seriema complains to Lord Blade about this. You ever notice how he lets her get away with stuff that he wouldn't allow from anyone else? Me, I reckon he's got a fancy for her – or for her money, more like.'

'More like,' Galveron agreed absently. 'Anyway, if she wants to complain she can please herself. Lord Blade can have my resignation any time he wants, especially after what I've seen today.'

'Fair enough, sir, if that's what you really want, I wouldn't blame you.' The Sergeant spat into the gutter with considerable force. 'All the same,' he added reflectively, 'you did a lot more good today as Lieutenant Galveron of the Godswords than you could have done as plain Galveron the slaughterman.'

'Slaughterman?' Galveron frowned. 'How does being a slaughterman come into it?'

'That's what that poor lass's lifemate did for a living.' Ewald glanced sidelong at his officer. 'Didn't you notice those knives? And he made as neat a job as I've ever seen of cutting that bastard's throat.' Suddenly his seamed face creased in an evil grin. 'Yes indeed, a real professional job. Slaughtered a lot of pigs in his time, I'll wager. One more was no problem to him.'

'Slaughterman, eh?' Galveron frowned. 'You know, I wonder if we shouldn't have confiscated those knives of his.'

'But why, sir? You'd be taking away his livelihood.'

'That's why I hesitated, Ewald. I decided to give the man the benefit of the doubt. After all, *anyone* would be consumed by rage and bitterness after what he's just been through. There was just something about him, though, that made me uneasy.' Galveron shook his head. 'Ewald – send one of the men back there. Tell him to follow discreetly and make sure that family really do leave the city. If I was convinced that Ivar the slaughterman would stick to livestock in future I wouldn't be worried, but if his mind has truly been twisted by this atrocity, there's no telling how far he'll go for revenge.'

Eight

Plans and Preparations

The hem of the thick, dark cloak swept the steps behind him as Zavahl hurried down the twisting staircase that led from the lofty Hierarch's quarters to the vestibule at the back of the great Basilica. Here his privacy was protected by heavy doors of oak, inlaid with bronze. Bracing his arms, he pushed the great slabs ajar to gain access to the Sacred Hall of Worship.

The echoes of Zavahl's soft, padding footsteps and the louder clatter of the raised heels that Gilarra wore in a hopeless attempt to increase her tiny stature diminished into the vast hush like the beating of distant wings as they crossed the wide expanse of floor. Zavahl soon outpaced her, emerging from the massive portals of the Basilica to breathe deeply of the cool, rain-washed air. After the deep, mysterious shadows within the vast Hall of Worship, even the gloom of a rainy day seemed dazzlingly bright. The Hierarch turned back to look at the fascia of the temple, staring up and up at vistas of soaring pillars, intricate arches and dizzying balconies that had all been carved out of the living face of the canyon's sheer wall. It was truly magnificent, a miracle, a wonder – but Zavahl always found it difficult to believe that it could be his home.

Hurrying past the chill shadow of the Godsword Citadel's

high, looming walls that had been sculpted like the temple, from the cliff itself, Zavahl followed the roadway, passing between the low, gracious buildings that housed the priests and priestesses on his right, and the library and attached school and scriptorium on the left, with the Hall of Healing beyond. Finally he passed by the gardens and orchard, and came to the high, curving wall and the gold filigree of the Inner Gates. Astonishment flickered across the impassive faces of the guards as he approached, and they snapped belatedly to attention as he passed them by. It had been many days since he had emerged from his lurking place within the Basilica, but who would dare question the comings and goings of the Hierarch himself?

The high wall of the Inner Sanctum divided the gorge across its width, cutting off the Inner Sanctum with its Temple. The outer part of the canyon, between the Inner Gates and the access tunnel, contained a pleasant cluster of neat dwellings, the homes and workshops of the extensive army of support workers who kept the Basilica, the Citadel, and the Sacred Precincts running from day to day. Beyond them, the canyon walls closed in on either side to join the narrow stretch of sheer cliff pierced with an arched tunnel leading to the Lower Town that sprawled down the mountainside beyond.

Hugging the inner canyon walls were other buildings serving the community of the Sacred Precincts: stables, mews, a laundry, a bakehouse and the workshops of all the artisans from silversmiths to seamstresses. Here, in this outer area of the Precincts, the atmosphere was less awe-inspiring and more comfortable – it had the look of a pleasant, prosperous village, with a large, grassy square in the centre which served as meeting-place, marketplace and a playground for the children of the artisan families who were fortunate enough to live here. Today was the children's lucky day. The Hierarch scowled to see a voluble crowd, apparently undeterred by the rain, who had gathered several deep around the tall, gaily painted wagon in the middle of the square.

Zavahl curled his lip in disgust at the sight of the gaudy vehicle, and the donkey with its little cart piled high with an assortment of goods. The two superb black horses, standing patiently and with colossal dignity, were the only creatures that loaned a certain air of respectability to the outlandish assemblage. Zavahl wondered where and how this pair of shabbily dressed, mud-splattered itinerants had managed to come by such magnificent beasts. The traders' ensemble looked as though a travelling circus had camped within the Sacred Precincts, and the effect was not helped by the crowd, which, the Hierarch noted with annoyance, consisted not only of children, but of junior priests, scribes and servants from the Sacred Precincts. They surrounded the entourage, coming as close as they dared to the four armoured Godsword guards who watched over the visitors.

Unless more were hiding in the wagon there were only three itinerants: a tall, dark-haired, dark-eyed man of middle years who stood beside the horses and, perched up on the wagon seat, the wife, a tiny creature, much younger than her husband but plain as a wren. Her eyes, wide with awe, remained fixed firmly on Zavahl's face in a fashion that he found both irritating and unnerving. She had her arm around a little girl who was looking at the Hierarch with a frank, bright, curious gaze, a welcome relief from the moonstruck stare of her mother. With some relief, Zavahl turned away from the woman and child, and approached the trader himself. For certain he would get more sense out of a man. He knew that, even for a Hierarch, he was being unspeakably rude.

Strictly speaking, these folk counted as his guests within the Sacred Precincts, and custom dictated that he should offer them refreshment and invite them inside, out of the cold, wet courtyard. Zavahl did not care. He had just over a day to live, and courtesy seemed of little consequence now.

The trader looked him straight in the eye – a calm appraising stare without a trace of deference. The Hierarch gazed back. 'Please,' he said softly. 'Tell me about this dragon.' And as this simple, honest-seeming man told his tale, a faint ember of hope began to glow once more in Zavahl's heart . . .

'What in Myrial's name is going on here?'

Zavahl jumped, inwardly cursing himself for doing so, as the rasping voice spoke right in his ear. While his attention had been fixed on the traders, Lord Blade had approached from behind on silent feet.

The Hierarch recovered himself. 'Why, my Lord Blade, have your sentinels not informed you? It's a sorry day when the Godsword Commander cannot rely on his men.'

'My sentinels told me a heap of arrant nonsense that no sane man would believe.' Blade's voice held a hard edge of contempt. 'I have no wish to discuss it before this superstitious riff-raff.' He flicked a quick, narrow-eyed glance at Zavahl. 'Besides,' he added, in a bland, insinuating tone, 'why must *you* stand out here in the rain and deal with this rabble? Surely if such a wondrous creature had appeared within Callisiora, Myrial would have informed his Hierarch first and foremost? You never *used* to have any difficulty finding out exactly what was passing in our realm.' He gestured dismissively at the crowd around the wagon and turned to his guards in some irritation. 'You! Don't just stand there, you idle slackers! Disperse that mob at once!' As he spoke, the loiterers in the vicinity of the wagon all remembered pressing business elsewhere.

Zavahl reacted to the taunt with a hot flare of anger that sank into icy fear. *What does Blade know? How much has he guessed? He cannot possibly know about the Eye's unresponsiveness – or can he?*

'Myrial sends his tidings in his own good time, and in his own way,' he replied smoothly. 'If he chooses this lowly trader as his herald, who are we to question his intent?' He hurried on before the Godsword Commander could reply. 'Now, Lord Blade, your arrival was most timely. I shall require an escort to accompany me up to the Snaketail Pass to investigate these rumours.'

As he was speaking, another notion flicked through Zavahl's quick mind. If there really *was* a dragon, he could always tell the populace that Myrial had alerted him to its presence. That should allay the widespread suspicion that the Hierarch had the God's disfavour. Blade knew better than to cause civil unrest by challenging him in public, and the silence of the Godsword troops was guaranteed, which only left the traders. If *they* pressed their claim to finding the creature it would ruin everything . . . Quickly, Zavahl turned back to Blade before he had time to leave. 'One more thing. In our absence, I would like you to avail the trader's wife and child of your hospitality – in the Citadel.'

For once, even the phlegmatic Blade looked startled. He drew Zavahl away, out of the trader's earshot. 'You want me to *imprison* them? On what charge? There's no crime in the city statutes that mentions telling a pack of lies about a mythical creature.'

Zavahl scowled. 'I don't want them imprisoned *officially*! But I do want to keep them safely in my hands for the present, and the Citadel is the best place to hold the others while the man shows me what he found. Time will tell whether or not they are telling the truth, but I want some answers, and until I get to the bottom of this business – whether it be chicanery or miracle – I don't want anyone vanishing. Nor do I want them blabbing their tale all over the city.'

'Not until you can release *your* version of the truth, you mean.'

'*I* am the Hierarch!' Zavahl almost spat the words at him. *I decide what constitutes the truth in Callisiora.* To his horror he almost heard the thought spill aloud from his lips, and strangled the words unsaid. With an effort, he brought his temper under control. 'The decision is mine.'

'For now,' Blade replied in a quiet, even voice, his expression stony. 'You're a fool, Zavahl. Whatever happens, this is a mistake. If you really want them silenced, you'll have to kill them.'

'Then see to it,' Zavahl said coldly.

Blade gave him a long, hard look, then shrugged. 'As you command, Lord Hierarch.' He stalked away stiff-backed.

A shiver ran down Zavahl's spine. He suspected that he had just made a serious mistake. So what? he told himself. I am the Hierarch – what can Blade do to me? Besides, he refused to let that thrice-damned butcher get the final word. 'Lord Blade?' he called. The Godsword swung round, for once betraying his annoyance at being called back in such a peremptory fashion. Zavahl smiled. 'One more thing,' he said softly. 'Get this damned menagerie out of my courtyard, and have a message sent to the stablemaster. Tell him to look after those horses well, and treat them with the greatest care. By the end of this day, they will belong to me.'

'No, Zavahl. By the end of this day, they will belong to *me*.'

Gilarra, startled by someone speaking so close to her,

spun to see Lord Blade standing a short distance away, his gaze fixed greedily upon the two magnificent black horses belonging to the traders. It was the closest thing to emotion she had ever seen in his face. 'I beg your pardon? Did you say something?' she asked him.

He looked at her sharply, then shook his head. 'No, Lady. I was merely thinking out loud. If you will excuse me . . .' With that, he hurried away. Gilarra shrugged, and went back to watching Zavahl with deepening concern as he supervised the preparations for the journey. Clearly the enforced delay was tightening his nerves as he waited impatiently for Blade's escort to assemble themselves, and for the traders' wagon and livestock to be accommodated. On Blade's instructions, the wagon was driven into the Citadel courtyard, and the animals were taken to the far end of the Sacred Precincts to be housed in the complex of stables, kennels and mews near the entrance tunnel. As the time sped by, Gilarra saw the Hierarch grow increasingly agitated. Unable to stand still, he paced back and forth across the courtyard, snapping and snarling like a cur-dog at anyone who got in his way. His eyes were focused inward, and his expression was tense and pale.

Poor Zavahl, Gilarra thought. He's right on the edge now. I should never have told him these ridiculous tidings of a dragon. It was just too cruel to raise his hopes. Had I been any kind of a friend, I would be helping him to face up to his responsibilities and accept his fate. It's bound to come to that in the end. Zavahl is destined for the sacrificial pyre. No matter how he pins his hopes on these mad rumours, he cannot escape his fate.

This was the dark side of the Hierarch's role, the antithesis of the panoply and power. Though only one unfortunate Hierarch in a hundred might be required to give his life

for the land he ruled, there was no escape and no appeal if
the worst should happen. A chill ran through Gilarra. How
close she had come! I always envied Zavahl his position, she
thought candidly – until today. Now I wouldn't be in his shoes
for every gem in these cruel mountains. I wonder how I would
be facing up to the prospect if our roles had been reversed, and
I was the one destined to die tomorrow?

She couldn't bear to watch him any longer. Gilarra turned,
intending to head back into the temple and pray for Zavahl's
tormented soul. Lord Blade was back again, and was standing
in her way. 'Lady Suffragan.' He bowed his head to her, his
demeanour quiet and respectful. 'I came to ask if you are
ready to take over from the Hierarch.'

During the last few months, everything had been leading
up to this moment – yet now that it had finally arrived, Blade's
words, brutal in their simplicity, still shocked Gilarra to the
core. *All my life I've been preparing for this moment. I thought I
would be ready* . . . With an effort, the Suffragan pulled together
her whirling thoughts. 'You believe, then, as I do, that this tale
of a dragon is nonsense?'

Blade shrugged. 'Whether the dragon be fact or falsehood,
alive or dead, it won't be enough to placate the Tiarondians.
They are expecting the Hierarch to be sacrificed tomorrow
night – indeed, they are convinced that their continuing lives
depend upon his demise.' He smiled bleakly. 'It's our responsibility to see that they aren't disappointed, Suffragan.'

Gilarra's instincts warned her that it would be a lethal error
to show any weakness in front of this man, as Zavahl was
finding out to his cost. She took a deep breath. 'Very well,
Lord Blade. What exactly are you suggesting? Do you wish
to prevent the Hierarch from setting out on this wild goose
chase?'

The Godsword Commander shrugged. 'No. I suggest we let him go. He'll find no live dragon up on the Snaketail – of that I'm certain. With such additional proof that Myrial has abandoned him, he must acquiesce to his fate. I will place him under guard – with your permission, of course – and bring him back to the city. You can announce tomorrow's ceremony to the people, and Zavahl's fate will be irrevocably sealed.'

Kanella was awestruck. Throughout her life her greatest support had been her profound, unquestioning faith in Myrial. Now, quite unexpectedly, here she was in the very Sacred Precincts of the Temple, with the most powerful and holy man in Callisiora! She forgave him for looking so dour and ill humoured; the Hierarch must have many important matters to preoccupy his thoughts. Had she been alone, she would have been too overawed to make any sense, so she was glad to leave matters to her pragmatic lifemate, who judged folk not by rank or title but by their actions. Just being here, part of this moment, was enough. She was content to stay in the background and let Tormon do the talking – unlike Annas, who had been forbidden to get down from the wagon box and was now twisting and fidgeting in her seat, growing restive and bored at all this pointless adult chatter.

Kanella felt a tug on her hand, and half turned to see her daughter looking up at her. 'Mama, why is that man so grumpy?' Annas asked in a typical child's whisper that was almost as loud as if she'd shouted. The trader's blood froze. 'Shhh!' she hissed urgently, terrified lest the Hierarch had overheard such rudeness. He gave no sign of having heard, however, and remained deep in conversation with

Tormon. 'And you're sure?' she heard him say. 'It was definitely some kind of living creature? You couldn't be mistaken?'

'No, my Lord.' Tormon shook his head. 'It was a huge, outlandish beast – that's for sure – but whether it was still alive, I couldn't tell. I doubt it could have survived this long, but who can say?'

'And you can lead me to it? If it is as you say, there could be a reward for you.'

'I'll lead you there, my Lord.'

'Good man.' The Hierarch – the Hierarch himself – put an arm around the shoulders of Kanella's lifemate. She almost burst with pride. 'Come then,' he was saying to Tormon. 'No need to drag your little family all the way back up the mountain. They can stay here in comfort, warm and dry, until we come back.'

At his words, Kanella felt a shiver of unease. She looked beyond the Hierarch to the cluster of unsmiling, heavily armoured soldiers and their grim, harsh-faced leader. The only one who didn't seem intimidating was the small, plump woman with the grey-streaked dark hair, and even she was scowling, her face tight with unspoken anger. Suddenly Kanella didn't want to stay here. The shadowy, steep-walled canyon with its solitary exit seemed too much like a trap. Firmly, she told herself not to be silly. If she couldn't trust Myrial's own servant, who could she trust?

Arrangements were made quickly. Kanella's timidly voiced concerns about her horses were brushed aside. Space would be found for them here in the stables. While runners were sent to the city's merchants to hire carts and strong oxen to climb the pass, Kanella saw her own animals settled comfortably, though she remained aware every moment of the Hierarch's brooding presence in the background, fuming with ill-suppressed impatience.

At last everything was ready. Lord Blade, the stony-faced Godsword Commander who would be accompanying the Hierarch and his escort of soldiers, had loaned Tormon a fresh horse and everyone was preparing to depart. Tormon hugged Kanella and his little daughter. 'This shouldn't take too long, lovey,' he reassured her. 'We'll probably be back by nightfall, or tomorrow morning at the latest, depending on how long it takes to dig the poor beast out. Once that's over, we can think about getting settled down for the winter.'

Kanella swallowed hard, and warned herself once again not to be an idiot. 'Hurry back,' she whispered. 'And Tormon – you will be careful, won't you?'

The trader grinned. 'Don't worry – I don't even plan to get my hands dirty. I'm going to let these hulking soldiers do all the hard work.' After one last hug, he mounted his horse. As the cavalcade rode towards the tunnel that pierced the cliffs and led into the outer city, she turned away, unable to watch any longer. The long dark passage looked too much like a gaping mouth, ready and waiting to swallow up the unwary.

'Come along, my dear.'

Kanella whirled at the touch of a hand on her arm, and found herself face to face with the small woman, who, she had already discovered, was the Suffragan Gilarra, second only to the Hierarch in Myrial's eyes. 'My Lady . . .' She tried to bow, but the woman pulled her up with a kindly laugh. 'Let's not be formal . . . Kanella, isn't it? Life's too short. Come along, my dear – you and your little one can come home with me. I have a son just about her age.'

Gilarra had begun to lead Kanella and Annas toward the

cluster of neat white artisans' dwellings, when suddenly a soldier blocked their way. 'I'm sorry, Lady Suffragan,' he told her, 'but I have orders from Commander Blade and the Lord Zavahl that these people are to remain in the Godsword Citadel until the Hierarch's return.'

Gilarra's expression did not change, though Kanella was sure she saw a glint of irritation in the other woman's eyes. 'And I have just changed those orders.'

The soldier shook his head regretfully. 'I'm very sorry, Lady Suffragan, but the Commander and the Hierarch both made their wishes very clear, and I must obey them . . . Perhaps you could take the matter up with them when they return?'

'You may be sure I will.' Gilarra's tones were clipped with anger, but when she turned back to Kanella she was smiling again. 'Those men! In their zeal to give you a place to rest, they never stopped to think you'd be far more comfortable with me than in that freezing great barracks.' She shrugged – a little *too* casually, Kanella thought. 'Never mind, dear, we won't get your escort into trouble. You go with him now and let him get you settled, and I'll come along and see you later.' She fixed the unfortunate soldier with a long, cold stare. 'You make sure they have every possible comfort, do you hear?' Then, before Kanella could draw another breath, she was gone.

The guard didn't look too intimidating, Kanella tried to comfort herself. She was reassured to see that he had a kind word and a cheery smile for Annas. He led the trader and her daughter past the artisans' village and through the high gold gates to the Inner Sanctum itself. Kanella was most surprised to find, beyond the looming wall, an orchard on her right-hand side, and a homely garden, with flowers and vegetables all battered and disintegrating in the rain, on the other. She didn't know exactly what she had expected, but surely nothing so ordinary . . . On the far side of the gardens stood more buildings, grander and more imposing than those in the artisans' village on the other side of the dividing wall. They were constructed from blocks of the same golden stone that formed the canyon's cliffs.

They passed the last of the buildings and emerged in the spacious courtyard before Myrial's Temple itself. Kanella gasped in awe at her first real sight of the imposing structure, carved in relief like a great mask on the face of the cliff. How could puny human hands have produced a miracle on so grand a scale? Surely the God himself must have had a hand in its creation. If the Lord Hierarch was pleased with the dragon, maybe he'd let her look inside . . .

'Mama – I'm all wet now.'

'Come on, mistress. Don't stand gawking in the rain.'

Kanella was unaware that she had stopped until the guard's gruff voice broke into her reverie, and she felt her daughter's urgent tug on her hand. 'Sorry,' she muttered. She turned to her left to follow the soldier – and stopped dead in her tracks once more. The building that must be their destination had also been carved from the cliff but, unlike the glorious fascia of the Temple, which had been intricately and painstakingly sculpted in loving detail, this place was clearly built for war. It loomed over her, as though it were about to crush her like an insect. The walls were utterly smooth and featureless, so no enemy could gain a foothold to climb them, she supposed. The only windows were arrow slits that looked like mean squinting eyes.

'Grand, int it?' The guard said proudly, mistaking her horror for awe.

Annas pulled back at her hand. 'Mama, I don't like that place!'

Kanella thrust the small bundle of clothing she had brought with her into the unready hands of their escort and picked up her daughter. 'Me neither,' she said with brisk honesty, 'but we've slept in worse places on the road. At least it'll be warm and dry – well, dry at least. It'll be all right, sweetheart. It's only till your dad gets back, then we'll go.'

As they headed for the grim entrance with its fearsome portcullis, the little girl looked glumly at her new, temporary home. 'I hope he hurries up, then,' she said doubtfully.

NINE

The Price of Silence

Within the thick-walled fortress that was the Citadel of the Godswords, even the officers' quarters made few concessions to luxury or comfort, Galveron thought, as he hurried along the bare and draughty corridor, the rhythmic tapping of his boots ringing with an echo from the exposed expanses of stone on walls and floor. Though the place always reeked with the masculine, martial smells of leather, oil, iron and sweat, nothing could ever eradicate the smell of old, chill, damp stone that permeated the entire building.

Not at all a suitable place to bring a little girl, let alone imprison her, the Lieutenant thought in disgust. How dare the Hierarch attempt this incarceration of a mother and child who had broken no laws and, as far as he could see, had done no wrong. And what was all this nonsense about a bloody dragon? It was most unlike Zavahl and Lord Blade to set off together on such a wild goose chase. Had everybody in the Sacred Precincts gone mad today?

Even before he had received this latest news, Lieutenant Galveron of the Godswords had been in no good mood. The endless rain was taking a dreadful toll upon the poorer inhabitants of Tiarond. This morning, on patrol in the Lower City, he had walked through a miserable collection of wretched hovels, noting the leaky roofs, crumbling brickwork and rotten doors and window frames. The back lanes were choked with uncleared refuse and, because the streets were so close to the rising river, the gutters had backed up and overflowed into the streets. The inhabitants, diseased, infested and famished, had gathered in their doorways to watch with hostile, hopeless eyes as the Godsword patrol, well fed and warmly clad in their heavy black cloaks, passed by.

Galveron shook his head in angry disapproval. These squalid riverside slums, along with a great deal of other property in the city, were owned by the Lady Seriema, easily the richest woman in the entire realm of Callisiora. All that wealth had done nothing to allay her greed, apparently. Over the last five years since her father's death she had been squeezing her tenants for every last copper she could extract, and clearly, Galveron thought bitterly, she didn't believe in wasting any of her precious fortune on repairs. He couldn't even take her to task over the matter; as second-in-command of the Godswords he lacked the authority. It would be up to the Hierarch or Lord Blade to intervene – and both of them were far too busy with their own private plots and schemes to give a hang about a bunch of verminous slum-dwellers.

Today, however, Seriema had gone too far. His heart bled for the poor families who had suffered so badly at the hands of her hirelings. It had not escaped his attention that lately she had been casting people out of their homes to free up tracts of valuable land within the walls of Tiarond. The areas concerned were usually close to either the river or the city gates, so he assumed that her plans had some connection with trade. Either she wanted more warehouse space ready for more fruitful times, or she planned some kind of new market area, with ruinous tolls on her fellow merchants for use of the space, no doubt, Galveron thought disapprovingly. Unfortunately, there was nothing he could do about the evictions. The land belonged to Seriema, and she was entitled to dispose of it as she wished. He would not, however, tolerate murder, assault and rape among her henchmen, and their practice of setting houses on fire to prevent the tenants returning must be stopped at once. It was only thanks to this accursed pernicious weather that the entire Lower Town, with its primarily wooden buildings, had not gone up like tinder.

On days like this Galveron wondered why he had joined the Godswords – and, more to the point, why he stayed. Ever since childhood he had loved the old stories and legends, learned at his grandmother's knee. His father had been a warrior, who had died when Galveron was just a boy. Undeterred by his parent's untimely end and inspired by the legendary heroes of his grandma's tales, he'd thought to join the forces of Good – Myrial's own elite – and set right all the wrongs of his poor land. It made him cringe to remember what a gullible young innocent he'd been.

The Godswords had turned out not to be the league of god-like heroes young Galveron had expected, but as flawed a bunch of mortal men as ever cheated at dice or took a bribe. Within the walls of the Citadel fierce competition flourished, with each man vying with his fellows for rank and favour. Bribery was commonplace and tale-bearing almost compulsory. In some cases, even back-stabbing was not confined to a mere figure of speech.

Galveron shook his blond head in disapproval. It was a source of constant amazement, to himself as well as his comrades-in-arms, that he had not only survived in this pit of corruption but had risen so quickly through the ranks that he'd made second-in-command at the age of twenty-five. He was so completely unlike Lord Blade, the ruthless, hard-bitten Commander, that he could not help but suspect he had somehow been set up as a dupe, to be used in one of Blade's ambitious schemes. Ever since he had been promoted to his current rank, he'd spent each and every day waiting for the axe to fall, but so far, it had never happened. Apparently Blade was more than happy to keep somebody honest and conscientious around, if only to do the dull and dirty work.

And speaking of which ... Galveron turned left as he reached a junction of passages, and hurried down the last long corridor that led to the prisoners' quarters. In the brief time since his return from the Lower Town, he had spoken to the Suffragan Gilarra, and his ears were still burning from what she had to say. He could only be grateful that her anger had not been directed at *him*. That did not help him out of a very difficult situation, however. 'What are you going to do about it?' the Suffragan had demanded – but what could he do? How could he disobey a direct order from the Hierarch, and what would happen to him if he did? Yet he could not live with his conscience if an innocent woman and child were murdered.

Zavahl's decision to imprison the wayfarers filled Galveron with alarm. Though he had no idea what was going on in the Hierarch's convoluted mind, of one thing he was absolutely certain. Whether a dragon was found today or not, the poor traders could measure the remainder of their lives in hours at most. If civilians were brought into the Citadel, it was almost always a one-way trip. In addition, few of the guards on duty had any knowledge of the traders' presence, and those who had been present when the woman and child were taken into the Citadel seemed most anxious to forget about it, to the point where Galveron had had considerable difficulty in finding out anything at all about the incident. No one dared actually to come out and say that the Hierarch had ordered these innocents killed, but their very reticence and the fact that the travellers had been brought deep into this little used part of the Citadel, all served to confirm Galveron's suspicions.

How could he face this poor woman, knowing what he knew?

At last Galveron had reached the room in which the trader and her daughter had been bestowed. Even as he was reaching for the door handle, he knew he was too late. A ghastly shriek tore through the air and cut off abruptly. A high, childish voice was squealing, 'No, no, no . . .'

Galveron burst into the room in time to see the woman slide from the soldier's grasp, her dead eyes staring in a face mottled and blue from asphyxiation. The child's screaming cut off abruptly as her mother thudded heavily to the floor, limbs still twitching. The little girl's eyes were empty and blank with shock, her mouth still open in mid-scream. The guard, absently coiling the cord of the garrotte between his fingers, looked up from the body, his mouth twisted with a vast distaste, to see his superior officer standing in the doorway.

As the frozen moment of horror passed, Galveron finally found his voice. 'Barsil! What in Myrial's name do you think you're *doing*?' He was scarcely aware that he was shouting. 'Why didn't you wait for my return? She was just a helpless woman, for Myrial's sake! An innocent trader!'

The soldier's eyes widened. 'Trader? But I thought Lord Blade said *traitor*! In any case, sir, it don't matter. This was on the Hierarch's orders. The woman and child must be silenced, he said. They must never talk . . .'

His words were cut off abruptly by the clatter of small feet in swift and sudden motion, as the little girl made a dive towards the half-open door.

Galveron, taken by surprise, made an ineffectual grab as the child squeezed past him, then she was gone, running like the wind down the passage. 'Shit!' Galveron snapped. Already she had disappeared round the corner, heading for the place where the passages joined. With the soldier at his heels, Galveron raced after her.

Toulac was awakened by the sound of a troop of riders passing by her house along the nearby trail. Pulling back the curtain, she peered out of the window – and decided that she must still be dreaming. Why, surely that was the Hierarch himself! She'd know that wry and permanently disapproving expression anywhere. And beside him, by everything holy, was that cold-blooded bastard Lord Blade! When they had passed her safely by, Toulac let out a breath she had not known she'd been holding, and sighed with relief. 'Why in the seven pits of perdition are they going up the mountain with all those soldiers?' she muttered to herself. 'Taking trouble to somebody, I'll be bound.'

With a chill, Toulac thought of the strange visitor who'd arrived in the night, and the even stranger creature that was housed, right at this very minute, in her barn. They said that the Hierarch knew everything that passed in his realm . . .

'Superstitious twaddle!' she told herself. 'If he had known, would he have passed by the house?' None the less, she couldn't shake the conviction that the two events were connected, somehow. Surely, this had to be more than mere coincidence?

Toulac worked the pump handle vigorously over the old stone sink, thanking providence that her mother had nagged her father mercilessly until he'd worked out a way to bring water *inside* the house. He had nearly broken his back sinking a well in the packed earth of the cellar, but it certainly saved a lot of messing about. She took a long deep drink, then scooped up a double handful of the clear, cold fluid and splashed her face. She desperately needed to clear her head. Though she had dozed for an hour or two this morning, uncomfortably upright in her chair, her thoughts still felt slow and blurred following her sleepless night, and she was worried about the weird woman – not to mention her *extremely* weird companion – that the fates had dumped on the doorstep.

Another abiding concern was the fate of poor Mazal. The horse had vanished, screaming, into the night, terrified out of his wits – and she didn't blame the poor beast – by that outlandish, dragonish creature. Toulac was desperately worried about her old companion, though he was in no danger from the big lizard, who had consumed most of Toulac's meat supply and was now asleep in the barn. There were other creatures in the mountains, though, bears and big cats and the like. She desperately wanted to go in search of him and bring him back to safety, yet she didn't dare leave the injured woman for the time it might take to find a terrified horse.

Still stiff from sitting all night at the bedside of her unexpected visitor, she hobbled over to the fire and dropped an armload of new wood on the sullen embers, before starting a fresh pot of the strong black tea sold by an old herbwife in Tiarond. The blend was a secret recipe, so old Manda claimed, passed down through many generations in her family. A combination of herbs, berries and bark, it packed a kick like a battling warhorse and had seen Toulac through many a long night's watch or early morning march. Wherever she had wandered, the warrior had always contrived to have a supply on hand.

While the tisane was brewing, Toulac ransacked her larder, wondering whether she had anything fit for *anyone* to eat, let alone an invalid. By Myrial's boundless backside, she had been letting things slip lately! Just as she was rummaging in the deepest, darkest recess at the back of a shelf, her heart leaped as she heard the sound of a shrill whinny coming from outside. 'Mazal!' Toulac straightened sharply and cracked her head on the shelf above. 'Bugger it!' Rubbing her reeling head, she rushed to open the door.

Because of the heavy overcast, it was impossible to tell the time with any accuracy, but it looked to be about noon or after, at any rate. Toulac peered blearily out at the new day, and found it grey and wet, as usual. Much more wonderful to her was the sight of her horse, who stood waiting for her at the bottom of the porch steps. Mazal looked a fright: muddy and scratched by undergrowth, his mane and tail matted into strings by the rain. Apart from that, Toulac noted with relief, he seemed unscathed. The warhorse flattened his ears and rolled his eyes as he sniffed the air. Clearly, he could still smell the giant lizard, but the creature was safely out of sight, asleep in the barn.

'Come on, you daft old thing.' Toulac walked the horse up and down a couple of times, to make sure he hadn't lamed himself in his frantic flight. Then, not without some difficulty, she coaxed him back up the porch steps and into the house. After his ordeal, she didn't want to leave him in the draughty, rickety lean-to woodshed at the back of the house, and he certainly couldn't go into the barn right now! Once she had managed to get him inside, and installed him back in last night's place in the corner of the kitchen, Toulac prepared a warm mash for the weary beast and rubbed him down to dry him and get rid of the mud. Leaving him to eat, she poured herself a mug of the strong black tea, and went back into her bedroom to check on the injured stranger.

The woman stirred and moaned a little as Toulac entered the room, but she did not wake. Now that it was daylight, she opened the shutters a little, so that she could see the face of her guest more clearly. She shook her head sadly at the sight of the scar that stood out as a livid brand on the stranger's pallid skin, like a frozen image of a zigzag lightning bolt that seared its way down the side of her face and continued along her shoulder and arm. There's nothing wrong with a few scars, the veteran thought – Myrial knows, I've collected enough of my own over the years. It's a shame, though, that she should have such an ugly wound right there on her face. When Toulac looked carefully, however, and saw past the scar, she realised that the woman's face possessed a curious, delicate beauty that seemed to throw the disfigurement into relief, making it seem worse than it actually was.

What in Myrial's name could have happened to mark her so savagely? It was like nothing Toulac had ever seen. What a tragedy, she thought. A vision flashed across her mind of the woman with her short, raggedly cut hair restored to length and lustre, her skinny body (it *was* skinny, not slender – she sprawled on the fleeces like a parcel of old bones) filled out and bedecked in decent clothing. Then Toulac looked again – at the grim lines, harsh even in repose, carved by grief and time and weather across the stranger's brow and around her mouth; at the severe, practical cut of the mud-caked leathers – now hanging over a nearby chair – which had clung flat to her whipcord-and-bone body; at the fighter's calluses and scars on her forearms and hands. This enigma was no town-maid, soft and fragile. She's a warrior, the veteran thought, with a jolt of excitement. A warrior like me!

Toulac put out a hand, feeling the woman's throat for a pulse. It still beat there, and maybe felt a little stronger now – or was she just imagining that? She hoped the woman would live. Over the years, she had gained a good deal of rough-and-ready battlefield experience in diagnosing and patching injuries. As far as she could tell there might be a cracked rib or two – certainly they would be bruised – but amazingly she couldn't find any broken limbs. The woman seemed half starved, which didn't help matters, but if she was tough enough to get through the exposure and concussion she was in with a chance. Shaking her head, Toulac touched the jagged scar with gentle fingers. It looked as though the poor girl had suffered through far worse than this and survived.

When she returned to the kitchen, it was clear that Mazal, who was trembling with fatigue, wanted to lie down. The warrior sighed. There was nothing else for it; she must make him a bed right here, and be damned to the mess in the kitchen! There's one thing, Toulac thought, looking around the dingy room. A good, thick bed of clean straw will hide the mucky floor at least and it can't make this place look any worse than it already does.

Toulac pulled her boots on and went out to the barn, her feet squelching in the mud. Despite the pouring rain, somehow she could not bring herself to hurry. She felt a little nervous, she supposed, at the thought of another encounter with the monstrous dragonish creature, though she knew she was being stupid. The creature had sought her out to help his companion, had he not? That required a certain degree of reasoning and intellect. 'Toulac, old girl, this clearly is not your average ravening monster,' she tried to reassure herself. 'The trouble is, he's just so bloody *big*!'

For a long time, Toulac stood just within the doorway of the barn, watching the strange creature she had sheltered. It had not so much as flicked an eyelid since she had entered. It was lost in the deep sleep of utter exhaustion. Nevertheless, the veteran reflected, the creature was showing a good deal of trust in her, a total stranger, by allowing itself such an unguarded slumber. Somehow, she was rather touched by that.

Now that it was daylight she could study the creature more closely. A peculiar-looking beastie it was, but she found a simple beauty in the elegant curves of its long body as it lay curled in the straw like a sleeping cat. Its hide gleamed with a soft sheen in the dim half-light that seeped through the open doorway, the scaly patterning somewhat reminiscent of a serpent's skin. The reptilian appearance was deceptive, however. Toulac had touched it the previous evening, and found it warm and limber beneath her hands.

Oh, how she wished this weirdsome, wonderful creature would wake! Though when it did, she realised with some dismay, it would very likely be hungry again. Luckily, she had been raising two pigs, one to eat and one to sell. That had been the plan, at any rate. Last night, at a loss for something to feed her huge visitor, she had given up one of the pigs, which had vanished down the throat of the giant lizard with alarming speed. Today the other would probably follow its brother down the same road, and that would be that. Oh well. Toulac shrugged. It had been a nigh impossible task to feed the wretched things anyway, so that would be one less thing to worry about. But what would this monster eat after the pigs had gone? What was its usual food?

The warrior studied the sleeping creature closely. What the bloody blazes *are* you? she wondered. Despite its considerable size and formidable appearance, it was clearly an intelligent being, more so, Toulac reflected wryly, than many of the big, dumb fighting men she had come across in her long and eventful life. Where in all creation had it come from? What was its connection to the strange, fey, injured woman it had brought right to her door?

Toulac was no fool. In the course of a lifetime's wanderings she had seen the Curtain Walls many times, and knew that they enclosed the whole of Callisiora. The priests might say they were the boundaries of the world, but the wily veteran had never believed that for a single minute. She had heard all the stories, told around the fire during long midnight watches, of outlandish, often horrifying intruders that were not native to Callisiora, but had seemingly broken through from ... What? Where? Nowadays, interestingly enough, those tales and rumours were becoming increasingly frequent and bizarre. Coincidence? Toulac didn't think so.

For much of her life, the veteran had itched to know what lay beyond those uncanny barriers of power and light. As she stood there, in the cold and dusty barn, looking at a creature outside all human ken, she experienced the old stirring of excitement in her blood, a feeling she had thought she'd lost forever. She felt the black and heavy cloak of age, despair and uselessness, which had weighed her down for so long, slip from her shoulders and vanish. Was this her last great chance? The longed-for opportunity to end her life in the midst of some grand and wonderful adventure? To go out fighting as a warrior should? Too right it was!

'Whatever is going on here,' Toulac vowed, 'I intend to be part of it – supposing it's the last thing I do.'

Just then, a small voice came from behind her: 'Help me – please.' The mysterious woman had awakened and ventured outdoors.

The monster opened its eyes.

Ten

The Fate of a Stranger

Barsil was loitering in the Citadel courtyard beside the trader woman's canvas-wrapped body. He was waiting for a cart to come across from the stable block at the far end of the Precincts, so that he could take the corpse away and bury it in the graveyard outside the city walls. Muttering sourly, the Godsword soldier pulled his hood up against the cold rain. He was not a happy man. Today seemed to be the day he got stuck with all the dirty work. It wasn't fair!

First of all he'd been given the job of putting away the trader woman and her child. The killing hadn't bothered him – it never did – neither did the sex of both his victims nor the youth of one. He had sense enough, he told himself, to prefer such nice, soft easy targets to, say, a great big eastern Reiver, armed with a battleaxe. It had been pure bad luck, however, that Lieutenant Prissy-Britches Holier-than-Myrial Galveron should appear at the worst possible moment and make a proper muck-up of the entire business. Luckily Barsil had just had time to finish the woman before the interfering bastard showed up, but the soft-hearted fool had let the girl escape, and she had vanished right into thin air, though Barsil had his own ideas about that. He and the Lieutenant had supposedly searched the Citadel from top to bottom. There was no way the brat could have escaped, not without help from Galveron. But who would get the blame if the Hierarch found out? Not the bloody officer, that was for sure!

To cap it all – as if Barsil's day hadn't been difficult enough already – the cursed lieutenant had ordered him to give the woman a decent burial. 'Why me?' he'd felt like saying. 'I already killed her, didn't I? Surely it's somebody else's turn to bury the bitch.' The bleak look in Galveron's blue eyes, however, had suggested very strongly to Barsil that he'd be wiser to keep his mouth shut and get on with the job. Under normal circumstances, of course, once Galveron was out of the way, he would have tried to bribe, blackmail or browbeat someone else into taking on the onerous task, but the Citadel was almost deserted today. Some of the troopers had gone up the mountain with Lord Blade and the Hierarch, while others were out on patrol in the city or had just returned and were in the messroom, eating scanty noonday rations that were still far better and more plentiful than anything available to the folk of the Lower Town. *Nobody* interrupted a trooper when he was eating – not these days – so Barsil knew that there was no escape. Unfortunately, he was just going to have to get on with the job himself.

Suddenly, it dawned on Barsil that he really *was* alone. He glanced around surreptitiously. The narrow courtyard between the towering outer bailey of the Citadel and the high, solid structure of the inner keep was filled with a dusky grey half-darkness even on the best of days, but this heavy cloud that hung over the city suffused the deep well between high stone walls with crowding, murky shadows and thick gloom. Barsil looked down at the trader woman's body, an idea forming in his mind. Might as well take advantage of the situation. This whole business had been a right old pain in the backside, so why come away empty-handed? Stooping swiftly, he unfastened the canvas wrappings and folded them aside.

He ignored the miasma of death, faint but already unpleasant, that hung around the body, and paid no attention to the hard, clammy feel of cold flesh. Now, he thought, let's see. You never see a poor trader – they're always worth something . . . It took a while to rummage through the many pockets in her leather jerkin, but his searching revealed nothing but a pocket full of grain, one full of shrivelled bits of chopped carrot, and another laden with hard, boiled honey sweets. Barsil cursed bitterly. Bloody horse treats! The bitch! He turned his attention to the pouch at her waist, but it held just a handful of copper and silver coins. Well, better than nothing, but not by much. She had hoops of gold wire pierced through her earlobes and a slender gold chain around her neck, and these he removed and dropped into the pouch with the coins. At least they would get him a night with one of the Lower Town whores.

There was nothing else. Her boots, of good, sturdy, supple leather, turned out to be too small to fit him, but maybe the leather jerkin had possibilities . . . Grunting with the effort, he rolled the corpse over and, with difficulty, stripped the jerkin from the stiff, cold body. Before trying on the garment, he wrapped the corpse back into its canvas shroud. It would only be a matter of time before someone came along, and the fewer awkward questions he had to answer the better.

With another quick glance around to make sure he was still unobserved, Barsil unclasped his black cloak, bundling it on top of the body to keep it off the wet ground. He thrust his arms into the leather jerkin and— 'Myrial's black arsehole!' he snarled. The bloody thing was too small again. Muttering a string of oaths, he dropped the jerkin on the ground beside the discarded boots and kicked the offending pile. He was just about to kick the corpse as well, for good measure, when the sound of hurrying footsteps stopped him with one foot in mid-air.

Flailing his arms for balance, Barsil whirled in alarm. To his relief, it was only young Scall, apprentice to Agella, the smithmaster of the Sacred Precincts, who crafted weapons beyond compare for Myrial's holy warriors and acted as farrier to the fleet mounts of the Hierarch's messengers and the mighty warsteeds of the Godswords. Everyone knew it was bad luck to cross a smith, and no one in the Citadel failed to respect Agella. The same, however, could not be said for her skinny, lackadaisical, wet-behind-the-ears apprentice, who was hurrying out of the Citadel, clearly returning from some errand or other.

At the sight of the lad an idea burst into Barsil's brain. Maybe the day needn't be such a dead loss, after all. 'Hey!' he hissed. 'Hey, you! Apprentice!'

The boy jumped like a beggar's flea. 'Me?'

The trooper sighed. 'Of course, you. Who else? Get your backside over here.'

Scall, scowling, sullen and plainly reluctant, shuffled across the courtyard, dragging his feet. His expression cleared a little when he saw that the other man was only Barsil, not someone of rank. 'What do you want? Mistress Agella told me to get right back. She'll be really angry . . .'

'Never mind *her*.' Barsil seized the youngster's arm. 'I've got something just for you,' he said in a conspiratorial whisper. Picking up the leather jerkin, he held it out for the apprentice's inspection. 'What about that, eh? Could have been made for you.'

Scall's hand crept out towards the jerkin. The apprentices

could never afford stuff as good as this. To Barsil's annoyance, however, the hand was suddenly snatched back. 'What's the matter now?' he demanded.

The boy frowned. 'This is stolen! It belongs to that trader woman. I was looking at it when she came in this morning.'

'Myrial in a midden!' Barsil swore under his breath. He thought quickly. 'Er – of course this belonged to the trader. She traded it to me, as a matter of fact.' He tried to summon up a jovial smile. 'You know what these traders are. Always trading . . .' As he spoke, he kept edging furtively away from the long, canvas-covered bundle in the shadows.

'Did she trade you those, too?' Scall pointed out the footwear that lay on the ground. 'Seems odd that anyone would trade their *boots*.'

Barsil lashed out and cuffed the boy around the ear, not too hard, however, because he still hoped to strike a bargain. 'Less cheek, you apprentice. Less answering back. Now, do you want this lovely jerkin – the likes of which *you* won't see again in a hurry – or not?'

'I was only asking,' Scall whined, his hand clasped to his ear and his lower lip stuck out like a shelf. 'You've no call to go hitting me.' At that moment, his eye fell on the bundle in the shadows. 'What's that?'

'Er – nothing,' Barsil said quickly.

Scall's eyes stretched wide. 'That's her, isn't it? She's *dead*!' His voice rose to a horrified squeak. 'You're trying to sell me a dead woman's clothes!'

'Shut your hole!' Barsil gave the apprentice another clip round the ear. 'Not so bloody loud, you idiot.' He spread his arms wide in a shrug. 'Look, all right, so she's dead. So she doesn't want her jerkin any more, does she? And that's a good quality bit of leather, that is. You don't see craftsmanship like that every day. Why, it would be a criminal waste to let a fine piece of gear like that be buried in a grave, and I'm sure she'd say the same herself, poor soul.'

The boy was still gaping like a stranded fish. 'How did she . . .' he whispered, but Barsil gave him a hard, fierce look that shut his mouth very fast. 'Listen, sonny. If you want to survive here in the Precincts for very long, you learn not to ask those kinds of questions – and you learn when to keep your mouth shut tight. Understand me? She met with an accident. It's very sad, I'm sure. Now do you want this bloody jerkin, or shall I take it elsewhere?'

For a little while Scall was silent as he struggled with temptation. 'What do you want for it?' he said at last.

Barsil grinned at him. 'Now *that's* better. You're learning to use your head at last!' He leaned close to Scall. 'Seeing as I know you're only an apprentice, and short of coin, I'm just going to ask a little tiny favour, out of the goodness of my heart. Now, I need a new sword, but the smith has a lot of work on, and even if I ask her now, it'll take her months to get around to me. You must know where she keeps her list. If you'll just sneak in, and put my name right at the top, then I will give you this beautiful jerkin, free and for nothing. What do you say?'

The apprentice hesitated. 'Agella's very particular about that list. She says her reputation rests on doing quality work and playing fair with her customers. Unless it's Lord Blade or the Hierarch, she's very strict about first come, first served. If she catches me tampering with her work list, she'll take the hide off me.'

'Go on – you can do it,' Barsil urged. 'A clever lad like you. Do it right, and she'll never know the difference. And . . .' He dangled the garment temptingly in front of the youngster's

eyes, 'you will be the proud owner of this lovely jerkin.'
He winked at Scall. 'This should fetch the girls, don't you
think? That pretty little brewer's apprentice I keep catching
you making eyes at?'

'I'll do it,' Scall said quickly. 'But what if I put your name
second on Agella's list? She'd be far less likely to notice that
I'd tampered with it.'

'Done!' Barsil clapped the apprentice on the shoulder, and
handed over the jerkin. 'Remember now, I'll expect you to
keep your part of the bargain. Don't make me come looking
for you.'

'I'll do it, don't worry. I'll do it as soon as I can.' The
apprentice went running off – and not a moment too soon.
He had to step aside to make way for the cart as it came
rumbling through the great arched gateway of the Citadel.

Barsil shook his head. I don't believe I was ever that young,
or that gullible, he thought. And for certain, I was never
that stupid.

'Help me – please. I'm going to be sick!' That was what
Veldan had tried to say, but half the words were lost as she
staggered down the porch steps, dropped to her hands and
knees, and threw up on the muddy ground. She felt dazed
and disorientated, her memory of recent events nothing but
a blur. With nothing but a blanket wrapped around her naked
body, she was shivering violently. She ached all over, her head
throbbed as though it was about to explode, and her retching
sent pangs of white-hot agony knifing through her ribs.

At this moment, the only good thing in Veldan's life was
the sight of Kaz, hurtling towards her, splashing great spat-
ters of mud in all directions and bellowing with relief and
delight. 'Veldan, Veldan! You're awake! You're alive!' Over

his shoulder, Veldan caught a glimpse of a barn and an anonymous person, who clearly had been knocked down by the firedrake's headlong rush, sitting on the ground.

Kaz ploughed to a halt beside her and Veldan, her face streaked with tears of joy, put her arms around his neck and clung on tightly as he took her weight and pulled her to her feet. 'Oh, Kaz – I thought I'd never see you again,' she told him, resting her face against his long, muscular neck. Transmitting the thought, even in the softest mental whisper, drilled fresh pain through her skull, and sent spots of lurid light dancing in front of her eyes. She wanted to be sick again, but luckily there was nothing left to come up.

Kaz turned his head to look at her. 'Dammit, sweetie, you're in an awful state. Stop scaring me like that! I thought you'd bought it this time for sure!'

'I thought we both had,' Veldan admitted, shuddering at the memory. Then she froze, her arms still locked in a death grip around the firedrake's neck. 'Kaz! The Seer? What happened to Aethon?'

'I'm sorry, Boss.' Regret darkened Kazairl's thoughts. 'I'm pretty sure he was dead when I left him, and if he wasn't, he must be by now. You've been out cold for almost a day. I couldn't save him, but I could help you, so I had to leave him. I had no choice.'

Veldan swallowed hard. 'Then we've failed again,' she whispered.

'For pity's sake, Veldan,' Kaz said fiercely, 'not even Cergorn himself could turn back a landslide! I—'

'Girlie, they must make 'em hardy where you come from. But you'd better put *something* on, or you're likely to catch your death of cold!' The woman's voice was as rough and deep as the growl of a she-bear.

Veldan looked around quickly, sending another flare of pain through her head and ribs. She was suddenly aware that her blanket had fallen to the ground and she was standing there, stark naked, in the freezing rain. She saw a sturdy woman of advancing years and medium height, with shrewd blue eyes and straight grey hair cut as short as Veldan's own. All the joys and sorrows of a long, eventful life were written in the lines of her face. She wore several layers of shirts and jerkins, sturdy breeches and an open sheepskin coat of advanced decrepitude. At this moment, she was engaged in a futile attempt to brush the mud from her backside, where Kaz had knocked her down.

Veldan tried to reach down for the fallen blanket, but her vision blacked out in a dizzy wave of nausea and pain. She clung one-handed to Kaz's neck, swallowing hard, her pulse throbbing in her temples. 'I can't see,' she whispered.

'Here. Let me help you.' The woman's rough voice sounded kind. Veldan felt her grasp loosened from the firedrake's neck as her arms were slipped, one by one, into the fleecy sleeves of the disreputable coat. In panic Veldan struggled weakly, groping to find Kaz, who, to her astonished indignation, had made no objection to the way she was being manhandled.

'She's all right, Boss.' The firedrake's voice cut in, bracing and reassuring. 'She gave me a whole pig last night.'

Taking Veldan's arm, the woman sat her down carefully on the porch steps. 'Now listen,' she said firmly. 'I understand that you want to be with your friend, but let's be sensible. You look like seven sorts of shit warmed over.' It was exactly the sort of comment that Kaz would have made, and Veldan found it immensely reassuring. Beside her she heard the firedrake's snort of laughter.

'By Myrial's broad backside,' the woman muttered to herself. 'He really *does* understand me!'

Now that she was seated, Veldan's vision began to clear again. The woman was sitting on the steps beside her, seemingly unafraid of the looming Kaz, who looked even bigger from this low perspective, though it had to be said that, with his muzzle in Veldan's lap, he didn't look particularly fierce.

'Seems like you and your friend didn't expect to see each other alive again.' The woman's blue eyes twinkled through the mists of Veldan's returning sight. 'Truth to tell, I had my own doubts, when you arrived last night. Girl, you must be tough as old boot leather! I admire that in a woman – it reminds me of myself!' She chuckled and held out a hand. 'I'm Toulac.'

'Veldan.' The Loremaster took the woman's hand. Despite the cold surroundings, their handclasp was warm and firm. 'And this is Kazairl – Kaz – my . . .' For a moment she floundered, wondering how to explain the firedrake without giving away the secrets of the Shadowleague. Yet there was something about the older woman that inspired instant trust . . . Oh, damn it to perdition, Veldan thought. I can't make a worse mess of things than I already have. 'Kaz is my partner,' she said. 'We talk by exchanging thoughts.'

Toulac's eyes widened. 'Well, may I be dipped in dog's dung! I can think of a thousand ways a trick like that could come in handy. You two ever tried gambling?'

Veldan and Kaz exchanged a look of chagrin. 'All the time,' the Loremaster replied drily. 'Mostly, with our lives.'

'I believe you, if you make a habit of playing tag with landslides.' Toulac put an arm around the younger woman's shoulders. 'Come on, girlie – you've got to come in now, out of the cold. It's going to snow like a son of a bitch before very much longer, and you're shivering fit to rattle your bones. Besides, you should still be lying down after that crack on the head. You don't bounce back too quick from that kind of injury.'

Veldan sighed. 'All right,' she agreed reluctantly. 'And Toulac – thank you for not starting out with a whole bunch of questions.'

The older woman chuckled. 'Just you wait,' she growled. 'I'm saving them all up for later, when you're feeling better.'

Though she knew it made sense to go back inside, Veldan lingered, caressing the firedrake's head. After they had come so very close to losing one another, she was reluctant to let her partner out of her sight, and she needed no mind-speech to know that he felt the same. Suddenly she understood a little better what Elion must be going through.

'I'm sorry your friend is too big to come inside with you,' Toulac said. 'He can't even stay on the porch and put his head through the doorway into the kitchen. For one thing, we don't want every nosy passer-by on that cursed trail to see him and come snooping into our business. And for another, he'll scare the horse into fits.'

'You have a *horse* in your *kitchen?*' Veldan interrupted.

'And what if I do?' the older woman snapped defensively.

The Loremaster gave a wheezy, painful chuckle, clutching at her ribs. 'You don't know how glad I am to hear that!'

Toulac, who clearly had gathered herself for another blistering retort, looked dumbfounded. 'Glad? In the name of Myrial, why?'

'I passed him when I came staggering through the kitchen,' Veldan admitted. 'I didn't like to say anything – I thought I was seeing things, after that bang on the head!'

'You don't think it's kind of – well, odd?' Toulac demanded, still suspicious.

Veldan shrugged, wincing with pain as she did so. 'Why?

MAGGIE FUREY

It's your kitchen, he's your horse, and the weather's atrocious. I'd probably have done the same thing myself.'

Toulac stared at her in disbelief, then both of them burst out laughing. And in that moment, a friendship was forged between the two women that only death itself could break.

Blade had passed the sawmill without sparing it a glance. His thoughts were elsewhere. I must take care of this business quickly, he thought, so we can get back to Tiarond. All day he had been aware that a change in the weather was on its way. Winter would be coming early this year. He looked up at the sky with some concern. It was the colour of a lurid bruise and darkening by the minute. A storm was on the way, and Mount Chaikar was a lethal place in a blizzard. Maybe I should have stayed down in the city and let Zavahl take his chance in the storm, he mused, though the Hierarch dead in a snowdrift would not have suited his purpose half so well as the Hierarch burning on a sacrificial pyre.

In reality, the Godsword Commander knew that staying behind in Tiarond had never been an option, not after the traders had brought their tidings of a dragon. From Tormon's description of the creature, he had known at once that the man was telling the truth, but it was important that he check the area of the landslide himself. Clearly, the dragon had been heading for Gendival, and if it had managed to penetrate so far into these cold, inhospitable mountains, it was a fairly safe bet that it had not been alone. The presence of Loremasters in Tiarond at this particular time could compromise his position badly. Any Shadowleague agents must be found and neutralised at once.

Despite the problems presented by the dragon's presence, Blade felt a pang of regret for the poor Dragonfolk. If they were

158

sufficiently desperate to risk sending one of their kind all the way into these cold, damp northern lands, their plight must be bad indeed. Bleakly he thought of the many thousands of beings who must be dying, right now, all over the world. All because one man had been brave enough – or mad enough – to tamper with the boundaries that had kept them safe for so long.

Panic seized him. His hands grew slick with sweat within their leather gauntlets. His horse tossed its head up and down uneasily, sensing his distress. Sternly, Blade brought himself back under control. *Don't start pretending you have a conscience at this point,* he told himself. *You knew very well when you tampered with the Curtain Walls that many thousands would die – from the grotesque and warlike Gaeorn to the wise and glorious Dragonfolk. Those deaths were necessary. They were inevitable. The inhabitants of this world may have been safe within their protected little enclaves, but they were also stunted, stultified and stagnating. Change was what they needed, and change is what they're going to get. It's too late to back out and change your mind. You've set a chain of events in motion that can't be stopped. And the strongest will survive. The strongest, the toughest – and the cleverest. They'll be free at last, to go where they will, and develop as they choose.*

Keep on thinking that way, jeered a small, insidious voice in the back of his mind. *Keep on telling yourself you're doing it for their sake. Maybe if you pretend for long enough, you'll make it true.*

Though the rain-soaked cloak lay heavy across the Hierarch's shoulders, his heart was soaring as he watched the soldiers dig out the dragon. Saved! He could scarcely believe his good fortune. Tomorrow he would not be forced to take his place upon the pyre, to be sacrificed for the glory of Myrial. The God had smiled on him after all, for now he would have this incredible creature to take his place!

Above, the skies were darkening ominously. Blazing, pitch-soaked torches had been set into the mud all around the dragon to give the men a better light for their excavation. Already they had managed to expose more than half the monster. Dead or moribund as it was, the creature was still a thing of extraordinary beauty. Though it lolled slackly to one side, the elegant head, with its long, tapering muzzle, could have been sculpted from purest gold. Zavahl wished he could see the huge eyes, but for all the soldiers' attempts to pry them open, they remained firmly closed. Judging from the length of the dragon's body that had already been uncovered, it would be of a size to impress upon the most persistent of Tiarondian malcontents that Zavahl the Hierarch still had the favour of his God!

He had seen enough now – more than enough – to satisfy himself of the traveller's claim. It was time to get rid of the man. Sidelong, Zavahl glanced at the trader who waited near by, his face shadowed by his deep hood as he huddled in his cloak, shivering in the raw wind and persistent rain. He watched the digging impassively, keeping a respectful distance from his betters. The Hierarch saw Lord Blade standing to one side and slightly behind the man. The Godsword Commander was tense and watchful, his cold grey eyes almost boring holes in the back of the itinerant's head. Zavahl caught Blade's eye. He nodded once, almost imperceptibly, and Blade's guards exploded into action.

The trader took to his heels, catching the soldiers by surprise. In a pack, they went after him. Zavahl barely spared them a glimpse. The silencing of the itinerant was Blade's responsibility, not his. Already he was hurrying forward into the ring of torchlight, eager for a closer look at his dragon.

Tormon had begun to bitterly regret this idea of bringing his find to the attention of the Hierarch. During the trek up the mountain he had felt increasingly uneasy. Despite his proud claim that he was never overawed by rank, he couldn't help but be intimidated by the cold, harsh demeanour of the two great men, the Commander of the Godswords and the Hierarch himself. The men-at-arms in the escort had been no help, either. Save for the squeak of their damp leather accoutrements and the occasional chink of metal against metal, they rode in a disciplined silence, looking right through the trader as though he did not exist.

Only when Tormon had taken the exalted ones into the narrow gully that led off to one side of the trail, and shown the Hierarch the dragon, had Zavahl's rigid stance and stern expression relaxed. The general atmosphere of tension in the group had slackened a little at that point, but not enough to put Tormon at his ease. The Hierarch's eyes were still shuttered, his face devoid of all expression. His voice, as he had thanked the trader, still lacked any genuine emotion or warmth. Lord Blade, at his shoulder, remained as taut, cold and menacing as a baited bear-trap.

Now, though the digging had progressed and a great deal more of the amazing creature had been laid open to view, Tormon's eyes were elsewhere. He had pointed himself towards the excavation as if watching with great interest, but was concentrating all the time on shuffling slowly but steadily sideways with an almost imperceptible stealth, trying to put as much distance between himself and the others without their noticing. His eyes, concealed within the shadowy recesses of his hood, were everywhere, keeping track of the positions of the Hierarch, Lord Blade and Zavahl's bodyguards, who had not joined in the digging. Desperately Tormon scanned the precipitous walls of the gully, green-slicked and slippery from the rain, in an attempt to find an escape route. If matters unfolded as he was beginning to suspect they would, he was going to need one.

As the endless minutes stretched on towards evening, it seemed that Tormon had been waiting forever for the threat to come. He was shaking now – he couldn't help it – with fear and tension. Not for one minute did he let himself think he had been fanciful and exaggerated the danger. He remained alert and on edge, ready to move.

The instant he saw Zavahl's slight signal the trader exploded into action, diving to his left, away from the guards' drawn weapons, and scrambling a frantic course across the debris on the gully, heading towards the bottom of the gorge, instead of back up towards the trail, where the horses were tied. His attackers would be expecting that. Instead Tormon ran across and down, breaking through the startled diggers and over the dragon's body, trying to put as much distance as possible between himself and his betrayers before they had a chance to collect themselves.

Though they slowed his escape, the piled boulders and jackstraw trees that jammed the lower part of the gorge offered Tormon some fortuitous cover. Arrows zinged through the air in a dark and lethal swarm, cracking against rocks, thudding into tree trunks and mud, close enough to make his belly knot in terror and coming nearer all the time as Blade's soldiers found their range. The sounds of pursuit came close behind the trader: the grinding scrape of rolling rocks, the crack of broken branches, and a good deal of panting, grunting and swearing. Sick with fear, fleeing for his life, Tormon prayed as he had never prayed before, for the mists to come down and hide him, for some secret escape route to open up at his feet, for a miracle, please dear Myrial please, a miracle . . .

There was the sick, meaty thunk of arrow striking flesh, followed by a ghastly, rending scream that seemed to go on and on. But that's not my voice, Tormon thought, as he went down. I'm not screaming. Then his thoughts flashed out in a blaze of pain. Darkness engulfed him, and all sound ceased.

Aethon, a creature of the element of Fire like all the Dragonfolk, could not be scathed by flame but, as his starved body absorbed the heat of the close-clustered ring of torches, he began to rouse, his thoughts clawing their way up to consciousness from the dark depths of oblivion. Soon, the dragon began to be aware of his surroundings: the damp, the mud and the biting cold. There was no sign of Veldan and Kazairl and, in his battered, dazed and weakened state, he could barely raise his telepathic voice above the feeblest of whispers. He was dismayed, but not surprised to hear no answer. It was more than likely that the Loremasters had perished in the landslide, and he himself had fallen into the hands of the Callisiorans – the race that Veldan had described as primitive, superstitious savages.

At last he came to understand the true horror of his situation. Though the nearby fire had awakened his mind, it could do little to restore his desperately weakened body, for such a miracle would require the pure, fierce energy of raw sunlight. Nothing else contained sufficient power.

Despair replaced dismay. The sentence was irrevocable. There was no possible way he could escape. Soon, in this place, Aethon, Seer of the Dragonfolk, was going to die.

Now that he was lucid once more, Aethon's mind began to race. Why had he not foreseen his own end when he'd undertaken this journey? True, he had been aware that something might go awry. Beyond a vision of the Snaketail Pass, all his impressions had been confusing and blurred, almost as though he were looking at the world through a different set of senses. But death? It seemed impossible! The dragon tried to gather his whirling thoughts before true panic set in. If he died now, not only would his unique talent be lost, but all his knowledge, the accumulated lore and wisdom of centuries, passed down through numberless Dragonfolk generations, which might well hold the key to what ailed the beleaguered world.

It would be a terrible thing to die a solitary death here in a foreign realm surrounded by these primitive, alien creatures. The Dragonfolk were never alone at the time of their death. Before its consciousness passed from the world, a dying dragon would give all the accumulated knowledge and experience of a lifetime to a nominated successor, transferring the information directly from mind to mind. That way nothing was ever lost. This was of great importance to a species who bore few offspring and whose population was always perilously low. Aethon, as a Seer, was unique among his folk. The loss of his skills could disadvantage the entire race, unless they could be passed on, as his predecessor had bequeathed them to him. Also, on an emotional level, he would be denied the comfort of knowing that some part of him would survive as his unique legacy to future generations of Dragonfolk.

Suddenly, it came to Aethon that there could – just possibly – be a way to save his memories from oblivion. As a Loremaster, his telepathic prowess was far above the level of most Dragonfolk. If he could transfer not just his memories but his entire consciousness into another body – and a sturdy, robust human form at that – he might be able to use it as a vehicle to get him back to his own lands, where he could pass his knowledge to a successor in the usual way, before finally letting his consciousness move on beyond, as was natural and proper.

Such a thing had never been attempted. Aethon didn't know if it *could* be done. But he was going to try. It was his only chance. Still and silent he waited, concentrating with all his might, waiting for one of the humans to come close enough, willing them to approach. There seemed to be some kind of commotion amongst the little knot of men within the gully. One was fleeing, the others haring after in pursuit . . . Aethon cursed to himself. Where were they going? Would they return? He couldn't lose them now – this was his one, last chance. No – it was all right. One of the humans had not followed the others. He was coming nearer, nearer . . .

As the man reached out to touch him, Aethon pounced. Though his body did not move a muscle, he gathered his whole mind, his entire consciousness, into a single, narrow bolt, and hurled it spear-like into the mind of the unsuspecting man. Even as he did so, he became aware of the proximity of another Loremaster – but it was too late. He was already committed. As a dense white shroud of snow dropped from the skies, the dragon's dying body writhed in a gargantuan convulsion. Within its new vessel, Aethon's consciousness let out a silent cry of triumph. Aloud, the Hierarch screamed.

ELEVEN

A LIFE FOR A LIFE

Gilarra, Suffragan, second only in greatness to the Hierarch himself, was enjoying an afternoon of much needed domesticity in her simple, comfortable home in the artisans' quarter. She had given her two servants a holiday so that she could be alone with her family as an antidote to her disquiet, firstly over Lord Blade's plans to remove the Hierarch and put her in his place, and secondly over the trader woman and her little daughter, who had vanished into the bowels of the Godsword Citadel as though they had never existed. Three times she had gone there to ask after them, and had been put off every time: they were bathing, the guards said, or eating, or fast asleep. Always the commonplace, polite facade, which somehow managed to imply that there was no need to be concerned. Always the excuse of the Hierarch's orders, or Lord Blade's instructions, which she lacked the authority to countermand. Always the armed guards who somehow, without quite making an *explicit* threat, managed to turn her back from the citadel door.

At least she had managed to waylay Blade's young Lieutenant and warn him of her concerns in no uncertain terms. Galveron's a good lad, she reassured herself. He won't let any harm come to them. Maybe it'll be all right. Maybe this threat exists only in my imagination. Dear Myrial, let it be so. Surely Zavahl wouldn't harm an innocent mother and child? He may be driven and demanding and fanatical in his beliefs, but he's never been an evil man, and rarely unjust – except towards himself.

Her lifemate, Bevron, who had also taken time off from his work as a silversmith, was sprawled on the hearthrug, playing with their little son Aukil. Gilarra looked up from the shirt she was embroidering as he began to speak. 'It's amazing what a difference it makes to the atmosphere in the Sacred Precincts when Zavahl is away. It's as though we all heave a sigh of relief and let ourselves relax.'

Gilarra, anxious not to break the peaceful mood of the afternoon, had managed so far to avoid the subject of Zavahl's impending sacrifice. This, however, was an opening she could scarcely evade without seeming to break the trust that had always existed between herself and her lifemate. Desperately she scoured her mind for a gentle way to break the news, then gave it up as a bad job. No matter how she broached it, Bevron wasn't going to be pleased. Best just to get it over with. 'If Blade has his way, you'll have plenty of opportunities to relax after tomorrow,' she told him drily. 'As of tomorrow night, you'll be sleeping with the new Hierarch.'

'*What?*' Bevron jumped up from the hearthrug, scattering wooden animals right and left, to an indignant wail of protest from little Aukil. 'You're planning to sacrifice Zavahl? Oh, Gilarra, no! It can't be true!'

Gilarra dropped the sewing from her lap and stood up with him, taking his hands in her own. 'It's not my idea, love. But you and I seem to be the only folk in the city who don't care for the notion. As far as the Tiarondians are concerned, and probably the rest of Callisiora too, the Hierarch has failed them. If Myrial has turned His face from Zavahl – and you must admit, it certainly looks that way – he's no longer any use to the people he represents, except as a sacrifice.'

Bevron gripped her hands so tightly that it hurt. 'And if he goes, you must replace him.'

'Love, we've always known it could come to that. I've lived with the possibility all my life. You accepted it when you became my lifemate.'

'Only because I never thought it would really happen,' Bevron growled. 'Damn Zavahl! It would never have come to this, if he hadn't been such a pious, conceited *fool*!'

'Oh, hush now,' Gilarra scolded. 'Poor Zavahl – I would hate to have his outlook on life. I've never seen such a lonely man. Half the time I feel desperately sorry for him, and the other half I want to hit him out of sheer frustration, because he brings so many of his troubles on himself. Ever since he was a child, he's always taken everything so *seriously*.'

'Daddy – play some more!' Aukil, his lower lip stuck out like a dinner plate, was tugging at Bevron's tunic. With a sigh, the silversmith let go of his lifemate's hands. 'No, lovey. You can't put the cows on the yellow square. That's the corn, remember?' This time he was addressing his son, who had discovered long ago that the hearthrug, patterned as it was with brightly coloured squares, made the ideal backdrop for his toy farm.

Aukil's lower lip stuck out even further. With his light brown hair and sturdy build, he was the image of his father. 'Can, too. S'*my* farm.' With an 'I dare you' glance at his father, he moved the little wooden cows back on to the yellow square. 'They like corn.'

Bevron shrugged. 'Suit yourself, matey, but your farmer will starve next winter.' He turned back to Gilarra, picking

up exactly where he had left off, she noted with a smile. Since
they had become parents, they had both become expert at
carrying on two conversations simultaneously.

'Why do you think Zavahl is the way he is?' Bevron was
saying. 'I mean, the two of you were brought up together in
the Basilica and the Precincts, but you've turned out so very
different, Myrial be praised.'

'Well, to be fair on Zavahl, our circumstances weren't
exactly the same.' Gilarra picked up her sewing again, nipping
the tip of her tongue between her teeth as she concentrated
on threading the needle before she resumed the conversation.
'He was brought up to be Hierarch, remember. I never
had that terrible responsibility to weigh me down. And old
Malacht, the priest who had charge of him . . .' Her vision
clouded and she shuddered. 'Now there was a real fanatic
if you like – a man made from equal parts of steel, stone
and vitriol. It was all right for me – I was raised in the
Priestesses' House, but Zavahl grew up under the domination
of that cruel, black-hearted despot.' She looked away from
Bevron, gazing back into the past, her forehead creased in
a slight frown. 'If the twisted old brute hadn't died in that
accident, I sometimes wonder what would have become of
Zavahl . . .'

'What accident?' Bevron interrupted.

Gilarra looked up in surprise. 'I was forgetting that, being
brought up among the artisans, you wouldn't know this. He
fell down the Hierarch's staircase in the temple, the one that
links the private quarters up high in the cliff with the areas
of worship.'

Bevron let out a low whistle. 'That's some kind of fall!'

Gilarra shrugged. 'He broke just about every bone in his
body before he finally hit the bottom. And do you know

what? There wasn't a single person in the Sacred Precincts who wasn't delighted.'

She scowled so fiercely that Bevron took an involuntary step backwards. A loud crunch came from underfoot, followed by an angry wail of protest from little Aukil down on the rug. 'Oops!' Bevron stooped, and picked up two wooden oxen, sadly the worse for wear. 'I'm sorry, son.' He ruffled the boy's hair.

'You killed them,' Aukil shrilled.

'No, lovey, they've just had a bit of an accident,' Gilarra told him soothingly. 'It's only legs and tails. Your dad will soon glue them together again, as good as new.'

'Of course I will. You run and find the glue pot, and I'll fix them for you right now.' As his son ran off, Bevron weighed the wooden figures in his hand. 'Broken like old Malacht,' he mused.

Gilarra shook her head. 'Thank Myrial, you couldn't glue *him* back together again. Anyway, after he died, Zavahl's life improved a thousandfold, but such a childhood had to leave its scars. I suspect I don't know the half of the abuse he suffered as a child, so I can't entirely blame him for being the way he is. Malacht never forgave him, you know, for being the son of a serving girl, instead of a priestess's child, as I was. You know the rule. Myrial's Voice must be the first child born within the Sacred Precincts following the old Hierarch's death, no matter what the mother's origins. I suspect though, that had there not been too many witnesses, Malacht would have throttled poor Zavahl with his own cord and waited for a candidate that he considered more suitable.'

'Which would have been you,' Bevron said softly.

Gilarra shrugged. 'Oh, I won't pretend I didn't play the "What if?" game often enough in the deep hours of the night, back when I was young and ambitious. It's just my luck that I'm going to become Hierarch now, when it's the last thing I want or need and when I'm left to sort out this unholy mess of Zavahl's making. I'm not too convinced about the purity of Blade's motives in all this, either . . . Why, whoever can that be at the door?'

Though Gilarra told herself not to be so silly, the knocking, rapid but soft, somehow had a furtive sound. Again she remembered the trader and her little girl being led into the forbidding maw of the Citadel, and a feeling of deep unease stole over her. 'I'll go.' She waved her lifemate back to his recumbent position by the fire, dropped her embroidery back into the basket and hastened to the door.

On the step stood young Galveron, Lieutenant to Lord Blade. One look at his face told Gilarra all she needed to know. She took a step back and sagged against the doorpost, but she had not spent most of her life coping with the city's human crises, passed on to her by an uncomfortable Hierarch, for nothing. As the habit of a lifetime took over, she pulled herself together. Only then did she realise that the young officer bore a burden in his arms, something he was hiding beneath the voluminous folds of his long, black soldier's cloak. He met her eyes and nodded. 'Get in – quick!' she hissed. Bundling him past her into the narrow passageway, she slammed the door, bolted it, and locked it tight.

Galveron glanced through the open door into the cosy room where Bevron and his son were happily at play. He grimaced, turned abruptly, and made for the kitchen instead, still without saying a word. He seated himself on a chair beside the long, scrubbed table, and let his cloak fall open at last. In his arms was the tousle-haired little girl, her face filthy and streaked with tear stains. The trader's child. Her thumb was in her mouth, and her dark eyes, so lively and merry when Gilarra had last seen them, were staring, blank and dead.

'Myrial have mercy!' Gilarra ran across the room and knelt by the young officer's side. 'Annas? Annas?' She reached out gently to touch the dirty face. The child screwed her eyes tight shut and flinched away, yet made no sound, not even the slightest whimper.

'She's been like that since I found her.' Galveron's voice was ragged and harsh. 'Her mother . . . she . . . I was too late. Executed on the Hierarch's orders. The little one saw everything. She ran, hid . . . We had the place upside down, searching. I was her only chance. If one of the others had found her . . .' He shook his head, breathing as though he had been running in a long, long race. As Gilarra looked into his eyes, she realised that he was not unmanned by grief, as she had first suspected. He was a soldier, after all, and not a complete innocent, despite the impression of pure goodness that shone in his frank blue eyes and open face. No, Galveron's lack of coherence and control came from anger – pure, incandescent rage – suppressed with great difficulty so as not to terrify Annas any further or alarm Gilarra's own child in the room next door.

'I found her in the courtyard at the finish.' Galveron had found sufficient voice to continue. 'Myrial only knows how she got so far without being caught. She was hiding in that ridiculous wagon of theirs.'

Gilarra noticed that he was clutching the child tightly enough to whiten the flesh on her bare arms, yet still Annas did not move, or make a single sound. 'Here, let me take her,' she said. Quickly, almost thankfully, it seemed, Galveron gave the child into her arms, as if, by doing so, he could relinquish the dreadful knowledge of how she came to be here.

Gilarra rocked the little girl, crooning softly, trying, with great determination, not to think who had ordered the poor child's death. *Not now, not yet,* she chanted to herself in rhythm with her rocking. First things first ... But even as she pushed the monster back down beneath the surface of her consciousness, she knew that it would re-emerge before too long, and she must confront the fact that Zavahl, whom she had known and loved as a brother all her life, had turned into a terrible stranger ...

Damn you, Zavahl, for this. She gritted her teeth and felt her heart grow hard against him. *Maybe you do deserve to die.*

'Galveron, will you fetch me a bowl of warm water, please? The kettle is there, at the side of the hearth.' Gilarra could feel herself beginning to shake. It was as though the Lieutenant had passed his anger across to her, when he had handed her the child. *Oh, Zavahl, how could you do this?*

Bevron put his head around the kitchen door, looked at the child and Gilarra's face, and ducked back into the other room to keep Aukil occupied. From the slight crease between his brows she knew that she'd have about a thousand difficult questions to answer later. None the less, she knew she could always count on his understanding. Patiently, she stripped the little girl and washed her gently, hampered by a great deal of difficulty in persuading Annas to take her thumb out of her mouth for two minutes together. Having dried her with a soft towel, Gilarra put the child into one of Aukil's nightshirts – then dressed her in another, following an accident with a posset of warm milk mixed with a sleeping draught, which dribbled back out of Annas's slack mouth to soak the original garment.

Gilarra gave up, hoping the child had managed to ingest enough of the potion to get some rest. She tucked the little girl into her own and Bevron's big bed and returned to Galveron, who had been pacing the kitchen like a trapped wolf, a cold light burning in his eyes. 'Why?' she asked him. 'Why would the Hierarch order such an atrocity? The murder of a mother and child in cold blood . . .'

The Lieutenant, young no longer, looked out at her from behind that open, pleasant face. 'You're the one who knows him best, Suffragan. I was hoping you could explain it to me.'

She poured a mug of tea from the pot whose contents simmered, black and lethal by this time, at the edge of the hearth, and made him sit and drink. 'You've taken a dreadful risk,' she told him softly. 'What will you do when Blade and Zavahl come back and there's no body to show them?'

He shrugged. 'Run, I suppose,' he said wearily. 'Otherwise it's a flogging, or imprisonment. Who knows, maybe even a traitor's death, with the Hierarch in his present mood.' He looked up at Gilarra, his eyes pleading. 'But I had to save her, Suffragan – I couldn't let her be killed, not a little child like that.'

Gilarra, already blaming herself, sank deeper into self-recrimination. This is my fault, she thought. I knew something was wrong. I should have insisted that Annas and her mother come with me. Kanella would be alive now if I had. Thanks to me, this fine young man's life is at stake, his whole future has been blighted. And having come so far, the Hierarch can't leave a witness alive to betray his perfidy. If there's no sign of her body, he'll turn the whole world upside down until he finds the child . . .

Except that Zavahl will no longer be the Hierarch.

Gilarra felt a weight lift from her shoulders. Maybe there would be advantages, after all, to taking the mantle of power from Zavahl. She patted Galveron's arm. 'Don't worry, my dear. When Lord Blade gets back, I'll make it my personal business to see that you come to no harm over this affair. You have my sacred word.'

The young man gasped. 'You're going to depose the Hierarch!'

By Myrial, but he was quick! 'You keep your mouth shut about this – do you hear me? The whole city will know soon enough.' She leavened her words with a smile as a new idea struck her. Once she reached her position of power, there might be more ways than one to protect herself from Blade and his machinations. 'Galveron – if I *should* become Hierarch, I plan to make a few changes. How do you feel about taking the job of personal bodyguard?'

The young officer's face broke into the first smile she had seen from him. 'My Lady – I would like that very much.'

Once Galveron had departed, Gilarra looked in once again upon the little girl, to find Annas fast asleep, her thumb still locked inextricably in her mouth. Looking down at the child – an orphan now for sure: Zavahl would not have scrupled to kill the father if he could spare so little thought for the mother and daughter – the troubled woman tried to settle her racing thoughts. There was nothing to be done now, but wait and hope that Galveron would get back to the Citadel before the Hierarch's return.

Gilarra wrung her hands. How could she face Zavahl, with her secret knowledge of his horrific deeds? What had happened to the brilliant, flawed, melancholy, vulnerable soul she had known, her brother while they grew up together, her lover once each year when they performed Myrial's Great Solstice Rite? I don't know you any more, Zavahl, she thought bitterly. Did I ever, really? Have I been wrong all these years?

Folding her hands, Gilarra knelt down beside the bed and its precious sleeping cargo. All she could do now was pray – pray for the life of this little one, pray to Myrial for the salvation of Zavahl's tormented soul.

The trouble with humans was that they moved so *slowly*! Shree, impatient to be getting on with the mission, had travelled far ahead of Elion, who was still toiling up the difficult trail that led to the Snaketail Pass and the city of Tiarond, which clung to the precipitous slopes of the mountain's opposite side.

The need to keep her partner in sight was a constraint that the wind-sprite, driven by her anxiety, could not help but resent. The Tiarond side of the Snaketail, as near as the Senior Loremasters of Gendival had been able to pinpoint the location, had been the place from which Veldan had sent her desperate plea for help. More than a day and a night had passed already since they had heard that anguished cry, and evening was beginning to close in again over the mountains. Surely, given the long silence that had followed Veldan's plea, there could be no survivors? Yet what if, by some miracle, there were? The wind-sprite could no longer bear to confine herself to the human's snail-like pace. Leaving Elion and his horse to drag themselves as best they could up the crippling slope, Thirishri ranged ahead, scouting towards the area on the far side of the pass.

A wind-sprite's vision differed from that of a human. The air was her element, as the earth was to a Gaeorn, and the water to one of the Leviathan or the lake monster Afanc. To Thirishri, invisible to human eyes, bodiless by any simple human terms, the element was her shelter, sustenance – even her means of conveyance as she rode the thermals and winds. The air could also be her weapon. Shree could change shape at will, using invisible tentacles to whip calm and limpid air into whirlwind or gale or storm. She could compress the atmosphere to form a solid, invisible barrier, though this difficult process took a vast amount of energy and concentration, leaving her spent for some time afterwards. She could also mould and manipulate the air, infusing it with the powers of will and memory, desire and imagination, to form illusions that were indistinguishable, until touched, from solid, physical reality.

The wind-sprite could *see* the air as a living, ever moving medium, just as a human could see movement – currents, ripples and waves – in water. She could also see where the air had been disturbed, for instance, where it had been displaced by the movement of an organic object such as a human or an inorganic force like a landslide. The trails left by a living creature would last several hours, even longer on a calm day, giving the wind-sprite a vision through time of all the recent events at a location. Such a cataclysmic event as a landslide would create a disturbance in the ether that remained for a number of days.

As soon as Thirishri had crested the summit's final ridge she did not need to see the long, black, muddy scar that slashed the mountain's flank to understand what must have happened. The vision of the landslide hung there in the air, waiting to be read by those with the skill to see. As Shree hovered above the pass and the trail that lay beyond, the events of the last two days were written in the air below, just waiting for her to disentangle the complex network of traces. Sifting through the layers of after images left around the area, she found ghost doubles of Kazairl, Veldan and the Dragon, and saw how they had been buried in the slide.

I have found the place, she sent back to Elion, not bothering to hide her dismay. *They were buried in a landslide, as we suspected.*

As the human opened his mind to reply, Shree caught the overspill of his strong emotional state, just a single glimpse before his controls snapped back into place. Regret, fear and concern were all present – and rightly so – but the wind-sprite was less happy about the other emotions that she found: a heart-leap of fierce exultation, the smug glow of revenge and, lurking beneath the others, a black and twisted abomination of sick envy at the thought of Veldan's death.

Thirishri fought to conceal her deep concern, so as not to betray what Elion had inadvertently revealed. *They may not be dead,* she said. *The trails are very confused at this place, but some seem to lead away down the mountain. I must get closer to interpret . . . Wait! What's that?* As the sprite swooped down, she saw a number of horses tied beneath the shelter of an overhanging ledge, and gained a clear view into the deep and narrow gully that branched off the main trail. *The dragon, Elion!* she cried. *And men – pursuing another man!*

One unarmed man was being hounded and shot at by a dozen warriors, who all seemed to be professional, experienced soldiers. Clearly this had been some kind of ambush or trap. Even from a distance, Thirishri could feel the shock and fear emanating from the fugitive, coupled with a bleak and bitter rage against such injustice. The archers were finding their range now: the hail of arrows was closing in on the target.

Shree found herself in the throes of a dilemma. The Seer of the Dragonfolk should be her first concern, but Aethon wasn't going anywhere, if indeed he yet lived. It was the nature – and the duty – of a Loremaster to intervene in such a situation as this ambush, yet she must not reveal her existence in this land to these primitive, superstitious natives, nor must she attack or harm the archers without discovering the true facts behind the incident. After all, the fugitive might be an escaped murderer, for all she knew. On the other hand, she could not risk allowing an innocent man to be killed – and for certain, her intuition told her he *was* innocent.

There was only one thing for it. Shree swooped down between the hunters and their quarry and closed in on the fleeing man. Staying at his back, straining with the effort, she compressed the air behind him to form a resilient shield that was dense enough to bar the entry of an arrow.

Not a moment too soon. The bolt struck the man right between the shoulder blades, hurling him to the ground and knocking the breath from his body. Though Shree had stopped the arrow penetrating his flesh, she'd been unable to dampen the whole force of impact. Its smack carried loud and clear in the rainy air. Good, the wind-sprite thought. The poor man will carry a bruise for ages, but the noise should fool his foes.

Now – she needed a distraction, or some form of conceal-ment. Well, the storm would be here soon, in any case . . . As though she were dropping a curtain, Thirishri reached up to the snow-laden clouds above and pulled the impending blizzard down into the gully in a whirlwind of hard-flung snow, concealing the man's whereabouts from his foes. She could hear their startled cries, and a lot of crashing and cursing as they blundered about. She adjusted her vision to peer through the thick swirling snowstorm, and watched with wry amusement as they stumbled in circles, barely able to find one another, let alone the man they sought. Just to make absolutely sure, Shree stirred up a small whirlwind and picked up a tangle of brushwood and broken boughs, which she dropped across the man's recumbent body. He would be stunned a little, she realised, by his fall and the force of the blunted arrow's impact, but he would not be deeply unconscious. She only hoped he had the sense to lie still until his pursuers were safely away.

A scream ripped out above the whistling wind. Cursing, Thirishri hurled herself towards the convulsing body of Aethon the Seer – and the air imploded in a thunderclap as she gasped with shock. By Aeolius, Father of Wind-Sprites – what had the dragon done? The human had dropped to his knees, his hands clasped to his head, and was still screaming fit to tear his throat out. 'Myrial! Myrial help me – it's in my head!'

Transferral of consciousness? Had the Seer, in his desperate extremity, achieved the impossible? Frantically, Shree tried to reach him. *Aethon? Aethon! Can you hear me?*

Nothing. The telepathic matrices held no sense whatsoever of the Seer's presence.

No, Thirishri thought. I must have imagined it. The whole notion is insane. Before she could investigate any further, the man disappeared from view in the midst of a knot of soldiers, who had come running at the sound of his cries. The screams cut off abruptly as their leader struck the victim's skull a glancing blow with the hilt of his sword.

'Enough,' he said. 'Evidently, the strain of the last few months has taken its toll upon the Hierarch. Worse, his hopes that Myrial sent this creature as a sacrifice are unfounded. Not only is the beast stone dead, but you saw it perish the instant Zavahl laid his hand on it. The message could not be clearer. Myrial has turned against the Hierarch, and therefore against the Hierarch's people. Tomorrow Zavahl must serve us in the only way remaining to him. He must become the Great Sacrifice, so that Myrial may smile on us once more.'

Dismissively, the man turned away from the figure on the ground. 'Bind him. Tie him to his horse and let's get out of here before this accursed storm gets any worse. If we don't get off the mountain soon, we won't get down at all.'

Thirishri, sunk deep in dismay, paid little attention to the humans. As she had feared, her examination of the dragon proved that it was dead. As she hovered, invisible in the blizzard, Elion's telepathic voice reached her. 'Shree? Everything all right?'

No, Elion – they could scarcely be worse, given the circumstances. Where are you?

'Close to the head of the pass. I've nearly burst myself getting up here, and in spite of the fact that I've been leading it, the horse is practically on its knees. I've had to drag the wretched brute every inch of the way up here, and now we've run into the great-grandfather of all blizzards. The weather is atrocious up here – I should just make it down before the pass snows up completely, and providence only knows how we'll get home again this side of spring. Be with you as soon as I can. What in the seven pits of perdition was that thunderclap?'

Nothing important. Elion, listen – I've found Aethon.

'What? Where? Is he still alive? What about the others?'

Not here. There are old traces from yesterday going down the mountain. Some are human, but I can't tell whether all of them are until I've had a chance to investigate. One thing is for certain – wherever we find Kaz, Veldan will be also . . .

At that moment, the wind-sprite's attention was torn away from the conversation by the departure of the men, who had bound their unconscious comrade and hoisted him across a

MAGGIE FUREY

horse. 'Let's move it!' she heard the leader shout. 'This cursed trail will block in no time.'

'Shree? What's happening?' Elion prompted. 'Is the dragon dead?'

Shree dropped down to touch the dragon. Aethon was stiff and cold, and her deep-sight could detect no aura. *Yes, Elion – the Seer of the Dragonfolk breathes no more.*

There was a long moment of silence before the Loremaster replied. 'Festering bloody damnation!' he snarled.

Had it not been for the missing Veldan and Kazairl, Thirishri would have sent her human partner back over the pass before it was too late, so that they could return to Gendival for the winter. It was her duty, however, to find the two strays and make sure they were safe, so there could be little chance of heading home now until well after the year had turned. Festering bloody damnation indeed. Shree couldn't have put it better herself.

Twelve

The Apprentice

Agella glanced up from the blade she was hammering. 'KEEP PUMPING!' she roared. From the corner of her eye, she saw her apprentice jerk out of his daydream. The rhythm of the wheezing bellows picked up pace, and the heart of the forge grew incandescent once more. With care, the smith placed the blade back in the fire, and watched with meticulous attention as it picked up heat and began to glow. She took advantage of the pause in her hammer's din to scold the boy again, for all the good it would do. 'Scall, how many times do I have to tell you that the work of a smith is all about paying attention? Timing is everything in this profession. You *must* be very quick and very precise, while the iron holds the proper heat . . .'

At that exact instant the iron *did* reach the right temperature, and Agella, who had never taken her eyes from the glowing forge, hooked the sword out with the tongs and placed it back on the anvil, hammering and folding with a skilful twist of her brawny wrist. What's the point? she wondered. This one will never be a smith if he tries for a thousand years – though at least if he *did* try, it would be something. If the gormless glaik wasn't my sister's boy, he'd be out of here on his backside so fast he wouldn't know what had hit him.

At her side, she glimpsed Scall pumping the bellows with frantic haste, an expression of ferocious concentration on his face. She sighed. 'Keep a STEADY RHYTHM, boy,' she yelled. 'You've got to KEEP IT UP!'

Again, the soughing of the bellows faltered as Scall spluttered, trying with no success whatsoever to contain his fit of giggles. Agella had a feeling that if it was not already crimson from the heat of the forge, his face would be beetroot with embarrassment. She raised her eyes heavenwards. It's your own fault, she told herself. Remember what it was like at his age? A memory surfaced of the sturdy, freckled, red-headed fourteen-year-old who had sniggered with her friends at every stupid innuendo and bawdy joke. Thirty years ago, and it only seemed like yesterday . . .

Myrial up a tree – the boy's got me *daydreaming now!* With a round, disgusted oath, Agella dropped the cooling iron into the water trough. A savage hiss split the air as steam rose in a cloud. She wiped her sweaty forehead with a scrap of spark-holed towel and turned to see her apprentice shrinking away from her, his features taut with apprehension. He always knew when he had mucked up, but it didn't stop him from doing exactly the same thing next time. 'Scall – will you *stop* that bloody cringing!' she growled. 'You'll have folk thinking I beat you black and blue – when the truth is I probably don't punish you half enough, you gormless lump!'

Scall bit his lip, his eyes fixed on his feet. 'Sorry, Smithmaster Agella,' he mumbled.

The smith shook her head. 'What are we going to do with you?' she asked in mild exasperation. In truth, she was quite fond of her cackhanded, woolgathering nephew, but it was high time the two of them faced facts. Scall was just no good – and Agella, as smith to the Sacred Precincts, including the

Basilica and Godsword Citadel – was up to her ears in work. She needed an apprentice who could *learn*, an assistant who would help, not hinder.

Scall's dark eyes, huge in his thin face, were fixed on her with the expression of a dog beneath a table. He was afraid to speak out loud, but she knew, none the less, that he was imploring her in silence not to cast him out. Agella couldn't blame him. Without her, his future looked bleak indeed. When he had first come to the beastquarters, some half year ago, his first sight of the Hierarch's stables, kennels and mews had left him incredulous and awed. He had only been thirteen then: callow, shy, surly and deeply resentful of both the mother who had packed him off to be an apprentice and the aunt who had given her the opportunity. Agella, the smithmaster to the Precincts had, in the absence of any offers from masters of other crafts, finally and reluctantly offered to take her sister's gangling daydreamer of a son off her hands, despite the fact that she and Viora didn't get along. Scall's mother had accepted with gratitude and almost indecent haste. Her lifemate Ulias had been, in his time, a tailor of no mean skill, until he had been stricken by the knotbone disease that had turned his hands to useless claws. Now he spent his days fighting crippling pain, no longer able to support his family. A bright and handy son might have been some help to the beleaguered family, but this clumsy, sulky, lackadaisical adolescent boy had proved one burden too many. Since Scall had – hopefully – been settled in a trade, with his food, clothing and shelter found elsewhere, Viora and Ulias had been able to move in with their daughter Felyss and her lifemate in the Lower Town. There was no room there for Scall, however. He was one too many for such a cramped little house, and his brother-in-law had no time for such a useless, unproductive daydreamer. If the boy's aunt and craftmaster were to throw him out now, he would find no welcome back at home. The streets would be his only option – and with the city in its current grim state, he wouldn't survive out there two days together.

Agella looked down at her skinny apprentice with pity. 'Go on, lad. Nip across to the brewmaster and fetch me a beer – and get one for yourself, while you're about it.'

'Don't like beer, Mistress Agella,' Scall muttered, his eyes still fixed on the floor.

'Well, it's high time you learned to like it! Don't be such a *weed*, boy! Fetch us a couple of beers – each – and we'll sit down quietly and consider your future.'

This time Scall did look up at her, and Agella caught the flash of stark terror in his eyes. 'It's all right,' she said kindly. 'I won't abandon you – and I'm not blaming you, never fear. But we might as well face facts sooner rather than later: you're just not cut out to be a smith. Don't look so miserable.' She clapped him on the shoulder with a big, freckled hand, almost knocking him on to his face. 'Run along and get those beers, then we'll think for a while and try to discover something you *are* good at.'

He was just about to run out of the door when something caught her attention. Something different about the boy . . . 'Scall,' she called. 'That jerkin is far too good to be wearing in the smithy with sparks flying around. Where did you get it?'

As he turned, she saw him flush crimson. 'Er – one of the Godswords gave it to me, mistress. It was too small for him, he said.'

Agella frowned sternly. 'You'd better be telling me the truth.'

He looked at her with wide-eyed innocence. 'But it is the truth, mistress. Honest. Every single word.'

Suddenly the smith wasn't really sure if she wanted to know any more. She flipped a hand at him. 'Off you go, then. And don't dawdle with that beer.'

Scall ran out of the smithy, and into the lower area of the Sacred Precincts, which housed the village of the Temple artisans on its western side and their workshops and meeting square here on the east. An air of abandonment and desolation filled the place today. The square, once so gay and pleasant with its flowers and trees, was deserted. No one sat on the benches by the central fountain, the bright blooms had long since wilted and mouldered away, and the trees were winter-bare.

Scall's first mistake, he realised as soon as he hit the open air, had been to forget to put on a cloak or his coat. After the sweltering heat of the forge, the cold of this bleak grey day sliced right through to his bones. His second error lay in cutting across the grassy square at an angle to reach the brewhouse in the shortest time.

'Hey! Get off there, you daft beggar! There's little enough turf left as it is!'

Scall ploughed to a halt and looked down at his bemired boots, then back over his shoulder at the trail of muddy footprints that scarred the waterlogged ground, then sidelong at the angry gardener. The heat of shame flooded his cold face. 'Sorry,' he muttered. 'I didn't think . . .' Even to himself, it sounded pathetic.

'That's the trouble in this place. Nobody *ever* thinks! Specially you bloody prentices! Rush here, hurry here, over the seedlings, across the turf, what does it matter? And us poor

groundsmen working from sunup to sundown to put everything right before the Hierarch sees the mess!' He thrust his
finger into Scall's face. 'You're Mistress Agella's lad, aren't
you? I'll be having words with her, I will . . .' With that he
stamped away, still muttering wrathfully.

Scall swallowed hard against the tightness of impending
tears. Why couldn't he ever seem to do anything right?
He wasn't stupid. The retired priestess who lived near his
parents' old tailor's shop and earned her living as a scribe
for the unlettered poor of the neighbourhood had begun to
teach him his letters, and had called him a bright young lad.
So why in this hard world, with work to be done and livings to
be earned, could he not seem to succeed at a single thing? The
harder he tried, the more flustered he became, and the more
mistakes he made. Even now, he suddenly realised. Because
he had tried to hurry in the first place, he had crossed the
ill-tempered gardener, then had become so flustered that now
he was going to be late with Mistress Agella's beer, thereby
earning himself another scolding. Scall sighed. It was going
to be one of those days when he couldn't do anything right.
He rubbed the back of his hand across his eyes then, walking
as lightly as he possibly could until he had reached the edge
of the grassy square, he sped to the brewhouse as fast as he
could run.

To Scall, the brewhouse held an air of arcane mystery,
with the brewers bustling about between barrel, vat and
still, performing their strange alchemical arts. As always,
the place was meticulously clean – whenever Scall came
in, the two apprentices, Kareld and Maryll, were sweeping,
scouring or scrubbing *something* – and the air was warm and
heavy with the aromas of fruit, hops and malt, though this
year there had been no harvests and Brewmaster Jivarn was

reduced to using old dusty, dried supplies that were having an uncertain effect on the quality of his wine and ale – not to mention his temper.

'Wipe your bloody *feet!*' somebody yelled as Scall came through the door. Again, he felt the shameful heat rise in his face. Why did he never *remember* the things that other folk seemed to think were so important? Luckily Brewmaster Jivarn was nowhere in evidence today. Maryll brought him Agella's favourite beer in two tightly corked flagons, then ticked off the amount on the blacksmith's slate, for the artisans of the Sacred Precincts had evolved a complex system among themselves, using barter and payment in kind for the use of one another's services. Agella's part of the bargain would be to make new vats and piping for the stills when needed, not to mention regular inspection and repairs of the gear in use.

As he took the beer from the girl, Scall realised that he was blushing again. Maryll was about a year or so older than himself, with long legs, hair like sunshine and a pretty, freckled face. On many a night he had dreamed about her, and the memory of those dreams left him abashed and tongue-tied in her presence. She smiled at him as he blurted out his thanks, and Scall dashed out of there as fast as he could, wondering all the way whether her smile had been kindly meant, or whether she had – oh horror! – been *laughing* at him.

With his head so full of Maryll, Scall was paying little attention to his surroundings, and had no idea that anything was amiss until he collided with Barsil the guard in the doorway of the smithy. With all the breath knocked out of him by the impact, Scall staggered backwards and sat down hard, still frantically clutching the flagons to his chest to save them. Despite his best efforts, one of the stoppers came out due to all the shaking and foaming beer cascaded everywhere, soaking through Scall's jerkin and breeches and forming puddles on the ground all round him.

Agella appeared in the doorway. 'What in the name of thunderation is going on here?' She looked from Scall to the guard in astonishment. She knew Barsil all too well, and the very fact that the weasel-faced, work-shy member of the Godsword rank and file had actually broken out of his usual shambling stroll was enough to indicate that something must be wrong. Barsil leaned wheezing against the door frame, trying to catch his breath. 'Smith – come quick!' he gasped. 'There's a demon horse gone mad in the stable! He's killed young Ruper!'

Agella swore. Ruper was the son of one of the stablehands, a big, powerfully built lad about Scall's age. Where her own apprentice seemed daft because he was a dreamer, poor Ruper was just slow-witted, understanding about as much as a five- or six-year-old child. He helped out in the stables, doing simple tasks such as mucking out and watering the horses, but normally there was someone around to keep an eye on him. How in the name of everything sacred could this dreadful thing have happened? The smith reached down without thinking and yanked Scall up from the ground, but her attention was all on Barsil. 'What horse?' she demanded. 'We've no killer beasts here in the Precincts!'

'Er – it's new. In the stables.' The guard's gaze flicked nervously away. Nobody dared lie to the smith, but Agella had a feeling that Barsil didn't dare tell her the truth, either.

'I *know* it's in the stables! You already told me that, you bloody fool!' Agella shouldered past the dithering man, seized his arm and yanked him after her as she raced across the yard towards the stable block. 'Stay there!' she yelled over her shoulder at her apprentice, who stood there, gaping and dripping, still clutching his flagons to his chest. She hoped the gormless young idiot hadn't managed to spill *both* of them. She had a feeling she would need a drink before much longer.

As she ran, Agella wondered what had made the horse turn rogue. Not the conditions, that was for sure. Most Tiarondians would be delighted to change places with the animals of the Sacred Precincts, whose quarters were warmer, more luxurious and in a far better state of repair than most of the human dwellings in the city. The Hierarch's stables, kennels, pigeon-loft and mews were draught-free, spacious and dry. Even in these hard times, the animals had a better diet than most Lower Town dwellers. Their bedding, changed each day, was thick, clean and dry. If an animal was injured or fell sick, several physicians near by in the Temple's Hall of Healing specialised in animal complaints. With all this pampering and attention, which horse could have turned wild enough to kill a lad? What could possibly be ailing the beast to make it do such a terrible thing?

As the master neared the stable block, the angry screams of the rogue horse could be heard quite clearly. A knot of folk – mainly grooms, falconers and kennelmen, plus a handful of Godswords in their black livery and mail – obstructed the doorway to the building. The bystanders fell back to allow Agella to enter, and she hurried down the wide central passageway edged on either side with spacious stalls, whose occupants represented the equine race in all its wide diversity. In the course of her work, the smith had come to know every one of them. There were steady, even-tempered riding horses bred for their smooth paces and ability to travel long distances; colossal draft horses capable of pulling enormous loads; a bunch of shaggy little pack-ponies, imps of mischief, the lot of them, but sure-footed on the steeper mountain trails; the slender, long-legged mounts of the couriers, built for stamina and speed; and the fierce, fiery-tempered warhorses of the Godswords – in Agella's opinion, the most likely candidates for the role of killer.

The pampered inhabitants of the Hierarch's stable were normally contented, sleek and calm, but today they were restive and uneasy, moving fretfully around their boxes, eyes rolling and hooves scraping the floor of their stalls as they banged against the wooden partitions with a hollow sound like drums. Their coats were stained dark with fear-sweat and their nostrils flared as they scented death and blood. Agella realised she'd been mistaken in thinking that one of the warhorses must be the culprit. As she neared the far end of the building, and the secluded stalls in which new horses were allowed to settle down, she saw that two of the boxes were occupied, and a knot of Godswords were clustered around them at a respectful distance. *New* horses? she thought indignantly. Nobody told *me*! Usually, Agella was one of the first to be asked to inspect any new arrival. Then the realisation hit her: one of the soldiers was aiming a crossbow at the horse.

'Let me through!' Agella did not speak loudly – she didn't have to. Immediately, the warriors stood aside to let her pass. Everybody knew it was bad luck to cross a smith. Then all other thoughts were wiped from her mind by the horses that occupied the two adjacent boxes, two flashing-eyed, flailing-hoofed ebony giants that took her breath away with their ferocity and splendour. One of them, she noticed, was a stallion. The smith came to a halt outside his box, safely out of biting range. 'Myrial's teeth and toenails!' she gasped. 'Sefrians! Where the blazes did *they* come from?'

A trail of blood led from the door of the stallion's stall, where a body had clearly been dragged out and away. Now the horse was attacking the very door with teeth and hooves, intent on destroying the barrier between himself and freedom. Fergist the stablemaster was looking on helplessly, his tall, bony body tense with anxiety, his brow creased with a frown below his thatch of greying hair. Over the banging of hooves, the angry screaming of the horse and the crunch of splintering wood, Agella managed to catch snatches of his low, hurried explanation. 'They were just brought in today . . . Ruper was taking them water . . . Must have tripped . . . Father went in there . . . We dragged him out . . . Slammed the door shut just in time, or it'd be loose in the Precincts by now . . . I daren't shoot them. You know how rare they are. I've special instructions from both the Hierarch *and* Lord Blade, if you please, to take good care of them.'

Agella shook her head. 'You may not have a choice. The brute will have that door in splinters before long – and *then* where will we be?'

'You needn't worry on *that* score.' The stablemaster's voice was stiff with indignation. 'These boxes are solidly built – I oversaw the work myself. The horse hasn't been bred yet that can smash its way out of *my* stable.'

The smith looked again at the stallion, taking in its white-rimmed eyes and the sweat that dulled its strong black neck. Beneath that pent-up power and anger, she realised, was fear. The horse had been taken away from its usual surroundings and left in this unfamiliar place, full of strange people and other stallions. Then poor Ruper had come along . . . Suddenly Agella's eyes narrowed as she looked away from the flashing teeth and the enormous forefeet that smashed repeatedly into the door of the box. The stallion's belly and sleek black quarters were striped with whip cuts. She rounded on the stablemaster. 'Who lashed him?'

'Dalvis. Boy's father.' Fergist shook his head. 'The horse wasn't so bad at first. Oh, he was a bit wild and fractious when he came, but we've had them like that before. But the odd thing was, he turned gentle as a kitten with young Ruper – like he was used to youngsters. That's why we let the lad go in there. But then Rupe stumbled, and went down under those big hooves, and his father panicked and went in with the whip.' He shook his head. 'The horse went right for Dalvis – he didn't stand a chance.'

'Hold on – I thought the *boy* was killed!' Agella interrupted.

'No, no – we managed to drag Rupe out while the stallion was busy with Dalvis. The lad was just knocked out by the fall. He's with the healers now.' He leaned closer to the smith. 'But you know the funny thing?' he confided. 'All the time that horse was pounding poor Dalvis into the floor – and remember that Rupe was lying there, right in the middle of the box – the beast never so much as stepped on the boy. It was like he—'

The door of the box burst open in an explosion of shattered planks. Agella, knocked aside by an avalanche of muscle and bone, went crashing into the wall, hitting her elbow and the back of her head. She pulled herself upright quickly and ran after the escaping stallion, jumping over the Godsword soldiers who were trying to pick themselves up out of the dung channel. Something crunched under her foot – a broken crossbow. The mangled weapon looked as though the horse had stepped on it first. 'Shut the doors!' she roared, but it was already too late. She arrived in the open doorway with the stablemaster breathing down her neck. Both of them emerged just in time to see the massive black beast heading straight for her hapless apprentice, who was standing right in the way.

The smith caught her breath, helpless to do anything other than watch as the killer bore down on Scall, who stood there, unmoving, his face pale and set. Horror twisted Agella's guts. Shit! she thought. He's frozen! But at the very last instant, the boy turned aside, stepped neatly out of the giant's path, and let out a long trilling whistle. The thundering behemoth ploughed to a halt, its shoes striking a shower of sparks as its hooves slipped and skidded, leaving long white scrapes on the paving stones. It wheeled round on its haunches and headed back towards the boy – but this time at a sedate and gentle trot. When it reached him, he held out his hand, and the massive beast dropped its nose into his outstretched palm then started to work its way up his arm, licking at the beer that soaked his sleeve.

'Myrial in a whirlwind!' The stablemaster's voice was shaky. 'Maybe the lad should be *my* apprentice, not yours. I've never seen anything like that.'

The smith let out her pent-up breath in a long sigh. 'Nor have I, Fergist. Nor have I – and I hope I never have to see it again.'

By the time they reached the boy – keeping a wary distance from the horse – Scall was standing there stroking the stallion's powerful neck, with a look of pure wonder on his face. 'Mistress Agella – he likes me!'

'Scall,' the smith said softly. 'How did you know to whistle at him like that?'

The apprentice flushed. 'I saw the two black horses come in with those traders this morning,' Scall explained. 'I heard the woman whistle to them then, and I guessed he would be missing her. I thought a familiar sound . . .'

'Well done, lad!' Agella lifted her hand to give him a vigorous clout on the back – then looked at the horse and thought better of it.

'Well done indeed,' the stablemaster added. 'That was quick thinking – but it seems to me you also have a rare instinct for these beasts. You and I may want to talk in a while – but first, do you think you could get this fellow safely back into his stable?'

Scall gave the stallion a final pat, and left him with his nose buried deep in his manger. 'I think he's all right now,' he told the stablemaster and the smith. He slipped quickly out of the loose-box, a new stall, next to that of the Sefrian gelding, for it had been discovered that the two horses settled better when they were together. By now word of the killer horse had raced through the Sacred Precincts, and a small crowd had gathered in the passage at a respectful distance, watching while the smith's no-good apprentice led in the killer horse as though it had been a lamb, then fed it and settled it down.

Now the stablemaster shooed them away. 'Go on now, everyone. There's nothing more to see here, and you're disturbing my horses. Haven't you all got work to do?'

'Aren't you going to destroy that brute?' someone called out. 'It *killed* a man, for Myrial's sake! This place won't be safe as long as it's around.' His question was backed by a chorus of voices, all raised in support.

Fergist bestowed on them a long, level look that Agella could have hammered out on her anvil, and waited until they fell silent. 'It's not up to me – nor you,' he said. 'These are rare and valuable animals, and they belong to the Hierarch. The decision is for him to make. We must wait for his return. Or would you care to dispute the matter with Lord Blade, who told me personally, just before he left for the mountain, to take all possible care of these beasts?' The thought of Lord Blade seemed to cool the indignation of the crowd. All at once, the bystanders began to drift away, most of them still muttering discontentedly.

Scall watched them go with a scowl on his face. Though he knew the horse had killed a man, it had come to him and trusted him, and he had fallen in love with the magnificent beast. He had seen the cruel whip-cuts on the stallion's flanks. Surely they would take into account that it had been provoked? But a few yards away, at the end of the passage, an apprentice was busy with bucket and mop, swilling the blood trail from the floor. The blood of a man who'd been alive an hour ago. Scall averted his eyes quickly, and turned to the stablemaster. 'Sir? This horse killed Dalvis. What will happen to him now – really?'

Fergist looked grave. 'As I said, boy – that's for the Hierarch to decide.'

'But what will you tell him?' Scall pressed. 'He'll listen to what you say.'

'Scall,' Agella put in firmly, 'the stablemaster and I are going back to the smithy now, to have a little talk.' Her face, usually so ruddy from working over the hot fire, still looked very white. 'Why don't you go and fetch us some more beer?'

'But . . .'

'*Now*, Scall. And you needn't hurry.' Scall gaped at her for a moment, then turned on his heel with a sigh and set off in the direction of the brewhouse. Everything was back to normal. For a fleeting space of time he'd been a hero – but nothing had really changed. And besides, he told himself, none of them know why the stallion obeyed me. I'm wearing *her* waistcoat, with *her* smell still on it. No wonder he came straight to me! But how can I explain that to them? I could never go and confess to the smith that I took a dead woman's jerkin in exchange for altering Agella's precious sacred list!

As he continued on his way towards the brewhouse, he didn't notice that he'd avoided the muddy grass instinctively, and wiped his feet as a matter of course on entering the brewers' lair. He *did* notice, however, that Maryll seemed to be taking a very marked and sudden interest in him. Before she allowed him to escape with the ale, she wanted to know every detail of his encounter with the killer horse. He was enjoying the attention so much that he was in no hurry to leave. It was quite a while before his cold and aching arms reminded him that he was still clutching Agella's beer, and should have delivered it some time ago. 'Maryll,' he gasped. 'I'm very sorry – I've got to go!' He excused himself hastily, and ran back to the smithy. As he ran, he heard the apprentice brewer calling after him, urging him to come back later. Scall smiled to himself. Well, maybe *some* things had changed for the better, after all.

There were far greater changes afoot, however, than Scall had realised. As he came into the smithy, the smith and the stablemaster were perched on stools as close as they could bear to the glowing fire, and Agella was talking. 'Listen, Fergist, that crowd went away once when you threatened them with Lord Blade, but they're hungry for blood now, and there's no telling what they might talk themselves into if the Hierarch doesn't come back soon.'

'The trouble is, I'm not sure they aren't right . . .' The stablemaster saw Scall enter, and shut his mouth quickly.

'I agree.' Agella took the beer from Scall, completely ignoring his mutinous scowl and mutterings of protest. This time, she didn't even offer him any. Thoroughly out of countenance, he took his own low stool away into a corner to sulk – but not so far away that he couldn't hear every word that was said between the two adults.

The smith handed one flagon to the stablemaster, who uncorked it and took a long, thoughtful swig as he picked up the conversation where he had left off. 'Though Hierarch Zavahl and Lord Blade do want to keep them, I don't particularly want those beasts in my stable – and I'm having a hard enough time stretching out the fodder for the beasts that are already here. If this horse-trainer friend that you mentioned can give the Sefrians a home until the trouble dies down, and if she's really as trustworthy and as good as you say – because if she mucks up it'll be *my* head that will roll – and if she can make them behave themselves in the process, it might be best for all concerned.'

Agella smiled. 'Oh, she's good – I promise. She may be getting on in years now, but Toulac has forgotten more about training horses than most folk will ever know.'

'How do you know her?'

'I've known her since I was about Scall's age.' Agella stared into the fire. 'My folk were eastern Reivers, before our clan were conquered and wiped out by the warchief Vlastor. My father killed his son, you see, and he vowed that he would never rest until every drop of our blood had been spilled.' She paused for a moment. 'The slaughter was terrible,' she said at last. 'I was hiding in a barn with my younger sister when Toulac, who was a mercenary with Vlastor's forces, discovered us. She smuggled us out as water-boys in Vlastor's own army, and I first started to learn my craft from his smith. Eventually Toulac brought us to Tiarond, and apprenticed Viora with the seamstresses and me with Master Eharl, who was smith to the Godswords at that time.' Scall gasped.

He'd had no idea that his mother and aunt had had such an adventurous past. Agella looked up at the stablemaster. 'So you see why I trust Toulac. I owe her everything: my profession, my prosperity – and my life.'

'She sounds like a remarkable woman,' the stablemaster said. 'And you really think she'll train the lad, too?'

'I'm sure she will, though she never had a lot of time for his mother. She may be too proud to admit it, but she could use some extra help up there – and some company. In fact, that's the main reason I want to send Scall. He may not be much good as an apprentice, but I'm not so heartless that I'd pack him off at the first opportunity. I worry about Toulac, living all alone up on that mountain. The sawmill isn't doing too well, she can't be making much of a living out of it, but she's so damn independent that she won't take any help from me. If Scall goes up there, though, I'll have a good excuse to send stuff such as food, extra clothing and warm blankets. You know – items that are available to us here in the Precincts but nowhere else for as long as this accursed rain lasts. It's a good arrangement, Fergist. You get the horses out of your stable, Scall gets a future as an apprentice to the best horse trainer I ever saw – and if he eventually comes back here, he should be very useful to you.'

Fergist nodded. 'You're right. It sounds like the ideal arrangement.'

Scall's mouth fell open. Why, without so much as a by-your-leave, they had rearranged his entire future! Agella turned to him. 'Scall,' she told him in her most no-nonsense voice, 'we have a job for you. We want you to take the two black horses out of the city, and deliver them to Mistress Toulac at the sawmill up the Snaketail trail. We want you to stay with her, if you suit each other, and learn all that she can teach you. She's a rare good trainer, and this could be a great opportunity for you. What do you say?'

She wasn't *really* offering Scall a choice – and well he knew it. The recent happy hopes of success with Maryll melted away like snow in spring. Curse you, he thought – I don't *want* to be stuck halfway up a mountain with some mad old woman! Though he didn't dare speak his thoughts aloud, his silence was eloquent.

'It might be your best chance to save that precious monster horse of yours,' the stablemaster put in.

Scall sighed. He wanted to ask why his mother disliked Mistress Toulac, but he didn't dare. He might as well give in gracefully right now. He knew it would save trouble in the long run. Mistress Agella didn't take kindly to being disobeyed, and everyone knew it was bad luck to cross a smith. It was a pity, he thought sourly, that the same rule clearly did not apply to apprentices. Besides, what choice had he? He was trapped. He couldn't tell the truth – that he didn't know a damn thing about horses, and all of this had come about because he was wearing the stolen garment of the animal's original owner! There was no way out. It was probably a judgement on him.

'All right,' he sighed. 'I'll go.'

Thirteen

Into the Fire

6H orse meat,' Elion muttered. 'Horse liver, horse stew, horse steaks . . .' The horse looked sideways at him with its usual dumb insolence, curled its lips back from its great, yellow teeth, and tried to bite. Swearing, Elion snatched his arm back out of the way, and those gravestone teeth met on empty air with a snap. Ever since they had left Gendival, the creature had been pure recalcitrance with four legs and a tail, not to mention those vicious teeth trying to help themselves to chunks of Elion's flesh.

Gritting his own teeth, the Loremaster took a firmer hold on the bridle and tugged as hard as he could, but he might as well have tried to shift the whole bloody mountain. A thin slick of icy slush had already formed under his boots, and he couldn't plant his feet steadily enough to keep up a decent pull. Elion cursed again. It just wasn't fair. He'd been forced to drag this wretched creature up every blasted inch of the precipitous trail, knowing all the while that there was a crisis on the other side and speed was crucial. Now they had finally made the pass, his legs were on fire and he was trembling with exhaustion, and this miserable, bad-tempered, ill-favoured, stupid bag of bones didn't like the look of the icy floodwater that ran down the trail on the other side and was refusing to go any further. Blindfolding it had failed. Hitting it had failed. It seemed they had reached an impasse.

Elion? What in the name of all creation is keeping you? Shree sounded anxious. *The men have gone at last, and I need your help. The man I rescued is already beginning to stir – what if he should awaken? We don't want him wandering off in this blizzard before we can speak to him.*

'I'm doing my best!' There was a snap to Elion's mental tones. 'I need *your* help, Shree. This bloody-minded bag of bones is refusing to come down the trail.'

He could hear the wind-sprite's sigh all the way up the mountain. *Very well. I'm on my way.*

Within moments, Elion felt a warm breeze touch his face. *Here I am.* To his surprise, he found himself warmed by a sudden glow of comfort and relief. It took him back to his childhood. When he had tumbled down or had broken a favourite plaything or was unable to complete a difficult lesson, his mother had always been there with a hug or a treat to comfort him. Her clever hands could mend anything except a broken heart, and her wise words of advice could make most problems go away . . .

Elion pulled himself out of that train of thought with a jerk. His mother had been dead these many years. He was grown now, and damn well ought to be able to solve his own problems, except that here he was, begging help from someone he couldn't even see. 'Can you get this vile-tempered lump of dog's meat moving?' he asked Shree brusquely.

I expect so. I'm not so sure about the horse, though! The wind-sprite dissolved into peals of laughter.

'Very droll.' Again, Elion clenched his teeth, wondering how long it would be before he wore them away completely. 'When you're quite finished . . .'

At your service, my dear Loremaster. Laughter still danced behind Shree's telepathic voice. *Now, go down to the end of the flooded area and wait to catch the horse.*

Wondering what the wind-sprite was planning, Elion waded into the cold, swift-running water. How would Shree get the horse to move? She might project an illusion – that was the most likely way. A lion or a bear – something to scare the stupid brute into motion. Elion began to worry. How much does an elemental know about horses? he wondered. This trail is very slippery under the water. If the horse is scared into a panic it might bolt down so fast that it falls and breaks a leg! I'd hate that to happen. I need the transportation . . .

He had reached the end of the flooded section where the trail widened when he heard the sound of hooves. To his utter amazement, it sounded as though the horse was moving carefully downtrail at a sedate, steady pace, and within moments it came into sight through the dither of snowflakes. Elion blinked. Around the final bend in the trail came not one but *two* horses: the Loremaster's evil, chestnut-coated nemesis and, in the lead, a little, nondescript brown mare. The irascible demon-horse followed her like a lamb, with ears pricked forward and shining eyes.

As Elion stood gaping at this miracle, the brown mare vanished. The chestnut whinnied piteously, looking around in puzzlement. Then, as the Loremaster approached and took hold of its bridle, it reverted to its former character, laid its ears flat and snapped at him once more. Irritating as the sprite could be, Elion had to give credit where credit was due . . . 'Shree, that was amazing. I've never seen anything like it. How did you manage to tame this brute – even for a while?'

A rainbow flickered momentarily through the veils of snow as the wind-sprite glowed with pleasure. *It was nothing, really – I just took the requisite illusion straight from your horse's mind. The other horse you saw was its mother.* She chuckled at Elion's chagrin.

Damning all wind-sprites, all horses and, just for good measure, all mothers to perdition, Elion looked closely at Aethon the Seer. He was dead all right – cold and stiffening already, his golden skin bleached to an ashen grey. Turning away with a sad and troubled heart, the Loremaster stooped to examine the innumerable imprints of booted feet that had been trampled back and forth in the mud and snow. If Kaz or Veldan had left this place on their own feet, there would be no way to tell. The landslide detritus that had blocked the trail had been partially cleared by the soldiers in digging out the dragon, and was piled high against the walls of the offshoot gully that slanted away from the trail. The floodwater was now draining back into the narrow canyon, clearing its own downward routes by carving runnels through the mud that covered broken trees and tumbled boulders.

Elion scrambled down into the gully in search of the fugitive that Shree had rescued. The wind-sprite hurried on ahead of him, blowing away the heavy skeins of snow as she went. Without Shree's help, the man would have been difficult to find. Elion had been expecting to hear a muffled cry for help, perhaps, or possibly a stream of profanities, but the stranger was either too badly hurt to call out or was suffering in grim, determined silence. Elion was both concerned and perplexed. Why was the wretch not moving, or uttering a single sound? Were his injuries worse than Shree had thought?

Bear a little to your left, the wind-sprite said. *The man is about ten feet away from you.*

The Loremaster approached with caution, and finally spotted the man, who lay face down in a muddy hollow, struggling to lift two heavy boughs and a miscellaneous collection of smaller branches that pressed down on his legs and back. 'Shree?' Elion said accusingly.

What did you expect me to do? You took such an endless age to get down here, I was afraid he'd run off and we would have to catch him all over again.

'Really, Shree – you should be ashamed of yourself. Is this an action worthy of a Senior Loremaster? Don't you think the poor wretch has been through enough? That's a terrible thing to do to anybody.'

It worked, didn't it? The sprite sounded completely unrepentant. Shaking his head, Elion hurried across to the struggling man. As he knelt down beside the captive, he was shocked into pity by the rictus of despair and terror that distorted the man's face. 'It's all right,' he said quickly. 'My name is Elion – I'm here to help you. You'll be all right now.'

The man shook his head violently. 'My family,' he moaned. 'Kanella. Little Annas . . .' His eyes brimmed with tears.

Elion looked away, disturbed by such profound pain, which came too close for comfort to his own raw grief at Melnyth's death. He patted the man clumsily on the shoulder. 'All right – don't try to talk now. First things first . . .' He paused to clear his throat. 'Let's get you out of this mess.'

Tormon, still stunned by his miraculous escape from the arrow, was beyond astonishment at the appearance of this dark young man with the shadowed eyes. He barely noticed as his unknown benefactor began to lift away the heavy logs that pressed his body down into the mud. His mind was filled with shadows of its own: hideous images that repeated over and over again. Kanella, slain. Annas, his bright-eyed baby, dead somewhere in the black heart of that vile mausoleum, that manmade monument to savagery, war and destruction. And over the trader's dreadful thoughts of murder, horror and blood, loomed the shuttered face of the Hierarch, arrogant and self-involved, the face of a man who had submerged his own humanity into the service of some greater power and, in doing so, had drowned his sense of responsibility for the lowly folk beneath his sway. Innocents murdered? Ordinary, trusting folk deceived and betrayed? Blame Myrial, not Zavahl. All of his actions were for the God's glory, and by the God's will.

Tormon knew there was no point in hoping. Already it must be too late. In the time he'd spent trapped here in this cold, bleak waste, he had come to the terrible understanding that the Hierarch had planned this ambush all along, had decided, for some reason, that *he* wanted to take the credit for finding the dragon, and had arranged matters so that Tormon would never be able to talk. Such base and ruthless treachery could only mean one thing: that the trader's lifemate and daughter, helpless captives in the Godsword citadel, had been silenced also. Annas and Kanella were already dead.

Tormon's thoughts went to the Hierarch. Suddenly his heart was flooded, his mind consumed, by a cold and killing rage. Never in his life had the trader deliberately harmed another human being, but that was about to change.

'Well, my girl, it looks like I coaxed you back into bed just in time.' Toulac spoke softly, so as not to awaken Veldan, and tucked the quilt more tightly around the sleeping woman's shoulders. The former warrior looked down at her oblivious guest and sighed. You might have waited a little longer, she thought. There was so much I wanted to ask, and while you were still weak and dazed, you'd have let slip more information, mystery lady. Next time you wake you'll be more alert and refreshed, and you'll be on your guard.'

Toulac had been disappointed – though not at all surprised – to find herself half dragging, half carrying Veldan back to bed. The little idiot had been crazy to get up and start moving about so quickly, though Toulac could sympathise with her need to see her friend and reassure herself that he was all right. She'd barely had time to eat a morsel of bread soaked in sweetened tea before she slipped back into oblivion, leaving the veteran more frustrated and curious than ever.

'Well, standing here looking at her won't help – unless this mind-reading stuff she talked about is contagious,' Toulac told herself. She had also been disappointed in her hopes of getting anything out of the dragon-creature – what had Veldan called it? A firedrake? Clearly it was considerably more intelligent than any normal beast, that was for sure and certain. If it had been able to write the word HELP on the floor of her porch, surely there must be some way to communicate with it . . . But all of this was pure conjecture on Toulac's part, since the firedrake, as she had discovered on a recent visit to the barn, was also fast asleep.

The worst of it was that she could understand and sympathise. So many times, in her warrior's past, she had drawn on all her reserves to keep going, on and on, through battle, bad weather and rough terrain. When everything around her was blurred in a fog of exhaustion, and she had been sure she couldn't strike another blow or march another step, sure that she must lie down in the soft snow and sleep for one last, long time – on each occasion she had found one last shred of courage or strength or hope that kept her a heartbeat ahead of death's cold grasp. And each time, when she'd come safely to the end of her ordeal, she had done exactly what her two guests were doing: slept and slept until she had replenished herself. And after I finally awoke, I used to eat and eat, Toulac thought, with some dismay. What in Myrial's name am I going to feed them on?

Well, the first job was to try to find some food in her neglected pantry that would be suitable for an invalid. Sadly a diligent search turned up very little: some onions, a few dusty potatoes, a cluster of tough, shrivelled carrots, some dried peas and a handful of barley in the bottom of a crock. Using the last of the cold beef joint and its bone, Toulac simply chopped everything up, threw the whole lot into her biggest stewpot, filled it with water, put it on the fire, crossed her fingers and called it soup. Though that's probably not what poor Veldan will call it when she tastes it, the warrior thought ruefully. Oh well, I never claimed to be any kind of cook.

As Toulac straightened up from the fire, wiping her hands on her breeches, she noticed Veldan's weapons: her scabbarded sword, two throwing knives and a very serviceable dagger, propped up with her own sword near the fireplace. Their immersion in so much mud, grit and water had done little good to the sword belt and scabbard, and the blades, too, were in dire need of cleaning and oiling. Her eyes went to the woman's leather fighting gear, draped over the back of a chair. It was finally dry now, she realised as she picked it up, but it certainly needed some repairs after being buried under half the mountain! Her careful fingers found two sizeable tears and several places where the leather had been badly scuffed and worn. Well, that could soon be fixed. Though she couldn't be bothered with sewing in the general way, she could repair leather gear in her sleep. She had spent so many hours over the years extending the life of her own fighting garb that the time probably added up into days.

The veteran rummaged about on dusty shelves until she unearthed oil and a handful of soft, clean rags, together with the old saddle bag that contained her mending equipment: needles, waxed cord and a lump of the special glue that was sometimes used for sticking down patches. She put the glue in her oldest pot and stood it in a bigger pot filled with boiling water so that the glue would soften. An old leather tunic, worn out to the point where it was now plugging a draughty hole in one of her shutters, provided the material for patches. Let me see – I'll start on the sword, I think . . . It turned out to be a well-balanced and finely crafted weapon, a delight to hold in the hand. With a happy smile, Toulac settled down in her comfortable chair by the fire and set to work, humming a bawdy song under her breath. This was just like the old days!

As the afternoon darkened towards dusk, the veteran worked with the swift efficiency of many years' practice and it seemed no time at all before she had dealt with the weapons and had turned her attention to the leather gear. Feeling in one of the pockets, she came across the lumpy shape of something hard. Curious, she pulled it out. It fitted neatly into the palm of her hand, a small globe, about the size of a hen's egg, that looked as if it were made out of some kind of cloudy glass. A shallow groove ran round its middle, almost like a seam that split it in half. The urge to twist the two halves against one another to see what would happen was almost unendurable, but the veteran restrained herself firmly. You could get some very nasty surprises that way. The firedrake in her barn was enough to tell her she had no ordinary kind of visitors, and the woman's belongings must be similarly strange. 'Anyway,' Toulac told herself firmly, 'dangerous or not, she won't thank you for nosing about in her pockets. And what if you break it, whatever it is? Don't be a busybody. Put it away.'

She tried to replace the mysterious globe in the deep tunic pocket from which it had come – but now it wouldn't go back in. Toulac rummaged again, and pulled out something small, dark and soft. Curious, she opened it out. 'What in the world . . . ?' She smoothed the black silk out with her calloused fingers, saw the eye holes – and felt her heart clench with pity. That poor, foolish, desperate child had been so self-conscious about her disfigured face that she'd stooped to hiding her scar with this accursed thing! The warrior wiped away a surreptitious tear, telling herself not to be so sentimental. 'After all, what is she to you?' she muttered. 'The way you're carrying on, anybody'd think she was your daughter!' But daughter or not – this nonsense would have to be sorted out. Toulac wasn't about to let the poor girl go through the rest of her life being afraid of her own face. Pushing the glass globe back into the pocket, she put the leather tunic to one side, then leaped up, brisk and purposeful, from her chair. Almost savagely, she hurled the mask into the fire and used the poker to stuff it right into the heart of the glowing coals. 'There,' she said firmly, as the silk shrivelled and flared. 'That takes care of that nonsense.' She only hoped that Veldan would forgive her.

Swinging the small bundle that contained his scanty store of possessions, Scall ran out of the apprentices' dormitory without a backward look. There was no one to see him go. The apprentices were all working at this time of day, and the weather, looking blacker by the moment, had kept everyone indoors. The wind had swung round to the north, and the rain was already turning to sleet. Scall looked around him as he ran – at the neat, tiled artisans' cottages, the stables and workshops. The leafless trees dripped dismally on the muddy gathering square. He couldn't bring himself to believe that he was leaving this place for good: everything had happened far too fast for him to take it in. Tomorrow he'd have a new home, a new mistress and a new profession. *I don't want this,* he thought – but no one had asked him.

In the smithy, Agella was waiting. 'Ah, there you are at last. Hurry now, Scall. Fergist has the horses ready for you, and there's no time to lose. The days are short just now, and you want to get up there before dark, don't you?'

Scall saw a solitary ray of hope. 'Couldn't we put it off till tomorrow?'

Agella shook her head, and the one last hope vanished. 'No. By the looks of the weather it's going to snow, and you might not be able to get up there at all tomorrow. Your only chance is to go right now, and don't waste any time on the road.'

'But Mistress Agella . . .' He knew she couldn't bear whining, but he was desperate to dissuade her from this plan. If only he could tell her about the jerkin! But the notion that he'd actually trafficked in the stolen belongings of a dead woman scalded him with shame. No one must ever know. He couldn't bear to go through life with such a stain upon his reputation. Instead he tried another tack, as near to the truth as he dared come. 'How can I become a horse-trainer? I barely know how to ride! You had to teach me to sit a horse yourself, remember, so I could run errands for you up to the mines. *And* I kept falling off!'

Agella's eyes flashed. 'For Myrial's sake, boy, no one expects you to *ride* the Sefrians! What do you think I'm trying to do? Kill you? Nor would I send you alone through the city in charge of so much potential horsemeat. I'll arrange for one of the Godswords to act as escort. Here.' She thrust another bundle – a sack made from thick, oiled cloth – into his arms. 'There's a good supply of food in there. We can't let you go up to Mistress Toulac empty-handed. And I've written her a letter – here it is, be careful not to lose it – explaining the situation.' She tried to smile at him. 'Toulac is an old friend. You'll be a great help to each other, and don't worry. She may be a bit gruff and crotchety, but underneath the steel and fire she has a heart of gold.'

I know what she is, Scall thought. I've heard of her. Everybody knows about the mad, cranky old witch who lives up on the mountain. He still didn't know why his mother hated her, and was afraid to ask for fear of what he might discover. He shuddered at the thought of the coming months. Because of the snow, he stood a good chance of being trapped up there with her and not being able to escape all winter, no matter what she did to him.

'Come on now,' Agella said sharply. 'Don't stand there dreaming. Let's get going.' But in spite of her own words, she hesitated, and put a hand on his shoulder. 'Scall, you've been a good lad,' she said in a gentler voice. 'You may not be cut out to be a smith, but I know you tried your best. I know you don't believe me right now, but this is a great opportunity for you. Truly.'

You're right, Scall thought, as she turned away. I don't believe you.

As Agella came out of the smithy, she almost fell over the Godsword guard Barsil. He gave her a casual salute and made as if to saunter off, as though he had just happened to be passing. Agella frowned. She knew perfectly well that he'd been eavesdropping; the man was a positive leech for other people's business. She disliked Barsil at the best of times, but today she found herself positively loathing him. 'Haven't you anything better to do today than loiter around the Sacred Precincts?' she demanded crossly.

'No, Mistress, I'm off duty today. S'not *my* fault there's nothing doing.' He began to sidle away, but the smith stepped in front of him, and stopped him in his tracks.

'I'm glad to hear you're free today,' she said, 'because Stablemaster Fergist and myself have an errand for you. I want you to escort my apprentice and the two new horses up to Mistress Toulac at the sawmill.'

Barsil's eyes narrowed with anger, but he put a good face on it. 'Of course, Mistress. You know I'd do anything to help *you* out. Er . . . I'll just go and fetch my other cloak—'

'Don't bother,' Agella said crisply. 'The one you're wearing is fine.' She knew perfectly well that once Barsil got out of her sight, that would be the last she'd see of him today. And tomorrow he would turn up, ever so apologetic, with some plausible excuse, having managed to weasel out of the whole unpleasant business. 'Come with me now,' she added quickly. 'You must leave immediately – there's no time to lose if you want to get back tonight. Hurry up, Scall. You've got both your bundles? Good. We mustn't waste any time about getting you on your way.'

There was nothing Barsil could do. He had already admitted that he was off duty – and therefore available – and the stable- and smithmasters far outranked a mere lowly soldier, even a Godsword. Clearly neither guard nor apprentice were happy with this new arrangement. Leaving the pair of them to follow her, Agella went briskly on her way, well aware that they were scowling behind her back like a pair of gargoyles. There, she thought. Maybe *that* will encourage that sneaking wretch to mind his own business in future. It's a bit hard on poor Scall, but most of the decent guards are on patrol in the city today, or have gone off up the mountain with the Hierarch.

Scall couldn't credit such misfortune. Every time he decided things couldn't possibly get any worse, another calamity befell him! He turned to scowl at Barsil and found the guard glaring back at him. Scall knew the Godsword was warning him not to spill the truth about the jerkin. The trooper's expression spoke volumes. *Just wait*, it said. *I'll get you for this!* The apprentice shuddered. Even supposing he *did* manage to stay on his horse, it didn't look as though he was going to make it up the mountain without a bruise or two.

When the smith and her apprentice reached the stableyard, trailed by the glowering Godsword soldier, they found the Sefrian stallion and gelding waiting for them, their halters fastened with long ropes to a sturdy ring bolted into the high yard wall. Scall noticed that everyone was keeping a very respectful distance between themselves and the two black giants. In spite of all the trouble it had caused him, he was glad he was still wearing the jerkin. Unable to resist showing off, he walked across to the animals, repeating the whistle that he'd heard the trader woman use. They pricked up their ears, and turned to him as far as their tethers would allow. Scall rummaged in his pockets for the grain and the wizened apples he'd filched from the brewhouse while saying goodbye to Maryll. The Sefrians crowded round him, whickering happily and nuzzling against him like gigantic puppies.

'Be careful,' the smith called softly. She was standing back, well out of reach of the tethered animals, and Scall was heartened by the look of amazement – and, he fancied, admiration – on her face.

After a moment Fergist came hobbling out of the stable. 'Ah, there you are,' he called cheerfully.

The smith affected not to notice that he was limping. 'Everything ready?' she asked.

'Just about – and I won't be sorry to see those big black buggers go.' The stablemaster glared at the offending animals. 'That bloody stallion kicked me – pretty near gelded me, in fact – when I was getting him out, and the gelding nearly took a chunk out of my arm.'

Agella's lips twitched. 'What have you got for Scall to ride?'

'Well, that's a bit of a problem.' Fergist seemed to be finding it difficult to look the apprentice in the eye. 'You see, horseflesh is at a premium in these hard times, and I don't want to risk letting one of the Precinct mounts go. Besides, I can't really spare a horse right now.'

'Well what do you expect the poor lad to do?' the smith demanded. 'Do you want a raw beginner like Scall to ride a monster that *you* can't even control? Or are you asking him to walk?'

'No, no,' said Fergist hastily. 'We have a mount for the lad, don't you fret.' He left them for a moment, and emerged again from the stable leading a small brown and white donkey with a wicked, rolling eye. '*This* came with the horses,' said the stablemaster sourly, 'and I might add, the little blighter has been pretty near as much trouble as the big ones.'

Scall's jaw fell open. In the background, Barsil burst out laughing. The apprentice was aghast. I can't go all the way through town perched on that little thing, he thought. I'll never live down the embarrassment! 'I can't go up the mountain on a *donkey*,' he protested aloud. 'Look at the size of it, for Myrial's sake. It'll never carry me!'

'Oh, I wouldn't worry about that,' Fergist said cheerfully. 'These creatures carry the most tremendous loads all the time. You shouldn't be too much of a problem for her if you take it easy. It's not as if you're a heavyweight.'

As the little beast approached Scall, it eyed him sidelong from under its shaggy brown fringe, then snaked its head out and nipped him on the arm. The apprentice jumped back with a yell, then stood rubbing his bruised flesh. After a moment he collected himself. 'I'm not riding that ... that ridiculous *creature*,' he said flatly. 'And that's final.'

Shortly afterwards, Scall found himself heading out of the Precincts through the tunnel, astride the narrow, bony back of the misanthropic little beast, wondering how he had come to be there and cursing his fate.

The ride down through the streets to the outskirts of the city was one of the worst experiences of Scall's short life. The two big horses were fractious and uneasy among so many buildings and strange people, and pulled this way and that on the ends of their lead ropes. Every other minute, Scall was sure he'd be pulled right out of his saddle. That was not the worst of it, however. Had he not already been aware of the ridiculous spectacle he made, with his legs trailing almost to the ground on either side of his midget mount, the brats and urchins of the Lower Town left him in no doubt whatsoever. He was the victim of boos and catcalls wherever he went, and only the rancorous presence of the glowering Barsil, who rode alongside with a loaded crossbow, saved him from a hail of thrown mud and other missiles of a far less wholesome nature. Though the Godsword's company was so unpleasant that the apprentice thought that he'd prefer to be covered in mud than to put up with Barsil's taunts, which tended to dwell on Scall's uselessness in needing a wet-nurse and which pointed out –

repeatedly – that the donkey was more intelligent and useful and considerably better-looking than its rider.

The road took the apprentice and his escort down through the Upper Town, with its spacious streets lined with the mansions of the affluent merchants, then through the commercial district with its shops, markets, counting-houses and the many inns that catered, in better days, to the needs of the pilgrims from the outlying reaches of Callisiora, who swarmed in droves to the Holy City each summer. At Meeting-House Square, with its shuttered and deserted taverns, Barsil took a right turn to take them down towards the city's western gate. 'Not long now, sonny,' he smirked, 'before we get you safely out of this big, bad city – you and your girlfriend there.'

Scall clenched his fists. He had no idea how he could possibly bear to travel any further with this nasty, shifty-eyed bastard – but the problem was academic. When they reached the west gate, the guards who manned the gatehouse were in the middle of a dice game. Barsil's darting, greedy eyes took in the players and the piles of copper on the guardroom table, then darted back to Scall and his charges. 'Listen, sonny,' he said. 'You're on your own from here. I have some business to take care of.' He gave the apprentice a leering, gap-toothed grin.

'What?' Scall gasped. He'd thought he was desperate to rid himself of this weaselly excuse for a guard but, now his wish had been granted, he was horrified at the idea of making the journey alone.

'It's all right, you pitiful little worm. I've nursemaided you through the town, and that's where the danger lay. Just turn right when you get out of the gates and follow the trail. Even a stupid little pipsqueak like *you* couldn't manage to get lost, and you won't meet anybody. No one in their right mind would be out and about on a day like this.'

'But . . . but you were supposed to take me all the way up to the sawmill,' Scall protested. 'Mistress Agella said so.'

'*Mistress Agella said so*,' Barsil mimicked in a high-pitched, sing-song voice. His expression darkened, and the breath froze in Scall's throat. 'Now listen here, you little turd. This is what's going to happen in the real world. I am going to stay here by this nice, warm fire and play dice. *You* can damn well take yourself up that trail, and stop pestering me. And . . .' Suddenly, a knife had appeared in his hand. 'If you ever breathe a word to her – or anybody else – about this, I'll come looking for you, do you understand? And I'll make you sorry you were ever born.'

Scall could only nod, his mouth too dry for speech. Unable to bear Barsil's menacing stare, or the jeers and mockery of the other guards a minute longer, he clapped his heels to the donkey's sides, and scurried out of the gate, the two great horses clattering along behind him. As he set off along the trail, the sound of raucous laughter echoed in his ears.

FOURTEEN

The Heiress

Seriema bent her head over the column of figures. Reluctant to break her concentration long enough to light a lamp, she found herself squinting to make out the rows of numbers as dusk thickened in the room. I'll see to it in a minute, she told herself, not for the first time, as she ran her eyes down yet another neatly penned inventory.

Numbers had always held a fascination for her, especially when applied to her own mercantile ventures. Even as a child, she had loved to keep her father, Trademaster Stemond – who held the leadership of the powerful Mercantile Assembly – company in his counting-house. She would perch on a high stool for hours at a time with unnatural patience for one so young, while she watched with fascination as his quill moved down the long rows of figures.

Sometimes, as a special treat, Stemond would show her his detailed, intricately painted maps, and talk to her of the gold and jewels, shining silver and ruddy copper torn from her own northern mountains, the feasts of meats, grains and greenstuffs from the fertile plains, and rich spices and exotic wines from the strange, faraway hills of the south, where the heat lay across the olive groves with their silvery trees like a mantle of heavy silk. With a careful finger, Seriema would

plan routes for the caravans of her imagination, while her
father, who still, at that time, was confidently expecting the
son who would one day take over his empire, would watch his
little girl with an indulgent smile that had gradually soured
as the years went by and, little by little, he came to realise
that Seriema was all he would ever have.

Following in her father's footsteps had not been easy for
Seriema, though she was well aware that most Tiarondians
believed she'd done nothing during Stemond's lifetime but
wait for his fortune to fall into her lap, and little more since
his death than sit on his money like a hen on an egg. In
either case, however, nothing could be further from the truth.
When she was seventeen, she'd fought tooth and nail against
Stemond when he had insisted she marry some capable young
merchant, a son of any one of several colleagues, so that there
would be a man to manage his concerns after his death, and
then hopefully a blood heir to succeed in him in the far-off
future. Their relationship had never recovered from that spate
of bitter battles: not even the death of her mother, worn down,
some said, by the continual feuding between her lifemate and
her daughter, had been enough to heal the rift. Stemond could
not excuse what he saw as Seriema's selfishness in failing to
provide for the future of his trading empire, and she never
forgave his seeming lack of trust in her abilities and his blind,
unthinking prejudice against her because she was not a man.
In the end, however, she had had her way – as she had always
known she must. There was no one else to inherit Stemond's
numerous enterprises save the rebel daughter.

Without delay, Seriema had set out to prove to the world
that she could not only be as good as her father, but even more
successful than Stemond or any other merchant in Tiarond. If
this had involved being harder, tougher, more ruthless than

her associates – well, she had soon learned to grow a thick
hide, and the other merchants, who had converged on her like
a frenzy of sharks following her father's death, had learned
their mistake very quickly – and usually the hard way. And
if, over the years, Seriema had found herself isolated and
bereft of friends, she had this satisfaction at least: those of
her fellows who did not like her respected her at least – and
if they lacked respect, she soon taught them to fear her. In
a very short time, she had fought her way right to the top –
bettering her father's old position by becoming head of both
the Mercantile Assembly *and* the Miners Consortium – and
there she planned to stay, despite every setback this accursed
weather tried to throw at her.

An ache behind Seriema's eyes made her realise that while
she'd been wrangling with gloomy factors' reports, shrinking
warehouse inventories and paltry trade figures, she had barely
noticed the darkness of the room as night drew in – not until
a brisk knock on the door made her tear her eyes from the
closely written pages with a sigh of exasperation as Presvel
entered. Seriema's assistant was carrying a cup of tea in one
hand and in the other a lamp that cast stark uncanny shadows
across his round, cheerful face, which obscured the fact that
his curling dark hair was thinning away from his brow.
Though he had both hands full and was moving carefully
so as not to spill the contents of the cup, he still managed to
convey his usual air of bustling efficiency. 'Lady, just look at
you,' he chided. 'You've done it *again*! I know you left orders
not to be disturbed, but you just won't remember to light
your candles, and you're absolutely *ruining* your eyes trying
to work in this dim light!'

Seriema, irritated though she was by the interruption, bore
the scolding patiently. She did not believe in punishing her

staff for being right. Besides, though she would never admit it aloud, Presvel's mother-hen fussing was one of her few emotional comforts in a lonely life.

'Here – I've brought you a nice cup of tea.' Presvel put down the lamp on a free corner of the cluttered desk and, with his free hand, swept a pile of documents aside to clear a space in front of her. Seriema suppressed a smile. She knew the flamboyant gesture was not as extravagant as it seemed. Her assistant knew better, by now, than to mess up her work. When she eventually returned to the papers and collected them together, not a single document would be misplaced.

'Drink it while it's still hot now – as if anything ever *stayed* hot for more than two minutes in this great draughty barn of a house.' Presvel set the cup down in the newly cleared space with a flourish. 'I'll wager you have a great-grandmother of a headache by now – and it serves you right, working straight through the day like that. I've told you and *told* you about taking time to rest every now and again . . .' As he was speaking, Presvel moved around the room, lighting the oil lamps and the candles in their sconces, scolding all the while. Seriema let the endless stream of words flow over her as always, enjoying the way they dispelled the arid silence of her workroom in much the same way as the shimmering golden candle flames dissolved the shadowy gloom.

Her assistant left after a short while, as Marutha, the housekeeper, came in to mend the sinking fire. A look from Presvel as he left the room silenced the bent old woman just as she was opening her mouth to begin to scold Seriema. 'It's all right, Marutha,' he said, 'you don't have to bother. The Lady and I have already covered in depth the subjects of overwork and the ruination of eyes.'

Marutha glared at his departing back, and knelt by the

hearth, muttering darkly about *some* people being too clever by half. Seriema sipped gratefully at the hot tea – and of course it *was* hot, despite Presvel's lugubrious mutterings – and chose to ignore the old woman. She stretched luxuriously, clasping her hands behind her head and pulling her elbows back to banish the taut ache across her shoulders and neck. Her eyes burned from scanning row upon row of tiny figures in the dim half-light, and she admitted to herself that Presvel had been right. Already her sight was blurred at a distance. She was going to wreck her eyes completely if she kept this up. She ought to relax and rest for a while – try to forget her worries . . .

Seriema's moment of quiet reflection couldn't last, of course. The old housekeeper had been bursting to speak since first she'd entered the room. After a few moments she looked up from the fire that she was mending and addressed the merchant in the annoyingly over-familiar tones of an old servant who had known her from the day she was born. 'You shouldn't let this nasty weather upset you so. It won't do you any good.'

'How very perceptive of you,' Seriema retorted in acid tones. 'And have you any *practical* suggestions as to how I might achieve this?' After her parents' death, the lonely young woman had accepted the housekeeper's cosseting in much the same vein as Presvel's solicitude. Once she'd become head of the Mercantile Assembly, however, and had taken on her new responsibilities, Marutha's continued lack of respect had begun to grate on her.

The old woman, thick-bodied and grey-haired, levered herself up stiffly from the fireside. 'There's no need to be like that,' she said huffily. 'It's not *my* fault if you've fretted yourself into a state.'

'Well, you're certainly making sure I stay in one!' Seriema snapped. 'Take yourself away, Marutha, for goodness' sake, and find something useful to do.'

'Sorry, I'm *sure*, my *Lady* Seriema!' As the old woman shuffled out, still muttering, an injured expression on her face, Seriema moved to the comfortable chair by the fireside and dropped her face into her hands, giving herself up to her worries once more. It didn't matter how carefully or frequently she perused the inventories and reports – the final conclusion was always the same. Trade was already on its knees – and if some miracle didn't occur soon to stop this foul rain, the entire Callisioran trade network, built and nurtured through centuries, would collapse completely. 'And when goods stop crossing the realm, armies will start,' she muttered to herself. A cold finger of fear trailed down her spine. She was looking not only at personal ruin, but at the disintegration of Callisiora.

Marutha's knock on the workroom door, so brusque as to be little more than a token, proved that the old woman was going to nurture her current sulking fit for hours, if not for the next few days. 'There's someone to see you, my *Lady*. She won't say who she is, and she's all wrapped up in a big black cloak so's I can't see her face. She doesn't talk like no beggar, though, and she says it's a matter of life and death. Will you see her, or shall I have Presvel throw her out? If you ask *me*, I wouldn't . . .'

'Nobody asked you, dammit!' To her horror, Seriema found herself screeching like a fishwife. Really, she thought, it's high time Marutha was retired. Then I could engage a housekeeper with a more respectful attitude. She took a deep breath and collected herself to address the business in hand. A caller at this late hour had not come on ordinary business.

Seriema's curiosity kindled. 'I'll see the visitor, Marutha. Where did you put her? In the drawing room? Very well, but fetch Presvel, and have him wait outside the door, within call.' Ignoring the housekeeper's resentful glare, she buttoned the collar of her brown velvet dress, which she had loosened as she worked, and headed briskly for the stairs.

Somehow Seriema had expected the mysterious stranger to be taller. She paused in the doorway of the drawing room, one hand gripping the edge of the doorframe, suddenly finding herself made hesitant by surprise at the sight of the diminutive figure swathed in, of all things, a soldier's cloak several sizes too big.

'Shut the damned door, will you?' The voice was low and raw, but definitely female and oddly familiar. Startled into obedience, Seriema stepped all the way into the room and let the heavy door swing shut behind her. The click of the latch dropping into place sounded portentous, as though the sharp sound had sheared the straight, even thread of her life, and she was falling with all her plans in tangles around her, towards some unknown future.

'Well, don't just stand there like a ninny. Help me out of this blasted thing,' the woman said sharply. 'Come on, Seriema, you idiot – give me a little assistance here, for Myrial's sake. My hands are full, and I haven't got all night.'

All at once, Seriema recognised the voice. 'Gilarra? Is that you? What in the name of wonder are you playing at?' She darted forward and released the simple brass clasp of the cloak – and gasped as it fell away to reveal the tousled, crimson-faced figure of the Holy Suffragan, bearing a sleeping child in her arms.

'She won't wake,' Gilarra said softly. 'I had to drug the poor little thing within an inch of her life.' She laid the dark-haired little girl down on a tapestry-covered couch and straightened her back with an exaggerated sigh of relief. 'Why is it that children are always considerably heavier than they look?'

While Seriema looked on, dumbfounded, the Suffragan stretched her arms above her head then swung them back and forth and rubbed them hard to get the circulation going again. Throughout the entire performance the child never stirred – not even at the sound of a sharp rap on the drawing-room door.

'I've brought some nice, hot tea for you and your visitor, my Lady,' Marutha sang out sweetly.

Gilarra gasped, her eyes widening in panic. 'Don't let her in! I mustn't be recognised!'

Wondering what in the name of perdition was going on, Seriema responded with equal sweetness. 'Leave the tray outside, Marutha. I'll fetch it myself in a minute.'

'Well! There has to be a first time for everything, I suppose.' The housekeeper's disgruntled muttering came clearly through the door, followed by the clatter of porcelain as the tray was set down, none too gently by the sound of it, on the little table in the hall. There was a long moment of silence.

'That will be *all*, Marutha,' Seriema said firmly.

'Bah!' came the mutter, followed by the sound of footsteps stamping away.

'I see that being Head of the Mercantile Assembly and the Miners Consortium isn't all it's made out to be.' Gilarra's shoulders relaxed as she left the child and returned to the fire, stretching her hands out over the flames and chafing her chilled fingers. 'Why don't you fetch in the tea, my dear? I'm absolutely perished.'

'As you wish.' Seriema, thoroughly irritated now by Gilarra's presumption, kept a firm rein on her temper, though she had always detested mysteries. The ability to keep at least a semblance of external calm had given her a great advantage over the years in dealing with difficult situations and shrewd opponents. Besides, her curiosity was already getting the better of her annoyance with Gilarra's dramatics and evasions. Why, after all these years, had Gilarra suddenly turned up on her doorstep? They had been friends for a time at school in the Precincts. For some reason that Seriema could never fathom, the older girl had taken it upon herself to champion the shy, lonely little merchant's daughter. Six years' age difference was a good deal, however, and as Gilarra, the Suffragan-elect, had grown into the benefits and responsibilities of her position, she had drifted away from her younger companion, leaving Seriema resentful and bereft, convinced that Zavahl had somehow been instrumental in taking her friend away.

As Seriema opened the door to pick up the tray she caught the eye of Presvel, who was loitering near the bottom of the staircase. She firmly gestured him away. After a long, reluctant pause he went but, judging by his apprehensive expression, she deduced that Marutha had instructed him to overhear all he could while he waited.

Seriema poured tea for herself and Gilarra, and sat down opposite the Suffragan. 'Now,' she said firmly, 'suppose you start explaining.'

Gilarra looked from Seriema to the sleeping child and back again. 'I've come to do you a favour.' Taking advantage of Seriema's astonishment, she pressed on quickly. 'You've got no time for men, Seriema – not only literally, because you work all the hours that Myrial sends, but also in a figurative sense, because you don't want some bungling lifemate interfering in your business concerns. But you haven't considered the future, my dear – an unusual oversight in one so clever.'

She leaned forward across the hearthstones and touched the other woman's arm. Seriema jumped a little and flinched away from the contact. She was unused to being touched by others, and it made her uncomfortable.

Gilarra withdrew her hand without comment, and continued as if nothing had happened. 'What happens when you die, Seriema? Who will benefit from all the years of dedication, all the self-denial and the grinding hard work? Where will it all go?'

The Suffragan's words came as a profound shock to Seriema. She was stunned by the enormity of such an oversight. Obsessed as she had been with bringing her empire through the difficult years following her father's death, she had not given a single thought to the future. Angry and dismayed, she turned on the Suffragan in a flash of outrage. 'And what is that to *you*? Since when have you ever cared about me? Oh, we were friends once, back in our schooldays, but since you grew old enough to take up your official duties with *him*, you haven't been near me once! You wouldn't be here now, what's more, if there wasn't some advantage in it for you!'

'Not for me – for her.' Gilarra indicated the little girl. 'And for you, I hope. I've brought you your heir, Seriema.'

For a moment Seriema was bereft of words and drowning in a welter of emotions that coursed through her. She felt curiosity about the child's antecedents and Gilarra's motives, mixed with anger at the other woman's interference in her life. There was also a flash of pity for the unkempt little waif, with her pale, pinched face and her thumb locked firmly in her mouth even as she slumbered. Most of all, however, Seriema was scared – terrified, in fact. For the first time in her life, she felt truly inadequate to the situation.

What do I do to take care of her? Where would I start? What if she falls sick – what if she already is? She certainly looks ghastly! Where are her real family? And what can I possibly say to a child that has just been dumped on me, like some discarded garment that has been passed on?

'No.' The word was out of her mouth before she was conscious of making a rational decision. 'I'm sorry, Gilarra – it's out of the question.'

'That's a pity,' Gilarra said softly. 'She's an orphan, you see. Quite suddenly, in the space of a single day, both her parents have been killed. On the Hierarch's orders.'

'Well, I can't help that ... *What?* But why, in Myrial's name?'

'Seriema, listen – just for a moment. Please. I brought the child to you because you're my best hope of giving her the care and protection she needs. I can't tell you everything ...' she broke off, looking obliquely at the merchant.

Damn her! How well she knows me, Seriema thought, her curiosity kindling. 'Go on,' she said, with a sigh of resignation.

'Her parents had information that Zavahl didn't want to become public. Her father – well, let's just say he met with a tragic accident. Her mother ...' Gilarra hesitated. 'Seriema, I'm putting a tremendous amount of trust in your discretion and in the loyalty of an old and long-neglected friendship by telling you this. The child's mother was killed by the Godswords.'

'*What?*'

'As I said, it was all on the Hierarch's orders,' Gilarra said hurriedly. She looked Seriema squarely in the eye. 'I think we are both well aware that Zavahl won't have the opportunity to do such a thing again. But it wouldn't foster confidence in a new Hierarch if such an atrocity should become public

knowledge at this time. I also expect that Lord Blade will want
to expunge any witnesses to the Godsword involvement in this
business – and that's where the problem lies. You see, Seriema,
the little one saw her mother die.'

Seriema felt the blood drain from her face. She looked at
the child with horror and new pity.

'There are those in the Citadel,' Gilarra continued in a low,
hoarse voice, 'who wanted to be rid of the only witness, but
a very courageous young soldier saved her. Between us we
managed to cover up her escape. Now she needs a haven,
where she can grow up in comfort and in safety, with her
true identity a deadly secret.'

A cold, bleak anger had settled over Seriema. 'Whose child
is she?'

'You know I can't tell you that. For your own safety as
much as hers.'

'Never mind my blasted safety!' Suddenly, Seriema was
on her feet. 'How dare you come strolling in here and drop
your damned problems at my feet, like a cat dragging home
some chewed-up bird! You don't give a damn about the
upheaval and turmoil and trouble you'll be unleashing into
my life by saddling me with some verminous, disease-ridden
slum-brat—'

'She's the trader Tormon's child.'

For a handful of heartbeats Seriema stood staring, robbed
of breath and thought and motion. Then she sat down slowly,
gripping the chair arm tightly with one hand while the other
was held up in repudiation, as though she could somehow
physically hold off the Suffragan's words.

'Annas is the daughter of the traders, Tormon and Kanella.'
Gilarra dropped the words deliberately, like stones on to the
deceptively still surface of Seriema's silence.

The merchant closed her eyes, unable to come to terms with the fact that the Hierarch should dare such a dreadful deed with one of her own. All right – it was true that itinerant, independent renegades like Tormon and his lifemate were outside the jurisdiction and the protection of the Mercantile Assembly. It was also true that the quiet, dark man with his ridiculous, multi-coloured wagon had been a thorn in Seriema's side for years, despite – or because of – the fact he was by far and away the most decent, hard-working, and successful of the independents. But she had truly liked the man. Whenever their paths had crossed he had treated her as a colleague, no more, no less. He had never tried to patronise or belittle her because she was a woman in a man's shoes, and, more importantly, he had never been aggressive, hostile or resentful towards her because she held such a position of power. He treated her in exactly the same way as he approached the other merchants: with courtesy, respect – and stiff but honest competition. Until this moment, Seriema had never realised just how much she had come to like him. She took a deep breath. 'Very well. I'll take the child. What did you say her name was?'

Kaz roused at dusk. To his surprise, his drowsy, half-waking thoughts encountered another mind. 'Senior Loremaster Thirishri? Is that really you? I don't believe it!'

It is I. How good it is to hear you, Kazairl. When we saw the landslide, we were greatly concerned. Are you well? Where are you? And Veldan – how does she fare? I sense from your thoughts that she is still alive.

'She'll recover. You know how fragile humans are. She took a lot of battering in the slide, and a real nasty bang on the head. I was worried at first, but now I'm sure she'll be all right, given a little time – and a chance to rest, Thirishri. We've found shelter with a former warrior, in the first house down the trail. She's a real tough old battleaxe – she and Veldan are the best of friends already. Which brings me to ask what *you* are doing here. Where are you now? You must be close if you've seen the slide. And you said "we". Who else is with you? Not Cergorn, surely?'

We are at the site of the landslide. We came in answer to Veldan's cry for help, but it seems we have come too late. With the Seer of the Dragonfolk dead, there is little to be done but escort you safely home – if the snow will permit. We will be heading down to you soon. As for my partner on this mission . . . Kaz detected the faintest touch of hesitation in the wind-sprite's mental voice. *I'm afraid that my companion is Elion.*

'*What?* That craven streak of misery? That ungrateful, whining fool?' Kaz snarled. 'How *dare* you? Tchaaa! If you bring that bastard offspring of a slime-viper anywhere near my partner I'll chew his limbs off and stuff them down his throat! I'll tear him into bloody, quivering shreds . . .'

*You will *not!** Even at this distance, Thirishri's blast of reprimand was enough to flatten the firedrake to the hard-packed earthen floor of the barn. *You are a member of the Shadowleague, Kazairl. You will put aside your personal grudge in the cause of duty, as you have been taught.*

'Oh, will I indeed?' Kazairl said, with an ominous rumble. 'Well, you just listen to me, Senior Loremaster Thirishri, because I want you to be absolutely clear about this. If that festering pile of rat's dung hurts my Veldan in any way, just once more, he's dragonbait. It would be worth being thrown out of the Shadowleague just to grind his miserable bones to powder in my jaws. One chance, Thirishri. That's all the lizard-livered patch of pond-scum gets. I suggest you warn him. He'll be very unhappy – very briefly – if he makes a mistake.'

'Boss! Boss!' Kaz's roar, followed by a crash and the sound of splintering wood, woke Veldan from an uneasy sleep filled with gruesome dreams. She opened her eyes to see the firedrake trying to squeeze his head into the aperture of the window. Bits of broken shutters, now reduced to kindling, adorned his horns and were scattered on her quilt and the floor beside her bed. It appeared to be growing dark outside. A bitterly cold wind was blowing into the room, and the little bit of sky that she could glimpse between the firedrake's head and the window frame was full of whirling snow.

'All right,' she grumbled sleepily. 'Keep your tail on. What's wrong?' She struggled to sit up, to wake up properly, to prepare herself for some unknown new emergency. Damn this knock on the head! Still, she seemed stronger than she'd felt the last time she'd awakened. 'What's wrong?' she repeated, aware that Kaz had fallen silent out of concern for her. She could hear his tail smacking into the mud outside as it twitched back and forth in agitation like the tail of an angry cat. It always betrayed his state of mind.

'Don't worry, Boss – I've warned him. He won't give you any trouble – not if he prefers to keep his guts inside his body . . .' Kaz's telepathic voice ended in a vocal sound: a long, chilling, drawn-out rumble of a snarl.

Oh no! There was only one person, to Veldan's knowledge, who could elicit that kind of reaction from the firedrake. The Loremaster's heart sank like a stone. 'Elion? He's coming here?' Her stomach clenched like a small, cold fist. Damn, damn, damn! All right – so they had made a complete muck-up of their mission – but Cergorn couldn't have come up with a worse punishment than to send Elion to witness the extent of her failure.

'What in the name of all creation . . . ?' said a voice from the doorway. Veldan turned quickly, ignoring a warning throb from her tender skull, to see Toulac standing there with a scowl on her weatherbeaten face. 'You!' she snapped at the firedrake. 'What are you doing, breaking up my house? Get out of there, you stupid lummox, before I make myself a new shutter out of your worthless hide! Go on! Get out of it!'

Protective as always towards her partner, Veldan felt a jolt of anger to see him so abused. She wanted to leap to his defence – except that she was truly grateful to this tough old warrior who had taken them in without question or hesitation. 'I'm sorry about your shutters, Toulac,' she said quickly, deflecting the seething woman's attention to herself. 'Kaz isn't designed for the average human house, and he got himself a little overexcited . . .'

'Overexcited?' Kaz's indignant bellow blasted into her mind. '*Overexcited?* Is that what you call it? When I found out you were still alive, I got *overexcited*.' The word was laden with sarcasm. 'Now that miserable string of slime is coming, I'm bloody, raging *mad*, is what I am!'

'It's all right,' Veldan said quickly to Toulac. The warrior, no fool, had seen the crimson fire of rage kindle in Kaz's eyes, and had prudently stepped back into the doorway, out of his reach. 'Someone is coming,' the Loremaster tried to explain. 'Another of my people. He's on his way down from the pass right now. There's . . . Well, there's a lot of history between us, and a lot of bad blood. Kaz gets a bit dangerous when Elion is around. It's because he's so protective of me.'

Toulac's face relaxed a little. 'Bad blood, eh? That I can

appreciate. It happens to warriors more often than you'd think. We spend most of our time in life-and-death situations, and that kind of danger doesn't increase our tolerance for our comrades one jot. There's too much at stake. Now, don't you worry, girl. As far as I'm concerned you and this lumbering critter are my friends, shutters or no shutters, and if this Elion starts any trouble, he'll be out on his backside. And as for you . . .' She turned to the firedrake, eyes twinkling. 'If *you* start anything, you'll have me to reckon with, understand? I prefer my house in one piece, thank you.'

'Just who does the stupid human think she is?' Kaz said in a low, irritated rumble. 'Doesn't she know what she's dealing with? Why, I could roast her where she stands, without moving a step!'

'I know, I know,' Veldan soothed. 'But it *is* her house you're breaking up, Kaz, and she has been very good to us. Let her dream, my dear. Don't forget, she's never met a firedrake before. She doesn't know what you can do.'

'You like her, don't you?' Kaz said sharply.

'Very much. Why?'

'So do I.' The firedrake smirked at her. He withdrew his head from the window and vanished, leaving the former warrior and a very astonished Loremaster alone.

There was a shrewd glint in Toulac's eye. 'I take it you're not going to tell me what happened between you and this Elion?'

Veldan sighed. 'There wouldn't be time and, to be honest, the details are still too painful to repeat. To cut it short, Elion hates me because his partner was killed and I stopped him from going to help her. It was hopeless, and *he* would have been killed too. Then he almost got *me* killed – which is why Kaz hates him so bitterly – and I hate him because he was responsible for me getting this.' Suddenly self-conscious, she put a hand up to the scar on her face, realising, to her utter amazement, that while in Toulac's company she had forgotten the disfigurement for the first time since she had been injured. What was more, the veteran warrior, far from showing curiosity, pity or disgust, had not reacted to the scar's existence by so much as an eyeblink.

Elion, however, was quite another matter. The mask! Where was the mask?

'Thanks for the loan of the shirt, Toulac.' Veldan strove to keep the betraying urgency out of her voice. 'Will my own clothes be dry yet, do you think?'

'Of course. I've done a few repairs for you, too. Your gear took a fair old battering in the slide.' Toulac smiled, but her eyes were oddly wary. 'I never thought I would see the day when I'd be patching fighting gear again.' She went out, and returned shortly carrying a wooden bowl in her hands, and Veldan's clothes draped over one arm. 'Here,' she said. 'Have some soup. It's about time you ate something.'

Veldan was glad to comply. She was ravenously hungry. As it turned out, this was just as well, for Toulac's cooking was anything but a treat. The warrior, who'd been watching Veldan's face like a hawk as she ate, suddenly burst out laughing. 'My, aren't you polite? Don't worry – I know my limitations. I'm afraid that in this house, hot and nourishing is about as good as it gets.'

'That's fine by me,' the Loremaster said as she finished the soup. 'I hadn't realised that I was so hungry.' Laying the bowl aside, she picked up her clothes from the bed and began to hunt through the pockets – casually at first, then with an increasing urgency bordering on sheer panic. The mask! Where had it gone? Had she lost it in the landslide?

'You won't find it,' Toulac said calmly.

Veldan whirled to face her, barely noticing the throbbing of her head. 'Where is it? What have you done with it?'

'I threw it in the fire.'

For an instant, Veldan's thoughts were blotted out by a mixture of emotions: fury, horror and despair. She came back to herself with the whoop of Kaz's laughter. 'Ohohoho! Nice *move*, Toulac! I could forgive the old battleaxe anything after that!' Then, sensing his partner's great distress, the firedrake lowered his voice. 'It'll be all right, sweetie – truly it will. Don't be angry with Toulac – she did the right thing. You had come to depend on that mask. If you'd kept it on much longer, you would have condemned yourself to wearing it for the rest of your life. It may be bad at first, Boss, but I'll always be there to help you through. That's one thing you *can* depend on.'

As the firedrake finished speaking, the grizzled warrior sat down on the bed beside Veldan, and put an arm around her shoulders. 'I don't apologise,' Toulac said firmly. 'We're going to cure you of this foolishness if it's the last thing I do. You can be as angry as you want with me, but it won't bring your mask back, so why waste the energy? It would be a crime to hide that lovely face any longer.'

'Lovely?' Veldan spat, recoiling from the other woman. '*Lovely?* How dare you mock me, you old bitch? I'm not lovely – I'm hideous!'

Toulac's eyes hardened. 'Were you not so deeply upset, that little tantrum would have earned you a good walloping, my girl. Now shut up, and listen to me.'

Much to her surprise, Veldan found that she'd shut her mouth and was listening, all attention. Toulac must have been a real terror in her time, she thought.

'I won't lie to you,' the veteran said firmly. 'That scar is not a pretty sight, but –' she held up an admonishing finger as Veldan opened her mouth to speak '– it's not near as bad as you think, and it'll be better still when it silvers out. No one but a complete imbecile would turn away from *you* in revulsion – and I can't see you scaring people into fits!'

'I don't want them to pity me,' Veldan mumbled.

'What? Pity *you?*' Toulac burst out laughing. 'My dear child, just take a look at yourself. You've a brain in your head, you're a warrior, and you have the air of a woman who knows how to take care of herself. You can talk with your mind, and you have that fearsome, magnificent creature out there to be your friend. And whatever you may think, your face is lovely. Granted, it may not be as flawless as it once was but, believe me, the plain old rest of us would gladly trade a scar like that to be as beautiful as you. Really and truly. So you see, Veldan, folk will *sympathise* with your injury – and that's fair enough – but no one is going to pity you longer than two minutes together. They'll be too busy envying you instead. Trust me.'

Veldan looked at her, and swallowed hard. 'All right,' she said softly. 'I'll try to do without the mask – in truth, I have no choice. I'll do it, Toulac – you wretched, interfering busybody. I'll manage somehow.'

Toulac grinned and clapped her on the shoulder. 'You'll manage magnificently.' Climbing stiffly to her feet, she headed for the door. 'It's time you were getting dressed, girlie. We're expecting company, remember?'

fifteen

Unexpected Company

Without Scall, the smithy was surprisingly lonely. It was astonishing, Agella realised, how much she had become accustomed, over the last few months, to the company of such a hapless boy. Exasperating as he could be, he was her sister's son – the nearest thing to a child of her own that she would ever have – and she had been fond of him. The smith sat down beside the dying embers of the forge and put her head into her hands. 'Blessed Myrial,' she sighed. 'I hope I've done the right thing.'

Now she had time for reflection, Agella found it little short of incredible that she had acted so impulsively and with such little thought for the consequences. Yet she'd had her reasons, she reminded herself. She had been losing sleep over Scall's future for some time, for it was all too clear that she would never make a smith of him. Now she came to think back, of course, he'd always had a patient, calming way with the animals that came into the smithy, but when the incident with the killer stallion had shown her that he possessed such an incredible influence over the beasts it had seemed just too good to be true. His way with the horse had reminded her at once of her old friend Toulac.

Agella had been worried about Toulac for some time – she

was sure the older woman wasn't taking proper care of herself, living all alone up on the mountain – but given the veteran's independent spirit, there had seemed to be no way she could help. When Scall had tamed the killer, it seemed to the smith that Myrial had dropped the solution to both of her problems right into her lap.

Toulac's situation had not been her only influence, however. There was something about the Sacred Precincts these days – an uneasy feeling, an unplaceable tension in the air, like the heavy atmosphere before a thunderstorm. It was no secret among those who dwelt in this cloistered place that the Hierarch was beginning to break down under the pressures of his failure to intercede with Myrial and stop the ceaseless rain. And not only had Zavahl lost touch with the god, it seemed, but he was also out of sympathy with the mood of the ordinary people. If the opinions of the Lower Town folk were any indication, never had a Hierarch been so unpopular. Lord Blade was up to something, too. Agella didn't trust that one as far as she could throw him. She had a bad feeling that events were coming to a climax – and tomorrow was the Eve of the Dead. 'That's when the trouble will start – you mark my words,' she muttered to herself. That being the case, when the unexpected opportunity had arrived to get Scall out of the Precincts, she'd seized it with both hands.

Nevertheless, I hope he'll be all right, she thought. Maybe I should have gone with him. What was I thinking of, to let him go up there with those enormous beasts? One of them actually *killed* a man, for Myrial's sake! A big, strong, adult, an experienced horseman besides. And I sent the poor lad off with only that whoreson Barsil, of all people, to depend on. I can't see *him* being much use in a crisis! If only I had some way of knowing whether Scall had managed to get there safely!

Outside the window dusk was falling, and that wasn't all. A fine sprinkling of snow was spinning down, getting thicker by the moment.

When the knock came at the smithy door, Agella leaped up as though her wooden stool had turned into holly boughs. 'Who is it? What's wrong?' She flung the door open to see one of the Godsword soldiers who'd been doing sentry duty in the tunnel when she had seen her apprentice off. 'Is it Scall?' she demanded. 'Has something happened to him?'

The guard looked at her as though she had grown an extra head. 'I dunno nothing about no Scall, Mistress,' he said with a shrug. 'I've a message for you from the tunnel gate. Your sister is trying to get in to see you – or some woman who *claims* to be your sister, at any rate. She says she's in terrible trouble, and she needs your help.'

Viora? In what kind of trouble? And how was Agella going to break the news to her sister that she'd sent her son away out of the city to some unknown fate? The smith struck her own forehead with the heel of her hand. 'Pestilence, plague and perdition! This is all I bloody need!'

The walk through the tunnel seemed longer than usual. The further Agella went, the more worried about her sister she became. What could have befallen Viora and her family? Had they been attacked or robbed? Was there sickness in the house? Goat Yard was not in the best of neighbourhoods, and the poorer parts of the city were far from safe in these hard days. It was slap-bang in the middle of the worst plague area and, judging by what she had heard from Scall after his occasional visits home, few households in the neighbourhood had been lucky enough to escape the blacklung fever altogether. Theft and looting were commonplace – though in truth, few folk in the Lower Town had anything worth stealing now. Or had

Viora somehow fallen out with Ivar, and been thrown out of his home? Though the young slaughterman worshipped his spouse, always treating her as though she were a delicate and precious treasure, his temper among other folk could be unpredictable and violent. Surely, though, he would not distress Felyss by driving her parents away? It made no sense.

The smith was secretly glad to see that Ivar was not among the little group clustered at the town end of the tunnel. Her relief, however, changed to dismay then horror when she came close enough to witness their distress. The roughly tied bundles on the ground beside them showed their fugitive status quite clearly – but worse than that, Ulias was stooped and defeated, Viora was weeping and dishevelled, and as for Felyss, with her face all swollen and purple with bruises, her clothing filthy, bloodstained and torn . . .

For an instant, Agella was back in her own childhood, when the enemy had ransacked her father's keep. They had put the warriors and male children to the sword right away, but they had raped the women, young and old alike, in an orgy of violence, before slitting their throats . . . When she saw the crazed, empty look in Felyss's eyes, she began to wonder if the invaders of those days had not been merciful, in the end, by destroying their victims . . . Then she pulled herself together and told herself not to be stupid. Felyss was a sensible girl. With help from her family, she would come through this.

At the sight of Agella, Viora burst into a fresh flood of tears. 'Our home,' she sobbed. 'Gone. Everything gone. The soldiers . . .' She glanced up nervously at the tunnel sentries, and said no more.

The smith ran forward to embrace her sister. 'Viora! My dear, come with me. Wait – don't try to talk now. Let me get you home first, then you can tell me what happened.' But when she came to lead the refugees back through the tunnel the guards stopped her short. 'Come now, Mistress Agella. You know we can't let unauthorised folk into the Precincts. Unless there's a service in the Temple, only folk who live here, their spouses and immediate families, and people with legitimate business are permitted to go inside.'

Viora whimpered. Agella took a deep breath. There was no point in losing her temper with the soldier. He was only doing his duty, and he was absolutely right. Nevertheless, she noticed that he and his companion were looking very uncomfortable at having to deny her. Thank Myrial, she thought, that they all think it's bad luck to cross a smith. She smiled at them both. They seemed so young, really, for the responsibilities of their position. 'You're right, of course,' she said. 'I know those are the rules, and I should know better. But just think about it for a moment. I have no spouse or children. These poor, distressed folk are the only immediate family I'm ever likely to have, and they would take up no more room than a spouse and children. Should I be condemned to always live alone? It seems to me that I'm being penalised in relation to, say, the Suffragan Gilarra, just because I'm unwed. Besides, lads, you can see the state they're in. What would you do if that was *your* mother weeping at the gate with all her worldly goods in a tattered bundle? What would you do if this poor lass was your sweetheart?'

She wasn't much good at producing a winning smile to order, but Agella did her best. 'Please, lads. It won't be for long, I promise. Just a day or two, until I sort out some alternative. And you won't find me ungrateful.' She tilted her head and winked at them. 'How would you like to own better swords than Lord Blade himself? I promise, you'll go right to the top of my list, and I'll do you such a job of work as you've never seen before. Go on – what do you say?'

The two guards looked at each other for a long moment, then both of them started to grin. 'Well, *I* never saw nobody,' said the one who had first accosted her. 'Did *you* see anybody, Armod?'

The other lad shook his head. 'Only folk on legitimate business, Brennek.' His grin was growing wider by the minute. With his eyes fixed firmly on a point somewhere above her head, he gestured for Agella to pass through with her family.

'Thanks, boys,' the smith said. 'I owe you – and you can rely on me to pay you back. You'll have your swords as soon as I can make them.'

The artisans' cottages in the Sacred Precincts were arranged to face each other in regular groups of three, so that each neat little house had two triangles of communal garden, one at the front and one at the rear. Paved paths ran through the spaces between each home and the next, resulting in a network of routes rather than the simpler grid pattern of the streets in the Lower Town. It took experience and practice to learn the positions of everybody's house and the easiest route to get there. Strangers often found themselves hopelessly confused, but few strangers were ever permitted within the Precincts.

The route to the smith's home was even more baffling in the dark. Agella could almost feel the confusion emanating from Viora and her lifemate as she led them through the network of streets. Felyss stumbled along, lost in her own private torment, quite unaware, the smith was certain, of where she was or why. Agella frowned. Shutting herself off from her immediate surroundings was a natural reaction, on the girl's part, to what she had been through. Her deep withdrawal was a form of shock, part of the natural defences of her body and mind against the outrages they had suffered. As long as the poor lass doesn't stay like that for *too* long, Agella thought with a frown. Eventually such a retreat from the outside world could prove dangerous.

Felyss, though clearly at the end of her endurance, was dragging a heavy canvas bag filled with tools of some kind. Agella could hear them clanking. Whenever she tried to take the burden from the girl, Felyss clenched her fingers round the handles in a grip of steel, and began to whimper in distress.

'Don't try to take it away from her,' Viora whispered with a warning shake of her head. 'They're Ivar's slaughtering tools. I don't know how she finds the strength to carry them, but she won't be parted from them – don't think I haven't tried.'

Agella frowned. 'But where is Ivar?'

Viora compressed her lips, her face set like stone.

'*Dead?*' Agella gasped.

Viora shook her head. 'Not now,' she whispered urgently, with a sidelong glance at her daughter. So the smith had to be content to wait until she had brought them safely back to her cottage and ushered them inside.

The fire was laid already, and the house was spotless, though this was not Agella's doing, for she worked much too hard at the smithy all day and sometimes half the night too to be bothered with house-cleaning. Instead, using the complex system of barter, bargaining, and traded favours by which life was conducted among the Precinct's artisans, she hired the kennelman's youngest daughter, Cetulia, a likely lass of sixteen, to come in daily, clean the place and leave the fire ready for lighting when the smith returned home, tired and hungry, at the end of a long and busy day.

Agella's cottage was one of the smaller dwellings, compact and simple, but cosy nonetheless. A small porch led into the main room – kitchen and living area together – which boasted a cooking range with a generous fireplace. A high-backed wooden bench, padded with bright cushions, stood in front of the fire, and a comfortable chair was set at one side of the hearth, convenient for coal-bin and wood-box. A lamp hung on a hook from the central beam of the low ceiling, and rag rugs brightened the polished wooden floor. The walls boasted several cupboards and a number of shelves, and against the wall opposite to the fireplace was a sturdy table with wooden chairs. Doors led off to the scullery, Agella's bedrooms and the tiny, cramped spare room.

The smith lit the lamp. It took no time at all to get a good fire going. Cetulia, good girl that she was, had made sure that the copper at the side of the hearth was filled, so there would soon be plenty of hot water. In this damp, raw weather, Agella kept an ongoing pot of soup at the side of the hearth, its ingredients replenished so many times that the original stock was a far distant memory. She swung the cauldron, on its iron hook, over the flames, and balanced the kettle at the side of the coals.

Viora had settled her daughter on the cushioned wooden bench in front of the fire. Felyss, though, would not be persuaded to lie down, but sat rigid and bolt upright, ready, Agella thought with pity, to spring up and run at the slightest sign of threat. The poor lass looked as though she might take flight any moment, except that one arm was still dragged down, anchored to the floor by Ivar's heavy bag of tools, which she would not relinquish.

Ulias, slumped in the smith's favourite chair by the fire, kept whispering in a harsh and broken voice, 'I couldn't stop them, I couldn't stop them, I couldn't stop them, I couldn't stop them . . .' over and over, until Agella's palm itched to slap him. With a slight frown, she glanced back at Felyss. She seemed to be lost in some private inner torment, oblivious of the world around her, but Agella doubted that. The girl needed her family to be strong now, and to *support* her, for Myrial's sake, not sink into the kind of spineless, self-centred self-pity in which her father was wallowing. Oh, she didn't begrudge him his distress. No blame to him for that – it was only natural – but he should be putting it aside just now, to avoid adding to his daughter's anguish. He would have plenty of time to indulge his own feelings later, in private, with his spouse.

Weak, the smith thought with stern disapproval. I always suspected that Ulias was weak. Then she caught herself back before her thoughts could stray any further down that road. He's a good man, she reminded herself, and he was an excellent craftsman in his time. He provided well for his family then. The knotbone has crippled more than his hands, I think, and I mustn't give Viora the slightest suspicion that I'm being critical. How she used to flare up at me – though I had the red hair for it, she was the quick-tempered one of the family – if I ever dared say a word against him. She'd accuse me of jealousy, because I had taken up such an unladylike profession that I'd never have a man of my own.

A small spark of amusement lit Agella's dark reflections as she thought of Fergist the stablemaster, a widower who shared her bed on a regular basis in a relationship that was informal but most satisfactory to them both. So much for what Viora knows, she thought smugly – and realised that her thoughts were wandering. I'm as bad as Ulias, she thought with a prickle of conscience. I'm so reluctant to face the horror that has befallen my sister's household that my thoughts will seize on any other subject. She was not the only one, she realised. Viora and her family, numb and shocked, seemed to have spent the last of their energies in reaching safety. Now they had finally reached a refuge, exhaustion had overtaken them, and the pain of the abuse they had suffered was truly beginning to set in. Damn, thought Agella. *And here I am standing like a bloody scarecrow, as paralysed and useless as the others. They came to me for help, and it's high time I took charge.* Yet what *was* the best way to deal with the aftermath of such a catastrophe? She shook her head. *I'm better with iron and flame,* she thought, *than this kind of thing.*

Quickly, the smith turned to her sister. 'Viora?' She put one hand on the sobbing woman's shoulder and, rummaging deep in her pocket with the other, pulled out the large piece of rag which had so many varied uses in the course of her working day, handkerchief included. She pushed the black-smeared rag into her sister's hand. 'Don't worry,' she said helplessly. 'It's only a bit of soot.' She was about to add that everything would be all right, but a glance at Felyss made her swallow her words. 'I'll take care of you,' she said instead. 'You're safe here.'

Viora blew her nose and breathed deeply, beginning to bring herself back under control, while Agella crossed the room and went into her little scullery. She found a flask of wine in the larder, thin, rather sour stuff, but wine at least, and the best that brewmaster Jivarn had been able to manage in this bad year. As she put the flask and four cups on the tray, she was reminded that one of Felyss's household was missing. *Where in perdition is Ivar?* she wondered. She'd received an impression from Viora that he wasn't dead, but if he's alive, she thought disapprovingly, then he damn well ought to be here with his lifemate. Shaking her head, she took the wine back into the other room and poured a generous helping for each of them. Taking one of the wooden chairs from beneath her table, she brought it close to the fireside and sat her sister down. 'Now,' she said gently, as she handed Viora her cup. 'Suppose you tell me what happened?'

Viora gulped the bitter wine. 'Seriema's bullies.' Her voice was thick with venom. 'They evicted us on her orders. All of Goat Yard. Burned the houses so we couldn't go back.' The cup shook in her hand as her voice rose shrill. 'I was keeping things calm! We would have got away safe, but then Ivar came back and tried to fight them . . .'

With horror, Agella listened to the ghastly tale and its aftermath, the hours spent trying to shake off the Godsword soldier sent by Galveron to follow them. The remainder of Viora's account was lost, however, for suddenly her daughter broke into a keening wail. '*No no no no no . . .*'

Agella, thoroughly alarmed, sprang up to slap her out of her hysteria, but one look at Felyss's battered face made her take pity. Instead she took the untouched cup out of the girl's hand, then grabbed her shoulders and shook her sharply. 'Stop that!' she snapped in a firm, authoritarian voice. Felyss was rocking back and forth, her movements growing ever more violent. The smith, at a loss, resorted to the bellow she'd developed over the years to be heard above the roaring of the forge. 'FELYSS! *STOP THAT NOW!*' There was a sudden silence, then the girl began to whimper quietly but, Agella noted with relief, the wailing and the frenzied rocking had ceased.

'You leave her alone!' Viora blazed, with a violence that shocked the smith. 'How dare you – after what she's been through!'

Agella was horrified by the savage expression on her sister's face. 'After what she's been through, she needs all the help we can give her.' She deliberately kept her voice calm, but inside, her own temper had been prodded. *She's got a nerve to speak to me like that, after I took them in! I had to put my own position*

*here in jeopardy by bribing the bloody guards, for Myrial's sake!
And this is all the gratitude I get.* Firmly she halted the stream of
angry thoughts. They wouldn't help. Ignoring her sister, she
knelt down in front of Felyss. 'After all you've been through,
my love, what you need is some of this nice wine.' She pushed
the cup into the girl's hand, then helped her guide it to her lips.
'Come on, now,' she coaxed. 'Just a little sip . . . Good girl! Now
another . . .'

Felyss grimaced as the sour wine stung her bruised, cut
mouth. Good, Agella thought. Another thing to help jolt her
out of her trance. 'Now,' she said, in the same brisk tone, 'you'll
feel better after a nice, hot bath.'

Leaving Felyss with her wine, she summoned Viora, who
would benefit from having something useful to do. 'I normally
bathe here in front of the range – when I don't use the Precincts
bathhouse – but I think she'll feel more secure in the privacy of
my bedroom. After that, we'll tuck her into my bed, and then
I'll slip across to the Hall of Healing. I've a friend there, one of
the physicians, and she—'

'Why must my daughter endure an outsider knowing of her
shame?' Viora interrupted.

'Viora, you *know* that's nonsense!' Agella was quickly running out of patience. Her sister had no right to react like this!
'Don't you *ever* talk of shame to poor Felyss! She has nothing
to be ashamed of! What happened was none of her fault. And
Evelinden isn't an outsider, she's a physician, and if ever Felyss
needed a healer it's now. I know you've been through a lot,
but do try to *think* – for all our sakes.'

Viora took breath for an angry reply, but the smith put out
a conciliatory hand to her. 'I know it must be very hard, but
try to stay strong for a little while longer, just until we get that
poor lass of yours safely settled. Then you can yell at me all

you want. Now, the tub's in the scullery. If you'll get it, while I light the bedroom fire—'

'You have a fireplace in your *bedroom*?' Viora demanded. Agella was shaken by her hostile tone. Then the smith remembered the cramped, damp, primitive housing in Goat Yard. 'We rarely get much sun here in the Precincts,' she explained wearily. 'We're hemmed in by those high cliffs. Except in the height of summer, this place is colder than a snowman's carrot. All the accommodation, from the Temple on down, was built with as many fireplaces, ranges, braziers, cressets and stoves as they could manage to cram in, and we're grateful for them all, believe me. Hurry up now, and fetch that bath. We must make poor Felyss comfortable.'

'All right, all right,' Viora said grudgingly. 'I'll fetch the cursed bath. I'll only be a moment—' Halfway out of the room she stopped dead, as if some new thought had struck her, and turned back to her sister. 'Where's Scall?'

Pox! Agella thought. I'll have to tell her, I know, but I was hoping to put it off a little longer. Her mind raced for a way to evade more trouble – for now, at least. 'He doesn't live with me, Viora,' she said evasively. 'Apprentices have their own house. You know that, or you should, if you've been listening to what he tells you on his visits home.'

Viora was undeterred. 'Well, wherever he is, I want to see him,' she said stubbornly. 'Once Felyss is settled, I want to see my son.'

The smithmaster sighed. There was no getting out of it now. Viora hated Toulac with a loathing out of all proportion because the older woman reminded her of her youth among the rough and violent Reivers; a time that Viora would much rather forget. Briefly Agella considered the notion of staving off the storm, claiming that the apprentices had a curfew, and that Scall would be asleep, but it would only make things worse tomorrow morning. No, might as well get it over with. She beckoned her sister into the other room, out of earshot of Felyss. 'I'm sorry, Viora, but you can't see Scall,' she said firmly. 'He isn't in the city – I sent him off up the mountain on an errand for me, to Mistress Toulac at the sawmill.'

Viora's jaw dropped. '*What?*' she shouted. 'You sent him to that coarse, uncouth, disreputable old baggage? All alone? Out of the city, where anything could happen to him?'

'No, no,' said Agella hastily. 'I sent one of the guards with him – an off-duty Godsword soldier. Now what could be safer than that?' A vision of the weaselly Barsil flitted into her mind and she shuddered. Thank Myrial that Viora had not seen the Godsword soldier in question.

'Then why couldn't you have sent the soldier alone?' Viora demanded. 'Why did poor Scall have to go? You know I don't want him mixing with mercenary ruffians like Toulac!' Her eyes flashed in temper. 'You sent my son off up the mountain on some fool's errand in this murderous weather – and then you have the effrontery to tell me how to take care of my daughter? If you ask me, it's a damn good thing you never did have any children of your own!' Viora stalked off to the scullery, and the smith could hear her banging and clattering, though all she had to do was lift the tub out from under the bench.

Agella clenched her fists tightly, and counted to ten – then realised it wouldn't help if she went right up to one hundred. With a sigh she returned to the bedroom, and set about lighting the fire. This night was going to be even more difficult than she'd thought. And where, in all of this dreadful business, was that wretched Ivar?

SIXTEEN

SHELTERS IN THE STORM

T oulac left her visitor to her dressing, and went to put the kettle on. As she came back into the kitchen, she was surprised to hear the sound of hooves on the road outside. Surely that couldn't possibly be Veldan's people already? If it was, they had been bloody quick about getting down off the mountain! 'Who the thundering blazes can that be?' she muttered, and went to the window to take a look.

'Myrial in a handcart! It's the Hierarch again!' Toulac gasped, peering out through the shifting snow at the peculiar cavalcade that was heading for her door. '*And* that miserable drab's bastard Lord Blade. And what in the festering pits of perdition are they doing *here?*'

Below Toulac's house the road ran round a jutting shoulder of the mountain, then straightened and sloped steeply, all the way downhill to the plateau in clear view of the city. It would be way too exposed to travel in a blizzard like this. The travellers would be forced to seek shelter . . .

'Bugger it!' Toulac muttered grimly. 'This is *all* I need!' The veteran dodged behind the curtain as the cavalcade drew to a ragged halt right outside her door. Toulac hesitated barely an instant – then grabbed her own sword and Veldan's weapons and dashed back to Veldan's room.

The woman was finishing her dressing at top speed. 'Armed men,' she said succinctly. 'Kaz told me. He's gone to hide at the back of the barn, so you should try to keep them out of there.'

Toulac nodded. 'It's the Hierarch and that misbegotten Blade. Wear my clothes – from the chest there. Get into bed – I'll tell them you're sick . . .' Her words were drowned by a thunderous knocking. 'Hide these.' She thrust the weapons at Veldan. 'Stay put.'

Veldan nodded. 'I'll warn Elion to stay away. I only hope he'll be all right in this snow.'

'Better than he'll be if Blade starts asking him awkward questions.' Glad that her guest had the sense to know when to obey orders, Toulac scurried back to the door. 'Coming, coming! Give these poor old bones a chance . . . Why, my Lords!' Dipping her head respectfully (she was damned if she'd bow to the slimy sons of bitches), she stepped back to allow them to enter. 'Come in, come in and welcome, my Lords,' she prattled, gesturing them towards the fire. 'It's an honour to shelter such grand folk, I'm sure.'

Mazal stood foursquare in his corner, his tail swishing irritably and his neck snaked out, ready to bite the first stranger who came near. Blade had stopped in his tracks in the doorway, and was staring at the warhorse, his mouth twisted with distaste. 'Old woman,' he said coldly, 'I am *not* accustomed to sharing my quarters with livestock.'

And Mazal isn't accustomed to sharing his quarters with such scum as you, you heartless, mean-spirited snake. Still, at least he hadn't recognised her from long ago, and that was the main thing. Toulac took a deep breath and unclenched her teeth. 'Sorry, my Lord, I'm sorry indeed,' she whined, 'but he's my livelihood, that horse, and my old barn just isn't safe. Why, the roof could fall in with the very next breath of wind . . .'

'So it isn't suitable to shelter my horses?'

'No, my Lord. Definitely not.' *It'll be unsuitable all right, if Veldan's friend gets peckish!*

Blade turned on her with a look of scorn that made Toulac's blood seethe in her veins. 'Well, where can I house my troop, you stupid woman?' he demanded. 'I have two dozen soldiers freezing out there!'

And as far as I'm concerned, you can stick them right up your . . . 'Well, my Lord, there's always the sawmill. It's warm and dry, and there's plenty of offcuts and chippings to burn, and a fireplace and all. Your men and their beasts'd all go in there easy.'

'Very well.' Blade went back outside, and Toulac heard him conversing in a low voice with the leader of his troop. After a moment, he returned. 'The Hierarch is with me, but he was taken ill up on the mountain, and will need some care. I will stay here in the house, with Lord Zavahl and two guards to tend him. The rest will shelter down in the sawmill. Now, you will kindly remove that stinking bag of bones outside, where it belongs. We may need it later, should we get snowed in here.'

Cold horror pierced Toulac like a sword blade through her guts. *Eat Mazal? I'll see you dead first, you son of a bitch. I'll tear out your beating heart with my own two hands . . .*

Blade was staring at her with that cold, mean-eyed look that Toulac remembered so well, and tapping his foot impatiently. 'Is there anyone else here with you?'

If you don't stop tapping that bloody foot at me, I'm going to cut it off – from the head down. 'Yes, if it please you, my Lord. My granddaughter is here, but she's very sick with the blacklung fever, my Lord. Don't worry, though. She's safe in her room, out of the way. You and the Hierarch *shouldn't* catch it from her. There's another room next to hers, at the back of the house, and then a lovely, cosy loft upstairs with a nice big bed.'

'I'll take the loft,' Blade said decidedly. 'The Hierarch can have the downstairs room.'

That's right, you snivelling coward – put some other poor sod next to the infection. 'As you wish, my Lord. I'll find you some clean bedding.'

'No, old woman, you will not. First of all, you will get that damned horse out of here!'

'As it pleases you, my Lord.' *And I hope your prick shrivels up and drops off.*

Toulac shrugged into her coat and led a disgruntled Mazal outside, praying that the warhorse wouldn't take a sly kick at Blade in passing, yet almost sorry when he did not. On the way out, she passed the Hierarch being half dragged, half carried into the house between a pair of burly soldiers. What could be ailing the man? He hung limply between the guards, his eyes rolling in his head, his mouth hanging open in an imbecile's leer.

A shiver of recognition ran through Toulac. She had seen men in that state before – frozen in battle, paralysed by terror, or when they had received a shock of such magnitude that their minds refused to countenance or comprehend what was taking place. The last time she'd seen anyone look like that, it had been Vlastor, a Reiver chieftain of the eastern hills who had hired her sword to assist in one of the clan wars that cropped up in that region with the frequency and inevitability of weeds. The chief, victorious in battle, had entered his enemy's fortress in triumph – only to find the head of his beloved son and heir impaled upon the gates. Toulac began to wonder. What happened up there on the mountain, she thought, to make the Hierarch look like that? Squash that curiosity right now, Toulac old girl, she told herself firmly. Don't go getting tangled in the affairs of the Hierarch and that bastard Blade, or it'll end in tears. We're in more than enough trouble already.

She turned to pat the neck of the warhorse. 'Now, old lad – where in the world am I going to put you?' Night was falling fast and the temperature dropping with it. Snow was already piling in great drifts against the side of the house. Thinking of the long, cold night ahead, the veteran snagged a passing soldier by the sleeve as he began to make his way down to the sawmill. 'Hey, you – sonny! The woodpile is behind the house. Fetch me a nice big pile of firewood, and get it inside quick, or you'll have Lord Blade to reckon with!'

The soldier and his companion hitched their horses to the porch rail and stamped off, muttering things that Toulac was glad she couldn't hear. If she *had* heard, she'd be forced to readjust their attitudes, and there was no time for that now. Hastily she pulled Mazal aside, just in time to prevent him from biting a chunk from the backside of the soldier's horse. Well, clearly she couldn't house him down at the sawmill with the other mounts. The stallion was far too territorial. The night would be too cold to leave him tied up under the shelter of the porch. Toulac looked doubtfully at the barn, and even more doubtfully at the horse. Then she made her mind up. There was only one thing for it – she had no other option. Besides, she couldn't have better protection for the horse if Blade did start getting hungry . . . 'Listen,' she told Mazal. 'You've got nothing to be afraid of. You're a big brave warhorse, remember? Now don't let me down.'

Toulac blinked in the darkness of the barn. As far as she could see, there was no sign anywhere of Veldan's companion. 'Kaz?' she whispered. 'Where the blazes are you?'

There was a stirring in the back of the barn. A mound that Toulac could, until a moment ago, have sworn was a pile of old manure, straw and general rubbish, heaved upwards and turned into the elegant contours of the firedrake.

'By Myrial's wide waistcoat!' Toulac gasped. 'How did you do that?'

Kaz cocked his head at her quizzically, his eyes kindling at the sight of the horse.

'Oh no you don't, matey,' Toulac told him hastily. 'Mazal is the last of my old companions, and he's very dear to me. I want you to guard him and keep him safe from that mangy cur-pack out there. *You* aren't supposed to eat the poor critter!'

Kaz dropped his head to the ground, and gave a drawn-out, piteous sigh.

'All right – I know you're starving. But not Mazal.' Toulac told the firedrake. 'Once the soldiers have gone I'll try to make it up to you, I promise.' Her words came out jerkily, for she was trying to hold the plunging warhorse, which was determined to put as much distance as possible between itself and Veldan's companion. Nevertheless she had a feeling that the animal was not so consumed by terror as he had been during his first encounter with Kazairl. Mazal was pretty intelligent – for a horse, at least – and he had a well-developed instinct for survival that had pulled both himself and his mistress out of trouble time after time. The firedrake had been around the place for over a day without threatening any harm, and his scent was all over Mazal's home range, mixed with the familiar, everyday odours of Toulac and the horse himself.

'Come on, Mazal – don't be an ass.' Firmly Toulac led the shying horse to a stall at the rear of the barn, strapped his blanket into place, and tethered him with more care than she had ever used in a long, careful life. As she settled the horse, she brought Kazairl swiftly up to date on what had been happening in the house. Finally she turned back to the firedrake. 'There we are. I think he's starting to get used to you. Hopefully, he'll be all right if you don't get too close or make any sudden, threatening moves.' Daringly, she patted Kaz on the nose. 'Thanks, mate – I really appreciate your help. This stupid lump of horseflesh means a lot to me.' Hurrying, before her unwelcome guests got it into their heads to come and search for her, Toulac headed out of the barn.

'Don't mention it. But remember – you owe me.'

The words dropped into her head just before she had reached the door. Toulac's mouth dropped open. She whirled back to face the firedrake, but he was studiously ignoring her as he watched Mazal with great concentration.

'Well!' Toulac left the barn with a great deal more to think about than when she'd gone in. 'I'm not so old that I can't tell the difference between what's real and what's imagination,' she muttered to herself. 'Well!' Firmly, she resisted the impulse to go back. 'May I be dipped in dog's dung!'

As soon as he left the sheltered gully, the gale tried to blow Elion right off the mountain. He could feel the bitter chill right through his snow-plastered cloak and several layers of clothing. Even the horse was too miserable to nip at him. It trudged along, head drooping, as though its rider – the trader rescued by the Loremasters – weighed as much as ten men put together. After no more than a dozen steps Elion began to doubt that they would make it. He understood the rules of survival in a blizzard, and right now this deadly wind constituted a far greater threat than the snow itself. Maybe it would be safer to go back to the sheltered gully and build a shelter. He had rations enough to last out a day or two, until this storm finally blew itself out.

Just at that moment he became aware of Veldan's mental voice, pitched to penetrate his preoccupied thoughts. 'Elion? Elion! Answer me, why don't you!'

'What do you want?' It was impossible to screen the hostility out of his thoughts.

'Can you find shelter up there? We have a troop of armed nasties encamped on us here. It's obviously the same lot you saw up at the landslide. You'd be better off—'

'Freezing my arse off on a bleak mountain trail in the blizzard of the century while you stay in a nice, safe, solid house with fires and blankets? That's your idea of better off? Who do you think you're trying to fool, Veldan? This is pure malice on your part, isn't it? You don't want me here interfering in your mucked-up mission. Maybe you'd prefer me out of the picture for good!'

'I'd prefer you out of my *life* for good, you stupid bastard – but I have no objections to your survival as long as you do it far away from me. Please yourself, then – come down here. But the last thing you'll hear when you're dying with an arrow through your guts is me saying I told you so!'

What is your estimation of the threat, Veldan? Shree's cool voice broke into the midst of the quarrel. *I trust your judgement of the situation, but please bear in mind the conditions up here. I believe we can get ourselves through the night, but for the humans, it will be neither easy nor comfortable.*

'Toulac – the former warrior who took me in – says that

Elion would be a damn sight safer out there in the blizzard than tangling with Lord Blade. I would say there's nothing she doesn't know about local conditions, and I believe we'd be wise to take her advice.' For a heartbeat, Veldan hesitated. 'Judging from Toulac's reaction to our visitors, I suspect I would be better off taking my chances up the mountain with you lot, but I don't think I could get out right now – not without being observed. Besides,' she added candidly, 'I like the old battleaxe and I owe her. I'm not just going to run out of here and leave her to cope with a troop of armed men all by herself.'

*Your loyalty does you credit, Veldan – but remember that first and foremost, you are a Loremaster and your first responsibility is to your fellow Shadowleague associates. At the first sign of trouble for you or Kazairl, I want you both to *get out of there immediately* and let me know at once. Hopefully, I will be able to assist your escape. We are returning now to shelter in the gorge where your partner dug you out of the landslide. I know you were unconscious, but Kazairl will know how to find the place. Be well, Veldan, and take care!*

The sense of presence that was Veldan faded from Elion's mind, leaving only the wind-sprite on whom to vent his spleen. 'Well, thanks a lot, Shree,' he groused. 'A night in a snowhole on a freezing mountain is all I need to complete a perfect day.'

A sudden gust of wind veered round from Elion's back and hurled a handful of snow into his face. *Always willing to oblige, my dear Loremaster!* Then the wind-sprite's voice dropped to a serious note. *This was probably the better plan in any case, as well you know. Veldan is in enough danger down there without us increasing her peril, and the sooner you frail humans get into shelter the better. Come, now, Elion

– stop sulking like a child. Delay could kill you. Turn around immediately, and let's get you back into the protection of the gorge, and under cover.*

Acknowledging – privately, at least – the sense of Thirishri's words, and stung more than he cared to admit by her accusation of childishness, Elion turned back into the teeth of the gale, dragging the reluctant horse behind him.

All at once he discovered the true killing strength of the storm. The wind blasted into his face, blinding him with driving snow as hard as grit. The cold shrilled in his ears and teeth, piercing the sensitive nerves with excruciating pain. Elion reeled and floundered, unable to find a way forward against the buffeting gale, which smashed into him with gargantuan strength. The Loremaster had put off his retreat too long. He gasped and choked like a drowning man, as the frigid wind snatched his very breath away.

Suddenly the gale was gone. Elion stumbled forward, thrown off balance by the abrupt return to equilibrium. Without the raw chill of the moving air ripping the heat from his body, his skin tingled and felt almost warm. Gratefully he took a deep draught of wintry air, and another. He rubbed his stinging eyes, with their snow-encrusted lashes. His ears were ringing; it sounded as though he could still hear the ravening howl of the storm . . .

Stop dawdling, you idiot! I'm only one little wind-sprite against the unleashed fury of the elements. How long do you think I can keep this up? Thirishri's telepathic voice sounded terse and breathless with strain.

The Loremaster blinked and looked around. On either side of him the snow was still streaking past just as thickly as before. Only a wedge-shaped section of still air, right in front of him, was free, clear and sheltered. Just as she had formed a shield to save the trader from his attacker's arrows, the wind-sprite was now protecting her partner from the brunt of the storm.

*Wretched human, will you *move*? We don't have all night!*

'Sorry!' Elion tugged sharply at the bridle of the long-suffering horse and started to haul it back up the trail. Even with Shree's protection, the journey was pure torment. His energy was dangerously low, and his hands and feet were frozen. Though the snow seemed to hold a slight glow of its own, marking the trail from the dark stone of the crags on either side, the night was blacker than a bandit's heart, and the Loremaster found it hard to see where he was going. He carried a good, efficient light source in his saddlebags, but such equipment was strictly for emergencies, and he was saving it for later, when the time came to build a shelter. The scouring wind stopped any drifting on this part of the trail, yet an impacted layer of frozen snow had formed all along the path and, because his numb feet could find little traction, his progress was uncertain and slow. He lost count of the times he fell, and the horse was little better, though it seemed to recover its balance more easily – probably because it had the unfair advantage of two extra legs, Elion thought with bitter envy. He was just about to turn around and tell it so when he realised that the cold and exhaustion must be making him lightheaded.

Just then there was a clatter and scrape of hooves behind him, and a shrill, terrified neigh as the stupid creature finally came down. An enormous weight struck Elion between the shoulders. He went crashing face down on to the rocky trail like a fallen tree, with the huge dead weight on top of him, pinning him to the ground.

For a panic-stricken moment, in half-stunned confusion,

Elion thought the horse had fallen on him and he would be forced to freeze to death where he lay. Then his burden began to move and, better still, to curse. With a curl of embarrass- ment inside, the Loremaster realised that the chestnut had pitched forward on to its knees and thrown the trader over its head to land on top of him. It was the first time Tormon had moved or spoken since they had started down the trail about an hour before, though to Elion it seemed like days. The trader seemed unable to help himself, and had simply sat silent in numb misery, slouching along on the back of the chestnut horse like a sack of dung. At least something has finally got a reaction out of you, Elion thought, then flinched at the nastiness of his own inner voice. He remembered how shocked he had been after Melnyth's death. Stunned and beaten down by the vast, unbearable weight of his sorrow, he had been in no better a state than the trader. Had it not been for Kazairl, neither he nor the badly wounded Veldan would have escaped the Ak'Zahar realm with their lives.

All at once, Elion's heart was moved to pity. With difficulty, he struggled out from beneath the trader, and the two of them managed to help one another to their feet. Despite the storm and darkness, Elion felt their eyes meet, and in that instant, they were joined by a bond of fellow feeling, then suddenly they were almost blown off their feet as the storm came howling around them in all its savage fury.

Sorry. I couldn't sustain the shield any longer. Shree's voice was faint with exhaustion. *But you're almost there, Elion. Only a few more yards . . .*

Those last few yards seemed the longest journey of Elion's life. Had it not been for the sturdy support of the trader at his side, he would never have succeeded – indeed, neither of them would have made it without the other. They had managed to get the horse up, but when Tormon had run an expert hand down its legs his palm had come away covered in blood. Cut knees, at least, then. Elion hoped the problem was nothing worse. It limped along behind them in a long-suffering and woebegone manner, its head drooping and its stringy mane plastered to its neck.

Now, Elion! To your left! Shree cried. The Loremaster couldn't believe they had reached the gorge at last. Pulling on the arm of the trader, he led his sorry little cavalcade down into the shelter of the gully.

Out of the gale, the air felt almost warm to his stinging face. Elion could have happily collapsed then and there and slept for a year or so, but he knew he didn't dare relax. Finding the gorge and getting out of the wind was only the first step. It would be just as easy to die here – it would take longer, that was all. Though the steep canyon walls provided a shelter from the howling gale, snow was still falling heavily into the declivity, and the piled detritus of the landslide was buried deep beneath a thick white crust. Elion knew that the feeling of warmth on his skin was merely an illusion caused by the absence of the wind-chill.

To build a shelter, they would need light. Elion groped in a saddlebag, his hands clumsy with cold and his fingers as numb and insensitive as blocks of wood. To undo the buckle, he was forced to remove a glove, and the frozen metal of the fastening burned like fire. The Loremaster rummaged through the contents, noting other items that might help them get through this cold night. 'Please,' he muttered, 'please don't be right at the bottom.'

As usual Elion had made a decent job of packing his gear. The glims were pushed down the side of the bag where he could reach them easily. He pulled out what seemed to be a sturdy glass tube about a foot long and the thickness of a broom shank, closed at either end, but in fact it was two tubes, joined in the middle by a cunning piece of glassblower's artistry. Elion had never dared to dismantle one to see how it was done – he was a Loremaster, not an Artificer – but on a regular basis he had cause to be grateful to those whose skills could create the glims. Taking one end of the tube in each hand, he twisted sharply in opposite directions. There was a sharp crack and a seal broke within the tube, mingling the contents of each separate half. A strong, greenish silver light leaped forth instantly, turning the spinning flakes of the blizzard into a globe of scintillating diamonds and sending shadows streaking across the snowy gorge.

Already Tormon was digging into the snow with both hands and scrabbling at the jackstraw pile of broken timber beneath. He turned sharply towards the flare of light, his mouth hanging open in astonishment, then practicality reasserted itself. 'Thanks – that should help,' he shouted, and went back to the vital task in hand. Elion was already hurrying forward to assist, sticking one end of the glim into the snow where it could illuminate their labours. By rearranging branches and hacking their way into the pile with sword and dagger, they finally managed to burrow beneath the mound and clear a hollow space within.

It was a dreadful task for two cold, weak men hampered by frozen hands and feet, especially as they needed enough space to get the horse inside. The task was too delicate and awkward for the wind-sprite; besides, Shree was so exhausted from her epic battle with the blizzard that she could do little more than keep the worst of the snow from them until she was rested. Sheer desperation kept the two men going. Somehow, as they laboured, it became a bizarre sort of competition to see which would hold out longer, and a matter of pride not to be the one who gave in first.

Time passed in a blur of hunger, cold and aching limbs. Elion kept going by working himself into a trance, sending his mind far away to happier times while his body dealt with the task in hand. The completion of the shelter almost took him by surprise. He looked around through a haze of weariness, hardly believing what he and Tormon had achieved. In the lee of the sheltering crags at the edge of the gorge they had burrowed into the pile of timber, chopping here, propping there, until they had formed themselves a rough chamber like a squirrel's drey, big enough, at a pinch, to take themselves and the horse. The floor was covered in a layer of springy pine boughs thicker than a mattress to insulate them from the cold, wet ground. The roof, like the walls, was formed from a tangle of interwoven branches, with a thick, insulating layer of snow above. The two men looked at each other for a long, silent moment – then shook hands, rightly proud of what they had wrought between them.

To Elion's surprise, the horse had more sense than to make a fuss about getting under cover – in fact, it almost trampled over the top of him to push its way into the shelter. It was forced to bend its head as it entered – there was barely room for it to stand upright as the branches of the ceiling scraped its back. Both men – even the shorter Elion – were forced to stoop. Once inside, Elion dropped to his knees, utterly drained and shaking with fatigue and cold. He rubbed his face to free his beard of the stiff crust of ice formed from frozen breath. When he rubbed his hands together to try to restore the circulation, bright flashes of hot pain stabbed his fingers.

When travelling in the mountains – standard Loremaster procedure, this – Elion carried a metal flask of water, honey and a little brandy, an elixir that made a good restorative in the cold. After a few moments, he found sufficient feeling in his fingers to grope in the inside pocket of his leather jerkin, where he kept the flask close to his body for warmth. He experienced some difficulty in uncorking the vessel, but finally managed to work the stopper out with his teeth. The first sip of the tepid, sticky concoction left a trail of glowing warmth down his throat. After another few sips, his head began to clear a little. He passed the flask on to Tormon, who was still upright, more or less, though he was leaning for support against the sagging horse.

After a few moments, the light came back into the trader's eyes. 'That helped,' he wheezed. He poured the last few drops into his palm for the horse, who licked at them gratefully. 'We should make some more of this.' With every moment, a little more strength was creeping back into his voice. 'Do you have all the stuff?'

'In my saddlebags – as long as the water in the big canteen isn't frozen.' Elion stood up stiffly, moving with care in the cramped shelter, and reached for the big canteen, still hooked to a ring on the saddle.

'Shouldn't be,' Tormon said. 'I tried to keep it tucked under my thigh when I was riding. Here – let me do that.'

Elion had been fumbling to unstrap the horse's burdens. The trader had the packs unfastened in an instant, and handed them over. He loosened the girths, swung the saddle off with a grunt, and wedged it off the ground, in a gap between the branches. Elion gaped at him for a moment. He remembered thinking, back on the trail, that Tormon was too far gone in grief to be anything but a burden – yet despite his pain and misery, the trader had still been capable of such a practical act as keeping the water from freezing. The Loremaster hardly knew whether to admire or resent such admirable – and knowledgeable – good sense.

Tormon patted the chestnut's damp neck. 'It's a good thing she's quite small,' he said. 'We'd never fit one of Kanella's great beasts in . . .' His words choked off abruptly, and he turned hastily away and busied himself with the animal, so that Elion could not see his face.

The Loremaster's heart went out to the trader in sympathy. All too well he understood the grief of losing a partner. In order to give Tormon time and space to get his emotions under control, he began to set about settling them into their less than comfortable haven. He had stuck the glim between two high branches to light the chamber. Now that the horse was inside, suddenly the shelter seemed very small indeed. Squeezing past Tormon once more, and very careful of the chestnut's quick hind feet – though right now it looked far too miserable and weary to try its usual shenanigans – Elion pushed a thick bundle of brushwood into the draughty mouth of the entrance burrow to block it.

Tormon looked around, his expression pale and set, but his feelings reined in once more. 'Don't forget the pole.'

Elion nodded and rummaged on the floor for the pole that Tormon had cut while they were building the shelter. It was a slender sapling, the longest and straightest he had been able to find, and from which he had trimmed all the branches. Between them, the two men raised one end and pushed it through the rat's nest of interwoven timber that formed the roof of their refuge, until the pole was propped upright, held in position by the ceiling of branches but protruding far beyond them, above the snow.

'That was a good idea,' said Elion. 'It'll mark our position if we need to be dug out.' He had forgotten that the trader did not know about the existence of Thirishri, or telepathic communication, or the proximity of his fellow Loremasters, sheltering in the house further down the trail.

Tormon looked at him strangely. 'The last thing we want is anyone from that accursed city digging us out,' he said bleakly. 'The important thing is that pole will keep an airhole open for us, no matter how much snow falls during the night.'

Feeling sheepish, Elion busied himself with his pack and bedroll, unwrapping the oiled canvas groundsheet that was rolled around the blankets to keep them dry. He was thinking only of getting warm and comfortable for the night.

'Got a drying cloth?' Tormon asked brusquely.

Glad that the trader seemed to have changed his mind about looking after himself first – for in truth, this tall, quiet capable man was starting to make him feel inadequate – Elion rummaged in his bag and came up with a generous square of soft flannel. Tormon took it with a nod of thanks and, turning to the horse, began to rub it down vigorously with the wadded cloth. 'Hey!' Elion yelped. 'That's the only one I've got!'

The trader looked down at him uncomprehendingly, as if mildly puzzled by such selfishness. 'She's the only horse you've got, too,' he pointed out. 'She's wet and chilled – do you *want* her to die?'

Elion thought about walking all the way back to Gendival. He shook his head. 'I'll dry myself on a blanket.'

Tormon's eyes crinkled at the corners as though he were about to smile. He said nothing, however, and turned back to the horse. Though his grey pallor and the weary sag of his shoulders attested to his own pain and exhaustion, he continued to tend to the animal, rubbing hard and briskly, paying particular attention to its legs and talking to it all the while in a soft, crooning monotone. 'There's my fine lady, brave as a lion and swift as the wind . . . You'll soon be warm and dry now, and pretty as a primrose . . .'

The horse's terrible, hunched posture had relaxed. Its violent shivering had almost ceased. Ears pricked, eyes brighter now, it was clearly responding to what Elion viewed, with some disgust, as a lot of unnecessary pampering. Fine lady, my backside! he thought. He hadn't even noticed, until Tormon pointed it out, that his mount was female. Just wait, he told the trader in the silence of his mind. Wait till that carnivorous monster is feeling better, and then let's see what a clever-pants horseman you turn out to be! Elion was sure that fate would prove him right. After a while, the horse stretched its head around, back towards the trader as he rubbed one chestnut shoulder. At last, the Loremaster smirked. I knew it was only a matter of time. The brute's going to bite him for his pains.

The mare gave a low, contented nicker, almost like a deep chuckle, and nosed gently at the trader's pockets, rubbing her long, bony muzzle up and down his coat in what looked very much like a gesture of affection. Elion's mouth fell open. In his mind he heard a chuckle from the wind-sprite, hovering out of the way somewhere just under the low roof. 'And you can shut up, too!' His mental voice was a savage growl – but it only made Thirishri laugh all the more.

'I thought you were making some more honey water,' Tormon reminded him gently.

'Sorry.' A somewhat chastened Loremaster rummaged in his saddlebags and pulled out the brandy flask and a small earthenware crock of honey. To be honest, he was grateful to have something useful to do that didn't involve wretched horses! Also, he was glad of the distraction. Right now, the chestnut mare was the last thing he wanted to think about.

After a while, the two men sat down, wrapped in blankets and eating jerked meat, rock-hard trail biscuits and sticky travel cakes of nuts, dried fruit, grain and honey. Unfortunately they could light no fire in the snow-shelter, for they depended on the insulating effect of their snow roof, and to melt it would leave them both wet and exposed to the violent elements once more. None the less, the heat of three bodies soon began to fill the cramped space within their den and, though they were not exactly warm or comfortable, Elion started to feel confident that they would survive the dreadful storm.

Tormon, now that he had taken care of both the horse and himself, was paying more attention to his surroundings. 'What *is* that thing?' he asked, pointing at the light source, which was growing dimmer now. Soon, Elion knew, he would have to break out another. Well, he told himself, with some resignation, your new companion is no fool. You knew it could only be a matter of time before he started to ask awkward questions.

'It's called a glim,' he said. 'I believe it's made from an extract of fireflies and some plant or other – don't ask me how.'

Tormon opened his mouth, then closed it again. *'You aren't from Callisiora, are you?'* With a telepath's intuition, Elion just *knew* what the trader had been about to say. He had no idea why the man had changed his mind, but he was glad of the reprieve. He didn't want to have to lie.

To deflect the difficult moment, Tormon turned back to the mare, who had been fed a ration of corn from the small bag in Elion's pack and was now lying on a thick bed of pine boughs that the trader had bundled together for her. He patted her chestnut coat, dry now, and flame bright. 'My, she's a pretty little thing,' he said. 'Neat as a cat, and brave, too. I admired the way she fought through that storm with us. Never balked or complained a single time.'

Clearly the trader had gone insane or was thinking of some other horse entirely, but as Elion was about to raise a protest he realised that Tormon had paused only for a moment, then had started to speak once more. 'This is just the sort of horse I wanted to buy for Annas, when she got a little older. Why, even at five, she could ride just about anything. Kanella started teaching her practically before she could walk . . .' He tailed off into soft reminiscences about his lost lifemate and child, his eyes bright with memory and unshed tears.

After a time, Elion was drawn to join him. 'You know, I never noticed before, but the red of that mare's coat is just about the colour of Melnyth's hair. Now you talk about a horsewoman . . .'

As the night wore on, and the storm raged and moaned outside, the two men shared their grief by exchanging tales of happier days with their loved ones. And at times, if neither one of them seemed to be listening to the other, no one seemed to mind in the least.

SEVENTEEN

NIGHT MOVES

Veldan's predicament was both unnerving and deeply frustrating. To be forced to lie in bed, hidden and helpless like a timid rabbit, while intruders roamed the house, was intolerable. Every time she heard voices or the sounds of movement she grew tense and held her breath, wondering whether Toulac was in trouble, or if Kaz had been discovered, or whether the door to her room would come bursting open and – and then what? Veldan realised, all at once, that she was letting her cursed imagination run away with her again. She was far from being without protection. Beneath the bedclothes she ran her fingers along the hard, reassuring shapes of the two swords, her own and Toulac's weapons. She adjusted her grip on the dagger she was holding, and indulged in an evil grin to bolster her confidence. 'There's nothing here you can't handle,' she told herself firmly.

She had disguised herself in Toulac's clothing, kitting herself out in similar fashion to the local woman with a sturdy pair of canvas pants and layers of shirts and jerkins. Her own clothes she wore hidden underneath, though she had taken care not to overdo the padding. Restricted movement was the last thing she'd need in a fight and, besides, she was boiling underneath the bedclothes, despite the frigid temperature in the room following Kaz's destruction of the window. That, however, was the least of her problems.

Keeping her ears tuned to the noises in the house, Veldan reached out with her mind to the firedrake in the barn. 'Kaz, is everything all right?'

'No, everything damn well isn't all right.' Her companion's waspish tones came back to her immediately. 'Your friend that cursed old battleaxe has left her miserable horse tied up here in the barn – *and told me to guard it*! Here am I, my belly sticking to my backbone, and she leaves that useless pile of walking firedrake fodder right under my nose to torment me! Veldan, this is killing me! How much longer do we have to stay here? I'm practically drowning in my own drool!'

From where she lay Veldan could see the snow, thick as swirled cream, driving past her window in the rising gale. She sent the firedrake an image of the storm. 'Looks like you'll have to grin and bear it, sweetheart. We'd be mad to try to leave here tonight.'

'We're mad to stay,' Kaz growled. 'Wretched humans poking and prying and snooping around. On the other hand . . .'

'What?' Veldan demanded sharply. She didn't care for that thoughtful tone. If Kaz was hatching plots and schemes, it usually boded ill for somebody.

'Nothing,' the firedrake said brightly. 'Nothing at all.'

Oh, no, Veldan thought. Now I *know* we're in trouble.

'My mind was wandering, that's all,' her partner went on. 'It'll be the onset of death by slow starvation, I expect.'

'Kaz, please – think about Toulac. She has to live here after we're gone. Don't start anything that could get us all into worse trouble.' The only reply Veldan got from the firedrake was an evil snicker. Under the bedclothes she clenched her fists. 'Just you wait until I get my hands on you!'

That Kazairl! There was never any telling what he'd think up next. Kaz the unpredictable, Kaz the unique – in a very literal sense. To the best of Shadowleague knowledge, there were no others of his kind, though admittedly their domain did not extend throughout the world. Even to the Loremasters, there were inaccessible places in the world where the Curtain Walls were impenetrable, their secrets determinedly concealed. One agent, however – Veldan's mother – must have succeeded in entering one of these hidden places, though she had not survived to tell the tale. Maybe my mother *was* the only one of her kind to find a way through, Veldan thought. But how did she do it? And why?

No one in Gendival had ever been willing, or able, to say much about her parents – not even the foster parents, Loremasters both, who had brought her up. They claimed her father was unknown – some outland human, a casual lover her mother had picked up during a mission and discarded on a whim. With a telepath's sure intuition, Veldan knew they were lying, especially when that story was laid side by side with the eventual fate of the only parent she had known.

When Veldan was still a babe in arms, something had made her mother quit her homeland, abandon her child and vanish without trace. Two years later, she was found on the borders of Gendival, returning from who knew where, so badly wounded that her life had drained away before she could reach her home and the aid she needed so badly. Her backpack was filled with a well-wrapped bundle, padded so thickly that it could only contain something truly fragile and precious. It did. A single egg, bigger than a human head, deepest black in colour with a changeful, iridescent sheen. A mother's only legacy to her daughter. Kazairl, the firedrake.

Lonely orphan, lonely hatchling: they had grown up insepa-
rable, learning together, eating and sleeping together, and
getting into mischief together – especially the latter, for the
firedrake's capacity for thinking up mischief seemed endless.
Only when she was grown, and a Loremaster herself, did
Veldan realise what a stir she and the firedrake had caused
among the Gendival community. Every Shadowleague member, from Cergorn the Archimandrite on down, were intrigued
by Kazairl's uniqueness, his rapid growth rate, his obvious
intelligence and his telepathic ability, for almost from the start
he and Veldan shared a rudimentary form of communication
that became increasingly extensive and sophisticated as they
grew older. Indeed, the Artificers had been determined to
take Kaz away for intensive study, but Cergorn's lifemate
Syvilda had forced the Archimandrite to forbid this. She
insisted that the child had already lost both parents, and
must not be deprived of another loved one. At the time, Veldan
had appreciated this intervention very much. Unbeknown to
the Archimandrite, his lifemate had kindled a great flame of
loyalty within one of his future Loremasters.

By thinking about the past, Veldan had distracted herself from her futile worrying about the present, but all the
while she had been straining to detect any sounds outside that might give her an idea of what was happening
in the rest of the house. Finally, after a period of silence,
she did hear something – and wished she had not. Loud
footsteps were approaching her door. Veldan froze. Once
again the image of the cowering rabbit flashed into mind.
Ruthlessly she crushed it, her hand tightening on the haft
of her knife. Rabbits might cower, but Loremasters did not.
Instead she concentrated hard on the sounds outside her
door. The more information she could glean now, the better

were her chances of saving her own life if trouble should arise.

There was more than one person in the passage outside: it sounded like three or maybe four. They were right outside – then they had passed. The Loremaster heard a click and a creak as the door of the adjacent room was pushed open, a murmur of low voices, and then a sound that wrapped tendrils of ice around her spine. A soft, high-pitched keening, a discord of confusion, abandonment and misery. The inhuman, desolate sound stirred an uncomfortable mix of emotion within Veldan. Fear and pity were predominant, but underlying them was the prickling urge of curiosity – the characteristic that Loremasters shared in abundance. The trait that, sooner or later, got most of them killed.

'Stop that noise.' The words were surprisingly unemotional for a command. There was the sharp, cracking sound of a blow, and the keening ceased abruptly. Then the same voice, cold and commanding, spoke again. 'You men don't need to stay in here and listen to his ravings.'

'But by your leave, sir . . .' This voice was hesitant and a little shaken. 'Surely we should be doing something more to take care of him? He's in a pitiful state to behold. And well, it *is* the Hierarch, after all.'

'It *was* the Hierarch.' Again, those dispassionate, offhand tones. 'Now it's nothing but the mindless wreck of a human being. Our responsibility now is to keep him alive, and get him back down to Tiarond in one piece before sundown tomorrow. He'll fulfil his last role as Hierarch then, when he is sacrificed to Myrial.'

Veldan's mouth fell open. What sick game were these superstitious primitives playing *now*? Sacrificing their own supposedly revered leader? Now I've heard everything, she thought. There's more to this than . . . The thought faded, unfinished, as the footsteps came out again into the corridor. She heard the creak-click as the other bedroom door was closed.

'Now,' said the steely voice, 'you'll remain at all times outside this room. Remember – no one, for any reason whatsoever, is to pass this door save me. If Zavahl sounds as though he may be in difficulties, one of you run and fetch me. It might help if you bear in mind that the Tiarondians *must* have a sacrifice tomorrow night. If the Hierarch is not available, then I will be forced to nominate one or two replacements. Do you understand?'

'*Sir!*'

One set of footsteps, moving briskly, receded along the passage towards the front of the house. To Veldan's relief, they passed her door without a sign of hesitation. The Loremaster pursed her lips in a low, soundless whistle. That, she thought, is one *extreme*ly dangerous man! In her experience, the cold, controlled, emotionless foe was always the one most ready – and able – to kill.

Kazairl was more than ready to kill. It was more than his impatient temperament could stand, having to lie here in this cold, draughty barn, camouflaged as a *midden*, for pity's sake – and all the while, less than a hundred yards away, his partner was trapped in a building occupied by a hostile force. If that wasn't bad enough, the hunger that gnawed at his belly was a constant distraction. His suffering was exacerbated by the fact that in front of him, right under his very nose, was a feast of succulent flesh that he must forbid himself to eat. He sighed. But there was no help for it. Like Veldan, he had discovered a great respect for the indomitable veteran Toulac.

Things would have to be dire indeed, before he'd distress her by dining on her old companion. If I eat her horse, he thought wryly, I'll have to eat Toulac, too – otherwise she'll probably eat *me*!

So the firedrake could do nothing but lie there, in his dungheap disguise, and wait for something to happen. He kept telling himself that, while everything remained quiet, Veldan was in no danger and that *was* the most important consideration. None the less, he wouldn't exactly be sorry, right now, to have something to fight.

The pair of snooping guards came as a gift from the kindly fates. Kazairl's head came up with a jerk at the first sound of voices beside the barn. As he listened, he realised that there were two men out there, walking along the side of the building, their voices pitched loud enough to be heard over the constant shriek of the snow-charged wind. In the way of soldiers the world over, they were bitterly bemoaning the bad weather, the spartan accommodation, and the tasteless, inadequate rations. This diatribe, of course, was rounded off by a brisk debate on the uncertain parentage, dubious sexual habits and heartless, sadistic cruelty of the tyrannical brute of a commander who had sent them out to patrol in the teeth of a blizzard.

Kaz had heard it all a thousand times before. During his life as a Loremaster, he had made a curious discovery. No matter the species – from humans, to the aquatic mer folk, to the sinister, insectoid Alvai, to the fierce and frightful Gaeorn – one constant, dependable, unifying characteristic prevailed. The complaints of the low-echelon soldiery were exactly the same.

The firedrake half listened to the conversation, letting the tedious, familiar details slip through his mind like a running stream, but always leaving a single strand of attention suspended in the flow, ready to hook any morsel of information that the men let slip. It took a while to come – by this time the men had gone right round the back of the barn and were heading down the other side of the building – but when it did, it made Kaz sit up.

'At least the sergeant said that once we've patrolled the perimeter, we can go into the barn and light a fire.'

'Aye, he's not a bad old bugger when all's said and done. Not like that flint-hearted whoreson Blade. Telling us to come out on patrol on a night like this while he's stuffing his miserable face, all snug and cosy in front of somebody else's fireside!'

The voices faded as the soldiers continued their patrol around the edge of Toulac's clearing. It was plain that, however much they complained about this Blade, and vilified him behind his back, they feared him far too much to think of disobeying his orders, even on a foul night like this. Well, that was one piece of useful information. The other, however, was far more urgent – not to mention interesting – to the firedrake. 'So,' he chuckled to himself, 'they're going to keep watch in my barn, are they? Well, we can't have that, can we? After all, I did promise to protect Toulac's horse . . .'

Silently, stealthily, Kaz slipped through the dark barn, giving the warhorse the widest possible berth so as not to scare it. When he reached the doorway, his dark, muddy coloration paled, flowing and fading beneath his skin to the dappled blue-grey-white of shadowed snow. He adjusted his vision to pick up the heat traces of the hapless guards. Yes, there they were. He could see their outlines clearly through the intervening blizzard. They were right where he wanted them – in the most dangerous and lonely part of their route, furthest from the house and closest to the forest eaves.

Heh, heh, thought the firedrake. Big mistake. I wouldn't go there if I were you, little guards. Drooling again, he licked his chops. Then, in an explosion of movement, he was a shadow blurring through the snow. Faster than a whipcrack, the firedrake pounced. The two men died in the same instant, without a single sound. One by one, they vanished into the dark, secret depths of the forest. A lashing tail obscured the disturbance in the snow, then disappeared into the trees. The swirling blizzard drifted into the curved track of the guards' footprints, and the other, strange, straight track that had intersected their path to such deadly effect. A smooth, white blanket settled over every trace of violence, leaving no sign that anyone had been there at all.

'Kaz? Kaz? Are you there?' Veldan swore under her breath. He's been quiet far too long, she thought. He's up to something – I just *know* it! 'Kazairl? Dammit, answer me! What's going on out there?

'Nothing to worry your pretty little head about, precious.' The firedrake sounded insufferably smug.

Veldan closed her eyes in dismay. She knew that tone all too well. 'What have you done now?' she demanded sternly.

'Just taking care of a couple of things.' The firedrake snickered. 'Truly, sweetie – everything's juuuuust fine. You worry about looking after yourself. And if you need me, I can be inside that house in a flash. There won't be much of Toulac's walls left standing, but we must all make sacrifices sometimes . . .'

The vast improvement in the firedrake's temper was obvious. No more gripes about being hungry . . . '*Kazairl!* You haven't gone and eaten Toulac's horse, have you?'

'*Veldan!*' Kaz sounded deeply injured. 'What kind of unprincipled monster do you think I am? That animal means a lot to Toulac. After she sheltered and befriended us, it would be a shabby trick to repay her by eating her horse. Imagine – my own trusted partner, who ought to know better, thinking that I'd—'

'All right, *all right* – I apologise. I'll mind my own business. I don't care what you're doing. Just don't get us into any more trouble.'

'I am sorely misjudged and maligned.' With his thoughts wrapped in a cloak of injured innocence, the firedrake withdrew.

Alone and undisturbed once more, Veldan was thinking hard. You didn't get to live long as a Loremaster unless you had contingency plans in situations such as this – and stuck to them. That was what went wrong last time, Veldan realised. The only possible last-ditch plan in the Ak'Zahar labyrinth was – if discovered, run for your life. If only Elion had stuck to the plan, I wouldn't have this. She ran a finger down the jagged scar on her face, hating the not-quite-feeling where the nerves had been destroyed on the surface of the skin. The wound – and the one on her shoulder – ached in cold, damp weather. They were aching now. If only Melnyth had stuck to the plan, the Loremaster thought bitterly, we might all have got out safely. Certainly, the end result would have been very different.

Absolutely. If Melnyth hadn't delayed the vampires, we might all have been slaughtered. Don't go down this road again, Veldan, you idiot. It's pointless. What's done is done. The Loremaster took herself to task, as she had done hundreds of times before. Firmly she shut off that avenue of futile speculation. But as always one last solitary thought escaped to lodge in the back of her mind like a poisoned thorn. *If only Elion hadn't . . .* Beneath her skin, the scars still throbbed.

This time, at least, Veldan had only herself and Kaz to take care of – and Toulac, of course. Any plan must include the indomitable veteran, though Cergorn discouraged such altruism among his Shadowleague agents. 'You Loremasters are rare and special individuals: telepathic, knowledgeable, highly trained, skilled and difficult to replace,' he always said. 'There's plenty of those other sheep out there in the world, and there'll always be more. Help them, save them and take care of them whenever you can – but *never* at the risk of your own life.'

Well, to blazes with Cergorn.

Veldan's plan didn't take much thinking out. As always, the options came down to fight or flight. Under the circumstances, flight was the only real prospect, unless she and Toulac wanted to fight nearly thirty men between them – a daunting proposition even with the help of Kaz A swift escape might well be required, however, and that was where the firedrake would excel. He could take the women further, faster and over far rougher terrain than human soldiers could hope to manage, especially on a night like this. The blizzard would be a great help in covering their escape – but on the other hand it would also prove the greatest danger. There'd be no point in escaping their enemies just to be frozen to death on the mountain.

Ears straining for a hint of a warning sound, Veldan slid out of bed and knelt beneath the window to rummage once more in Toulac's wooden chest. Working with feverish haste, she amassed a pile of whatever additional clothing seemed practicable, wrapping it in spare blankets from the chest and from her bed. She strapped the bundle with a couple of worn old leather belts that she'd found right at the bottom of the chest.

Veldan tipped the unused stuff back into the chest and closed the lid. Staying low, below window level – there was always a faint chance of someone on patrol outside looking into the lighted room, and though Kaz would probably have warned her she wasn't taking any chances – she crept across to the little table by the bed and blew out the solitary lamp. After letting her eyesight adjust, the Loremaster stood on the chest so that she could lean out of the window. There was no need to bother opening it, following its earlier meeting with the firedrake's skull. Careful not to disturb the layer of snow that coated the windowsill, she dropped the bundle outside, down by the wall, where it promptly vanished into the drifted snow.

This time, there were no footfalls in the passage. Veldan didn't hear a single thing, until Toulac's gruff voice – overlaid with an exaggerated crone's quaver – suddenly sang out. 'It's only me, dearie. I've brought you some supper.'

With a gasp, the Loremaster took a single dive from the top of the chest to her bed, landing so hard that, had the two swords not been sheathed, she would have been skewered. Hurling the blankets over herself, Veldan lay there with her heart threatening to burst out of her chest. As it turned out, she need not have panicked. There was a scrabbling at the latch, the sound of a muffled profanity. 'No thanks, sonny – I can manage,' she heard the veteran say – then the door burst open on the impact of a sturdy kick.

'Bloody latch!' Toulac muttered. 'Been meaning to fix it for ages. Could never manage it with my hands full.' The voice went back to the quavering old woman's whine. 'Why, bless me, dearie, has that nasty lamp blown out? Let old Toulac light it for you . . .'

'You're overdoing it, Granny!' Veldan hissed as the former warrior approached the bed.

In the darkness, Toulac chuckled softly. 'What have you been getting up to in here?' she whispered. 'It's blacker than Blade's heart. Is it all right to light the lamp again?'

'It is now. I've been hiding some warm clothing outside, in case we need to get out of here fast and hide up on the mountain. I'm not sure what's going on here between Blade and the Hierarch, but what I've overheard makes me very uneasy.'

'Tell me – but stay where you are. There's no way of locking this door, so look sick, in case someone walks in. We should be all right, though. Lord Muck has taken himself off to bed in the loft, but keep your voice down for the guards next door. There are four more, but I've settled them in the kitchen with a five-gallon jug of rough cider I was saving for a rainy day.' She grinned. 'They'll be quite content for a while, I expect.'

In the rekindled lampglow, Toulac sat on the edge of the bed while Veldan quickly outlined what she had overheard. 'I don't know enough about the local power struggles to be certain,' she finished, 'but apparently Blade has decided to seize control. That's fine as long as the Hierarch stays as he is, but if he should suddenly recover his sanity then he'll most likely meet with a sudden accident, sacrifice or no. Blade wouldn't risk losing everything at that point – and he'd be damned sure not to leave any witnesses.'

'Whoa, steady there!' Toulac held up a hand. 'I'm hearing a lot of ifs and maybes, girlie. Now most of your journey is fine, and I agree with where you're headed – but what about your starting place? I saw Zavahl when they brought him in, and he looked pretty far gone to me. Why do you think there's a chance he might regain his sanity out of the blue?'

Veldan bit her lip. 'Because I think it might just be trauma. Intense, profound, debilitating shock. You see, I know what Zavahl saw up on the Snaketail Pass. If he truly believes in the religion he preaches, then the creature he dug out of that landslide – and what it represents – has just shattered his view of his world into a million pieces.'

Toulac leaned forward. Her blue eyes, star bright with suppressed excitement, were fixed on Veldan's face. 'Something like you and Kaz?' she breathed. 'Something from beyond the Curtain Walls?'

Veldan nodded, somehow unsurprised that the veteran had worked things out so fast. She knew she was violating her Shadowleague vows of secrecy, but . . .

Kaz cut in, just as she was about to speak. '*Veldan!* What in the name of all perdition do you think you're *doing*? I like the old battleaxe, but this is a serious infringement of Shadowleague law!'

'I don't care, Kaz. Toulac is my friend. She saved my life. She can be trusted with our secrets. She's sensible and wise, and experienced in the ways of war. She knows the local situation far better than we do. She's helping and sheltering us, and doesn't deserve to be lied to. Besides, she's already *seen* you, Kaz. I think she's worked out that we aren't exactly from around here! We're safer if we include her. We owe her that much.'

The firedrake sighed. 'And you were nagging *me* about not getting into trouble! All right. Have it your own way. But you mark my words – it'll end in tears . . .'

'Kaz, shut up.' Veldan turned back to the expectant veteran. 'You're right, Toulac. I can't tell you everything now, but beyond this land there are other realms inhabited by all kinds of strange beings. Some of them would make Kaz look very ordinary indeed.'

Toulac's gnarled, strong hand fastened around Veldan's wrist in a grip that made the Loremaster gasp. 'Will you take me? Veldan, will you?'

Cergorn is going to kill me for this! None the less, the decision was one of the easiest that Veldan had ever made. 'Yes, Toulac,' she said firmly. 'Kaz and I will take you. First though, we have to get through tonight . . .'

Her words were cut off by a piercing shriek from the adjacent room.

The snow fell on the Sacred Precincts, covering the paths and buildings in a soft, muffling shroud of white. When Felyss was finally settled, the smith put on her warmest cloak and waded off through the deepening drifts, heading towards tall, golden gates that guarded the Inner Precincts. She took deep, refreshing draughts of the icy air, and felt the stiff set of her neck and shoulders beginning to relax. It was such a relief to get out of the house for a while. The tense atmosphere of grief, despair and impotent rage was close to unbearable, especially for one accustomed to living alone. Her sister was becoming increasingly irritable and snappish, and Agella was finding it harder and harder to keep her patience and curb her tongue. *I can understand,* she thought. *Viora can't vent her anger on those who had caused it, so she must find another outlet for all that pent-up emotion – but does it have to be* me?

As she went on, however, Agella began to replace the fretting about her sister with another worry. She was horrified to see how bad the storm had become. The air was thick with whirling white flakes, and already her boots were sinking ankle deep into the chill white mass that covered the ground. Oh, Scall! she thought, ashamed to realise that the arrival of the rest of his family had driven the thought of her poor absent apprentice right out of her mind. Dear Myrial, she prayed, let him be resting safely now in Toulac's house!

There was no guard at the gates of the Inner Precincts, though there should have been. Clearly, someone had taken one look at the weather, decided that no one would be out and about to catch them in their dereliction, and sneaked off to a warmer place. Typical, Agella thought. With Lord Blade and the Hierarch away, discipline goes to pieces in no time! That guard must be pretty confident they won't be able to get back tonight, though. I wouldn't like to be in his shoes if Blade turns up unexpectedly! She wondered what had befallen the Hierarch's party. She had seen their horses being brought out that morning, and later, Fergist had told her that they'd set off up the mountain for some reason or other. A shiver ran through her. If two great Lords and two dozen Godsword troopers had been trapped up there, conditions must be bad indeed. She didn't give a fig about the two great Lords – frankly she had no high opinion of either of them – but again her thoughts went out to Scall. If only he'd managed to get to shelter before the storm became too bad!

The physicians had their own dwellings behind the Hall of Healing, in a tranquil garden planted with the many herbs they used in their trade, all laid out in a delicate mosaic of neat little beds with mossy paths between. Sadly the herbs had been half drowned this year, much to the detriment of the city's well-being, despite the frantic efforts of healers and gardeners alike to save the precious plants, and tonight, to compound the disaster, the little plots were buried beneath a mantle of thick snow. The smith kept carefully to the main paths, staying well clear of the cultivated areas. It would be far too easy to stray into the herb beds by accident, and enough damage had been done already by the weather.

Evelinden's low white dwelling, one of a cluster of healers' homes, was larger than Agella's cottage. In addition to the usual rooms, the physician's house had another bedroom of generous proportions, a compact stillroom with its own water supply and stove for concocting medicines, and a study lined with books and scrolls. Evelinden shared it with a fellow physician a little younger than herself and about the same age as the smith, a slight, effervescent woman named Kaita, with shrewd, sparkling eyes and an irrepressible mass of springy dark curls. It was she who came to the door in answer to Agella's knock. 'Why, Agella, what a lovely surprise! Come in quick, and get yourself warm!'

The two women were just finishing supper, and Evelinden leaped up from her place as the smith came in. She was a small, bird-boned woman: serious, iron-willed and dedicated, delicate, quick and plain as a sparrow, with a smile that transfused her face with a transcendent, fleeting beauty. Her chief glory, a mass of dark brown hair, richly threaded with silver, lay across her shoulders like a shining cloak tonight, though through the day she wore it tightly braided and tied to keep it out of the way while she was at her work. As she hurried forward to embrace Agella, she was frowning with concern. 'My dear, I've never seen you look so worn out and wan! Is something the matter?'

The smith shook her head. 'No, Evvie, I'm fine. Just a bit tired. I didn't come for myself, but I do need your help—'

'Is it an emergency?' Kaita interrupted. 'Will anyone die if you sit down for a few minutes?'

'No, it's not that urgent—' Agella had no chance to continue. Before she quite knew what was happening she found herself sitting with the women at the table, devouring a large bowl of hot stew that was fiery with spices and pungent with unusual herbs. After the first astonishing mouthful, which sent her groping for the water jug, she dug in with alacrity, her spoon speeding up in pace. It had been a tumultuous day. She couldn't remember when she had last eaten and she'd never had the time to realise that she was so weary. The day's events had taken their toll, but with each mouthful of Kaita's stew she felt new warmth and energy flooding back into her body. 'This is amazing,' she said with her mouth full.

Kaita beamed. 'I'm glad you like it. I've been experimenting lately with various herbs and spices in combination, looking for some kind of tonic that might boost our people's defences against all this disease. I think I've found the right formula at last – and tonight I had the sudden urge to combine my discoveries with cookery.'

'Yet another one of her hare-brained ideas,' Evelinden put in, smiling. 'And like most of her wild schemes, it seems to work. I'm never sure whether she's a lunatic or a genius.'

'Well, it certainly works for me.' Agella's spoon scraped the bottom of the empty bowl. 'In fact, it worked wonders. Thank you, Kaita. I really needed that.'

Evelinden smiled at her. 'I know. That's why we insisted on feeding you first. When you came through that door, you looked absolutely drained.' She reached across the table and took Agella's hand. 'Now, my dear, what can we do for you? I know you wouldn't have come trekking out in all that snow for a simple visit. Kaita will pour you some tea, and you can tell us all about it.'

By the time Agella had completed her story, the two healers were looking very grave. 'Don't say it,' the smith sighed. 'I know I shouldn't have them here, and I know I could get into trouble for it – but what could I do?'

'Not another thing,' agreed Kaita. 'Especially on a night like this.'

'All the same, they can't stay here for long,' the cautious Evelinden reminded them, 'or you really will get into trouble, Agella. You don't want to lose your place here – especially with things as they are in the rest of Callisiora.'

'There's something else, too.' Kaita was frowning now. 'Agella, I know you want to take good care of your folks, but they mustn't be allowed to find out about the food that's stockpiled for the Precincts. If word of *that* gets round the Lower Town, we'll have a howling mob up here before we know what's hit us.'

The women looked at one another, then looked away. Trust blunt, impulsive Kaita to bring up a subject that was so uncomfortable for all three of them. Evelinden was the first to break the awkward silence. 'All right, we none of us like the notion of others going hungry while we eat, and as a healer, I suppose I ought to be ashamed of myself—'

'Well, I'm not,' Kaita butted in. 'I bloody well earned my position in the Hall of Healing. They may train us all, but you know as well as I do that they only have us back here for a permanent placement if we're the very best. And to earn my place here, I worked my fingers to the bone in a little backwater hole down on the southern coast. I studied, slaved and sweated for those people. I sat up all night with their old folk and children until I was dropping with weariness.

I gave them the food off my plate, and the clothes off my back. It's not as if I've lived a life of wealth and privilege like the Hierarch. I *refuse* to feel guilty about a bit of extra food. If we gave it all away to the hungry folk of Tiarond, let alone the rest of Callisiora, it would barely feed them for a day—'

'I know, my dear, I know,' Evelinden interrupted her friend. 'It's the Hierarch's ruling, not ours, and we all swore a vow of secrecy. It wouldn't do anybody a bit of good if we refused to eat our share.'

'You can be sure the Lower Townsfolk wouldn't see it like that, though,' Agella reminded them grimly. 'And who could blame them? You're right, Kaita – I can't afford to let my family find out – and unfortunately, I think Viora is already beginning to wonder.'

'There's only one thing for it, then.' Evvie got to her feet, brisk and decisive. 'We must get them back on their feet, and find a place for them down in the city as fast as possible – tomorrow, preferably. Come along, Agella. I'll go back with you now.'

When the smith returned home with the white-mantled healer, Viora pounced on her as Evelinden was hanging up her cloak. 'What took you so long?' she hissed.

The physician's hearing must have been very acute. She turned swiftly. '*I* took her so long, goodwife Viora. I had private matters to discuss with Smithmaster Agella.'

Viora glared, but did not dare to insult a physician. Agella hid a smile to see Viora so well and truly squashed – for a while at least. She had a feeling, however, that she would pay for it later.

Evelinden insisted on seeing Felyss alone. To Viora's annoyance, she drove the other women from the room, but when the girl's mother objected, she was firm. 'Your daughter needs to talk about what happened today. Without that, she'll never come to terms with this business, and the healing process can't even start. As a stranger, I'm safe. She can speak freely in the knowledge that it doesn't matter a bit. She'll see me a time or two, then I'll be out of her life. She won't have to encounter me every day, aware that I know the horrors of which she must unburden herself.'

For a moment, Viora's defensive manner fell away. 'And it will help her?' Agella suddenly saw how much of her sister's shrewish temper was due to worry over her daughter, and felt ashamed that she'd let herself get so annoyed.

The healer patted Viora's arm. 'Don't worry. It'll help. And afterwards, I'm going to give her a draught guaranteed to make her sleep halfway into tomorrow. A good long rest is what she needs – just as you do. So you had better start right now.'

Eighteen

The Enemy Within

The upper room, tucked beneath the sloping roof of the house, might once have been a cosy, comfortable place, but years of neglect had resulted in many of the overlapping wooden shingles cracking or slipping out of place. A handful were missing altogether, and the cold wind, mixed with an occasional scattering of finely powdered snow, came whistling through the gaps. The long attic room was a maelstrom of swirling draughts that slipped in through every crack and cranny, causing the lamp flame to flicker and flare. Against the walls, the shadows – of chair and bedstead, and the attic's stored boxes, bags and other miscellaneous junk – flexed and leaped, adding to the disturbing atmosphere of constant, restless motion. At the far end of the attic, one long, dark outline obscured the others, swooping back and forth along the wall. The silhouette of a pacing man had joined the mad whirl of the shadow dance.

At the best of times, Blade had little use for sleep. Never one to waste the slightest advantage, he had trained himself, over the years, to make do with ever decreasing amounts until a mere hour or two of rest would meet his needs. He had discovered long ago that the still hours of darkness, when most men were sunk in brutish oblivion, were an ideal time to study, manipulate and plan, leaving the busy, active daylight hours free for carrying out his designs.

Tonight Blade had much to think about. Before this storm had trapped him here, he had planned to be in Tiarond with the Suffragan Gilarra, discussing the details of tomorrow's ceremony, which would finally send that pious, whining fool Zavahl back to his precious god. Also, he mused, there were one or two plans to be set in motion to ensure the Suffragan's complete co-operation. Plans of which she would never know, unless she started to prove difficult.

Still Blade did not intend to waste his time worrying over matters that could not be helped. Though the storm had kept him here when he needed to be in the city, the snow should not present too much of a setback. Such a blizzard, so early in the season, ought to have blown itself out by morning. He had two dozen sturdy men-at-arms with him, easily enough to clear a blocked trail from here to Tiarond's gates.

It had long been Blade's plan to remove the stranglehold of its ridiculous religion from around Callisiora's throat. Only by eliminating the divine authority of the Hierarch – the mandate of a superstitious populace – could he take control himself. And once Callisiora belonged to him, Gendival would follow. This realm would be the perfect base from which to oust that fool Cergorn and renew his own claim on the leadership of the Shadowleague.

Sternly Blade reminded himself not to run before he could walk. Gendival was still a long way off in terms of effort, distance and time. His first concern must be Callisiora – and so far, everything was going very well indeed. His scheme, an intricate construct that had taken years to set up, was unfolding at last, with even better results than he had expected. He had planned to break Zavahl, to undermine his confidence with himself, and to rob him of the trust of his subjects. The one factor Blade had not reckoned with was Seriema's intense hatred of the Hierarch. Her idea of the Great Sacrifice, a bizarre, barbaric relic dredged up from the city's murky past, had been timely indeed, and now, with his hysterical, panic-driven actions of the last few days, Zavahl had done everything but hurl himself on to the pyre. Everything was going according to plan, he told himself – except for one vital, unanticipated detail. The appearance of the dragon.

Why would one of the Dragonfolk be passing through Callisiora? There could only be one answer. The desert-dweller must have been on his way to Gendival, to confer with Cergorn over the disintegration of the Curtain Walls – and if a dragon was taking that kind of risk, then it looked as though the Archimandrite was finally preparing the unwieldy Shadowleague to take action at last.

Well, this time Cergorn would be too late – but to give himself the best chance of success Blade knew he must keep his movements secret for as long as possible. Unfortunately, the dragon's presence could only mean one thing. He could never have made his way through such inimical territory without assistance. Unless his companion or companions had been killed in the landslide – and a painstaking search of the area by Blade's Godswords had revealed no further bodies – there was at least one unknown Loremaster wandering loose in this area.

Abruptly Blade stopped pacing. Whether or not he was actually recognised – unlikely, considering that most active agents in the field would be too young to remember him – there was still a chance that he could be exposed to Cergorn before he was ready to oppose the League openly for the second time. Over the years of his exile, he had taken great pains to hide his true identity – that was one reason he'd waited so long to make a move. In Callisiora, as in other realms, resident Shadowleague agents had settled here and there, recruited from the native species and living ordinary, everyday lives, their true identities kept secret even from their families. They were Cergorn's way of keeping in touch with what was happening across the world, and when Blade had first come here, they had been his greatest threat – a danger that he had with time and patience managed to eradicate.

Not everyone in Gendival had agreed with Cergorn. Blade had many sympathisers, who, seeing the fate of their leader, had abandoned their rebellion, deciding that prudence was the only possible course. Many remained loyal, however, despite the passing of the years. Gradually, carefully, he had managed to send messages to key individuals, and as the existing Shadowleague agents based in Callisiora had died – in some cases, with a little assistance – Blade had been replacing them with his own sympathisers until Callisiora was his, and he'd thought it safe to go ahead with his plan. But . . .

Why worry? The storm will take care of it. Suddenly, Blade smiled. Of course! Even if this unknown Loremaster had lived through the landslide, the interloper would have difficulty surviving these blizzard conditions on the mountain. All was not lost – not by a long way.

His attention was suddenly wrenched from his thoughts by the sound of screaming from the floor below. It sounded as though Zavahl was still causing trouble. *And he will probably continue to do so until the flames consume his pyre,* Blade thought wryly. He turned to hurry down the rickety, ladder-like staircase – then thought better of it. He had been mystified by the Hierarch's sudden seizure in the Snaketail Pass, but now an idea had come to him . . .

Let us see how he reacts when he thinks he's unobserved, Blade thought. Taking a blanket and the lamp with him, he moved swiftly to the far end of the long attic, to position himself above the room in which Zavahl was imprisoned. Kneeling, he examined the floor minutely until he found a gap between the boards, and laid the folded blanket down alongside. Unfortunately it was too dark in the room below for him to see what was taking place. But if Zavahl started to rave again, who knew what simple listening might reveal? Blade blew out the lamp and settled down to wait.

'No, no! It's in my head! Get it out – get out! OUT!'
There was a monster inside Zavahl. He could feel its hideously alien presence in his mind, casting doubt on his every thought and action. High on the lonely mountain, his world had come crashing down around him with as much violence and devastation as the landslide that had trapped the dragon. Myrial's abandonment had left him defenceless – open to attack from some malevolent and discarnate power. He had been possessed by some unnameable evil, which had transferred itself to him from the creature on the mountain. He could feel its presence crowding into his head, which felt ready to burst from the pressure of conflicting thoughts – some recognisably his own, others half-glimpsed, incomprehensible shapes that slipped in and out of his awareness, like strange fish swimming in the depths of a dark sea of conflict and confusion. His head throbbed from the constant, unrelenting pressure of too many thoughts, memories and emotions crammed into one inadequate vessel. It was like trying to walk in a smaller man's boots.

In the dark room that was his prison, the Hierarch continued to struggle against his bonds, though in truth, he wondered why he did so. It did no good to fight – he should have learned that by now. Each time he had tried to combat his fate, his battles had only made matters worse for himself in the end. Why bother to resist? he thought. There's no point. Truly, Myrial's curse is upon me. This time I'm finished. By tomorrow night it will all be over – and probably that's just as well. How could I continue to live with this demon trapped inside me?

A shudder passed through him. As Hierarch, Zavahl had always denounced the notion of demons, dismissing their existence as mere folk tales and superstition. Again he had been mistaken, as he had been proven wrong so many times of late. Again, the flood of events had inundated the mountain of his faith. More of his beliefs had been eroded, had crumbled and been washed away without trace.

The worst of it was that he had only himself to blame. He had approached an unknown, alien creature with no more caution than a three-year-old child wandering up to the family dog. How could he have been so stupid? Had these difficult days robbed him of all sense of self-preservation? He was Hierarch; it was not for him to risk himself against the unknown. Why else had he brought Blade and his troop of armed brutes? But no – he had been so anxious to examine the damned creature, and so certain it was dead, that all prudence had deserted him. In that moment, Zavahl had been blinded by sheer dismay. He'd been counting so heavily on the creature still being alive. His own life depended on it. In addition, curiosity had lured him – even mudcaked and dead, the dragon was an incredible, awe-inspiring sight.

As he had approached, he had felt *something* leap from the monster to himself. The world around Zavahl had vanished for an instant in a blinding flash as a presence, foreign and inimical, exploded into his mind in a starburst of pain. The impact, forceful as a physical blow, had been hard enough to drive him to his knees.

How will I ever find the strength to bear it? Trapped and crippled in this alien prison to the end of the creature's days . . .

What was that? Zavahl stiffened, his throat closing with panic until he could barely breathe. It was no thought of mine! Oh, Myrial, what's happening to me? The demon is starting to take over my thoughts!

I would be better off dead!

Had that been his own thought, or that of the intruder? Suddenly Zavahl realised that it did not matter. Wherever it had come from, it was the absolute truth. He remembered the moment when he had approached the dragon and the evil had possessed him. How quickly Blade had pounced to take advantage of his plight! It was as though he had been waiting for just such an opportunity. Zavahl had been too immersed in the pure terror of the moment to pay attention to the Godsword Commander's treacherous words. Now, in this instant of extremity and helplessness, they came back to him.

'The strain of the last few months has taken its toll upon the Hierarch . . . His hopes were unfounded . . . The beast perished the instant Zavahl laid his hand on it . . . Myrial has turned against the Hierarch . . . Zavahl must play the part of the Great Sacrifice.'

Bitterness curdled in Zavahl's stomach. Blade! That cunning, manipulative, treacherous swine! All along, he meant me to die – and if this dreadful thing had not happened he would have found some other way to put me on the sacrificial pyre. No matter how hard I tried to avoid my fate, it seems my death was meant to be.

Well then, so be it. At long last, with a feeling close to relief,

Zavahl had accepted the inevitable. At least his own demise would spell the end of the monster that lurked within him. If Myrial and his subjects required that Zavahl lay down his life then he would do so with no more whining or evasions and with no regrets – except one. He wished – oh, how he wished – that he could take Blade with him.

Human eyes were different, their vision flat and restrictive. The human body was a puny, weak, ill-balanced miscreation, its vital systems fragile and inefficient. And the mind! Confused, underdeveloped and grossly underused – a muddied maelstrom of thought and emotion without form or organisation . . .

No wonder Aethon was drowning.

Had he known what was in store, the dragon would rather have died than catapult himself into such a hideously alien environment. His complex intellect and the deep, all embracing store of his racial memory did not fit within this primitive, limited mind, which was bursting apart beneath the strain. The pain was inordinate and excruciating

like trying to walk in a smaller man's boots.

How had that alien concept intruded? Aethon cried out in alarm, but only a man's thin voice shrieked into the night. Contamination? Were the human's thoughts starting to bleed across into his own? Suddenly Aethon's struggles stilled. He was frozen in his shock like a fish in a winter pool. How did I think this could possibly work? he thought. How could the consciousness of two individuals from different species share the same mind?

With great determination, the dragon fought his way through the barrier of distracting pain and tried to take stock of his strange new situation. That traumatic period of mental turmoil and disorientation had blocked out the corporeal world completely, so firstly he needed to evaluate his surroundings, for this new body was far less robust and formidable than his true form, and physical dangers posed a far greater threat.

To his surprise, he was no longer in the open, on the high mountain trail. His new human body, aching and stiff, was lying on a soft, lumpy surface with an acrid smell of dust and damp. He struggled to rise, but could not. His limbs were firmly bound. Darkness surrounded him – he was blind and helpless!

Once again the tide of panic threatened to overwhelm Aethon. To a dragon's senses, it was never dark like this. Their vision encompassed the widest possible spectrum, including heat traces and adjustable focus over a tremendous range. Their glittering, bulbous eyes were set high and wide so that they enjoyed all-round sight, apart from a single, narrow blind spot behind their skulls.

Yet for Aethon, another revelation, far more horrifying, lay in wait when he continued to test the limits of the strange new brain that housed his mind. Sometimes the physical realm and the realm of the mind were not so very different. Just as he would have registered the loss of a wing or a limb from his dragon body, he discovered now that his host had absolutely no telepathic ability whatsoever – and therefore neither had he. Aethon was mind-deaf and mute, and that was how he would stay. How will I ever find the strength to bear it? he thought despairingly. Trapped and crippled in this alien prison to the end of the creature's days . . .

I would be better off dead . . .

Again, the dragon battled his own terror until he had grappled it down into submission. Think! he warned himself.

Think of your responsibilities to your own kind. Think of all the knowledge that you bear. If you'd been able to take the easy way out, you could simply have died quietly in the pass. Now, Seer – calm yourself. Analyse the situation in a rational manner, or all will most certainly be lost. The darkness, the total absence of any weather, the musty reek of the still air and a static, subliminal feeling of boundaries told him he was no longer outside but imprisoned within some kind of structure. He must have been brought here, all unknowing, during the whirl of confusion that had followed his transition. Again the thought sparked fear within him. What if the condition should recur? Another period of insensibility such as this could prove fatal.

Suddenly he became aware that his borrowed body was twisting and writhing, trying to roll over without any conscious effort from himself. With a start he remembered the other mind, the true owner of this form, who was also clearly awake and trying to assert himself. So far, Aethon had given little thought to this unknown human whose body he'd usurped but, though he felt a slight prick of shame, he still shied away from the mere idea of investigating his fellow inhabitant. The threat of contamination – of an indissoluble mingling of personalities – loomed too large in his mind.

Something must be done, however. This human form was displaying signs of increasing physical distress as its true owner grew more agitated and terrified, and his struggles increased. Fear of damaging the fragile vessel brought Aethon to a quick decision. He forced himself to relax and lie quiet, and tried his best to relinquish any attempt at control. In a rational sense, it was surely the best thing to do. After all, the human was the only one of the pair who had the slightest notion of what was happening to them. Hopefully, his actions and reactions could best ensure their mutual survival. By the Light, though, such helplessness came hard!

He had made the right decision. As the body rolled over, Aethon saw, down at floor level, a hair-thin streak of lamplight. Knife-edge slips of gold at either side outlined the shape of a door. Though it did not admit sufficient illumination for him to make out any details of his surroundings, the mere sight was a tremendous comfort, dispelling much of his sense of abandonment and blind disorientation. With his eyes fixed on that faint but comforting glimmer, the dragon could concentrate on his other senses, though there was little point in dwelling on the dank smell of the room, the rasp of thirst in his throat and the burn of hunger in his belly, the throbbing in his skull and the ache of cramped muscles in his bound limbs. Somewhere near by, he could hear a low murmur of voices, but, no matter how he strained, he could not make out what they were saying. Curse these limited human senses!

As the Seer looked at the light, a memory flashed through his mind like a lightning bolt across the night. The mountainside. The terror of looking out through an alien pair of eyes. A group of men-at-arms who surrounded him, towering over him as he cowered, shrieked and writhed. The ring of soldiers broke apart, and another figure stepped into the remembered scene. Though the lesser men fell back respectfully, such evidence of his authority was not needed. He possessed an aura of power and strength, of control, authority and complete assurance, that turned his fellows into insubstantial shadows by comparison.

Suddenly the dragon was swamped in a flood of hatred, resentment and stark, cold fear – clearly not his own emotions, but the feelings of his host-mind towards this man. Aethon felt no surprise. Something was beginning to stir within his own mind, swimming up through the deep well of his memory towards the light of consciousness. At first, with a pang of alarm, he was convinced that his host's memories were polluting his own once more. After all, he knew no one in this harsh, hostile human land.

But the conviction grew.

In the scene of his recollection, the man stepped forward, looming over him like the dark, brooding peak of the mountain. A hand came up to strike – and in that last instant before the memory snuffed out in pain and oblivion, Aethon knew. *'Amaurn! YOU!'*

The darkness echoed to the screams of man and dragon.

Now that Elion and his new companion were safely settled for the night, there was no point, Thirishri decided, in simply hovering around the shelter. The men had shared a small meal from the travelling rations in Elion's pack and were now nodding where they sat, but wind-sprites did not sleep. She'd be far better off doing something useful in this case, something to help Tormon. She had stayed while the trader gave Elion an account of what had happened to him, and was shocked, as she had so often been before, by the human capacity for treachery and violence. Moved by his distress, Shree vowed to herself that she would go into Tiarond right now, and try to discover the fate of his missing spouse and child. It should be safe enough for me to slip away for an hour or two, she thought. Clearly, nothing much is going to happen up here in that time.

Elion? She gave the Loremaster a sharp mental prod before he drifted any deeper into that weird, unresponsive limbo that humans seemed to need so much (though wasting so much time in oblivion served no purpose as far as *she* could see).

'What?' With an effort, Elion dragged his eyes open. 'Is something wrong?'

No – at least not that I'm aware of. And since we haven't heard from Veldan or Kazairl for so long, I presume they are all right too. Probably fast asleep by now, I should think, and I don't want to risk waking them.

'I should say not. That bloody firedrake attracts trouble like a corpse attracts flies.'

Elion! There's no need to be so unpleasant! Shree reprimanded him. *What you just said about the poor firedrake would be better applied to you humans, in my experience! Things seem quiet enough up here,* she continued, *so I think I'll just drift down the trail to Tiarond, and take a good look around the Sacred Precincts. Maybe I can find out what happened to Tormon's lifemate, and his child. You can always call, if you need me.*

She could already feel Elion gathering his thoughts for an objection, so without waiting for a reply the wind-sprite rose up out of the shelter and adjusted her vision for this dark and stormy night. With no humans to hamper her, she wouldn't bother to go down by the trail, which took a broad loop around the mountain's skirts. It would be far quicker to fly directly over the top of the ridge. Snatching up a skein of swirling snowflakes, she whisked herself away on the wind, heading for the city.

The city streets were quiet as Presvel went out, muffled in a thick, fur-lined cloak. An anonymous figure in the stormy night, he made his way down from Seriema's mansion, in its spacious enclave of the powerful and wealthy, to the cramped and huddled terraces and tenements and the twisting narrow alleys of the real Lower Town. What different values we can give a name, he thought, as he trudged along through the deepening snow. In the Sacred Precincts, they call every part of Tiarond but themselves the Lower Town, and despise it all alike. In the opulent dwellings around the Esplanade, however, we call the rest of Tiarond the Lower Town, and look down our noses at the honest labourers, for the most part at least, who have to live in the cramped and overcrowded rooms down here. Yet I grew up in these streets, and I should know better now – but it makes no difference. It's odd how we all need someone to look down on. The workers who live here call the Shambles and the riverside slums the Lower Town, and hold themselves aloof from the poor destitute wretches forced to eke out an existence in those damp and derelict hovels.

Presvel had to smile at himself. That was the worst of having an analytical brain. You couldn't just switch it off when it was inconvenient. He was supposed to be going to meet his lover. He should be flying along on hastening feet, his heart borne up on the wings of passion, according to those trashy novels that Lady Seriema didn't realise he knew she possessed – the ones she kept locked up in her bedroom drawer and read in secret in the night while munching on clandestine bits of cake.

The trouble is, he thought ruefully, that while the language might be overflorid and pretty daft, the actual sentiments those stories described were not so far off the mark. This girl *did* fill him with a kind of euphoric insanity, the likes of which he had never known before. He would dare anything for her, give her anything, take any risk – yet she was nothing but a common little whore from the lowest part of the Lower Town, and Presvel paid her for her time.

That's not true, and you know it! he told himself angrily. *She's not just a common little whore!* But he had to admit, if he were honest, that he was hardly in a position to judge. Tonight would only be their third encounter. Yet, he thought, though it sounds like a line from one of Seriema's dreadful novels, I feel as if I've known her all my life. I know she works hard, at any rate. He had seen her hands; though she seemed very young for her profession, they belonged to a woman much older, the nails worn down and broken, the fingertips blistered and peeling, the backs streaked with old burn scars and callused across the knuckles from wielding washboard and worn-down scrubbing brush. Presvel knew those marks. His mother, who had died of overwork before she'd had time to get old, had hands like that. When he had commented on them, the girl had turned on him like a cornered rat.

'Do you think this is *all* I do?' she had blazed, and then had shut up quickly, afraid of offending a customer and losing his business. It had taken some coaxing, but eventually she'd told him of her working day. The hours and sheer amount of toil had made his blood turn cold. She looked so young and small and slender! She had seemed as delicate as a primrose – and in reality she was far tougher and more worldly than himself, a grown man almost twice her age.

Presvel knew he must be crazy. After all, these visits to the Lower Town whores were not a new thing for him. He had been coming down here for years, on his rare free evenings, because he'd been deprived of normal female companionship by Lady Seriema's jealousy. Though their own relationship was not sexual in any way, he knew his employer very well by now. He had made himself indispensable over the years by assiduous study of her every mood, so that he could anticipate her needs – and he knew for sure that one of her most substantial needs was to be the only woman in his life. He had to be seen to dedicate himself completely to her, almost as if he *had* been a spouse or a lover. She would never, ever, consider sharing his attentions with another woman – in fact, he was afraid that she would react with such anger that he or his new partner might not survive the encounter.

Until now, Presvel had always considered the cost to be worth the benefits. Apart from her one unfortunate quirk of possessiveness, Lady Seriema was not an exacting employer for someone as tactful and efficient as himself. True, his clothing was very plain, but it was of superb quality and made by the best tailor in the city. He lived a life of luxury and authority in the finest mansion in Tiarond. Apart from this matter of women, he could eventually talk Seriema into giving him whatever he wanted and persuade her that the idea had been hers all along.

Until now, he had always considered the benefits to be worth the cost.

Until now, he had always kept his secret, by limiting himself very strictly to a single encounter with any one of the women he bedded, and by varying his routine and visiting a different part of town each time. This girl, however, had enchanted him. He had seen her twice now, and could not wait to see her again.

Presvel turned the corner, and saw the lighted windows of the inn ahead, and its painted sign, a huntsman with a bow, illuminated by the lamp that hung above the door. For a moment he did not see her waiting as they had arranged, and his heart sank. Had she found a better offer? Another customer who would pay her more? For the first time in his life, he knew what it was to feel true, consuming, jealous rage, and cursed the black-hearted fickleness of the whore. Then, as he was about to turn away she stepped out of the shadowy alley at the side of the building, pale and shivering in a thin, patched cloak, her fine, curling hair of palest gold gleaming in the lamplight and starred with a diamond-scattering of snow. His spirits went up with a bound once more, and his anger turned upon himself for keeping the poor lass waiting in the cold.

Presvel ran forward, calling her by name. For the first time ever, he had found out the identity of the woman he was bedding. Her name was Rochalla – and more than anything in the world, Presvel wanted to take her away from her wretched life, and give her all the security and comforts she had never known.

Much to her surprise, Rochalla was glad to see her customer, though she wasn't sure if she was comfortable with the notion. Men were a living to her, nothing more. She couldn't afford to let her feelings become involved, and she did not dare to let herself depend on someone else. She was used to taking care of herself, and until these last black months of rain and sickness she had taken care of her family, too. Her father, a miner, had died two years ago in a rockfall, and her mother, prostrated by grief, had followed him to an early grave, leaving Rochalla, then aged thirteen, and five younger brothers and sisters, one no more than a babe in arms.

With no one to help her, the girl had toiled like a slave to support her family. Each day she got up before sunrise to work in the Temple laundry in the Sacred Precincts, washing the linen and vestments of the priests and priestesses. Later, her hands still wrinkled from hot, soapy water, she trailed wearily across the city to the Gryphon, a sizeable inn near the gates, where she turned from laundrymaid into kitchen maid. The work was hard, but vital to the survival of Rochalla's little family. Arusa, the head cook, had the disposition of a nest of hornets, but her hasty temper hid a generous heart, and she always made sure that the girl had enough leftovers to take home to her hungry brothers and sisters.

After her shift at the Gryphon was over, Rochalla went home to the cramped little house among the knot of narrow alleyways that marked the oldest part of the town. She fed her family, then once they were all safe in bed she donned a tattered silk gown – left, long ago, by a careless customer at the inn – and took to the dark streets to ply her other, secret trade. After all this time, the notion of selling herself still filled Rochalla with horror and disgust, but she had promised her mother to care for the little ones . . . Somehow, she endured, and tried her best to shut her mind away while some rough man was using her body.

And in the end, it had all been for nothing. The rising before dawn, the endless days of gruelling labour in the laundry, the blows and scoldings in the kitchen. All those winter nights spent freezing on dark street corners, the stink of sweat and cheap ale, the mauling hands and slobbering mouths of her rough and drunken customers. All for nothing. Within a handful of days, the blacklung fever had taken the children one by one.

Last night Rochalla had been reluctant to leave the last sick child – but she knew that unless she earned some coppers she would be unable to obtain the medicine that might help. This afternoon, after leaving the laundry, Rochalla had visited the herbwife and parted with last night's meagre earnings in exchange for some new and nameless potion. Anxious about the child, she had rushed straight home with the medicine before going on to the inn – and had found Briede, the old woman who lived next door and minded the young ones in her absence, waiting at the door with tears running down her wrinkled cheeks. Derla was dead.

It had all been for nothing. She had loved the little ones, had sworn to care for them and protect them. She had slaved for them until her fingers bled, had sold her body on the streets, had endured pain, scorn and humiliation. For them she had buried her pride, bartered her youth and blighted any hope of a respectable future. And all for nothing. Her family were dead. She was the last.

She had set out that night in a haze of numb misery, letting her usual routine carry her along. Old Briede had been horrified at her going out on the streets tonight, with her little sister lying stiff and cold, but Rochalla had her reasons. She had seen the pyres of the dead, smouldering on the open plain towards the west of the city. There was no room left in the graveyard, and the citizens of Tiarond were no strangers to the stink of charring flesh as the fires smouldered in the wet and refused to burn. Derla would never end up there – not if her sister could help it! She was such a little child. Maybe the gravedigger could be persuaded to find just one small space, if he was given a good reason. She had come out tonight to her only generous patron, to make the money for a bribe. But this will be the last time, she told herself. After tonight, never again.

Nevertheless, at the sight of her mysterious, rich patron, she was astonished to find that she felt comforted and safe. Dangerous thoughts indeed, for one in her position! Rochalla lingered in the darkness of the alley, stunned by this revelation. Don't be stupid, she told herself. Just get through tonight, and then it's over for good. She was horrified to feel the faintest pang of regret. Unlike all the others – vulgar, stinking, rough and almost always drunk – this man had been gentle with her, always careful and kind, treating her with courtesy and consideration, as if she were a human being and not just some anonymous body to be used.

Dismayed by these revelations, Rochalla took herself firmly in hand. He's nothing to me, she told herself. None of them mean anything, nor ever will. They're a living, that's all, just another way of surviving these hard times. And if she wanted to make a living tonight, she reminded herself, she'd better hurry instead of dawdling here in the shadows like a silly fool. Another minute, and he'd get tired of waiting and be gone. Rochalla put on her brave, smiling, professional face. Sure that she had her disquieting emotions well under control now, she stepped out of the alley – and a moment later was horrified to find herself in her patron's arms, sobbing as if her heart would break.

Nineteen

Through Windows

Tiarond had changed. Thirishri, who had seen the city many times in the course of her long life, could feel the difference as soon as she came over the high ridge of the mountain. In the old days the place had been bustling, even after dark, but now the streets held a desolation and a hush that had nothing to do with the night-time and the snow. With a wind-sprite's vision, she could see that the warm golden stone of the buildings was dulled to a dismal ochre by the saturating rain, and the place looked grim and sullen in the stormy night. A pall hung over everything: a miasma of decay and disease, gloom, desperation and despair.

The wind-sprite was deeply concerned. The weather during these last seasons had been bad indeed, but the harshness of climate and landscape in these high mountains had magnified the problems. And if matters were this serious in Callisiora, what must be happening in other realms, where the normal, everyday climate was more extreme? What had become of the inhabitants of those lands? As always, when these feelings of gloom crept into her mind, her thoughts turned back to Gendival, and Cergorn, her much missed partner. She hoped he was managing without her, and had matters under control.

The Sacred Precincts, the apex and focus of the city, were

set high up on the side of the mountain, at the top of a network of steeply sloping alleyways and thoroughfares. Switching her vision between long and short range and the deepsight that registered the heat traces of the city's inhabitants, Thirishri took a close look around the streets below. As far as she could see, no one was stirring. Tiarond's populace seemed too dispirited, downtrodden and underfed to be active after dark, the wind-sprite thought. She would speed up to the Sacred Precincts and see what was happening there. Perhaps she could pick up the trail of Tormon's lifemate and his child. Shree flashed a quick thought to Elion, back in his den on the mountain, to let him know her intentions, then picked up a hot-air swirl from a cluster of smoking chimneys below and rose up smoothly above the huddle of dark rooftops.

As the wind-sprite floated higher up the broad, terraced mountain face, the layout of Tiarond became visible in its entirety. It was shaped like an arrowhead driven up into the mountain's flank, compressed between the two great spurs that ran down from peak to plateau, widening as they descended. The lower regions, which contained the poorer, more squalid streets, spilled out on to the plateau itself, where the city was bounded by a great looping wall that ran from spur to spur. There were two gates, one facing south and the other west, each one close to the crossing-point of one of the rivers. The western river boasted a magnificent arched bridge, and the waters that came down from the mountain's eastern face were crossed by a sturdy, cable-strung ferry.

In the lower areas of the city, the buildings were very old, crammed together in narrow streets as though the builders had tried to squeeze as many structures as possible into the increasingly constricted space between the two protective mountain walls. Porches, balconies and additional upper storeys of wood had been attached wherever possible to the ancient, crumbling stone of these houses – anything that would buy a few extra feet of precious living space. Many of these upper floors overhung the streets at crazy angles, giving an almost warren-like effect.

The overcrowding must be horrendous, Thirishri thought, as the resulting stench – more like a taste to a wind-sprite – rose up on the breeze. Each species to their own, I know – but I'll never understand how the humans can live like that. No wonder Tormon said the city is rife with disease. Maybe someone else had the same opinion, the wind-sprite noted, for in several locations there were gaping holes among the overcrowded buildings where many of the old houses had been torn away. Here and there, cleaner, more spacious new structures had been built.

Shree wondered where the residents of the crowded warrens had gone. The city walls would not contain a crowd of homeless folk for long. Surely they must soon begin to spill out on to the plain, in a haphazard collection of ramshackle shanties, which would be so inadequate that many would die. Yet if the overcrowding were to be alleviated by clearing the old buildings, then the inhabitants must go somewhere . . .

Oh, the fools! the wind-sprite said to herself. *Don't they ever learn the consequences of such profligate overbreeding?* The heretical thought flashed across her mind that perhaps the current climatic imbalance was nothing more than some natural form of planetary population control, not necessarily so undesirable as it initially seemed.

At least the upper regions of the city diverted Thirishri's mind from such uncomfortable notions. The large, spacious, beautifully constructed buildings, with their pleasant parks and generously proportioned avenues, were far above the crowded, squalid Lower Town in every respect. Here, far fewer people dwelt, in cleanliness, order and luxury.

These wretched humans! I'll never understand them! Shree thought. Why is it that they find such imbalance so necessary to their functioning? No wonder they tend to be so belligerent!

The wind-sprite came at last to the apex and focus of the city, where the two gigantic spurs of rock converged and were connected by the rearing cliffs of golden stone that protected and concealed the Sacred Precincts. Thirishri saw the dark maw of the tunnel that pierced the cliffs, and scorned it for the human rat-run that it was. Catching the breeze, she lifted herself higher, rising like a bonfire spark on the updraught that swirled about the massive palisade of stone. At the top of the cliff, the wind-sprite saw a sight that few humans had been privileged to view. Both sides of the city of Tiarond, the sacred and the profane, were laid out before her.

The clifftop ran back for about one hundred yards or more, sloping gently down towards the gorge of the Sacred Precincts. The rocks at the top of the palisade had been weathered by wind and rain into deep clefts, which looked as though mysterious writings had been incised there. From this height, Shree could see the canyon of the Holy City for what it once had been, long aeons in the past: a vast, deep lake, set into the mountainside like a jewel.

In her mind's eye, the sprite could see the shimmering waters that lapped the top of these very palisade cliffs, and see the broad deep ledges on the gorge's opposite side, far above the Basilica of Myrial, where there had once been beaches and bays. She could imagine the dark, weed-enshrouded lake bed, a hundred fathoms deep, where now stood the formidable mound of the Godsword Citadel, which had clearly been an island in its time, and the Scriptorium and Library, the Hall of Healing and the other, more mundane buildings of the Holy City. The wind-sprite felt a stirring of cold horror deep within her as she looked at the dark maw of the entrance tunnel, enlarged from a natural aperture in the rock, and tried to imagine that day when some tremor or shift of the earth had opened the fault and released the gathered waters to pour down the mountainside below.

With a sudden chill of prescience, Thirishri realised that sequestered canyon with its protective cliffs was still acting as a dam for pent-up forces – not a simple lake of water, this time, but a cauldron of violent emotions. The Sacred Precincts contained a seething turmoil of old rivalries and grudges, seasoned with anger, bitterness, envy, ambition and greed. With horrified clarity, Shree recognised that the coming of the Dragon Seer was just such another cataclysmic event as the long-ago earthquake that had released the lake, and that soon now – very soon – this festering mass of gathered violence would come crashing down upon the city.

Shree swooped down into the Inner Sanctum and made a low pass over the Citadel entrance. She hoped she could do something to help the poor distressed human whom she and Elion had rescued. Having saved his life, the Senior Loremaster now felt responsible for him. Humans were so vulnerable: both physically and mentally. Shree looked at the daunting bulk of the Citadel. The trader could never penetrate this grim fastness to seek out his lost family. If I go, the wind-sprite thought, I can find out what Tormon needs to know, and get word to him via Elion. If, by some miracle, his child and spouse are still alive, maybe we can think of some way to rescue them.

Having made her decision, Shree drifted through the Citadel's dark portal, across the courtyard, and into the fastness itself. Once within, she found movement less easy than usual. The air inside the building felt cold, dank and dead, as though it had been trapped unchanging for centuries within this oppressive mound of stone. Echoes of ancient treachery and violence seemed to seep from the very walls, like the blood of innumerable victims leaking through the stone. This is another dark side to humans, Shree thought, sickened by the miasma of ancient – and recent – horrors. How can they bear to live like this? She had to fight hard against the temptation to stir the old, dead air into a hurricane, to drive it before her through the crooked corridors and pull in fresh, new air behind her, until this vile place could be washed clean.

Mercifully it took little time to pick up the energy trace that was the woman. She had gathered all the information she needed to identify Tormon's lifemate from the trader's mind. Kanella's ghostly trail still lingered – only to be cut off abruptly in the chamber where the poor woman had met her end. Thirishri's thoughts darkened with sorrow. Though this was not an unexpected development, she did not look forward to confirming Tormon's deepest fears. What of the daughter, though? Ah, this was interesting . . . Clearly, the little one had escaped this room at least! Her pace quickening as hope inspired her, Shree set out to track the child.

The wind-sprite made a long and fruitless search of the Citadel, during which she scoured teaching rooms and offices, innumerable barrack rooms, with their bunks and lockers, and the huge, echoing space of the gymnasium, with its ropes and wall bars, and a roped-off indoor sparring area with a sanded floor. In her explorations she found two mess halls – one considerably more pleasant and salubrious than the other – and some kind of recreation room where Godsword soldiers lingered over their ale cups, many of them occupied in the various games using cards, dice, counters and boards with which the humans were wont to amuse themselves. Nowhere was there any sign of a child.

How could I have lost the trail so completely? Thirishri wondered. What in the world has become of the poor little wretch? Baffled and dismayed, she left the fastness and, with dwindling hopes, began to search the courtyard with its high enclosing walls. There, in a corner, was the tall, brightly painted wagon that she recognised from Tormon's memories – and just beside it the time trace suddenly reappeared. The wind-sprite's spirits leaped. It was clear that someone had come here and discovered the child's hiding-place, but there was none of the violent atmospheric disturbance that always accompanied a death. Instead the trace was joined by another. This is ridiculous! she thought. What can have happened here? She looked more closely. Yes, an adult had come here and left again – with the child. Concentrating hard to trace the individual lifelines in the tangle of tracks that led across the yard and through the gate, Shree followed the trails of the little girl and her abductor out of the Citadel, and across the Sacred Precincts.

The double trail ended at a house, indistinguishable from the others among the clustered dwellings of the Temple artisans. Shree circled the building, looking for a way in, but the windows and doors were all shut tight against the storm. She decided that the chimney offered the easiest access and, fighting the strong updraught caused by the fire, she made her way down into the black maw of the flue. She emerged into a cosy room, lit by lamp and fire, with a brightly coloured rug before the hearth. A man sat in the chair by the fire, carving a small but detailed cow from a piece of wood. A woman stood across the room at the window, looking out between the parted curtains.

Shree's arrival had sent a puff of smoke out into the room, and brought a handful of soot pattering down into the hearth. The man swore mildly, got out of his chair and brushed the oily black powder off the hearthstones and into the bottom of the grate. 'Must be some freak downdraught off the cliffs,' he said. 'That's the trouble with living in this place.' Receiving no reply, he went to the woman and put an arm around her shoulders. 'Don't worry, love. They're certain to be sheltering somewhere safe. It would take more than a bit of snow to finish Zavahl and Blade.'

'But what if they got trapped somewhere? What happens tomorrow night if there's no sacrifice?' The woman half turned, and Shree was surprised to recognise her as the Suffragan Gilarra. It had been some years since the wind-sprite had seen her, but she had changed very little – a matter of a few silvery strands in her hair, and some lines of care and laughter in her face.

'We'll worry about that tomorrow morning if they don't turn up – but they will, you'll see.' The man – Gilarra's lifemate, Shree presumed – spoke soothingly. 'It's no good you fretting yourself into a frazzle, love. That won't help. Come on, sit down by the fire. I'll make you a hot drink.'

'All right, Bevron. I'll do my best.' Gilarra let him lead her to the chair he had just quitted, and lowered herself gratefully into the soft cushions. '*Ow!*' She jumped back up as though she had been stung. 'What in Myrial's name . . .' She reached behind her, and burst out laughing. There, in her hand, was a half-carved wooden cow. She handed it to her lifemate. 'Yours, I think.'

'Sorry,' Bevron said sheepishly.

After a careful search among the cushions, Gilarra sat back down again. 'It's the horns that get you,' she said ruefully. 'I only hope that son of ours appreciates it.' She looked up at her spouse. 'Maybe, when you've finished this, you could carve some animals for little Annas. The poor child is going to need every possible comfort we can give her.'

Bevron shrugged. 'Of course I will – but what about Lady Seriema? Surely the richest woman in Callisiora will be able to buy Annas far better toys than I could make?'

Gilarra sighed. 'I'm not so sure. I only hope I did the right thing leaving her there. It seemed the safest place – Seriema has the wealth and power to protect the child – but she's such a cold fish! I'm afraid poor little Annas might be very unhappy there . . .'

Thirishri heard no more. Already she was hurtling up the flue. She exploded out of the chimney pot in a shower of soot and sparks, and headed out of the Precincts in search of the grandest house in the entire city.

Lady Seriema's mansion was on the edge of the great square, at the far end of the tunnel. Shree could scarcely recall the woman – a sulky-looking child, as she remembered, always in her father's shadow. Anyway, who cared about the woman so long as the child was here? She circled the upper storey of the house, peering as best she could between the slats of the shutters. A child that young would probably have a light of some kind burning . . .

At the fourth window, she finally found the object of her search – a small, tousled black head almost buried in a mound of soft pillows. The shutter, with its catch a little loose, banged in the breeze of her passing as she slipped inside for a closer look, and the child stirred, half turning in her sleep. Well, her breathing was fine, and there was no physical damage that Shree could see. She couldn't wait to bring the news to Tormon. He would be so delighted! The shutter clattered again as the wind-sprite left the room and soared high into the stormy sky. As she flew over the city, she decided to go back by way of the trail. Nothing would be moving on a night like this, but she might as well check while she was out here. As she skimmed along, she decided to defer her good news until she got back to the shelter. She was only sorry that *she* couldn't tell the trader, but Elion would have to do it for her. She could, however, be there to see his face when he received the news.

'Myrial up a pole! What was *that*?' Toulac muttered. 'Sounds like they're murdering him next door.'

Veldan had had enough of inaction. The fatal curiosity of the Loremasters had finally won out. 'I don't know,' she replied, 'but I think it's time we found out.' The raving madman in the adjacent room had been involved in the exhumation of the dragon. Surely there *must* be some kind of connection? One way or another, she would have to know. Aethon was dead — he must be dead — but still she wanted to talk to this man who had seen him last. Ducking out from under the veteran's restraining hand, she slid out of bed. 'Open the door a chink and keep an eye on the corridor for me. Warn me if there's any danger.' Already, she was halfway over the windowsill.

'Come back, you idiot! You're getting into danger for nothing! The affairs of these blasted highfolk are no concern of ours! Who cares if Blade *is* murdering Zavahl?'

'Me. Something peculiar is going on — and I intend to get to the bottom of it.'

Veldan lowered herself over the sill and stifled a squeak as she dropped into a drift of waist-deep snow. Well, of course it's bloody freezing, she told herself impatiently. What did you expect? Keeping close to the wall – where, unfortunately, the snow was deepest, but the signs of her progress would be least visible – she waded along, clenching her teeth to keep them from chattering until she was below the adjacent window. She knew the catch was broken on the shutter; for the last two or three hours she'd had nothing to do but lie in bed and be irritated by the racket as it banged in the wind. Pushing the window open, she hoisted herself – not without a certain amount of difficulty from her painful cracked rib – over the sill. Feeling down in the darkness with a careful foot, she discovered that there was a chest, similar to the one in her own room, beneath. Using it as a step, she came down, cat-footed, into the room.

From her place near the window, Veldan could see little more than a thin outline of lamplight that delineated the position of the door and, between herself and the light, the faint, humped silhouette of someone lying huddled on a bed. From the lack of any reaction to her presence, she guessed that his back was towards her, and had not heard her enter over the shrilling of the wind. Silently she crept towards him, reached over his shoulder and clamped a hand across his mouth. 'Keep quiet!' she warned in a piercing whisper.

Relief, joy, incredulity: Aethon was overwhelmed by a flood of emotions at the sound of Veldan's voice. His spirits, which had sunk so low, shot up abruptly. By her own miraculous survival, she had brought hope with her into the room. He tried to turn, to look at her – and in that instant real-ised that the body of his host was fighting the confining hand, kicking and thrashing as hard as its bonds would permit.

'Stop that, you fool!' hissed Veldan. 'You'll harm yourself! Stay still and let me help you.'

'It's me,' the dragon wanted to tell her. 'It's Aethon. I'm trapped here in this human's body.' But he could not. With horror, he realised the extent of his predicament. This might be the only chance to tell Veldan what had happened, but he could not mind-speak with the Loremaster, nor could he communicate with her in the human way. His host still retained control over bodily functions, movement and speech, but even if Aethon should find a way to wrest that control from the other, he had scant idea of the mechanism of human speech and how it was performed. Air was forced out of the body and somehow made to vibrate – that much he knew – but how exactly this was achieved, and how the words, in all their vast complexity, were actually shaped and formed, he had no idea.

For that, he would need his human counterpart.

Despite the dreaded risk of thought contamination, they would have to communicate.

When the hand clamped over his face, Zavahl was overwhelmed by terror, shock, and dread, exacerbated by the unspeakable things that had already happened to him in the course of this day and intensified by sheer unfamiliarity with such physical danger. As Hierarch, he had been safe for the past twenty years from the threat of such assault – ever since the unlamented death of Malacht, the tyrannical old brute who had raised him. Now, however, the pain, the fear and helplessness brought back memories of his childhood. Within a flash of recollection, the years of his adulthood dropped away and he was back in those nightmare times. It was Malacht who loomed over him on the bed, and the small, strong sinewy hand across his mouth had tuned into the old priest's wrinkled claw. There was no escape. There never was. Zavahl thrashed and writhed, beyond rational thought. Without the hand clamped tightly across his mouth he would have screamed aloud.

Then, like a door opening in a dark room, another image flashed into Zavahl's mind – a hand, his own hand, in the centre of the old Malacht's back. One sharp push – the stooped, black-cloaked figure of the priest vanished from sight. Shrieks. Thuds. The snap of breaking bone. An empty stone staircase, some of its steps smeared with blood, and a well of dark shadows far below.

Zavahl's world grew still. Though he was still dreadfully afraid, the pain and the unreasoning terror were gone.

Malacht's death was no accident. I did it. I killed him so I would be safe, and I was – until now.

The Hierarch had pushed that memory far down into his mind and buried it deep. Over the years, he had convinced himself that Malacht's death had been the result of a simple fall, that he himself had been nowhere near. But Myrial had known. Myrial, it seemed, had not forgotten. In the events leading up to this night, retribution had come at last.

Though his mind was reeling, Zavahl still struggled instinctively against the confining hand. 'Stop it, you fool!' a voice said. 'You'll harm yourself! Stay still and let me help you.' To his surprise, his assailant sounded female. To his utter astonishment, he found himself obeying her low, authoritative tones. As he let himself go limp, he felt the hand beginning to relax against his mouth. The voice whispered again. 'Before you shout for help, just remember that *I'm* not the one who tied you up.'

Awkwardly, Zavahl rolled over. Whoever she might be, she wasn't rash enough to start untying him at this point. He could barely see the figure perched on the edge of the bed, but he could feel her stirring as though rummaging for something. 'Damn,' she muttered. 'I *know* I had a glim in my pocket. All these clothes are in the way . . . Aha . . .'

There was the sound of a soft click, and the woman's face sprang out of the darkness, lit from below with a ghastly radiance. Zavahl gasped, barely preventing himself from crying out. This was a nightmare creature, disfigured and deformed, not only by the shadows but by a vicious scar that slashed the left side of its face, twisting and distorting the features.

Zavahl flinched, averting his eyes from the sickening sight to look down at the small, glowing object in the apparition's hand. The radiance had an odd, greenish glow: unearthly, unnatural and obscene. Had she some connection with the demon in his mind? 'In the name of Myrial,' he gasped. 'What manner of creature are you?'

A thunderbolt silence fell between them. After a long moment, the stranger spoke, her voice low and stricken. '*Creature?*'

He heard her swift, ragged, indrawn breath, almost like a sob, and looked up again to see that she had hunched in on herself and was trembling visibly. The upswept shadows cut sharply across a face drawn and haggard with pain.

Then her eyes flashed up and met his. It was as though she had slashed him with a sharp, bright dagger. 'Pretend I'm just a nightmare.' Her voice was hard now, and whetted with bitterness. 'Answer my questions and I'll cut you loose – fair trade. Then you're on your own, and you'll be free of the sight of me.'

'What questions? Who are you?'

Her hand shot out and grabbed a handful of hair at the back of his head. Pulling and twisting until the pain brought tears to his eyes, she turned his head until his face was close to her own. 'Never mind who I am. Just answer me! What happened up there in the pass, when you saw the dragon?'

Zavahl stopped breathing. She *knows*! She *is* a demon! Then his thoughts scattered, knocked aside by what felt like a series of scrabbling blows inside his skull.

Fool.

He heard the word distinctly, though it spoke within his head. The voice was not the familiar vocalisation of Zavahl's own inner thoughts, but a different sound, reverberant and inhuman, the words oddly slurred and fluid, formed from honeyed music strengthened by a hard, underlying metallic edge. As it spoke, Zavahl saw, within his mind's eye, patterns of flickering light that blossomed and faded in amorphous, pulsing, many-coloured shapes that seemed, in some indecipherable way, to be connected with the words.

Blind fool.

'Get out!' Zavahl hissed, through gritted teeth. 'Demon! Get out of my head!'

Listen.

'What?' The room darkened as the woman dropped her light on to the counterpane. Her hands clasped the sides of Zavahl's face, her fingers digging into his skin like claws and wrenching his head round to look at her. Even in the gloom, he could see the fire in her eyes. 'What's in your head, man? What?'

'Demons,' he whimpered.

Me. The voice spoke at the same time. *Aethon.*

The woman was shaking his head violently from side to side. 'Tell me!'

Tell her. Aethon. Aethon, here. Tell her, tell her, tell her, TELL HER!

'No! NO! Leave me alone! HELP MEEEE!'

The scream tore out of Zavahl, loud enough to bring all the guards in the world. Veldan gasped out a horrified curse and let go of his head as though it had turned red hot. She snatched up the glim and sprang towards the window, moving so fast that she was halfway over the sill before the door burst open, spilling soldiers into the room. From overhead there came a thunder of feet, hurtling down the stairs.

'Hey you,' a voice yelled. 'Stop or I'll shoot!'

Veldan dived headfirst out of the window. The drift beneath was thick enough to break her fall – she rolled and came bursting out of the deep snow, miraculously back on her feet. From the corner of her eye, through the veils of the blizzard she saw another figure – Toulac, she hoped – leap through the adjacent window. Then she was running, zigzagging towards the shelter of the trees. 'Kaz! Quick!'

'Coming!' With relief she heard his reply. Crossbow bolts were zinging through the air on either side, far too close for comfort, already finding their range. Praying that the swirling snow would confuse the aim of the marksmen, Veldan dodged and doubled, the icy winter air searing her lungs. Deep snow clung round her legs, hampering her movement and cutting down her speed. Time seemed to stretch to an eternity, with the dark, safe trees at the edge of the clearing a million miles away. A bolt came whistling past the side of her head, so close that the skin of her cheek prickled. Shit! Now they had the range . . .

A roar like a thunderclap split the air of the clearing. Kaz erupted out of the trees to Veldan's right, eyes blazing like blue lightning, red mouth agape and aglow from deep within. He ploughed to a halt in the snow, inhaled a mighty breath, and exhaled a jet of searing flame. The fire shot across the clearing and exploded like a starburst against the wall of the house below the window, charring the damp wood and spraying a fountain of sparks for yards on either side. Flame caught hold of the flapping shutters and one edge of the window frame, streaking and spreading in the wind. Darkness fled to the forest's brink, driven back by the flickering saffron light.

Suddenly, there were no more arrows.

In her mind, Veldan heard the whooping laugh of the firedrake. 'Jump up, sweetie!' He half turned and she leaped up on his foreleg. With an effortless shrug he used her momentum to throw her up on his back in a single, fluid movement. He wheeled back sharply, sideswiping with his tail to sweep a dramatic plume of snow into the air, and Veldan knew he was thoroughly enjoying all the stir and consternation he must be causing among their enemies within the house. She herself could not resist being swept up in the tide of his savage, gleeful joy. Dear Kaz! He throve on this sort of action!

Behind the house a horn blared out, answered by another from the sawmill down below. 'Time to go,' Kaz snapped. 'They're calling up reinforcements.'

'Get Toulac first!'

'Of course. Would I leave the old battleaxe?'

Toulac was finding the snow hard going, though her face was set in a grimace of fierce determination as she ploughed on gamely, weighed down by the bundle which Veldan had dropped out of the window. Veldan reached down and took it, then extended a hand to help pull the veteran up on to the firedrake's back. With a grunt of effort, the warrior came up behind her in a scrambling rush and clung like a leech, her chest heaving against the Loremaster's back with each wheezing inhalation. Veldan could hear the harsh rasp of her ragged breathing, and suddenly regretted the rash actions that had put the older woman at so much risk.

Shouts rang out over the sound of the screaming wind as a bunch of soldiers came running into the clearing around the side of the house. Their headlong rush came to an abrupt halt when they caught sight of the firedrake.

'Shoot, you idiots!' came a bellow from the window through which the Loremaster had made her sudden exit. She glanced back and saw a face in the burning window, harshly illuminated by a halo of flame. He glared out at her as fiercely as a hawk baulked of its prey, ignoring the heat and smoke as though they did not exist. The man was as tense and contained as a coiled snake, and Veldan was overwhelmed by an emanation of menace and brooding power. Grey eyes met grey across the clearing and clashed like two steel blades, sparking strong, conflicting emotions in the Loremaster: half lure and half repulsion. Time was arrested in its tracks as between them the two unmoving figures spun a web of curiosity, challenge – and some deep, unplaceable sense of recognition. Then the man broke the tableau. He inclined his head, an enigmatic smile touching his stern lips. A hand lifted to her in a wry, mocking salute.

Suddenly, Veldan was very afraid. 'Let's go!' She thumped Kaz on the neck with her closed fist. The spell that had held time suspended in the clearing was broken. The soldiers were lifting their bows.

'Hold tight, ladies!' In one great bound, the firedrake reached the edge of the woods, some two dozen crossbow bolts hissing and clattering among the trees at their heels.

From the house behind them came a sound that turned Veldan's blood to ice. Again, she heard the Hierarch scream, just as loud as before, when he had summoned the guards. *'Veldaaaan – wait! It's Aethon! It's me!'*

'Kaz – Kaz, stop!' The Loremaster thumped fruitlessly at the firedrake's neck. 'It's Aethon. He's not dead! Somehow, he's in that man's mind.'

'Yes, I heard.'

'Then we've got to save him. Turn back, Kaz!'

'In your dreams, Boss.' Without breaking stride, Kaz continued to plough uphill through the forest. 'We'll have to rescue Aethon later. You know I only get one flame-blast at a time. It'll take at least an hour for me to recharge myself for another – and we are *not* taking on two dozen crossbows without help.'

'But . . .'

Kaz increased his speed, hurling clouds of snow aside as he ploughed through them, whipping his long sinuous body in and out of the trees. 'Don't waste time arguing, partner. I'm right, and you know it. Now, you'd better ask Toulac if there's any shelter up here on this forsaken great pile of rock. Right now our chief worry is surviving the rest of the night. Mind your eyes.'

The firedrake charged headlong through a thicket in a welter of snapping twigs and cracking branches. Veldan threw up an arm in front of her eyes to protect them, and felt Toulac's face pressing into her back. It was hard to hear spoken voices over the whistle of wind in the trees, but that was just as well. She was willing to bet that the veteran was doing some spectacular cursing right now – and with good reason. Kaz was right, Veldan realised. They were in big trouble. And thanks to her reckless visit to the Hierarch, so was Toulac – and oh, mercy – what about Mazal, left behind and tied up in the barn? The veteran would be heartbroken at the loss of her only companion.

'Sometimes risks are necessary,' the firedrake reminded her. 'If you hadn't gone, we would never have found out about Aethon.'

They continued up the mountain flank at an oblique angle, to stay in the thick band of forest that was sheltering them from the brunt of the blizzard. If they wanted to put a safe distance between themselves and the soldiers, however, they would have to go beyond the treeline. Blade would have his guards out searching, there was no doubt about it. Losing men in the storm would mean nothing to him. When Veldan had looked him in the eyes, an understanding had passed between them. She knew he would come after herself and Kaz. She knew he would not rest until they had been caught. It was vital that they get far away from him, as fast as possible. Yet how could they survive a night on the exposed flank of the mountain?

Twenty

Within Walls

Annas awoke to a loud, repetitive clatter. A shutter, she realised, was banging in the wind. She could hear the shrill, whistling roar of the gale; a tremendous storm must be blowing outside the wagon ... But no – this wasn't a wagon! Confused, she looked around her in the lamplight. The room was large but cosy, with creamy walls painted with a frieze of pink roses. Opposite her bed, with its pink quilt and hangings, a fire glowed red in the hearth, pulsing like a heartbeat as the gusting wind sucked the draught up the chimney. The window – again, pink curtains – was over to her left, with a pink-cushioned seat underneath and a table near by that bore a ewer and bowl decorated with rosebuds.

Everything was very pretty, but Annas had never seen this place before in her life. Where am I? she thought. Why did I think I would be in a wagon? Only then did she realise that she didn't even know her own name.

There was a wall in her head. It was smooth and shiny, made of glassy black stone. It went up and up beyond all imagining, and stretched away forever on either side. She had a feeling – a vague sense – that a great many important things were lost on the other side, where she couldn't reach them. She didn't care. The wall might be a prison, keeping her away from the other thoughts and memories in her head, but it also kept her safe. Bad things lived on the other side of that vast, black barrier. Things she didn't want to face.

Just then the door swung slowly and silently open, and a strange woman entered.

'Annas? Annas?' The voice was soft, uncertain. 'Annas? Are you awake?'

Am I Annas? Does she mean me? Quickly, she screwed her eyes tight shut. She wanted to ignore the voice – she wanted it to go away and leave her alone, in peace, behind her wall – except that she was ferociously hungry, and bursting to the point where she would wet this bed if she stayed in it much longer.

Oh, all right. I'll be Annas. She opened her eyes, to see a woman with mousy brown hair and a very plain face. Who are you? I don't know you. You're not nearly as pretty as . . . The wall reared up, black and hard, in Annas's head, and the rest of the thought was trapped behind it. She turned away from the barrier and thought about other things.

The strange woman stretched out a hesitant hand, then jerked it back again. 'How are you feeling, child? Are you hungry? I've brought you something to eat.' She gestured at a bowl on the nightstand by the bed. Annas couldn't see what was inside it, but it didn't smell like anything good. She opened her mouth to answer, only to discover that no sound came out when she tried to speak. The words, too, were trapped behind the wall.

Oh, but this strange woman was hopeless! She just stood there, hovering uncertainly by the bed, as if she didn't have the faintest idea what to do next. It made Annas very nervous. She might not be able to remember much, but she understood that grown-ups were supposed to *know* this stuff! At a loss for a way to explain her needs, she scrambled out of the big, high bed and got down on her hands and knees, scrabbling underneath. It was with great thankfulness that she pulled out the half-expected chamberpot.

Annas gathered up the skirts of the nightgown that seemed to be too big for her, and settled herself in blessed relief. As she did so, she caught a glimpse of the stranger's face, bright crimson, before the woman turned primly away. 'Oh – oh, I'm so sorry,' she muttered. 'Of course, you've been asleep so long . . . I should have realised . . .'

Oh, for goodness' sake! Annas thought. The woman was absolutely hopeless! She put the lid back on the chamberpot and pushed it carefully back under the bed. Remembering the jug and basin on a little table in the corner, she went over to wash her face and hands – at least she tried. Somehow, while she had been asleep, her legs had turned all wobbly. She took two or three staggering steps – then suddenly she was falling.

Strong arms caught her and held her tight for a moment, squeezing her too hard. Annas found herself eye to eye with the strange, plain-faced woman, who without the slightest warning scooped her up and bundled her back into bed. *Just as if I were a baby!* Annas thought with great indignation.

'Don't worry,' the stranger said, with an odd, false heartiness, which Annas saw through at once. Some grown-ups sounded like that when they were trying to hide something.

'You've been asleep a long time,' the woman went on. 'You're bound to be unsteady on your legs at first.' Wringing out a washcloth from the basin, she began to wipe Annas's face and hands, her touch rough and clumsy.

I'm not *a baby!* Annas snatched the cloth away from her tormentor and finished her own wash, glowering blackly. She was beginning to feel really scared now. Nothing in this place was familiar to her. She knew – just *knew* – that she had never been in this place, with its cream-painted walls and flower-patterned curtains, in her life. Nor had she ever seen this woman before. She had no idea what lay behind the shiny wooden door of this room – and that was scary for sure. There could be *anything* out there! Monsters . . .

Annas began to tremble. She had no idea what lay on the other side of the wall in her head, either, and for some reason that was the scariest thing of all. She bit her lip fiercely, to keep from crying, but despite her best efforts, she could feel her eyes burning and her throat thickening around a sob. She gulped hard. A tear escaped and went rolling down her face, followed swiftly by another.

'Oh, please – don't cry!' The woman, who was absolutely no comfort at all, seemed very worried now. She was knotting her hands together and looking wildly around her, as if for help. 'Here – are you hungry?' she gabbled. 'Have something to eat. You'll feel much better . . .' She thrust the cooling bowl into Annas's hand.

Annas wiped her eyes with the back of her other hand and looked down into the bowl with a sinking feeling of dismay. Porridge? Ugh! She *hated* porridge. Cold, watery, *slimy* porridge, with a skin on top . . .

Suddenly it was all too much for Annas. Her temper snapped. This stupid woman who just stood there, wringing her hands together – it was all her fault! She was a grown-up. She was supposed to be in charge. She was *supposed* to know things! I hate her, Annas thought wildly. She's useless! She gives me cold porridge and rough washes and treats me like a baby! Who is she? What is this place? Why am I here? I want – I want my . . .

The wall in her head reared up all around her, shiny and black, looming over her as if it were about to fall on her and crush her with its weight, trapping her in the dark for ever . . . Annas let out a shriek that was misery and rage and frustration, all mixed with deepest terror. In desperation, she threw the bowl of porridge at the only possible target for her despair.

As the sticky contents splattered the woman's face and hair and began to trickle slowly down, Annas burst into noisy tears.

Seriema paced her workroom restlessly, cutting across the rich crimson carpet at an angle from the window to the fireplace and back again. Normally her mood could always be soothed by this plain, wood-panelled, workman-like chamber, richly comfortable but free of any feminine frills, its furnishings of desk, cabinets and bookshelves unchanged since her father's occupancy. Tonight, however, she was unable to settle herself. Following her encounter with Gilarra, and later with the child – this ghastly new responsibility that the Suffragan had wished upon her – she had been too tense and worried to return to any constructive activity, too agitated to relax, too anxious to eat, and far too distracted to go back to the pile of waiting documents that snowdrifted her desk.

Gilarra, come back, she thought wretchedly. I've made the most dreadful mistake.

She wished now that she had sent a maid to the little girl. At the time she'd thought it better if she should be the first to speak to her, considering the horrific scenes that Annas had witnessed that day. Whatever the child blurts out, she had reasoned, it's better if I hear it first, and not some feather-brained, gossiping maidservant who'll have a lurid, distorted version of the tale all over town before tomorrow morning's out.

Pausing to draw the thick, wine-coloured curtains aside, Seriema peered out at the thick skeins of snow that streamed past, blown almost horizontal by the gale. A stray draught from the window sent a chill along her skin, where her new-washed hair lay damp against her neck. It had taken forever to get all the porridge out without help but, Myrial be thanked, she had dismissed Presvel and Marutha for the evening before the humiliating debacle had taken place. In her mood of agitation and doubt, her assistant's hovering, solicitous presence would have been nothing but an irritation. As for Marutha . . . Seriema realised that she was clenching her fists. The old housekeeper's shrill, frank and vociferous disapproval of her actions in taking in the orphaned child of itinerant traders had already almost driven her to despair.

And what defence have I? Seriema thought despairingly. We both know very well that she's right. What will I do with a little girl? I don't know anything about children — I never wanted to! I don't even *like* them as most women seem to. Already I've made a mess of things. She's miserable, she hates me . . . Oh, great Myrial, however will I cope with this?

The merchant was ashamed of herself, and at her wits' end. Here she was, the richest, most ruthless, most power-ful woman in the whole of Callisiora, and one hysterical little girl had been enough to confound and terrify her. In sheer, cowardly panic she had fled the room dripping porridge, slamming the door behind her and locking it on the sobbing child within. What a way for a grown woman to act, her conscience reproved her. Angrily, Seriema buried the thought. Already she almost hated the child for exposing such a weakness in her.

'It's no good, you know – you'll have to go back in there.' The voice was such an echo of her own thoughts, it hardly seemed as though she'd heard it at all. With a gasp, the merchant spun away from the window. Presvel stood in the doorway, with a tray in his hands holding a decanter and two glasses. Seriema groaned and dropped her face into her hands. 'Damn you – how much did you see?'

'Enough to deduce the rest.' There was a chink of glassware as her assistant set his tray down on her desk. As Seriema dropped her hands, she saw his grin and felt her face grow warm with embarrassment. Ignoring her discomfiture, Presvel poured brandy and held out the glass towards her. 'Here – drink up, Lady. It looks as though you're going to need it.'

Presvel poured a generous measure of brandy for himself. Oh, dear Myrial, he thought despairingly, I can do without this tonight. He had just returned from his liaison with Rochalla, which had torn his normally tranquil emotions apart. He had been distressed beyond measure by the poor girl's grief, horrified by her story of unremitting poverty, hard work and the tragic deaths through sickness of her little family. The thought of her going all alone down to the graveyard in the morning with the body of her younger sister tore his heart, yet apart from giving her all the money he'd been carrying, he had been helpless to assist her or even ease her sorrow. Then, to make matters worse, she had told him that she would never see him again. For the first time since his childhood, events had gone out of his control. His life was falling apart, and now he had to deal calmly and cheerfully with this storm-in-a-teacup little crisis of his pampered mistress. Sometimes it was almost more than a man could bear!

Seriema's assistant, however, was nothing if not a thorough professional. He took a deep breath, made sure that none of his despair was showing on his face, and proceeded to act as if nothing was wrong in the world. Perching carelessly on a corner of her desk, he took an appreciative sip. 'Thank Myrial I work for a purveyor of wine and fine spirits,' he said lightly. He enjoyed being the only one who could lighten her bleak moods and flattered himself that he was the only person in Callisiora who had any influence with her at all. But his Lady trusted him – in fact he was the only one she *did* trust. He was indispensable to her, and thus retained his own position of importance. The other merchants knew by now that if they wanted any concessions from Seriema, her assistant was the man to approach. Their tokens of appreciation had mounted up to such a sum that he could afford to leave her and be independent – save that he had no wish to go. He enjoyed his paramount position in her household, and the authority and power that his influence gave him.

'Never mind the fine spirits!' Seriema snapped. 'What did you see, Presvel?'

'I didn't *see* anything much. The child woke me up, bawling – you can thank your stars, by the way, that Marutha is a lot more deaf than she cares to let on. I came along the corridor just in time to see you come hurtling out of that room like a hare with its backside on fire.' He struggled to suppress a grin – and failed completely. 'You seemed to be covered in porridge.'

Finally Seriema seemed to accept that it was far too late to save her dignity at this stage, and gave up the struggle. She flopped down heavily into the armchair beside the fire, almost slopping the brandy out of her glass. 'Oh, Presvel,' she wailed. 'What am I going to do?'

'Drink up, Lady, for a start.' Presvel settled into the opposite chair. 'Now, let's take a long, calm look at the situation. After all, you face far worse crises than this every month of the year, and I've never seen you beaten yet. She's only a little girl, after all. How bad can it be?'

That's easy for you to say, Seriema thought glumly. The damned child isn't *your* responsibility. 'But I don't know the first thing about children,' she protested.

Presvel leaned forward in his chair. 'Ah, but that's where you're wrong, Lady Seriema. You know a tremendous amount about little girls – of course you do. From personal experience.'

'*What?*'

'Well, you *were* a little girl, not so many years ago. Think back to what it was like.'

Seriema gaped at him, and took another deep swig of the brandy. 'But she hates me,' she said feebly.

'Think back,' said Presvel patiently. 'How would you have felt, suddenly waking up in a strange room – home gone, parents missing? In fact, didn't Gilarra tell you that she saw her mother killed? No wonder the poor thing became hysterical.'

'Damn it, Presvel!' Seriema scowled. 'Were you listening at the door again when I was talking to Gilarra?'

He shrugged. 'So, dismiss me. Come on, Lady – think. What did you say to the child? What did *she* say to you?'

Seriema frowned. 'Come to think of it, she didn't say anything. Not a single word! She just *glared* at me – it was so unnerving. She tried to walk and fell over, so I picked her up and put her back into bed. And she just kept on glaring

– I could *feel* her hating me.' In a single deep, fierce swig, Seriema finished the brandy. 'When I tried to give her the porridge she threw it at me, and started all that dreadful crying.' She frowned. 'Up to that point, though, she hadn't made a single sound.'

'Strange.' Presvel frowned. 'But shock can affect people in strange ways, or so I've heard. Anyway, we should go back and make sure she's all right. Considering she threw the porridge at you – and I don't blame her, by the way, it looked absolutely disgusting – she should be pretty hungry by now. Let's go and raid the kitchen. Working as I do for an unregenerate midnight nibbler, I know where the cook hides all the goodies. You know – the stuff she's been hoarding through the bad times and rationing out to us like a miser . . .'

'*Goodies?* Have you lost your wits entirely?'

Presvel sighed. 'Lady Seriema,' he said patiently, 'remember what I said about thinking back to your own childhood? When you were a little girl, did you *like* porridge?'

'Why, no. Now you come to mention it, I loathed the stuff when I was a little girl. I'm still not overly fond of it.'

'Exactly! So let's go and load ourselves up with things that she *will* like. There's no crisis in the world so desperate that it won't benefit from a nice big piece of cake.'

Seriema leaped briskly to her feet. 'Very well, Presvel – we'll do it your way. At this point, anything is worth a try.'

'You can count on me, Lady, always to have the situation under control.' Presvel smiled smugly. He had done it again. They would go upstairs and bribe the child with some sweetmeats, and this time there would be no fuss. Seriema would go to bed happy and, as usual, his standing would increase in his Lady's eyes.

'Good.' Suddenly, the usual iron was back in Seriema's voice. Presvel stiffened in alarm. When she used that tone it boded ill for someone – and this time there was no one here but himself.

'Since you have everything so well under control, *you* will go upstairs to deal with the child.' Seriema's eyes had turned flinty – Presvel recognised the danger signs. None the less, he didn't miss the sly gleam of triumph. With a sinking feeling of chagrin, he realised that she had manipulated him effortlessly and outmanoeuvred him completely. He leaped to his feet. 'What? *Me?* Take care of a *child?* All *alone?*' His voice rose to a squeak of dismay. 'But, Lady . . .'

'As you said yourself, I can always count on you – can't I?'

'But – but she's supposed to be *your* ward – surely you're coming with me?' He took a deep breath, trying to regain lost ground. 'Lady, this is a mistake. If you don't face her now, and get to know her, you'll only find it harder as time goes on.'

Lady Seriema's face turned as stony as her voice. 'That won't be a problem. I didn't get where I am today by doing my own dirty work, and this situation is no different. I'll give the child a home because I promised Gilarra, but I don't have time to start fawning over the brat. Deal with her yourself tonight. In the morning, hire a competent nursemaid. That will be all.'

She sprang to her feet. Pulling the curtain aside, she stood with her back to him, staring out of the window. 'I said that will be all.'

'Very well, Lady Seriema,' Presvel acknowledged quietly, and let himself out of the room. There were times, he knew, when it was best to shut up and do as you were told. He wouldn't have lasted as long in Seriema's service without knowing exactly, to the last inch, how far he could push her – but this time he'd miscalculated. He had seen her vengeful, wrathful, stubborn, troubled and cruel – but he had never thought he'd see the day she was afraid.

A moment later, as he hurried down to the kitchen, a smile began to grow on Presvel's face. An idea – a wonderful, marvellous, ingenious idea was forming in his mind. This is it! he thought, barely able to contain his excitement. This is how I save Rochalla and bring her to this haven of safety and comfort! If she'll consent to be the nursemaid to this child, she'll live here, and Lady Seriema will take care of her, as she takes care of all of us. She'll have good meals, and clean warm clothes, and she won't have to work and slave and wear her fingers to the bone . . .

And what about her other profession? asked the small voice in the back of her mind. You can't bring her here to this haven under the pretext of helping her and still expect her to be your whore. Presvel felt a pang of sorrow – the first of many, he knew, if he managed to carry out his plan. Unless, in the course of time, Rochalla should turn to him of her own free will, he must be content to take a benefactor's role. In any case, that might prove to be the safest course. They would have to be incredibly careful not to betray the fact that they had known each other before. Seriema would be aghast if she discovered that her nursemaid had been a Lower Town whore, and would certainly not look kindly on the former association between the girl and her assistant. Worse still, if she should discover any clandestine activities going on under her roof, her rage would know no bounds, and both Presvel and his beloved would find themselves out on the street.

*   *   *

Outside Lady Seriema's opulent home, in the storm, a new dark shape lurked among the shadows near the mansion's gateposts. As the curtain lifted at the window, sending a bar of light down on to the snow, hostile eyes watched from the darkness, looking up at the woman's face, outlined in lampglow. 'Make the most of this night, Lady Seriema,' muttered a voice, low and savage. 'For what you did to me and mine, it's going to be your last.'

Ivar watched unblinking, until the curtain fell once more. 'Don't worry – you won't die quick,' he promised. 'That would be too easy. I swear, you'll know exactly what my lifemate suffered, before you breathe your last.'

It was late when Evelinden finally let herself out of the smith's house, but at least her work was done. The homeless family were at rest now, sleeping peacefully with the help of a sedative brew. She had even managed to slip some into Agella's wine, and had stayed with her friend until she'd nodded off in the fireside chair. No doubt she'll be vexed with me when she wakes, the physician thought with a smile, but that's all right. As long as she's had a good night's sleep first, she can get as mad as she likes in the morning. As she trudged off through the snow, Evvie reflected that she might well need a sleeping draught herself tonight, after listening to that poor girl's grim tale.

With a sad shake of her head, the physician set off back towards the Inner Precincts, glad of the lamps set on tall poles between the buildings, to light her on her way. A sharp gust of wind tugged at her white mantle, and she pulled it more tightly around her. By Myrial, but it's cold tonight, she thought. She tried to quicken her pace as much as the deepening snow would let her. She was looking forward to getting home. Kaita would be waiting up for her with tea, or hot mulled wine . . .

Something heavy struck her between the shoulders, slamming her down into the ground and pinning her there. Her nose and mouth filled with choking snow, and she began to flail helplessly in panic. There was a sound of rending cloth as her mantle was torn away from her shoulders. Something gripped the back of her head, pushing her face further down into the snow to muffle her cries as agony like white-hot knives tore into her unprotected flesh.

Suddenly she was seized and turned over as easily as if she'd been a child's rag doll. Evvie caught a glimpse of the snow all round stained dark with her blood. Somewhere in the back of her brain, the physician, analytical and calm, told her there was little hope. Then she looked upon the face of her assailant – and all hope was gone. Corpse-white skin stretched tight across a narrow skull, and eyes that glowed with a feral, blood-red light. Its black lips were drawn back in a savage rictus, baring long and jagged fangs, and behind its shoulders, like a shroud of night, rose a pair of great, black wings. Dear Myrial – this was nothing human!

Then the face swooped down. In a blaze of choking agony, the fangs tore deep into her throat – and then she knew no more.

As soon as Bevron had left the room to make her the promised hot toddy, Gilarra was out of the chair and back at the window, where she stood unmoving, watching the snow come spinning down. The steep cliffs of the canyon cut off the vicious winds that she knew would be raging over the mountain above. The Sacred Precincts looked enchanting, each ledge, contour and carving on the lamplit buildings outlined by a layer of scintillating silver. A smooth white carpet covered the ground, scattered with diamond sparkles.

Softly, silently, the snow continued to fall. How soft and pretty it looks, Gilarra mused. From her vantage point inside this warm room, it looked like a blanket of thick white wool – but out on the city streets, she knew, there would be no room for such fancies. This innocuous-looking stuff was a predator, a stealthy killer in the night. Out there beyond the Sacred Precincts, the blizzard would be howling like a wolf pack through the streets. Many of the city's poor would not wake to see another day – and they might not be the only ones. A shudder passed through Gilarra as she contemplated what conditions must be like up on the mountain. If Blade and Zavahl had not found their way to shelter, it was likely that they were already dead.

And then what? In her heart, Gilarra had always harboured a secret longing to be Hierarch. Now, at last, she would achieve the power, if not the title, for many years to come – for, of course, when Zavahl died, the first two newborns, male and female, in the Precincts would be nominated to the roles of Hierarch and Suffragan. Until he had ordered the murder of the trader woman she had pitied Zavahl, but such callousness and brutality on his part had gone a long way towards easing any regret or sorrow over his death. Having watched, with increasing frustration over the last months, while Zavahl let his hold on Callisiora slip, she had been looking forward to the chance to serve her people in a more active and compassionate fashion – until the last few hours, when this storm had come sweeping down from the north and changed everything.

Now, for the first time, Gilarra had been made to understand why Zavahl's responsibilities always weighed so heavily on him. All those folk down in the city, dying in the snow.

Tomorrow their lives would be in her hands. She would be accountable – but not for long, if Blade and Zavahl did not return.

Whether Zavahl was alive or not, tomorrow was the Eve of the Dead. The people would demand a Great Sacrifice, especially now that the snow had come so early. There was no way out of it. And if Zavahl was no longer available, Gilarra was the next candidate in line.

Outside, the storm still swirled round the city. On this snowy night, the streets of Tiarond were much quieter than usual. The usual shadowy night-time denizens of these lamplit streets – whores and carousers, gamblers, cutpurses and night-soil collectors – were all safe under shelter. In the deserted Sacred Precincts, a shadowy, winged shape lifted from the blood-stained snow, and circled upwards to squat like a gargoyle on a high ledge of the Basilica. It had fed well tonight, and planned to rest here for a little, before heading home.

The creature lifted the bauble that hung swinging from the chain clutched in its taloned claw. It stared long and hard at the trophy, mesmerised by the sparkle as the red gem caught the light from the lamps below. It had taken the trinket from the body of its prey, and neither knew nor cared that the pendant with its little heart-shaped ruby was the physician's sigil, and that all the healers wore one as a mark of their profession. Among the Ak'Zahar, adornments with sparkle and glitter were greatly treasured – and this one, with its stone the colour of rich, delicious blood, was an especially precious prize.

Ah, but this was a fine place! Tonight's kill had been easy, and the creature could sense that there were many others of the same kind: more than enough life here for its purpose, hidden within these many buildings. Life. Sweet flesh. Rich blood. Soft creatures, vulnerable and weak. It looked down through slanted red eyes that could see as easily in the dark as in the daylight, and what it saw was good.

The creature had no idea what kind of lives the Tiarondians led. Such things were completely outside its experience. All it understood was the presence of warm, quivering flesh and hot blood, vibrant with life. Food! So much food, just there for the taking. This place could have been made for us, it thought.

The creature had seen enough. Spreading its leathery black wings, noiseless in the dark, it flew off in the teeth of the blizzard towards the north – over the cliffs, over the city's Sacred Precincts, and into the mountains, heading back to the source of the storm – the place where a long stretch of the Curtain Wall had disappeared.

Back to its own land, to alert the rest of the Ak'Zahar to the rich, ripe prize that lay waiting for them, ready for the taking.

TWENTY-ONE

RENEGADE

Toulac had no idea why Veldan had taken such risks and caused such a commotion – with such disastrous consequences – back at the house. At first her anger at the younger woman's foolhardy actions had flared fierce and hot, but it had soon died away as quickly as it had come. It was stupid to go shouting and ranting over something that had happened when you didn't know all the facts. Apart from that daft business with the mask, Veldan had struck her as being level-headed. Not at all the sort to go jumping around through windows in the middle of the night, taking insane risks and poking her nose where it didn't ought to be – not without good reason. Though it had better be a *damn* good reason!

Who needs a reason, Toulac? Go on – admit it. You're enjoying this! From the back of her mind came the voice of her younger self – the hardy, reckless adventurer she'd thought was dead and gone forever. What's more, it was right. Though her face was stiff and aching in the brutal cold, Toulac was suddenly suprised to find a grin there. The iron carapace of isolation and unhappiness had been shattered. She felt as though the last desolate, desperate years were being whirled away by the wild wind. The excitement of the escape had quickened her blood like a draught of strong wine. Toulac felt alive again, vigorous and younger than she had felt in years. Veldan and her strange companion had performed a miracle. At last, against all likelihood, she had been given back the adventure that she had craved so much, and never thought to see again.

Riding Kazairl was an exhilarating experience. She would never have believed a creature could move so fast across such a rough landscape of forest and rock. It took all her strength and balance to stay in place. She was thrown from side to side as the firedrake whipped his lithe body back and forth to zigzag between the close-set trees and snow, shaken loose from the upper branches by the force of their passage, dropped on her head in hard, wet clumps. Again and again, she was forced to tuck her head down or risk losing an eye as they crashed headlong through underbrush and thickets in a shower of splintered twigs.

They were not completely blind in the deep night – Veldan was carrying some kind of peculiar small, pale light, which cast a faint glimmer over the immediate surroundings – but on the whole Toulac was grateful for the darkness that hid so much of the terrain. Luckily it seemed that the firedrake's night vision was better than her own. With a swoop and a rush he would go scuttling up a rock face so steep that it was almost vertical, like a spider up a wall. Sometimes they would drop down into a hollow with a jarring thump that cracked her teeth together and threatened to drive her backbone out through the top of her skull. The only comparable experience in Toulac's life was the time, some thirty years ago or more, that she had shot the rapids of the great Tharascani River on a raft, for a bet.

At first, the warrior just let herself go and enjoyed the

experience. Everything had happened too suddenly for her to assimilate all at once, and she'd not yet had time to start worrying about the repercussions. Presently, however, she was forced to remember a truth that she had conveniently forgotten during the tedious years of her retirement. Adventure always has its price. Though she had been wearing her thick sheepskin coat when she'd escaped – she'd been wearing it ever since Blade and his men arrived – her ears and teeth ached with the cold. Warmth soaked up through her thighs from the firedrake's warm body, but she could no longer feel her feet and fingers – and she fervently wished she could no longer feel her backside, which was being battered to a pulp from all the violent bouncing about on the firedrake's hard back. In addition to her physical discomfort, there was the pain of leaving Mazal behind at the mercy of Blade's rough soldiers – but Toulac told herself that there'd be plenty of time to grieve for her old companion if it turned out to be necessary. Right now there was absolutely nothing she could do to help him, and she had other, more pressing worries, the survival of herself and Veldan being paramount.

Toulac could feel by the slump of Veldan's body that the younger woman was tiring. This was a rough ride for someone already carrying a collection of injuries. She had a feeling that Kaz was also aware of his partner's weakening condition, for he had begun to slow down, examining the terrain more carefully than before.

After a few more moments the firedrake shouldered his way through a thick tract of bramble and holly, with the two women tucked down low on his neck to protect their faces from the thorny, whipping branches. A bank dropped down steeply, and at the bottom the undergrowth thinned and died away. Veldan lifted up her small, mysterious glowing globe to reveal a small, stony hollow, barely large enough to accommodate Kazairl, with tall firs standing sentinel above and thick hollies pressing in all round. Though they still could hear the howl of the wind, its voice was muted in this sheltered place. There was no more than a thin sprinkling of snow on the ground, and Veldan's light picked up only the occasional scatter of airborne flakes spinning lazily down, dislodged from the trees above.

The firedrake coughed once or twice, as if to rid his lungs of the wind-chilled air. The two women straightened, unclenching cramped and shivering limbs and shaking snow from their hair. Stiffly, Toulac slid down. Veldan followed, stumbling as she landed. She turned to the older woman, her face a picture of dismay. 'Toulac – I'm sorry . . .'

'What a ride!' the veteran cut firmly across the attempt to apologise. 'I wouldn't have missed that for a fortune in diamonds!'

'But I've gone and got you into all this trouble,' Veldan protested wretchedly.

'Girlie, trouble's been my middle name for most of my life.' Toulac was busy untying the bundle that Veldan had brought with her. She tried to grin at the younger woman, found it impossible with a face that was frozen stiff and settled for patting her arm reassuringly instead. 'These last few years, trouble's what I've been missing. When you feel as if there's nothing left to look forward to but death, a bit of trouble comes more than welcome.' She handed Veldan her share of the extra clothing: a flannel shirt, a thick, knitted tunic coming unravelled around the hem, and a patched but sturdy leather jerkin. 'Here – put these on.'

'But thanks to me you've lost your house and everything,' Veldan insisted. Her fingers, clumsy with cold, fumbled at the buttons of the shirt. 'I don't see how you can go back now. And what about poor Mazal?'

'Girl, if you are going to go through life apologising for every damn action that you take, then you might as well slit your own throat right now,' Toulac snapped. She had the great satisfaction of seeing her companion's expression turn from distress to startlement. 'You're a warrior, supposedly. Don't act like a wet chicken! You made a decision back there and clearly, you had your reasons. Don't you go worrying about me and Mazal. The horse will be all right, I hope. Blade's men already butchered my last pig, so they won't need any extra horsemeat tonight. I'd be sad indeed to lose him, but it's too late to start fretting about him now . . .'

At this point the warrior realised that she was talking to herself. Veldan slumped back against the firedrake's flank, her eyes glazed and unseeing. Shadows leaped as the tiny, puzzling globe of light dropped from her hand into the snow. With a sharp expression of startlement, Toulac reached for her, grabbing her just before she could slide to the ground. To her dismay, the girl was barely conscious.

Kazairl whipped his head around, bellowing with alarm. 'Shut up!' Toulac hissed urgently. 'You'll give away our position to every soldier on this blasted mountain!'

'Plague on the stupid soldiers! What happened to Veldan?'

This time there was no doubting what she had heard – not with her ears, but in her mind, just as plainly as though she *had* heard each word spoken aloud. She stared at the firedrake, wide-eyed and stunned. 'I *knew* you were talking to me earlier!'

'You can *hear* me!' Even though Toulac was only listening to him with her mind, the firedrake had a distinctive voice of his own, and the gruff tones had ended in the upward lilt of astonishment. 'Most dumb humans can't,' he went on, 'and I can only hear you when you speak aloud – but never mind *that* now! Tell me what's wrong with my Veldan!'

'Of course,' Toulac said. There would be plenty of time later to marvel at such an amazing development – supposing they all got through this night. Carefully she checked the younger woman's heartbeat and breathing as best she could, with Veldan sagging in her arms like a bundle of sticks and rags. 'Here – help me prop her up against you while I get the rest of these clothes on her,' she told Kaz, 'then if I can wrap a blanket or two around her . . . I think the girl just overtaxed herself,' she went on as she worked. 'All this exertion and excitement isn't good after that crack on the head she took – and the cursed cold isn't helping at all.' She frowned. 'If only she'd had the sense to stay put in bed tonight . . .'

'Don't you dare judge her, *human*! You don't understand. She had no choice.' The firedrake's voice sounded like the snapping jaws of a steel trap in Toulac's head. Red sparks kindled in the depths of his eyes, and the veteran realised that she was treading dangerous ground. Nevertheless . . .

'Maybe I *don't* understand,' she retorted sturdily, 'but I bloody well mean to, before much longer. And if *Veldan* is no longer in any condition to tell me, *you'll* have to do it instead.' She glowered at the firedrake, who glared right back – a formidable sight, which Toulac firmly ignored. 'In the meantime, if you've finished playing silly buggers, let me get her up on your back again, and I'll guide us to a place where we can sort ourselves out in safety and in shelter.'

'And food?' Kaz asked plaintively. 'And a fire?' His tone had changed abruptly from belligerent to wistful.

Toulac grinned. 'Lots of food – I promise – and a fire for sure.'

'Then what are we waiting for, woman? I'm freezing my damned tail off here!'

'This is the place, sir.' Though the sergeant was muffled in a heavy cloak, Blade could clearly see that he wore the wary mien and rigid stance of a man who knew that his news would not be well received. He gestured out from the forest's edge, over the exposed, snowswept expanse of talus-littered rock that formed the mountainside above. 'This is where we lost the trail. It's just too dark, sir, and the men are just about frozen to death in this cold. We can't keep torches alight in the accursed gale. Even if we *could* see, the wind and snow are filling in any prints long before we can reach them.'

With an effort, Blade unclenched his jaw. Unlike that of his troops, his own night vision was excellent, but there was no point in getting angry with the men. It wasn't their fault that they had failed. This search had been ill fated from the start. Had the women been on foot, the outcome would have been different but, even in thick underbrush, a firedrake could move with alarming strength and speed when pressed, though its fierce bursts of action could not be sustained for long.

There was a brief lull in the gusting wind, and the bombardment of hard-flung snow died away momentarily. The Godsword Commander looked again at the rearing swell of boulder, cliff and scree that loomed above. The firedrake, with its powerful, low-slung build and flexible clawed feet could negotiate such terrain, but Blade knew it would be nothing short of murder to send his men up there on such a night as this, with the wind ravening like a howling, ice-fanged demon and the precipitous rocks treacherous and slick with ice and snow.

'S-sir?' The sergeant's teeth were chattering so hard that he could barely get the word out. He was hunched and miserable with cold. Blade could hear the muted plea in the man's voice, and looked behind him to the troops who were gathering by ones and twos into miserable, ragtag groups in the minimal shelter of the spindly trees at the forest's edge. Though they were afraid to disobey his orders, it was clear that they were desperately reluctant to venture out into the open on those cruelly exposed upper slopes. He nodded brusquely to the sergeant. 'Very well. Gather up the men and send them back. It looks as though we've lost our prey.'

'*Sir!*' With more enthusiasm than he had shown during this entire operation, the sergeant hurried off to round up his scattered men from the fringes of the forest. Once his sub-ordinate was out of earshot, Blade flung one vehement curse at the mountain and its escaping fugitives. To his darksight, the upper reaches of the mountain were a barren expanse of broken ground outlined in a chiaroscuro of sable and silver, pewter and pearl. One of those stretches of shadow, he knew, must conceal his prey. He couldn't hope to find them up there tonight, however – unless they should expose themselves by crossing one of the pale snowy stretches of open ground . . . He shook his head. An ex-mercenary and a Loremaster would never make such a foolish mistake. No, they could remain up there, concealed from their hunters by storm and darkness – until they froze to death.

I don't want her to die.

Unbidden, the face of the firedrake's grey-eyed rider arose in Blade's mind. *Who are you, girl? Why do you take me back to the past from which I so narrowly escaped?*

Well, there was nothing to be done now. Hopefully, the fugitives knew what they were doing. Hopefully, with the troops gone from the mountain, the firedrake would get them to shelter before the elements killed them. Hopefully, Blade would find them soon, and solve the mystery of the grey-eyed Loremaster. She must not die – but neither must she escape him, not before he had obtained some answers.

The troops had already gone, and Blade found himself standing alone at the forest's edge in the storm and darkness. The gale was picking up again, and its new-whetted edge seemed more deadly than before. Swiftly the Godsword Commander turned on his heel and followed his men back down through the forest towards food and shelter. A fierce headache was beginning to pound behind his eyes, partly from exertion in the cold, he knew, but also from anger, frustration, bewilderment and shock. In the whole of his life he had never expected to see a firedrake again. How and why, in the name of all creation, had it managed to turn up *here* – halfway up a mountain in Callisiora? Blade didn't question *where* such a creature had come from. Firedrakes were found in only one place. The land of the Magefolk. The land of his own birth. And that made its appearance tonight all the more alarming, significant – and utterly impossible.

As far as Blade knew, he was the only one to have ever escaped from the realm of the Magefolk. The Ancients, no doubt wary of such powerful beings, had surrounded their land with impenetrable boundaries that would also nullify their magic. Angry thoughts, born of an anger and frustration as old as this world, raced through his mind.

Why did the the creators of this world, whoever they may have been, bring Magefolk here, then deny them their magic? They had us caged and gelded like lowly animals! They brought us down to the most primitive of levels, and robbed us of the knowledge that we needed to advance and evolve – but they did the same to all races of this world. Towards

us, the crime was greater. They took away our entire reason
for existence, and imprisoned us behind barriers that made
the Curtain Walls look as flimsy as a piece of gauze. Then
they created the Shadowleague as gaolers to keep not only
us, but *all* the captive peoples from reaching beyond themselves, and developing to their true potential. The accursed
Shadowleague! *They call themselves Loremasters, but they are
no better than the keepers of a menagerie . . .*

Memory struck him with the force of a mailed fist. Those
were the words he had said to Cergorn, more than twenty
years ago. The words that branded him renegade, and condemned him to die a traitor's death. It had been a very near
thing – his escape, scant hours before his execution, had been
due to the courage of the only member of the Shadowleague
who knew his real origins – for the Ancients had kept the
existence of the Mages secret even from their precious sheep-
dogs – and the only one who *truly* believed in him.

Well, before Blade was finished, the whole world would
know about the Magefolk. The destruction of the Curtain
Walls was only a start. He would use the knowledge that
he gained to help him discover how to breach the stronger
barrier that held the Magefolk and suppressed their magic –
even here, so very far away. He believed he had a destiny –
that his life had been spared in order to fulfil this one great
scheme and see it through to fruition, no matter what the
cost. He had escaped to Callisiora and lain low in Tiarond
for more than twenty years, nurturing his plans, until now –
only now – had he dared to make his move at last. The world
and its denizens needed to change, to develop, to evolve – and
the end result would be worth the horrific cost in lives. Blade
was absolutely certain of one thing. Ultimately, destiny would
prove that he'd been right.

Blade strode on through the deep pinewoods, a grey and solitary figure, his thoughts far away from the darkness, the freezing wind and the snow-shrouded forest that surrounded him. Forcing the anger from his mind, he brooded instead upon the mystery of the firedrake and its rider with the oddly familiar face.

He found his way down among the crowded pines by long-developed instinct, barely seeing the underbrush and brambles through which he forced his way, or the dips and deadfalls he avoided with care and skill, and the aid of his cat-like night vision. Though he was still subliminally aware of his surroundings, all his attention was concentrated on the mysterious appearance of that creature from another life, that brought with it a crowd of memories of a land inaccessible and far away. Though it was difficult, however, Blade kept his thoughts fixed with great firmness upon the puzzle of the firedrake's appearance. That way, he would not have to think about its rider – the waif-like dark-haired girl with the piercing grey eyes, and the face that came directly from his past.

By the time Blade had returned to the old woman's house, he was more weary and drained than he had been in years. After checking with Zavahl's guard – the prisoner was either asleep or unconscious, and at this moment he could not bring himself to care which – the Godsword Commander went directly to his bed in the draughty attic room.

There, at last, he found the peace and solitude he needed to take himself back into the past, some twenty years before, when he had borne a different name in another land, and had been younger, far less wise and wary – and about to die . . .

The elements had provided a spectacular final sunset. From the high vantage of the Tower of Tidings, the sun appeared to be sinking slowly into the ferment of cloud that hovered above the Upper Lake, turning the dark shroud into a robe of glorious crimson and flame fit for a king. A fine and glorious farewell to the condemned man, Amaurn thought bitterly. Just to make me truly sorry that never again will I see the damned thing set. One last dawn is all that's left to me. That is, if I'm fortunate enough to get a final glimpse of the sun before they execute me.

At least he had managed to put Cergorn and the rest of his spineless Shadowleague bootlickers to some inconvenience. Lacking any building that resembled a prison, the Loremasters had been forced to displace the usual listeners from the Tower of Tidings and house their captive there, with enough guards on the only exit to stop a rampaging firedrake. There were advantages to being incarcerated here, however. There was an airy, open aspect to the circular tower room, with its windows looking to all four points of the compass, so that it did not feel much like a prison. Because it was normally occupied by teams of listeners who must keep their minds open at all times for any faint telepathic summons, the chamber was a model of warmth and comfort, with a generous fireplace, a heavy curtain across the doorway to keep out the draughts, thick, brocaded hangings on the curved stone walls, deep carpeting on the floor, a table for writing and dining, and soft chairs and couches designed for relaxation and comfort.

I can't imagine that Cergorn has any idea of the conditions up here, Amaurn thought wryly. He'd probably have ripped up the carpet, thrown out the couches and chairs, and made me sleep on the bare stone floor. Fortunately the tower was tall and slender, and the room in which Amaurn was being held was accessible only via a wicked corkscrew of steep and sharply twisting stairs. There was no possibility that Cergorn, with hooves instead of feet and his ungainly warhorse body, could manage such a tricky climb in so constricted a space. At least I've been spared further scorn and condemnation from the Archimandrite, Amaurn thought – not to mention an endless series of virtuous lectures about saving the wretched denizens of the world from their own innate drive towards self-destruction.

When the sun was quenched in cloud and dusk crept silently down the valley, Amaurn turned away from the window, put another log or two on the fire, and lit the candles on the table. They had brought his supper not long before, and now he uncovered the dishes to find soup, smoked trout, roast goose with vegetables and, to follow, wine-steeped woodland berries and a generous wedge of the local cheese. Amaurn applied himself to the food. In accordance with a tradition as old as the hills, his final meal was a feast indeed, and he saw no point in letting such good food go to waste. Besides, though his future seemed bleak and brief, he found it impossible to give up hope entirely. The notion of his own death seemed utterly inconceivable, and would remain so, he knew, right up to the very instant he drew his final breath. If, by some miracle, he were to escape this night, or against all odds be rescued, it wouldn't do to flee on an empty stomach.

Amaurn laughed aloud at his own folly. Sentenced to die at dawn, and still thinking of food and rescue! Well, maybe it was thus with all condemned men. He took a sip of the excellent wine, wondering why anyone would waste rare vintages on a man they planned to kill only hours later. With a shrug he lifted his goblet in a toast to Aveole – the only one who truly understood and cared for him. What were *her* thoughts tonight? If this tower was the only prison in Gendival, where had Cergorn bestowed her? Out of cruelty they had brought her to witness her lover's final humiliation today. He could remember little of the trial save Aveole's drawn face, grey and ill-looking against her crow-black hair. Though her slender body was slumped in wretchedness, her grey eyes still held a spark of defiance that none of her fellow Loremasters – not even Cergorn himself – had been able to quench.

They had held the trial in a clearing by the brink of the sinister Upper Lake, whose chill, bottomless waters were as grey and dark as the permanent overcast of lowering cloud that hung above the bleak, mountain-ringed tarn. The surroundings, framed by dark and sombre pines, were entirely suited to the occasion, Amaurn thought. Besides, such a momentous gathering, dealing with matters that affected the entire Shadowleague, must be held in the open, for the majority of the Loremasters were not of human shape. Many were too large to fit comfortably in buildings constructed on a human scale, and others, such as the Afanc and other water-dwellers, were unable to leave their own element.

So many eyes were looking at Amaurn: from the clearing, from the dark reaches of the water, from the trees and from the misty air between. The Afanc floated in position, his head held high above the water, his long green-black mane streaming down the length of his flexible, shining neck, his expression lugubrious and grave. Though the Selke and Delfini could not venture so far upriver to the inland lakes, there were several Dobarchu in the shallows, a cluster of round, furry faces whose bright, dark eyes lacked their usual merriment and mischief.

In the deeper waters, keeping a prudent distance from the shore, was a Nereid, the only representative of her kind permitted by Cergorn to attend. Though the Archimandrite, like most other air-breathers, despised and feared her kind, even *her* pale, pointed, waif-like face was cold and set with disapproval. Her siren voice was silenced, her mind, for once, on something other than luring land-dwellers to their inevitable death underwater to assuage her relentless drive for sex.

In the clearing itself, the small group of centaurs – Cergorn's lifemate and their son and daughter – were looking at Amaurn with real hatred, though he could scarcely blame them. He thanked providence that the alien, chitinous faces of Gaeorn and Alvai never altered in expression, though the glittering red eyes of the Gaeorn and the coiled-spring stances of the two great mantis-like Alvai indicated their hostility.

Some of the air-dwellers were also present. Wind-sprites were a fleeting shimmer in the corner of Amaurn's eye. Angels zigzagged lazily back and forth across the sky above the clearing, their wingspans stretching the length of two tall men. Their streamlined bodies, unsuited for hovering long in one place, swooped long-tailed and graceful as children's kites, their broad, flattened forms bearing an uncanny similarity to the ray-fish of the ocean.

The Dragonfolk, dependent as they were on powerful sunlight, rarely left the broiling desert of their homelands – but in this case they had made an exception. Their gleaming golden bodies took up the greater part of the clearing, and seemed to bring a glint of desert sun into this drear, gloomy place. To represent the Firefolk, two Dragons were present, a singular honour, Amaurn thought sourly, particularly since one of them was Chahala, the aged Seer. So many years lay upon her that her stiff old body was shading from gold to silver. Amaurn knew the long, gruelling journey must have cost her dearly, and wondered at her coming. She would die soon, he realised with a pang of sorrow, and would pass on her vast accumulation of memories to a young successor who was also possessed by the Seer's talent – or curse. As her gaze fell upon him, Amaurn thought he could detect a softer hint of sympathy for himself in her glittering ruby eye – or was it just his imagination?

For those Shadowleague members who were physically unable to attend – such as the mighty Leviathan of the ocean and the fiery, shape-shifting Salamandri in their volcano homes – the trial could be seen by means of the alseom. These globes of crystal, slightly larger than the head of a man, were remnants of the Ancients' technology (or magic) whose workings no one fully understood. Sounds and images could be passed, by some arcane means, from one globe to another: what one globe could 'see' and 'hear' would be echoed by the others, no matter how far apart they might be situated.

In those beings who could be said to have faces in the human sense of the word, all expressions were hostile, accusing, condemning. Out of the entire throng, maybe some three hundred Loremasters and Artificers, only one person was on his side – and she would be made to suffer for her loyalty, if the Archimandrite had his way. Though some of his followers were absent – facing punishments of their own, no doubt – Amaurn recognised many who once had been loud and vociferous in his support. Clearly, they had recanted when Cergorn had won the struggle and retained his high position as the Archimandrite of the Shadowleague.

It was odd, how little Amaurn could recall of what had passed at his trial. He remembered irritation at the way they spun out what was essentially such a simple matter: he had quarrelled with the Archimandrite over the basic purpose of the Shadowleague, and when Cergorn would not concede, he had recruited his own followers – not so very few, at that – and had led an insurrection that had tried to displace the leader. He would have succeeded, had the coterie of Senior Loremasters not been such a bunch of chicken-hearted cowards, preferring to lurk within the safe boundaries of custom and tradition. Only the fiery-tempered Gaeorn had been swift to back the renegade Amaurn, but had backed down just as swiftly when he found that all his fellows were against him.

Amaurn still burned with anger at the memory of Cergorn's final, condemning words to him. 'Your treachery knows no bounds. We took you in, a homeless stranger, and gave you a place among us, our shelter and our trust. In return you have plotted sedition and rebellion. You have betrayed your companions in the Shadowleague, and broken every vow you made, every oath you swore. Worse still, you have threatened the well-being of every living creature under our sun – the very individuals you were pledged to nurture and protect – by plunging this world of Myrial into anarchy and chaos!'

'Into evolution and growth, you purblind fool! *You* would keep this world swaddled in its cradle for all eternity . . .' That was all he had managed to get out before they had stopped him. Cergorn's will, reinforced by the power of the other Senior Loremasters, had clamped down on Amaurn's mind like a band of iron, clogging his throat and sealing his mouth as effectively as a gag.

Then Cergorn had pronounced the sentence. 'Amaurn, there is no denying what you have done. Your renegade notions are a danger to the entire world, and you cannot be allowed to live.' The Archimandrite took a deep breath. 'It is the will of the Senior Loremasters that you must die. Tomorrow at dawn you will be executed, in a manner of our choosing. I hope that you and your misguided followers will spend your last hours in serious contemplation of the error of your ways.'

Fleeing the memory of those words, Amaurn dragged his thoughts back to the present. He looked dazedly around the tower room, his prison, like someone newly awakened from an evil dream. His hand, holding his wine glass, began to shake. The final part of the Archimandrite's message had been unmistakable. If any of the renegade's adherents decided to perpetuate the cause of their fallen leader, they too would suffer the same fate. It was as well that the others had never known Amaurn's true identity – and that neither they, nor Cergorn had been able to guess at his ultimate goals. Only Aveole knew all his secrets and, understanding them, still supported him, believed in him, and loved him. Oh, how he needed to see her – just once more. Cergorn had already blocked any telepathic communication between Amaurn and any of his fellows, but surely even the Archimandrite would not rob a condemned man of the chance to say a last goodbye to the one who had become his soulmate? He waited, tense with longing – and yet, when she did come, she was in the room before he had the slightest hint of her approach.

She was a Loremaster, trained in stealth, and so silently did she arrive that he never even heard a footfall on the stairs. Out of nowhere there came the soft snick of a latch as his door was opened, and the heavy green curtain that hung across it blew outward in a draught. Then Aveole was in the room with him, slipping around the edge of the curtain, soft-footed and lithe as a hunting cat, as pale and silent as a wraith. For a timeless instant they regarded each other across the remains of Amaurn's supper – then he was on his feet and she was in his arms before either of them could be aware that the other had moved.

They stood there, wordless, straining together as though they were trying to meld their separate selves into a single individual; their bodies locked together in a tight embrace but their minds carefully shielded. How alike we are, Amaurn thought. Neither of us will inflict our own pain upon the other. What true soulmates we have become. He needed no words to savour the sinewy strength of the arms that embraced him, the perfume of her hair and the rough silk of her skin, patterned here and there with the silvery ridges of a warrior's scars.

For a time they drank each other in, storing memories, then, as if by some unspoken signal, they stepped apart. Aveole swung hastily away from him – Amaurn thought he glimpsed the glitter of tears on her face – and turned to look out of the window at the darkening valley beyond. A single thought leaked through her shielding. *That is my future. Nothing but darkness.*

Standing behind her, Amaurn watched with increasing pride as she mastered herself, even as he tried to quell his own overwhelming emotions. After a moment her head came up and her shoulders went back, and when she turned back to him again, her eyes were dry. 'They won't let me stay too long,' she said softly. 'For a while I thought they weren't going to let me come at all.'

From somewhere, Amaurn found a smile. 'When it comes down to a battle of wills, I'll put my money on you every time.'

'Do you think so? Then why can't I win the most important battle of all, and persuade them to spare your life?' Aveole's fists were clenched at her sides. She was beginning to tremble with the effort of holding herself under control. 'After tonight I'll never see you again.'

Though she was only a scant handful of inches shorter than

Amaurn, she looked small and vulnerable as she stood there. They had taken away her practical, comfortable Loremaster's leathers and garbed her in a shapeless white gown of some gauzy fabric that offered no protection to the dank chill of an autumn night. On her feet were flimsy slippers that would fall apart in no time on wet or stony ground. Presumably the clothing was only to keep her from running away, but the stark white of the dress leached the last bit of colour from her pallid face, making her look gaunt and ghostly. The long, loose robe gave her the appearance of a victim going to the sacrifice. From the day they had met, Amaurn had loved her, but he'd never realised just how much – until now, just before the end. It was as though his heart had been poured brimful of a warm, limpid light that cast a benison over all his deeds and days. Now, when it was too late, he regretted his confrontation with the Archimandrite. Had it not been for his pride and folly, he and Aveole would have had a future together! How he wished he could run away with her, and go somewhere – anywhere they could be alone together and safe.

Amaurn's feelings must have showed on his face. Even as he took a step towards her, Aveole darted across the room to him, moving with the customary swiftness and grace of a swordswoman born. They embraced once more, with bruising kisses that left them dizzy and gasping for breath. Then, tearing at one another's clothing, they coupled in a desperate frenzy, a wild maelstrom of love and grief, need and anger, passion and despair.

When finally they reached the calmer waters of fulfilment, Amaurn and Aveole snuggled together on one of the soft, wide couches, relaxed and drowsy, gentled and replete. Aveole cupped his face in a calloused hand, her fingers tracing the plane of his cheekbone and the curve of his jaw, committing his face to memory with deliberation and care.

'In my heart,' she whispered, 'we'll always be together like this.' And that was the way they stayed, savouring each precious moment together, until the guards came to take her away.

Aveole had been brave right to the end, refusing to sob or cling to him, and firmly holding on to her own dignity and that of her lover in the presence of the guards who had once been her Shadowleague compatriots. He had tried to give her his cloak to protect her from the raw autumn weather, but she had refused him firmly. Only later that night did he discover the reason: she'd known he would be needing the warm garment himself. Instead he gave her his ring – an heirloom of his house wrought of Mage-gold, which glittered with its own internal fire as though the metal were alive. It held sleeping powers, accessible only to one of his blood, which she could never discover or use, but that did not matter. Amaurn would need it no longer, and it was more important that she should have something to remember him by.

When it was time for the guards to escort her away, she half turned in the tower doorway, her hand extended and the gold ring gleaming on her finger like a flame. Her grey eyes were already shining with the tears that would be his only other legacy to her. That was Amaurn's last memory of Aveole. He had never seen her again – until tonight, when he had been transformed into that cold-hearted stranger, Lord Blade, and his lover's sweet face had reappeared, a scarred travesty of its former self, on another woman who had appeared from nowhere, and vanished into the storm.

TWENTY-TWO

The Tithe Caves

⁶Oh, why did I ever think that coming up here would be a good idea? I must have been mad!' Toulac made the mistake of glancing back over her shoulder. Though Veldan's weird little light globe illuminated only a few feet of space around the grey-haired warrior and she could see next to nothing in the darkness and driving snow, looking back reminded her of the fathoms of empty air that lay behind. She felt her stomach clench. Way back down there, somewhere, hidden below the treeline, was her house, and right now the old place seemed more desirable than it had in years. Longingly she thought of her bed, and her fire, and her jug of whiskey . . .

Don't be so feeble! Only yesterday you were pining for adventure, remember? The veteran gripped tighter with her knees around the firedrake's heaving sides, shifted the grip of her aching arms around Veldan's slumped body, and turned her eyes resolutely ahead, where, according to Kazairl, another three hundred yards or so of broken, bare, precipitous rock and scree stood between themselves and the top of the ridge.

'Not long now.' Even in his thoughts Kaz sounded as if he was panting, and Toulac struggled to balance their need against her guilt. After all, it had been the poor firedrake, not his riders, who'd done all the work during this stiff climb. His flanks moved in and out with each deep, rasping breath as he gulped in air to replenish his starved lungs. Taking deep breaths – more out of sympathy with the firedrake than because she had been exerting herself – Toulac looked around, but could see nothing.

'Let me try to help you.' It was the firedrake. 'At least this works for Veldan . . .'

'Myrial save us!' Suddenly, in her mind's eye, the landscape leaped into focus.

'You're seeing what I see.' Kaz sounded smug.

'Well, may I be dipped in dog's dung! Now I've seen everything!'

'Stick with me, and soon you will,' the firedrake snickered.

Toulac rubbed ice from her eyelashes and took a good look around. The high ridge they were climbing was, in effect, the shoulder of Mount Chaikar. The summit, a truncated peak, towered above her on her right-hand side. She shivered. Up here the snow was practically horizontal in a bitter, persistent wind, the kind that always seemed to haunt these high places. It found its way, with chill, prying fingers, through every layer of her threadbare old shirts and jerkins; not even the fleecy sheepskin could keep it out entirely. The cold sapped her energy, making her teeth chatter, her muscles stiffen and her bones ache fiercely. Such intense, deep chill could be doing poor Veldan no good at all. 'Are you rested yet?' she asked Kazairl. 'We shouldn't be dawdling up here.'

'I'm ready. Is Veldan still all right?'

'She's holding her own for now, I think, but the sooner we get her into shelter the better.' Even as she spoke, Toulac felt Kaz gather himself once more. 'Hold tight,' he told her. 'Here we go again!'

Toulac's head snapped back on her neck as the firedrake lurched forward in a fast, scuttling dash. His long, prehensile feet with their sharp claws dug into the stone to give him purchase, and his momentum carried him up the steeply sloping rock face like a gecko up a wall. Toulac heard the clatter and scrape of rock on rock as an avalanche of small stones, dislodged by the firedrake's progress, went slithering back down into the valley they had left behind. The firedrake halted for a moment where a fault in the face, sloping upwards at a steep angle, gave him a temporary resting place. Then, almost before Toulac had time to gather her thoughts, he was off again, dashing up and forward in one last muscle-wrenching, bone-cracking surge, with just enough power and speed to take them right to the top of the ridge.

'Well done! We made it!' Knowing that the firedrake would need to rest, Toulac took a tight hold of Veldan and slid them both to the ground, relishing the feel of solid, welcome, *level* rock that jarred against her bootsoles. She held the younger woman against her, propping her upright as best she could, trying to ignore the shakiness of her own legs, whose muscles were cramped from gripping so tightly. Veldan stirred and moaned in her arms, roused by the jolt of their landing or perhaps the renewed assault of the wind, more bitter chill and fiercer than ever here on the exposed knife edge near the mountain summit, which had had the same effect as a dousing with ice-cold water.

Kaz staggered and wheezed. 'Air, air – give me air . . .' he gasped in piteous, overly dramatic tones. Toulac leaped out of the way, pulling Veldan with her, as he folded his short, strong, sturdy legs and crashed down on to his stomach with a thud that the veteran felt right through the soles of her feet.

*　　*　　*

Roused by some inner alarm, Veldan snapped into full wakefulness as the firedrake went down. 'Kaz, what's wrong?' She struggled out of Toulac's grasp and staggered across to her recumbent partner. Kazairl lifted his head and supported her in a curve of his long neck, shifting his body a little to shield her from the wind. 'It's all right, sweetie, I'm fine. Just out of breath, from hauling you girls all the way up this accursed pile of rock. But what about you? Are *you* all right?'

The Loremaster was shivery, weak and aching all over and a savage throbbing drummed inside her skull, but she was careful to conceal most of her physical misery from her worried partner. 'I've felt better, but I'll live. Where in the blistering pits of perdition are we?'

'We're practically on top of the mountain. Your friend said she knew a good place for us to shelter – though she didn't think to mention what a difficult business it would be to get there.'

'That's right. I didn't want to put you off.' Toulac had to shout to be heard over the howling of the wind. 'And it'll be a far more difficult business getting down the other side, so we'd better be moving.'

There was something strange . . . Veldan frowned, trying to concentrate through the pounding in her head. 'Toulac? It seemed as though you understood what Kaz was saying.'

The older woman grinned at her. 'I did! How about that, girlie? When you passed out back there, Kaz and I needed to talk – and we discovered we could.'

Veldan could only gape at her, utterly stunned by her companion's unexpected talent for mind-speech. Toulac, however, was still talking. 'Come on now, Veldan. We can't mess around up here. We need to get you into shelter. You might be putting a brave face on it, but you look bloody awful to me. Kaz? Are you all right to go on now?'

'The sooner the better.'

'Come on, girl, I'll give you a leg up.' Toulac grunted with the effort as she helped hoist Veldan on to the fireddrake's back, and the Loremaster felt ashamed to need the help of someone so much older. Gritting her teeth and vowing that she'd regain her strength before much longer, she held out a hand to the veteran, who scrambled stiffly up behind her. 'At least it's all downhill from here,' Toulac said. 'Unfortunately, most of it's vertical.'

Toulac's reservations were well founded. The descent of the far side of the ridge proved a far more risky undertaking than the ascent. Wherever the ground was anything like level, they were forced to plough their way through deep drifts of snow. Mostly, however, the going varied from steep to precipitous, and the firedrake was forced to inch down carefully, zigzagging to and fro across each steep cliff face. Coming round on to Mount Chaikar's northern side, they took the full brunt of the snow-laden northerly winds. They were trying to work their way across the northern slopes and then bear round towards the eastern face, but Kaz was obliged to go wherever he could find a ledge or a foothold. The scramble down the craggy peak cost the veteran a few more grey hairs, but the firedrake's strong claws always managed to pull them up out of danger or anchor them before they could fall.

The last part of the trek was a long and toilsome battle. Even the sturdy Kaz was bitterly weary, and Veldan beginning to droop again. Toulac could feel that she'd stopped shivering – a sign, the veteran knew, that she was beginning to succumb to the deadly cold. She poked Veldan hard in the back, and felt her jerk upright again. 'Stay awake,' she bawled in the younger woman's ear. 'Just until we get there. It won't take much longer.' At least I hope not, she thought. If we don't get there soon, we probably won't make it at all.

Eventually, to Toulac's relief, they managed to pick their way round to the mountain's eastern side and struck a narrow goat-track ledge that seemed to be heading in the direction she wanted. At last she began to hope that the journey's end would soon be in sight. The vicious northern wind was at their backs now and, though it was hard to tell for sure, she thought there was something familiar about the surroundings here.

Then, to her disappointment and frustration, their progress was halted when the ledge petered out completely, with walls of smooth rock continuing for some considerable distance both above and below. To their left was a sheer drop down into a valley, far below, and to their right was a cliff as vertical and featureless as the wall of a house.

Veldan lifted her head, looked around, and cursed. Kaz made a low, angry growling noise deep in his throat. 'That's it,' he said flatly. 'We can't go any further.'

'Plague, pox and pestilence!' Toulac muttered. She could tell from his tone that the firedrake was beginning to lose faith in his guide. She thought hard for a moment. 'Kaz, can you back up a little way?'

'I hope so!' the firedrake snorted. 'It's either that, or sprout wings.' Slowly and carefully he began to shuffle backwards along the narrow ledge.

'I *know* it's around here somewhere,' Toulac muttered. In her own ears, her voice sounded slurred. She knew they didn't have much longer now. The intense cold was slowing her thinking, and her body was shutting down. She only hoped that Kazairl felt more alert than she did. This was no place to make a mistake. As he inched backwards, she held up Veldan's light to illuminate the cliff face to her right. Then she saw what she'd been looking for: a patch of darkness where no shadow should have been. 'There it is!' she yelled – just as the firedrake's hind foot slipped off the edge of the path with a rattle of sliding stones.

Suddenly the firedrake's hindquarters were teetering over the edge of the drop as he scrabbled for a foothold. Both women yelled. Toulac, holding her companion from behind, winced as Veldan's grip on her arms spasmed tight enough to bruise. With a bellow Kaz gathered himself and made a desperate lurch forward. Toulac dropped the globe and it shattered against the rock in an explosion of green-white phosphorescence. For an eternity that lasted a few heartbeats, they clung there, suspended and unmoving, on the brink of the precipice. Then, with a bone-cracking effort, the firedrake hauled himself back up on the ledge. Once he had regained his balance and his footing, there was utter silence. No one moved a muscle – except Toulac could feel how hard all three of them were shaking.

It was Veldan who finally spoke. 'There *what* is?' she asked in a quavering voice, and Toulac remembered what she had spotted just before their almost fatal slip. 'I saw it! The entrance to the caves! Just before Kaz missed his footing.' She peered blindly into the darkness. 'Oh, bugger it. I wish I hadn't dropped that light.'

'Let me look,' Kaz offered. 'Where am I looking, and for what?'

'On the rock face. There should be a darker place, a vertical shadow where a crevice angles sideways into the rock. It's hard to explain, but the cliff sort of folds over on itself to make a kind of corridor . . .'

'I think I see it.' The firedrake stretched out his long neck. Looking through his eyes, Toulac could see the shadow. He poked his nose towards the darker area, and she felt his surprise as he encountered nothing but empty space.

'Here it is at last!' Toulac cried. 'Thank Myrial for that. I was beginning to think I'd missed the place!'

'About time, too!' Kaz snorted. Moving very carefully, he squeezed between the two slabs of stone. The gap was so narrow that the two women had to tuck their legs up on his back to make room. The crevice was about twice the length of the firedrake's body, and very dark, but using Kaz's remarkable vision the veteran could just make out the blacker outline of a cavern mouth.

'Will you be able to fit in there, Kaz?' Veldan asked anxiously.

'I'd better.' Toulac was surprised by the vehemence of his reply. 'You're not leaving me behind this time, Boss. I don't care if it's a bit of a squeeze, but we're never going through *that* again.' At that instant they came to the end of the crevice and his tones changed to surprise. 'Why there's a gate here. An enormous iron gate! I just hit my nose on the wretched thing!'

'Sorry,' Toulac said. 'I should have warned you about that. Here, keep still and let me past.' Not without some difficulty she half climbed, half scrambled around Veldan and slid down the firedrake's shoulder. With stiff, clumsy fingers she rummaged in a deep shirt pocket and fished out a key, then, groping in the darkness, she ran her hands over the freezing iron of the heavily barred gate until she found the lock-plate and keyhole. It took a minute or two to fit the key inside – and then it would not turn. Toulac swore. 'Wouldn't you know! The bloody lock's frozen!'

'Maybe I can help,' Kaz said. He lowered his head down to

the lock and blew, very gently at first, then a little harder. A jet of flame spurted from his jaws and exploded against the lock-plate in a shower of sparks. Toulac leaped back with an oath, flattening herself against the crevice wall. 'Sorry,' said Kaz, a little sheepishly. The metal made soft pinging sounds as it cooled rapidly in the icy mountain air.

'Be *careful*, you clumsy great lump! You don't know your own strength, you don't,' Toulac muttered. 'It's lucky you didn't melt the whole damn mechanism. *Then* where would we be?'

'I'm *never* clumsy with my fire!' Kaz sounded hurt. 'Typical bloody humans! They've no gratitude at all . . .' He was still grumbling to himself as Toulac thrust her key into the lock and gave a sharp twist. With a shriek like souls in torment, the gate swung open.

The veteran stepped just inside the tunnel entrance and groped along the wall at about head height until she found the niche she remembered, with its tinderbox and oil lamp. She lit the lamp with shaking fingers, shielding the flame from the savage draught in the cave mouth with her body. As the lamp flickered into life the growing circle of light revealed a long tunnel, stretching away into darkness. In some parts its sides were the rough and uneven walls of a natural cavern, but in other places it was much more even and had clearly been hewn by hand.

Kaz was still waiting outside the entrance, with Veldan a hunched shape swathed in a blanket on his back. Resting the lamp back in its niche for a moment, Toulac reached up a hand to help her down. 'Come on, girlie. We're here.' Exhausted, weak and chilled to the bone, the two women staggered into the tunnel. Behind them the firedrake crept carefully along, his belly almost flat to the floor. About a dozen yards from the entrance, on the right-hand side and just where she remembered it should be, Toulac found a doorway, an open arch without a door. 'In here,' she said, fighting a ridiculous urge to whisper. 'This used to be the guardroom.'

Leaving Kaz outside, Toulac and Veldan lurched inside on their numb feet. The swinging circle of lamplight revealed a room with a generous fireplace, a table and chairs, and four bunks with threadbare curtains recessed into one wall. 'Here you are.' Toulac put the lamp down on the table, and helped Veldan into the nearest bunk.

The younger woman curled up into a shivering ball and closed her eyes. 'Just one minute,' she muttered. 'I'll just rest for a minute.'

Toulac covered Veldan with another blanket from the bunk and fought the temptation just to crawl in beside her. She felt sick and dizzy from hunger and exhaustion. Her muscles seemed to have turned to string and she felt oddly detached from the world around her, as if seeing her surroundings through a faint grey haze of mist. Resolutely she turned away from the bunk. 'Come on,' she muttered. 'Hang on just a little while longer. We've got to light the fire.'

Metal bins beside the hearth held kindling, coal and hard dry blocks of moorland peat. Toulac stacked them clumsily in the fireplace, straining to remember how to lay a fire. Then she couldn't remember in which pocket she had put the tinderbox. When she found it, she made five or six attempts to strike a light, but her hands were too numb and the flame would not catch in her badly stacked kindling and kept blowing out in the draught from the chimney. Her movements gradually became more forceful and abrupt as she began to lose her temper, until finally she struck so hard that both flint and steel striker went spinning from her shaking fingers and clattered away into the shadows. Toulac let out a despairing cry. Tears of weakness and frustration sprang into her eyes. It's hopeless, she thought despairingly. I just can't do it. Maybe I *am* too old for adventuring . . .

She had forgotten all about the firedrake. Suddenly from behind her there came a series of booming blows, followed by the crack and crash of falling stone. Kazairl, unable to fit through the guardroom doorway, had dealt with the problem in his own inimitable style. In order to enlarge the doorway to fit him, he had simply crept a little further down the passage then, twisting his sinuous neck to look back over his shoulder and take aim, he had given the stone around the edge of the doorway half a dozen sharp blows with his heavy, powerful tail.

Toulac, through a cloud of dust, saw his long body backing up again, then his head poked through the new firedrake-sized doorway. 'What in the festering pits of perdition do you think you're *doing*?' she demanded.

Kaz squeezed halfway into the chamber, shoving the table and chairs aside to make more room. He fixed her with a smoking glare. 'You promised me a fire, remember. Just because I'm not one of you *humans*, did you think I should sit out there in that draughty corridor, freezing my backside off?' He glanced worriedly at Veldan, deeply asleep on her bunk. 'Besides, I already told you. Last time was more than enough. I'm not being separated from my partner again – and *especially* not in an accursed cave!'

Before Toulac had much time to wonder what had actually happened last time, Kaz looked into the dark, dead fireplace and then at the tear streaks and the smudges on her face. 'Having trouble?' he snickered. 'Allow me.' Thrusting his snout into the fireplace, he exhaled a long, sustained burst of flame that set the heap of fuel ablaze. Flames went roaring up the chimney, and Toulac could feel the heat on her hands and face immediately. Also, she had to admit that the firedrake's body was very effective at blocking the draught from the open archway. At this rate, the room would be warm in no time.

'Not bad, eh? For a clumsy great lump,' the firedrake smirked.

'Thank you, Kaz,' she told him sincerely. 'I'm sorry I insulted your fire, and I won't ever do it again.'

Toulac threw on a few more blocks of peat and knelt by the hearth, letting the heat soak into her chilled body and staring at the hypnotic dance of the roaring flames. Oh, but she was weary, and the warming air was making her feel more drowsy. She mustn't go to sleep yet, though. Nor just yet . . . Her body slumped forward. The hearthstone made the hardest of pillows, but she scarcely noticed the discomfort. This is wrong, she thought. We need food. I must stay awake . . . Then she was asleep.

Ivar dared not sleep. He was not dressed for the freezing Tiarond night, and had eaten nothing all day. Though he had been convinced that his hatred would suffice to sustain him, he could feel his energy dwindling as the hours progressed, leached away by the merciless cold. Eventually, however, the night brought a stroke of good fortune. One of Lady Seriema's kitchen maids crept out of the house, carrying a basket, and went off in the direction of the Lower Town.

This was just as well for Ivar. His initial plan had been to get into the cellar down the coal chute, but when he tried it he had discovered that the grating was locked down into place. While sneaking around the back of the mansion, looking for another way in, he had almost run right into the maidservant, who was just letting herself out of the back kitchen door. Though she closed it behind her, there was no snick of the latch clicking into place.

Ivar, who had melted back into the shadows, felt like shouting aloud his relief. As the sound of the maid's footsteps died away, Ivar stole across the yard to the back door and waited for a moment, his ear pressed to the wood, listening hard. Not a single sound came from the kitchen now, though there had been all kinds of commotion earlier, when lamps had been lit all over the house and, from his listening post below the kitchen window, he'd heard a cook who sounded half asleep and far from happy with her lot, complaining about making porridge at this hour of the night. Now, however, all was still and silent once more, and had been for some time. Ivar decided to take his chance. He pushed the kitchen door open and stole inside, carefully wiping his snowy boots on the mat as he entered, so as not to leave a tell-tale trail of footprints behind.

The kitchen was very dark, for the fires in range and stove had been banked for the night. Groping his way along, Ivar collided with the corner of the big table, which scraped along the stone-flagged floor with a penetrating sound partway between a shriek and a groan that sounded, to the intruder, as loud as a yell in the stillness of the night.

Ivar froze like a hunted wolf, torn between the urges to flee or to attack, but ready to explode into action at the first sound of a footstep from the floor above. After a long, tense moment, he began to breathe again. He thanked providence that these houses of the rich were so big and of such solid construction, with high ceilings and good, thick walls; sound did not carry very far. He had watched the house, counting the folk who passed and repassed the windows, for so many hours now that he knew how many people were within, and where they were sleeping. There were four maids – three at the moment, since that brainless girl had gone out with her basket – and a cook. All of them must sleep in the high attic rooms, for he had seen lamplight up there earlier and counted shadows behind the blinds. The housekeeper, Seriema's assistant, and the bitch herself all slept on the floor below, in the upstairs bedrooms. That had been fairly easy to establish. Only one thing bothered him. There was clearly another room with an occupant, where a low light had been burning all evening, and earlier, at about the same time as the cook's complaints, there had been a disturbance, with folk moving about and slamming doors. That worried Ivar a little. Who was the mystery sleeper? Somebody sick? A child? But the bitch Seriema had no children, and she was too hard-hearted to be caring for someone who was sick. Anyway, it was not important now, though it might affect his plans for tomorrow.

The house was so quiet that Ivar decided to risk a candle. There wasn't much chance of someone upstairs being wakened by a light, but another loud noise such as the last might send all his plans crashing into ruin. He found a small stub of candle on the table, so small that when he lit it, the hot wax ran down and burned his fingers, but its light lasted him long enough to discover where the cook kept the household supply. He lit one new candle and pocketed another, then continued his search of the room.

The cook's fat tabby cat, clearly employed to keep down the population of rodents and black beetles but just as clearly, from its girth, the kitchen's pampered pet, blinked up at him from its warm spot on the hearthrug. A pot of porridge, with the ladle left sticking upright in the glutinous stuff, had been left on the corner of the hearth after being taken off the fire.

Its contents were still fairly warm, and Ivar spooned up great mouthfuls straight from the pot, eating with the voracity of a starving dog. He devoured about half the porridge, fairly confident that its loss would not be noticed in the morning, and then headed for the pantry, where he helped himself to bread – noting sourly that Seriema, unlike the Lower Town poor, could still get hold of flour – a chunk of white goat's milk cheese, which was all that anyone could get hold of nowadays, and a slice of cold meat pie.

Dropping his booty into one of the cook's small soup kettles, so that he could carry it easily, Ivar filled a jug with water from the pot set by the hearth and found his way down to the coal cellar, which opened out of the kitchen via a door next to the pantry. Creeping carefully down the steep stone steps, he headed for the dry end, furthest from the grating, where the firewood was kept. He made himself a concealed and cosy nest in the darkest corner, behind a large pile of logs and kindling, and settled down to rest at last. And wait.

Now that he was safe inside the house, there would be plenty of time to rest. Ivar's initial plan – to break into the house after nightfall, quietly dispatch the bitch whose bullies had raped his lifemate, get out again and take his chance – had changed with the announcement of the Great Sacrifice. All the town would be expected to attend, and it would take a very long time indeed to conduct them all through the narrow tunnel that was the only access to the Sacred Precincts. Seriema's staff, as common folk, would have to leave the house much earlier than the bitch herself – and then Ivar planned to strike. He would have more than enough time to carry out his plans for her.

The slaughterman fingered the two knives, the tools of his trade, that he had brought with him: the big, heavy knife for butchery, and the lighter, more flexible blade for skinning. Both were honed to lethal sharpness. Ivar tested the edges with an experienced thumb. I wonder how long a person would survive, he thought idly, if she were being skinned alive? Maybe it would be interesting to find out. A simple gag should smother all the screaming. Before Seriema was missed, the job would be done and he would be long gone.

In the darkness, Ivar smiled to himself. They always said, down at the slaughtering pens, that he was a master of his trade.

Twenty-three

Hope Renewed

I wonder what's happening to Veldan and Kazairl? the wind-sprite thought as she neared the sawmill on her journey back above the mountain trail. They've probably been asleep for hours, I expect. The sawmill, set back from the track, was hidden in a sheltering declivity of ground, a small valley that ran up for a little way into the forest before being lost in the steeper slopes of the screes. Though she could not see the buildings yet, Thirishri did have an unobstructed view for some distance up the trail. She had been paying little attention to the steep mountain path – for after all, who would be travelling on a night like this? Humans were a strange, irrational breed, but . . . But it seemed that they were even more irrational than she'd thought. Something was moving down there, struggling along with deadly slowness in the teeth of the howling gale.

Any hopes that the remainder of the night would pass without trouble vanished like a puff of smoke. *Now what?* Shree demanded irritably. Just when she wanted to get back up to the shelter with her good news . . . She descended a little, for a closer look. *By great Aeolius! Those look like Tormon's beasts!* By now she felt decidedly familiar with the appearance of the horses. As the trader had recounted his tale, his distress

390

had been so strong that the wind-sprite had repeatedly picked up images from his mind: visions of unusual clarity to come from a decidedly non-telepathic human. She was sure she recognised the two black giants, but it was the donkey that really settled the matter. Animals of that piebald colour were unusual in any case – and how many lowly donkeys travelled around in such magnificent company? Well, Shree thought. This is a turn-up! But how did they get here?

The wind-sprite was sorry for the trader's grief and for a joyous moment thought she must have made a mistake back at the Citadel and that she had found his missing spouse, not murdered after all. By some miracle she must have escaped, and come in search of him. Shree was just about to call to Elion, when caution prompted her to take a closer look. There was something odd about the lanky figure struggling along at the donkey's head. It didn't seem to match the image that she'd picked up from the trader's mind. Better make quite sure, before getting Tormon's hopes up too high – and besides, he'd want to know whether she was all right. And surely she wouldn't have left her child behind?

The wind-sprite swooped down towards the toiling group – and realised at once that she'd been mistaken. She thanked providence she hadn't blurted out her first impressions to Elion. This was not Tormon's lifemate! The poor trader would be devastated when his animals came back without her. As well as the disappointment there was also a puzzle. Who was this strange youth? The trader, in his account, had never mentioned any boys at all, and there had certainly been no image of this lad in his mind. Shree knew humans well, and as far as she could judge, this one seemed barely competent to be in charge of such great beasts. And why would he be bringing them up here on this dreadful night? He must be heading for the sawmill, she decided. Whether or not that had been his original plan, it was now his only hope of shelter and survival. And the sawmill was in the hands of Tormon's would-be killers. Was he in league with them – and if not, what in Aeolius's name *was* he doing, wandering around the mountains in a blizzard with someone else's livestock? One thing was for certain, he must be diverted from his intended destination . . .

All right, young human, the wind-sprite muttered. *You may not know this, but you're about to undergo a change of plan!* She sent a quick thought back to her fellow Loremaster. *Elion? Brace yourself. You'd better start enlarging that shelter . . .*

Having left her partner duly stunned and wondering how to explain the news to the trader – especially since Tormon still knew nothing about Thirishri herself – she considered her options. The boy had nearly reached the sawmill and would soon be able to see the glimmer of lamplight in the windows. Some quick distraction was needed . . . There was little she could do about the boy but, remembering her trick with Elion's chestnut, Thirishri reached out to the minds of Tormon's animals. She took the vivid image of his lifemate that she'd picked up earlier from the trader's memory and projected it into the minds of the three beasts. Suddenly the ears of the Sefrians pricked up. The weary little donkey lifted its drooping head. They could see and hear their mistress, standing further up the trail. She was calling to them, and whistling in her familiar way. In a flash the animals seemed to shake off their weariness. Bounding forward, they pulled their tethers from the hand of the unsuspecting boy and took off up the trail after the receding vision, leaving their new would-be master lying sprawled in the snow, knocked off his feet by the charging beasts. The lad let out a wail of despair and floundered after them, his feet slipping and stumbling through the churned up drifts.

Thirishri chuckled. *That should do it,* she said to herself. *I'll just slip down and blow the worst of that snow off the trail, to give them all a nice clear run.*

Scall was at the limits of his endurance. Getting himself and the horses up the mountain trail had been a fearful struggle. His troubles had begun as soon as he was out of the city and on the open road, where he had met a cart laden with human dead. Now that the graveyard was choked to overflowing, the gravediggers were trying, without much success, to burn the bodies on the open ground to the west of Tiarond, between the river and the city walls. Hindered by sodden fuel, the waterlogged ground and all the moisture in the air, the pyres did little more than smoulder and stink, thickening the air with choking, greasy smoke laden with the noxious stench of charred human flesh.

Agella's former apprentice was paying little attention to his charges. As a precaution he had fastened the horses' tethers to his belt but, now that the animals were out of the city, they seemed to have settled down, trotting obediently behind the donkey with their great hooves throwing up fountains of mud with every step. Scall, however, barely noticed the spattering he received. This dismal, dispiriting slough, with its smouldering pyres, was the perfect background for his thoughts. He was sunk in despondency as he rode along, his mind awash in a stream of doubts and fears. What's going to happen to me now? he thought. Just because the stallion took to me, it doesn't mean that I'll be any use at training horses. What if Mistress Toulac doesn't want me? Surely if she *wanted* an apprentice she would have one already? Nobody even thought to ask her. They're just casting me off like a useless piece of garbage, and hoping for the best. For ages now, Agella has been looking for a good excuse to get rid of me, and today she grabbed her chance. That's what this is all about. Because she's my aunt, she couldn't very well send me back to my mother – not that *she* wants me either. Scall sniffed, feeling very alone and woebegone. Not a single one of them wants me, he thought, and it's all because I'm *no good*. Mistress Toulac won't want me either. And if I can't control the horses she's bound to send me packing right away – and then what will become of me?

At this point, Scall had proved to himself just how bad a horseman he really was. As they neared the pyres, the animals – not that he could blame them – were becoming increasingly distressed by the stifling miasma of death. As the rising wind sent a cloud of heavy smoke rolling across the trail, the donkey snorted, sidestepped and gave a series of bucks, almost doubling her spine like a bow. For the first but by no means the last time on that miserable journey, Scall flew over her shoulder and landed with a juicy splat, face down in the mud, right under the enormous hooves of the Sefrians. For a bowel-loosening instant of pure terror, he thought he would be trampled. The two great horses, however, seemed to view his abrupt arrival as the final outrage. They snorted, plunged and then, as one, picked up those heavy feet and went charging off across the plain dragging Scall behind them, their tethers still firmly attached to his belt.

Scall ploughed face first along the slippery ground, throwing up a wave of liquid muck on either side. Mud filled his eyes, leaving him blind and helpless. He retched and spluttered, fighting for breath, as glutinous filth clogged his nose and mouth. The mud hid sharp stones and potholes in the track that battered his aching limbs as he was jolted along. A stone struck him in the mouth, and he heard the sickening crunch of a broken tooth.

The horses finally stopped running when they reached the river. They paused to drink, glancing warily around them, their black coats steaming in the chilly air. Slowly, shakily, Scall picked himself up and spat out a mouthful of bloody ooze. The next thing he did was to unfasten the tethers from his belt, though the knots had pulled so tight that he was forced to slice through the leather with his knife. The horses, their muzzles plunged deep into the cold water, took no notice, but at that moment Scall was past caring whether the misbegotten lumps of dogs' meat ran away again or not. He knelt down on the riverbank and washed the blood from his mouth and the muck from his face with icy water, though he had no objections to the blessed mud. He knew all too well that if he'd been dragged like that on stony ground, he would have been badly injured, possibly even killed.

A hard nudge in the middle of his back almost sent him flying headfirst into the river. Following her stablemates, the donkey had come back. Scall hardly knew whether he was glad or sorry. He couldn't stay here, however, and it was better to ride than to walk all the way. He hunted for some of the hard little honey-sweets in the pockets of his jerkin, in the hopes of bribing the horses into a better mood. Then, with a brief, unprecedented prayer to Myrial, he picked up the dangling tethers once more and dragged his aching bones astride the donkey's narrow back. As he headed back from the river towards the track that led up to the Snaketail Pass, the snow began to fall.

Scall soon discovered that his problems were far from over. When the gradient of the mountain trail grew steeper, the donkey decided she was no longer prepared to carry him. After being thrown from her back a dozen times and kicked, bitten and trampled for good measure, he had decided to let her have her way. But as the snow fell and the cold intensified, the going became increasingly difficult, and his progress grew slower and slower. Night fell when he was still a long way from his goal, forcing him to inch his way along, almost blind in the darkness. By this time, a full-scale blizzard was raging. Scall was frozen, exhausted and despairing, but he was too afraid to stop. Having grown up in a mountain city, he'd heard the grim tales of folk who stopped in the snow and never moved again. He kept on taking one dogged step after another, praying he'd reach shelter in time.

I can't believe any of this, Scall was thinking, as he stumbled along. When I woke up this morning, it was just a normal day. How did I get to be halfway up the mountain in the middle of a snowstorm, all alone except for two killer horses and an evil-tempered donkey, on my way to a new life with some mad old woman that I've never met? It wasn't fair. He hated everybody – the old witch Toulac, the damned donkey and the accursed horses, his mother for sending him off to be an apprentice – and most of all Mistress Agella, who had found such a rotten, callous way to get rid of him. He was trying to think of sufficiently painful fates for the lot of them when, without warning, the animals stampeded off up the trail, knocking him from his feet and leaving him flat out and dazed in the snow. To add insult to injury, the blasted donkey had trampled on him again . . . Then the true horror of the situation sank into his cold-dulled brain. The horses were getting away! Why would Mistress Toulac take him in if he turned up empty-handed? With a wail of despair he scrambled to his feet, and set off in pursuit.

*   *   *

'Your horses are coming,' Elion told Tormon. *Please, please don't ask me again how I know!* 'Better nip outside and get ready to catch them – they're on their way up the trail right now.'

The trader stared at him. 'How can you know such a thing?'

The Loremaster's heart sank. He could almost feel the slow, fierce anger kindling within Tormon, burning brighter by the moment. He could not meet the look in the trader's eyes.

'Elion, you saved my life,' Tormon growled, 'and for that reason alone I spare yours now. How could you stoop so low as to make sport—' The confrontation was interrupted by a loud whinny from the chestnut mare. Her head was turned and her ears were pricked as she listened intently. Then Tormon heard it himself – the muffled thud of hooves on the snowy path. In a flash he was out of the shelter, scrambling up through thigh-deep snow until he reached the trail itself. Elion scrambled out behind him, following him with the glim. Though the pale light threw the trader's shadow out in front of him, making it hard to see where he was putting his feet, it was better than groping around on such a black and filthy night.

Out of the darkness the Sefrians came, trailing their tethers, and Tormon called them to him. In the light of the glim, Elion could see the stunned expression on his face. He was not the only one. 'Great jumping fireballs!' the Loremaster gasped. 'I never realised horses grew so big! Where are we going to put them?'

'They're bred to be very hardy.' Tormon was forced to raise his voice, as the younger man had done, to be heard above the keening wind. 'It wouldn't be the first time they've had to stay out in the snow. There's a place down in the gully where the cliff overhangs a little, and it's fairly sheltered from the snow. Maybe we could stack up a bit of brushwood to make a windbreak. If you can spare them a mouthful or two of grain, they'll get through all right till morning.'

Though he was tempted to tell Tormon to take care of his own bloody livestock, Elion accepted the extra work in the cold without complaint. His sympathy and fellow feeling for this poor bereft man wouldn't let him do otherwise. 'Let's hurry, then,' he shouted. 'The sooner we get on with it, the quicker we'll get back into the shelter. We're freezing our backsides off out here—' His words were bitten off as a small brown and white donkey came hurtling out of the storm and nearly knocked him flat.

Tormon, with a cry of delight, caught hold of her bridle and made much of the little creature. 'She's Kanella's pet,' he began – then Elion saw his face change, and his heart went out to the trader in sympathy.

He knew that feeling. For a little while you almost forgot, then something brought the hurt back out of nowhere, like a knife in your chest. 'Come on,' he said gruffly. 'Let's sort out a place for these monsters of yours. I expect we'll find room for the little one in our own shelter.'

The Loremaster was concentrating so hard on building the cursed windbreak, so he could get back under cover himself, that he'd forgotten the horses had been accompanied. He was helping Tormon prop the fractured trunk of a slender pine to make a support, when Thirishri called to him. *Elion? Quick! The boy has gone right past you!*

Horses, boys . . . Was there no end to it? Snarling a curse, Elion left the startled Tormon fumbling in the dark. Lifting his glim high, he stumbled up the gully to the trail. There was a new line of footprints in the snow, heading uphill. 'Plague take it!' he muttered.

He hasn't gone far, Shree reassured him. *He's too exhausted.*

Elion followed the trail. It was easier for him, for he could use the furrow that had already been ploughed through the snow. Clearly, the mysterious horse thief was too far gone in exhaustion to realise that the tracks he'd been following had turned aside. The Loremaster soon caught up with his quarry. The boy was exhausted but was still stubbornly moving, crawling along the trail on hands and knees. Good for you, lad! Elion thought. You never gave in.

He grabbed the boy by the collar, hauled him upright, and ducked down to let the youngster collapse over his shoulder. Luckily it wasn't far to carry his burden, the lad was a bag of bones, and it was downhill all the way. He laid the boy down in the snow-shelter, covered him with both blankets, then poured some honey water down his throat and thrust the flask containing the remainder into his hand. 'Try to keep sipping on that,' he said. 'I'll be back shortly. Don't worry – you're all right now.' At least I hope he will be, the Loremaster thought, as he hurried back to the trader. If he can't give a good enough explanation of how he came by Tormon's animals, he might wish he had died out there on the trail.

Scall awoke to confusion. He realised that he was trembling from head to foot, but surely he had stopped shivering ages ago, during the blizzard? There had been pain, then numbness – then nothing. He noticed that the dismal howling of the wind was muted now, and he could feel the comforting weight of a blanket on his body. I suppose I must have reached the sawmill, he thought – but wouldn't there be more blankets, and a softer bed? And would the place smell so strongly of horse? He could see nothing in the darkness, but it didn't *seem* as though he'd reached the mill. Well, who cared? There was no wind here, or snow. There were blankets, and something reviving to drink. And Myrial be praised, there were no great killer beasts in his charge, or wretched donkeys with sharp teeth and hard little hooves. I don't care where I am, he thought. It's good enough for me.

Scall drowsed for a little while. When he awakened, aroused by the sound of voices, the violent shivering had abated somewhat, and there was light instead of darkness, and all around him the walls and low ceiling seemed to be made of entangled branches and twigs. There was fiery agony in his fingers, ears and toes as the feeling began to return, and he welcomed it gratefully. Anything was better than losing them through frostbite.

Two men had entered the rough shelter. One of them, the older of the pair, was wearing a thick, fleece-lined coat of black-dyed leather such as the eastern hillfolk favoured, and he had an angry, scowling face. His movements were jerky and abrupt, as though he was holding in a tremendous rage. With a chill, Scall recognised him as the trader he'd seen in the Precincts that morning, the former owner of the black horses and that blasted donkey. The other man, shaking snow from a long, dark cloak, he did not recognise.

Where am I? Scall thought. Why are these people here? He turned his throbbing head a little to the right, and realised that the two black monster horses had turned into a slender chestnut mare. The donkey, however, had somehow managed to get into the shelter, and Scall's heart sank. Luckily, the men were preoccupied with shaking the snow from their outer clothing, and settling the donkey beside the chestnut horse. They hadn't noticed yet that his eyes were open. Scall shut them quickly, afraid of the trader's pent-up rage. He recalled the apprentices' first law: *If anybody's angry, it's bound to be with you.* In any case, they were bound to want some explanations. If he feigned sleep, it might give him time to think of a way out of this predicament. In his exhausted state, however, he did not need to pretend for long. In no time at all, he was genuinely asleep.

It seemed as if Scall had only closed his eyes for an instant, then suddenly someone was hitting him in the face, over and over, with a big, hard hand. The shock of pain did more to bring him out of his cold-induced stupor than anything else so far. He squinted up through watering eyes to see the trader bending over him. The true owner of the two black horses. The man whose lifemate was— Scall let out a groan.

'Where did you get that jerkin?' The trader punctuated each word with a stinging slap. The blows increased in force each time he asked the question. 'Answer me! Where – did – you – get – that – jerkin?'

Scall knew an instant of pure terror. They were alone in the shelter. The other man had vanished – if he'd ever been there at all. There was no one to help him. Nobody to save him from his questioner's rage. He looked at the trader's face, contorted with fury and pain, and the memory of that long, canvas-wrapped bundle in the Citadel yard flashed through his mind. The man had already guessed the truth, but he looked, none the less, as if he'd blame the bearer of such dreadful tidings. *How am I going to tell him?* Scall whimpered with more than the pain of his burning face. If only the cursed man would stop hitting him for a minute, and let him think!

At that moment, he heard the other man come back into the shelter. 'On my life,' he said. 'You've got to be a brave man to try to take a leak out there tonight!' Then the light tone of his voice changed abruptly. 'Hey! Easy, Tormon, easy. Give the lad a chance. He won't be able to answer your questions if you knock his head clean off his shoulders.'

The trader kept his eyes bent with fearful concentration on Scall's battered face. 'You mind your own concerns,' he retorted harshly, lifting his arm to strike again.

A lean, brown hand came over his shoulder and caught his wrist. 'Tormon, I understand what you're going through, you know that. But remember that it was the Hierarch who led you into the ambush. This young scarecrow barely looks capable of taking the top off a boiled egg, let alone—' He bit the words off sharply.

'Murdering my wife and child,' the trader finished in a broken whisper. His shoulders slumped and the fierce light went out of his eyes.

'Let me question him,' the other said softly. 'You shouldn't be putting yourself through this, Tormon. I'll get the truth out of him, I promise.'

There was a long silence. Scall held his breath. Then, the trader shook off the other's grip, lowered his arm slowly and moved away, closer to the animals. 'All right, Elion. You get him to talk if you think you can. I hate to even look at him. But make him take off Kanella's jerkin first.' His voice thickened with tears. 'Get it away from him.'

'I will.' Suddenly, there was a new face hovering above Scall – that of a younger man, bearded and dark-haired. Scall flinched away, in fear of what would be done to him now. His head was spinning, and both sides of his face were ablaze with pain. His mouth stung where a tooth had cut through his lip, and blood from his nose was trickling down the back of his throat. He knew he was snivelling like a beaten infant, but he couldn't seem to stop himself. Suddenly the whole dreadful day came crashing down on him, and he burst into a torrent of sobs.

'Oh, great steaming cesspits!' The man gave an exasperated sigh. 'This is all we need!' Then a hand, firm but gentle, was wiping Scall's face with a cloth dipped in cold water. 'What a mess you're in,' the man muttered. 'Mud, blood, snot and tears. By all that's merciful, lad, your own mother wouldn't recognise you tonight.' He slipped an arm behind the apprentice's shoulders, half lifting him and propping him into a sitting position. 'There we are. That's better. With a nosebleed like that, you shouldn't be lying flat, or you might choke.'

'With any luck.' The trader's harsh voice came from the other side of the shelter. 'I thought you were going to get the truth out of him?'

'All in good time.' Deft hands unfastened the accursed jerkin – the garment that had landed him in this mess – and pulled off the damp, mud-caked garment. Scall was fervently glad to see the back of it, but the cold air in the fireless shelter made him shiver. A blanket was draped around his shoulders, and he snuggled gratefully into the warm wool. He mopped at his nose with his shirt sleeve and tried to take deep breaths. Finally he was getting his shameful weeping under control.

Then, without a word, his rescuer turned and left the shelter, leaving him alone with the feared trader. Scall felt the clutch of panic, but in the space of a couple of breaths, the man was back, shaking snowflakes from his shoulders and hair. 'Here.' He had taken the cloth he'd used to wipe Scall's face, and packed it with snow. He thrust it into the boy's hands. 'Hold that to your face until it all melts – and try not to soak yourself in the process. It'll stop your nosebleed and help keep the swelling down.'

He settled back on his heels, seemingly prepared to wait

until the boy was good and ready before questioning him. Though the fast-melting snow helped numb the pain so that Scall could think more clearly, he still had no idea what to say to his questioner. It would be easier trying to explain things to the younger man, that was for sure, but dealing with tragedy and death was quite outside his experience. Scall was terrified of what the trader would do when he discovered that the apprentice had profited from his spouse's death by taking her clothes. And what was worse: how did you tell a man you had seen his lifemate's corpse?

On the other hand, the last thing Scall needed was the trader getting the information out of him with more blows. This was Myrial's punishment for sure, he thought with a shudder. He had made a bargain he'd known was wrong, to obtain the property of a dead woman to which he had no right. Now he was being made to pay. He was going to have to face up to his responsibilities – because if he did not, the alternative looked as though it might be very painful. Besides, he had brought the trader's horses back to him. Surely that would count in his favour if beatings were to be handed out?

As he waited for the snow to melt, Elion looked at the youth: skinny, mud-caked and trembling, his face already turning black and blue. The Loremaster fought against pity for the lad.

Don't be ridiculous. The brat's probably a thief at best. How else could he be running round in Tormon's lifemate's clothes?

The Loremaster jumped. 'Shree, don't *do* that! Creeping up on people . . .'

*Wind-sprites don't *creep*.* Thirishri sounded affronted.

'Well, you know what I mean. Anyway, I'm glad you're here. I want to ask you a favour.'

What kind of favour? Shree asked warily.

Though he was only speaking mentally, the Loremaster took a deep breath. 'I want you not to tell Cergorn something.'

What have you done?

A blast of wind roared through the chamber, making Tormon jump up in fright. 'What was that?' he demanded.

'Just a freak draught, I expect,' Elion said aloud, and did his best to look innocent. 'Shree! Calm down. You'll have the shelter down around our ears! I haven't done anything yet – but I want to go into this boy's mind and find out what happened to Tormon's lifemate.'

What? But Elion, you know that's forbidden!

'That's exactly why I don't want Cergorn to find out. He would nail my hide to the Tower of Tidings.'

Yes, he would – after he'd thrown you out of the Shadowleague. How can you consider such a dreadful thing? Forcing your way into the minds of non-telepaths! Rummaging around. It's wrong and perverted.

'But listen, Shree,' Elion pleaded. 'The trader needs to know what happened to his family. We need to know what's going on in the city. The sooner we get at the truth the better. After what Tormon did to him, the boy's too terrified and distraught to talk. Go on,' he coaxed. 'Let me try. I know it'll be unpleasant for him, but—'

Wait! Shree interrupted. *There's no need for this. I can tell you most of what you need to know, the important parts, at any rate. I managed to trail Tormon's family down in Tiarond. Sadly, his lifemate is definitely dead, but Elion – his daughter lives! She—*

'Sir?' The boy broke into the Loremaster's thoughts. 'Sir – I didn't steal the horses, honest. And I didn't steal the jerkin, either. I know I was wrong to take it, and I'm sorry. Please don't let him hit me any more.'

Elion heard Thirishri laugh. *Well, well. There's no need to use force after all, my friend. You seem to have accomplished your goals by kindness.*

Elion was almost disappointed. To a telepath, the temptation to snoop around in unguarded minds was always there in the background. That was why such actions were strictly forbidden. For a moment, there, he'd almost had a legitimate excuse, but on reflection it was probably just as well he'd been prevented from carrying out his plan. If his deeds had ever come to light, Cergorn really *would* have thrown him out of the Shadowleague. It was far too great a risk to take, especially now he knew that Tormon's child was still alive. Now that was a piece of good news, at any rate. He wondered whether the boy really knew anything of the mother's death. Now, if only this wretch could be counted on to tell the truth, it would make life very much easier. In spite of his misgivings, he did his best to give the youth a reassuring smile. 'What's your name, boy?'

'S-Scall,' said the lad in a quavering voice that was thickened and slurred by his swollen mouth.

'Don't be afraid, Scall. My name is Elion, and I'm not going to hurt you.' He passed the water bottle across, so that the youngster could wash the blood out of his mouth. 'Now,' he said. 'Tell me how you came by those horses and, more importantly, whatever you know of the trader's lifemate.'

Scall took a deep breath, relieved that he was talking to the younger man and not the other. I'll just tell this fellow, he thought, then *he* can tell his friend. After all, it probably would be better if the dreadful news was broken through someone else. Even if the older man simply overheard him, it would be better than breaking the news directly. And then something made him look across at the trader, who sat hunched and wretched, with his arms clasped around his knees. His dour face was a mask of misery. *It's cruel to leave him in suspense, not knowing.* The realisation hit the boy like a blow. *The only decent thing to do is tell him myself.*

Levering himself to his knees, Scall shuffled across to where the trader sat, and knelt before him. 'Sir?' *Oh, dear Myrial, help me to do this!* In stumbling words, he described how he had seen the woman's body, and how Barsil the guard, while he was trying to trade the jerkin, had confirmed her identity.

Tormon gave an anguished cry and buried his face in his hands. After a moment he looked up again, his face ravaged and terrible in its grief. 'And Annas?' he whispered. 'What about my little girl?'

The apprentice shook his head. 'No, sir. I never saw nor heard anything about a child. And there was definitely only one body.'

The trader's mouth fell open. 'Do you hear that, Elion? That means there's still hope. Annas might still be alive!'

The younger man smiled at him. 'She is alive, Tormon – and again, please don't ask me how I know. Let's say I come from a family with a history of second sight, and leave it at that. Furthermore, I can tell you exactly where she is. Safe and sound, at Lady Seriema's house.'

'*What?* My Annas is alive?' Tormon let out a wild whoop of joy, and tried to jump to his feet, forgetting the low ceiling of the shelter.

Elion pulled him down again. 'Hold on, man – where are you going?'

'Back to Tiarond – at once!' The trader tried to pull his arm from his companion's grasp.

'Now hold on a minute,' Elion said firmly. 'Not in this storm, you're not. Besides, you're a wanted man in Tiarond now. You don't want to make an orphan of the poor child altogether. We'll think of a plan, and we'll go in the morning to fetch her, I promise.'

It's not so very far from morning now, Shree put in. *You humans will get some rest, if you've any sense. We have to work out a plan for tomorrow, for we daren't let the soldiers get back to Tiarond with the Hierarch. Think how difficult it would be to rescue Aethon from the city. We'll have to find a way to ambush them on the trail—*

'What? Two dozen guards?' Elion yelped. 'What do you think I am?'

I think I can take care of most of the guards, the wind-sprite told him, *the trouble is that if I deal with them in the vicinity of the Hierarch, I'm more than likely to kill him too. When I use force, it's too wild and powerful to let me pick and choose. We need to draw them off somehow, so see if you can think of some kind of diversion while I'm away. I'm going down to the sawmill now, to find out what is happening there. I want to talk to Veldan, and see if she has any suggestions. It helps to have the firedrake on our side.*

'All right,' said the Loremaster. 'Be careful, though. Don't get into any trouble.'

Wind-sprites never get into trouble, Thirishri snapped. No one had ever warned her about the human superstition of speaking too soon.

TWENTY-FOUR

AMAURN'S LEGACY

Kaz was worried. Though the room was warming up at last, he knew that the two women should not have gone to sleep before replenishing the energy their bodies had lost in fighting the deadly cold. I'd better wake Toulac, he thought. There was no hope of her hearing his mental voice as she slept, so he poked her hard with his nose. Nothing happened. She didn't even stir. And what about Veldan? By now, the firedrake was becoming deeply concerned. Twisting his head around in the cramped confines of the guardroom, he examined his partner with care. Her breathing, though steady, seemed shallow, and her body still felt icy cold to his touch. She ought to eat, he thought. Really, she should have something hot, but I couldn't manage that. Anything would do . . . Then he remembered Toulac's words, back on the mountain. *Lots of food – I promise*, she had said. Without wasting another moment, the firedrake began to back, very carefully, out of the room. If there was food in this place, he meant to find it.

As he crept down the tunnel, adjusting his vision for the darkness, Kaz wondered whether he should report their whereabouts to Thirishri. He decided against it. Who needed a nosy sprite and that stinking piece of offal Elion prying into the business of Veldan and himself? It's not as if they could be any use to us, he thought. That miserable human couldn't even get up here without my help, and what can a stupid wind-sprite do that *I* can't?

It wasn't long before the firedrake's nose told him he was on the right track. Bacon! he thought. Beef and cheese . . . What in the name of wonder *is* this place? After a time, the tunnel forked, the right-hand passageway climbing higher into the peak and the left-hand tunnel sloping down. Good smells were coming from the lower fork of the divide: herbs and spices, cheese, root vegetables and fruit. The upper tunnel, however, was more attractive to a firedrake. The mouth-watering smell drifting on the downdraught was made up of the savoury aromas of various types of meat. It took enormous self-control for Kaz to turn away from the promised feast and go the other way. He was hunting for Veldan now; the last thing his human partner wanted at the moment was raw meat.

After a few hundred yards, the lower passage opened out into a spacious, echoing chamber with walls that soared higher than Kaz's darksight could penetrate. The firedrake wasn't looking at the roof, however. He stopped dead in amazement, then began to explore with feverish haste. Food was piled everywhere he looked: crocks of butter and honey, casks of flour, sacks of root vegetables, crates of wizened apples, cheeses like great yellow wheels, and more, much more. In one corner, he found a sack of dried herbs that smelt like the strong black tea that Toulac liked to brew, and felt very pleased with himself. Just wait till the old battleaxe sees *this*, he thought. He also selected a bag of raisins, a crock of honey, and a big, round cheese – food that would give a human quick energy – and then stopped, felt foolish, and wondered how in perdition he was going to get his booty back to Veldan. Unlike human hands, with their useful thumbs, the feet of a firedrake just weren't built for picking things up.

Kazairl looked round for inspiration. 'Come on,' he muttered. 'Don't stand here wasting time – there's none to waste. Veldan needs food *now*!' After a moment's hard thinking, the solution came to him. He found one of the wooden, iron-bound casks of flour, and clawed at the end until it came off. Manipulating it clumsily, he turned it upside down to tip the flour out – then jumped back in an explosion of violent sneezes that shot random bursts of flame across the cavern, half melting several cheeses and incinerating two piles of carrots and a sack of beans. 'Great steaming centaur turds!' he swore. 'Blasted powdered grass seeds! Only humans would think of eating something so ridiculous!'

The firedrake had a dreadful time trying to juggle his chosen foodstuffs into the barrel, but between his claws and teeth he eventually managed without doing too much damage, if you overlooked the odd toothmark in the cheese. At the last minute he noticed a rack of dusty bottles in the corner. Wine? Knowing that humans, Veldan included, were fond of the ghastly stuff, he added a bottle to his supplies. Picking up the barrel delicately in his teeth, he made his way back up the tunnel to his partner and her friend.

Veldan was awakened by a hard snout poking into her shoulder, and a blast of hot, rank breath in her face. 'Kaz! Ugh!' she protested drowsily. 'That's disgusting. What in perdition's name have you been *eating*?'

The firedrake looked at her with wide-eyed innocence. 'Oh, that. Ah – I had a little snack earlier, back at Toulac's house. Heh heh.'

An image formed in Veldan's mind: two of Lord Blade's

Godsword guards being snatched away into the darkness of the forest. 'Oh Kaz! *Really!*' she scolded. 'How many times have I told you about that kind of thing? I don't know what Cergorn would say if he ever found out. You only have to be suspected of eating people, and we're in serious trouble!'

Kaz tilted his head and licked his chops in a firedrake's leering grin. 'Oh, come now, Boss. It's not that bad. Meat's meat, when all's said and done – and you know I never eat friends. Now *that* would be a disgusting habit! Besides, it *was* an emergency. We were in a dangerous situation, and I had to be ready for anything, not all weak and faint with hunger. Where do you think I got the energy to carry you ladies all the way over this hulking great mountain?' He cocked his head the other way, and his tongue flicked out again. 'I wish I hadn't promised you I'd only eat enemy warriors, though. It's *such* a chore to get them out of the chainmail.' He opened his formidable jaws. 'I haven't chipped a tooth, have I?' he asked in worried tones.

The Loremaster dissolved into hoarse and wheezy chuckles. 'Oh, you! You're incorrigible, do you know that?'

'True – but I'm charming with it. Not to mention incredibly handsome, and a good provider too. Look, sweetie, see what I've got for you. Some far better stuff to eat than enemy soldiers.'

Veldan swung her legs out of the bunk and struggled into a sitting position. An aching cold seemed to have seeped into her bones, and she was aware of a ravenous hunger. 'Right now,' she told her partner ruefully, 'I could eat an enemy soldier myself, and come back for second helpings.'

'That's my girl,' chuckled Kazairl. 'We'll make a firedrake of you yet. But I've found you something easier to eat.' He poked a wooden barrel toward her with his snout. The outside was gouged with deep toothmarks, and streaked with shiny saliva, and she wrinkled her nose.

'It's all right. I was very careful not to dribble *inside* it.'

'That's all right, Kaz. As long as there's food inside it, I'm not about to get fussy over a little bit of drool.' She plunged her arm into the open barrel up to the elbow, and began to pull out items one by one. The contents were better than a birthday and just as surprising, but the Loremaster was too preoccupied just then to bless her good fortune. She beamed at the firedrake as she stuffed down handfuls of raisins and cheese. 'Kaz – you're the best friend a girl ever had.'

Kazairl snickered, highly pleased with himself. 'That's not all, sweetie. Just wait until you see what else I found. I couldn't carry everything at once. How would some nice fried bacon go down?'

An enormous grin began to spread across Veldan's face. 'I think I must be dreaming! Kaz, if you can produce some bacon I will be your slave for life – and you can eat all the enemy soldiers you want.'

'Thanks for the thought, Boss, but if it's all the same to you, I'd rather have some bacon too.'

When the firedrake had returned to his foraging, Veldan levered herself off the bed and wrapped a blanket round her shoulders like a cloak. She built up the fire as high as she could, wondering whether she should wake poor Toulac, who was fast asleep with her head pillowed on the hearthstones. She decided against it. I'll wait until I have something hot for her to eat, the Loremaster thought. She'll have a stiff neck as it is. I can't make things any worse now.

The first thing to do was make some nice, hot tea. She hunted around the room until she found pure, cold water, in a stone cistern at the rear of the chamber, and some dusty cooking utensils at the back of a shelf. Soon a pan of water was heating at the edge of the fire. While she waited for Kaz to return, Veldan decided to contact Thirishri. She must tell the wind-sprite that Aethon, Seer of the Dragonfolk, had survived – or at least, his mind and personality lived on in the body of an unwilling human. Unfortunately for Aethon, he had picked a human who was in dire trouble himself. She remembered overhearing the cold, harsh voice of Lord Blade, as he pronounced the fate of the poor dragon's host: *'It's nothing but the mindless wreck of a human being. Our responsibility now is to keep him alive, and get him back down to Tiarond in one piece before sundown tomorrow. He'll fulfil his last role as Hierarch then, when he is sacrificed to Myrial.'*

If the Loremasters didn't take swift action, the Seer would be lost for good. Though he had been able to launch his mind out of his previous form, he would not be able to repeat the process from the body of a non-telepathic human. His only hope, as far as Veldan could see, would be to get the Seer and his human host back to the land of the Dragonfolk. Aethon's own people would know how to deal with such a difficult situation.

Veldan sighed. Why couldn't it have been a straight-forward mission this time? Just for once? Considering the near hysterical condition of Aethon's unwilling host, the Loremasters were going to have an exacting and eventful time trying to take him anywhere. *That's supposing we can manage to rescue him first,* she reminded herself. *If only the Seer could have identified himself sooner! If I could have managed to get him out of there tonight, how much easier life would have been!*

With an effort, Veldan pulled her wandering thoughts together. Easy or not, something must be done, and soon.

Finding space beside Toulac, she sat herself down cross-legged in front of the fire and stretched out her thoughts to the wind-sprite on the other side of the mountain. 'Thirishri? Are you there?'

Veldan? Are you all right? I'm on my way to the sawmill now. What's happening down there?

'Shree, I don't know how to break this to you, but we aren't down there any more. So much has happened in the last few hours, I hardly know where to start . . .'

As briefly as she could, Veldan told her fellow Loremaster what had happened in Toulac's home, how they had been forced to flee from Lord Blade and his Godswords, and how, at the very last moment, she had discovered that the essence of Aethon had survived, trapped in the body of a non-telepathic human who was a prisoner of the other men. When she brought the tale up to date, there was a long moment of silence from the wind-sprite, but when Shree finally spoke, she sounded very calm. *Veldan, you stay where you are for now. You have food and shelter, and you're in the ideal place. I'll tell Elion what has happened, then I'll go down to the sawmill and check on the situation. After that, I'll come to you.*

'Will you be able to find us in the storm?' Veldan asked doubtfully.

Don't worry. The storm is blowing itself out now, and it will soon be starting to get light, though that makes no difference to me. To the vision of a wind-sprite, you'll have left a trail across the mountain that will last for days. Don't worry. I will join you soon, and then we'll think of a way to rescue the Hierarch – and poor Aethon with him.

I admire your confidence, Thirishri, Veldan thought. I only hope you're right.

*   *   *

When the sergeant came to wake him, Blade still had not closed his eyes. Though the man apologised profusely for disturbing him, he was relieved, in a way, at the intrusion on his privacy. His thoughts did not make comfortable bedfellows, and this night had seemed as long as years. 'It's all right,' he told his subordinate. 'I haven't been asleep. Now you're here, what did you want? Is anything wrong?'

'Not wrong, sir. Not as such. I came to tell you that the blizzard's just about over. It won't be light for a while yet, but I was wondering if you wanted to make an early start, sir. If there's going to be a lull in the weather, it might be wise to take advantage of it, and get down off the mountain as quick as we can.'

Blade climbed quickly out of bed, where he had been shivering beneath the blankets despite wearing all his clothes except his boots. It's not surprising I was cold, he thought. The draught in this room seems worse than ever this morning. 'Good work, sergeant,' he said aloud. 'You're absolutely right. Tell the men to get ready to leave as soon as possible, but send a couple of them back uptrail to the landslide site to find the trader's remains. I don't like leaving unfinished business behind me. Though I doubt that a wounded man would have survived last night, I would feel much happier if we could find a body.'

'Sir?' the sergeant asked hesitantly, 'what shall we do with Mistress Toulac's horse? Do you want to take it with us? It's a good warhorse, sir, and it's not too old yet. It would be a shame to let it starve up here. What Mistress Toulac doesn't know about horseflesh just isn't worth knowing, and she seems – seemed – to think an awful lot of the beast.'

Blade looked sharply at his subordinate. 'Sergeant, you're right. Well done. She *did* think highly of it, to the point where the mad old bitch had it living in the house. I wonder if she values it enough to come back for it?'

'But sir, she'd be mad to—'

'If you ask me, the doddering old fool is half senile in any case. You never know, the animal may just be enough to tempt her back. Sergeant, select two men to stay behind – no, better make that four. Tell them to stay out of sight, and keep watch in case Toulac and her companion return. The creature they had with them must be shot – there's no safe way to capture something of that power and size – but I want those women brought back to me alive. Make absolutely sure they understand that.'

'Yes, sir,' said the sergeant without enthusiasm. 'I'll see to it at once.'

'Good.' Blade, already heading out of the door, turned back in the doorway. 'Don't waste any time, sergeant. I want to get out of this place and back to the city as soon as possible. Come and tell me when we're ready to go. I'll be talking to the Hierarch.'

The Seer of the Dragonfolk had come to the end of his patience, after a night spent trying to reason with the rightful owner of the body in which he was now incarcerated. This Zavahl – this wretched human – was impossible! Aethon, helpless and frustrated, cursed his bad luck. He couldn't make his host listen to him; the man kept raving about madness, or being possessed by demons. What passed for his mind was a seething morass of primitive fears and superstitions, a swamp of guilt and self-doubt. If that wasn't enough, he was the captive of one of the Shadowleague's worst enemies and condemned to die the following day. If I had searched the world over, the Seer thought, I couldn't have made a worse choice to carry my essence forward. Oh, *why* did this idiot have to be the only one who wandered close enough for the transfer to be made?

Why indeed? Unfortunately, though he could not seem to influence the mind, neither could Aethon detach himself from the discomfort and pain of this fragile human body. He ached from sleeplessness and thirst and hunger, and his muscles screamed with cramp from being tied all night in the same position. At no time in his life as a dragon had he ever felt as wretched as this. He was beginning to wonder whether it would not have been a better idea to have died after all. And yet still, while he continued, there must be some hope of getting out of this predicament – or so he thought, until the door opened slowly, and Aethon saw the man who now called himself Blade.

The Godsword Commander hoisted his captive up into a sitting position and propped him against the wooden head-board of the bed. Producing a flask of water strongly laced with wine, he held it to the Hierarch's lips and let him drink his fill. Zavahl gulped the welcome fluid eagerly, though Aethon, who could feel the wine warming a track all the way down to his empty belly, wondered at the wisdom of such an act. The captive was already feeling lightheaded from sleeplessness and hunger, and the wine was already making matters worse. Someone whose life hung in the balance, the dragon thought disapprovingly, should not be acting with such little regard for the consequences of his rashness.

When Zavahl had finished drinking, Blade sat down on the edge of the bed. 'That girl,' he began abruptly. 'The young woman with the scarred face, who was in here last night – what did she say to you?'

Zavahl hesitated. Aethon could feel his host's fear of saying the wrong thing. The Godsword Commander leaned forward. *'Answer me!'*

The Seer's world exploded in a blaze of pain as Blade's fist lashed out and hit Zavahl below the ribs. He doubled over, fighting for breath, but Blade grabbed his hair and pulled his head up so that he was forced to look into his captor's eyes. 'Do you want me to prove to you, at sundown, just how long it can take for a man to die?' Blade said softly.

'I . . .' Zavahl gasped. Somehow, in panic, he found enough breath to speak. 'She told me to keep quiet,' he gabbled. 'She said she'd free me if I answered her questions.'

'Oh, you accursed coward!' Aethon cried to his host. *'You craven fool! Don't tell him anything! Don't betray her to this monster!'*

Blade's eyes were boring into the Hierarch's face. 'What questions?' he demanded sharply. 'What did she ask you?'

'Don't tell him!'

'Only one,' Zavahl muttered. 'There was no time. She asked me what happened in the pass, when I saw the dragon. She knew about the demon in my mind . . .'

'Oh, you fool! You wretched fool! Don't talk about the demon! Anything but that!'

Blade nodded slowly. 'Tell me more about this demon, Zavahl. Does he speak to you?'

The Hierarch nodded. 'He called me a fool. He told me not to talk to you. Last night he told me to trust the woman.'

A cold smile spread across Blade's face. 'Well, well. Who would have thought it possible? So that's what happened to you, dragon. You can transfer to a human mind at need, and I get two captives for the price of one.'

Though he could not remember Blade, Aethon carried the memories of the Seer Chahala, his predecessor, who had attended the trial of the renegade. To the dragon's surprise, she seemed to remember Amaurn, not as the black-hearted villain that the Shadowleague described, but as a sadly misguided, rash young man, whose planned execution, though possibly necessary, had been a tragic waste.

Pain brought the Seer abruptly out of these thoughts. Blade was gripping the Hierarch's face, so hard that his fingers dug deep into the flesh, turning Zavahl's head so that the captive was forced to look into his eyes. 'I want to talk to your demon, Zavahl,' he said. 'Now. I am going to ask some questions, and *you* are going to tell me what he says. Do you understand?'

'*No! I won't speak to him! Tell him that!*'

Aethon could feel Zavahl's fear as he passed the message on. Blade's face grew very, very still, and the two minds, so different, who shared the Hierarch's body, felt the same cold clasp of fear.

The Godsword Commander spoke again, very softly. 'I think you seem to have forgotten, dragon, that you also dwell in this body now. If Zavahl feels pain, you will feel it too – and I suspect that this fragile human form will re-educate you as to the meaning of the word. I would also remind you that you can go no further now. If this body were to perish, then you would die with it. You must hold some position of authority among the Dragonfolk to be travelling with a Loremaster. Surely you have a responsibility to survive as best you can?'

'*Do you take me for a fool? I know you're going to kill this body at sunset, whether I answer you or not!*'

'No!' the Hierarch cried aloud. 'I can't tell him that! The demon won't answer you, Blade. He won't.'

Blade let go of Zavahl, and reached for the candle that stood in its holder on the table by the bed. He brought it up to his captive's face and held it there, so close that the smoke from the burning wick rose stinging into Zavahl's eyes and the heat of the flame began to redden his skin. 'Then for your sake,' he said coldly, 'the demon had better reconsider, before I start taking further steps to make him change his mind.'

Thirishri, who had followed Blade into the chamber, listened to the exchange with growing horror. She had come down to Toulac's place, counted the number of soldiers in the sawmill, and found an entry point in the roof of the house where two of the wooden shingles had been displaced. Once inside she had found herself in an attic room – and when she had seen its occupant, the shock had almost been enough to make her betray her presence.

Amaurn! After all these years, it turned out that the renegade who had vanished mysteriously on the eve of his execution had been hiding out right on Gendival's very doorstep. No wonder everything was falling apart in this land, the wind-sprite thought bitterly. *This monster spreads dissension and discord wherever he goes.* Her first thought was to contact Cergorn, but at this distance she would have to make any telepathic linkage very powerful to reach the Archimandrite. It would be almost impossible to keep her thoughts narrowed down to the private mode, and any leakage would betray her presence to Amaurn – the last thing she wanted at present. When dealing with an unprincipled blackguard such as this, even the slightest advantage was of the utmost importance.

Shree had overheard Amaurn's conversation with the sergeant and it had given her an idea. Hearing that two men were on their way up to look for Tormon's body, she passed on the news to Elion, with the suggestion that he and the trader might use the Godsword uniforms as a disguise to get into the city. It had taken some fierce arguing – why did humans have to look on the *black* side all the time? – to convince him of the sense of her plan, but she had won her way at last. Then, hoping to catch a glimpse of Amaurn's prisoner, she had followed the renegade downstairs.

She had been appalled by the beaten, ravaged appearance of the human captive. Was *this* raving wreck the only vessel Aethon could find to carry him? Worse and worse! Why, this wretch barely looked as if he'd last till sunset! Thirishri comforted herself with the realisation that if Amaurn needed the Hierarch as a sacrificial victim when the sun went down in order to further his schemes, he would make absolutely certain that the man survived that long, even supposing he had to give him the blood out of his own veins.

It's truly a pity that Amaurn is so misguided. What an Archimandrite he would have made! The unguarded thought shocked the wind-sprite to the very core. What in the name of Aeolius has come over you? she upbraided herself. You think it's a good idea to have someone so unpredictable and driven, so cunning and charismatic, in charge of the Shadowleague? Have you lost your mind? Yet, just for a moment, the thought had been so alluring that she was glad to wrench her attention back to the renegade and his tormented captive.

With deep dismay, Thirishri learned that Amaurn had deduced for himself the presence of the dragon. A thousand million plagues! That meant he would guard his prisoner all the more carefully – and if he suspected that the dragon might recognise him, he would be even more determined to slaughter Zavahl, the human host, at sunset.

He must not be allowed to learn the truth! For a wild, panic-stricken instant, she thought about killing him where he stood – but the force she'd need to use would also kill the prisoner and Aethon would perish with him. The wind-sprite's mind began to race. Maybe she could produce a diversion of some kind, without giving herself away?

To her intense relief the situation was saved by another human. An older man, thickset and weatherbeaten, entered the room. Shree recognised the sergeant again. 'Sir?' he said. 'Lord Blade? Sorry to disturb you, but you said to come and tell you when we were ready to go.'

The Commander barely glanced at him. 'Yes, yes – in a moment,' he said impatiently.

The sergeant swallowed hard. 'Begging your pardon, sir, but we don't know how long the lull in the weather is going to last. If you want to get down in time to prepare for the Great Sacrifice, it really would be advisable to go at once.'

Shree saw the angry flash of Amaurn's eyes as he put the candle down, and braced herself for the storm – but when he spoke, his voice was mild. 'Very well, sergeant. You're the expert. I'd be a fool to ignore someone born in these mountains. We'll do it your way, and get the journey over while we can.'

In spite of herself, the wind-sprite was impressed. It took a good leader to play to the strengths of his experienced men, and listen to their advice – especially when that advice went against his own wishes. But as the sergeant left the room, Amaurn turned back to back to his prisoner and shattered her grudging approval. 'Very well, dragon,' he said, 'you're reprieved for now. But think on this as we travel back to the city: the questioning is only put off. I'll have all day, until sunset, to extract the answers from you that I need.' He smiled mirthlessly at his captive. 'Come now, Hierarch. You may as well co-operate with me. Your sacrifice will not have been in vain, for when I take your place as ruler of Callisiora – as the power behind the Hierarch Gilarra, of course, though eventually *that* may change – the realm will prosper a great deal better in my hands than it ever did in yours. I have something here that will make a difference to our poor beleaguered land . . .'

At this point, had Shree possessed ears, they would have been pricking up. What had Amaurn discovered? There had never been any doubt about his cleverness. Had he found the reason for the failing Curtain Walls? Puzzled but extremely intrigued, she drifted closer.

From his pocket, Blade pulled out something square, flat and shiny. It was just big enough to fit into the palm of his hand. The wind-sprite felt the itch of curiosity. *Something that will make all the difference*, he had said. The renegade was as cunning and as tricky as a bag of rats – but how had he succeeded where all the Shadowleague had failed?

Amaurn was unfolding the tiny silver square, which grew bigger and bigger in his hands. Thirishri, deeply fascinated, inched closer. What in the world could it be? The strange item, when completely unfolded, appeared to be nothing more than a large sack of a soft, silvery fabric, smooth as frogskin, seamless, with no sign of a weave that the wind-sprite could detect. Shree sank down lower still, anger beginning to spark within her. This object had never been crafted in Callisiora. Surely it must be some artefact of the Ancients that the renegade had stolen from Gendival!

Laying the silvery object down on the bed beside him, Amaurn turned his attention back to the Hierarch. 'You see?' he said. 'Pretty, isn't it? In the bottom of that bag, my dear Hierarch, lies the salvation for all of Callisiora—'

As he was speaking, his attention elsewhere, Shree darted

down to the bed and slipped inside the sack. Just one little look—

Suddenly the bag was seized. Utter darkness fell around the wind-sprite as the neck closed tight. In panic she struggled to free herself, not caring, now, whether she betrayed her presence to Amaurn. The extent of her folly came home to her as she realised that he'd known all along that she was there – and he had snared her neatly, using her own curiosity as bait.

What *was* this accursed thing in which the renegade had trapped her? It was no ordinary bag, not from the inside, at any rate. Shree was in a place that was not merely dark; it was lightless, soundless, without boundaries she could reach. Terror seized her. She had never been completely blind before. Her array of wind-sprite senses had always found some medium or other to which they could adapt. Here, there was nothing – nothing whatsoever. Where were the sides of the bag? She floated, suspended, in complete and utter nothingness.

Faintly, Shree heard something: a voice that sounded vague and indistinct, and came from very, very far away. Her starved senses clung gratefully to the sound, but the words did not make pleasant hearing.

'Well, wind-sprite? How do you like your prison? It heartens me to see that Cergorn's spies are as inept and gullible as ever they were. You are enclosed within an artefact of *my* land now – a legacy from *my* ancestors. Ingenious, is it not? We used them for transporting awkward or heavy loads. The silver material sets up a field that moves the contents just slightly out of the reality that we know, not quite in this world but one step removed. That way, its contents weigh nothing and take up no space in the physical world until the bag is opened again. I thought you'd like to know that, since you're going to be in there for quite some time. The foreseeable future, in fact. Oh, and by the way, thoughts cannot cross the boundary between the two realities, so it's no good setting up a telepathic howl for help from your little Loremaster friends – though you're very welcome to try, if you like. After all, you won't have anything else to occupy your time.'

Thirishri loosed a blast of rage that, under normal circumstances, would have flattened an entire building. Here it had no effect whatsoever on the dark nothingness that surrounded her. There was no way out. She was utterly helpless, just when her companions would need her most. The wind-sprite seethed with anger in her prison – at Amaurn, for trapping her so neatly, but mostly at herself, for being so easily trapped.

Twenty-five

A Change of Plan

6 'Wake up, Toulac. Wake *up*!'

Toulac groaned. Despite a glorious smell of frying bacon, a sharp ache in her neck, and somebody shaking her shoulder, it was hard to open her eyes. With a wrench, she shrugged off the hand. 'Buggroff,' she muttered. 'Sleeping!'

'*Toulac!*' Somebody poked her hard in the ribs.

'*What?*' the veteran demanded crossly. Opening her eyes, she saw Veldan bending over her. '*You* should be resting!' She sat bolt upright, and there was a loud crack as two skulls knocked together.

'I've rested enough,' the younger woman told her with a rueful grimace, rubbing at her forehead. 'I'll be all right – that is, if you don't knock me out again. How do *you* feel? Kaz woke me up in the first place, because he couldn't wake you. He was worried.'

Toulac rubbed the back of her aching neck, and cursed herself for being so stupid as to fall asleep on the hearthstones. 'Nothing that a jug of whiskey and a twenty-year-old lad couldn't cure.' She gave her companion a leering grin, and they both laughed together.

'*That's* a medicine I haven't tried for a long while . . .' Veldan's laughter tailed away.

Toulac glared at her. 'I don't have to be a mind-reader to know you're worrying about that accursed scar again, you idiotic girl! I told you before – *it's not going to make any difference* – and just to prove it, as soon as all this mess is sorted out, I'm going to take you into the city and get you thoroughly laid!'

'If you can manage to do that without paying somebody for the privilege,' said Veldan bitterly, 'I'll forgive you for being such a damned old interfering busybody.'

'Less of the *old* when you're calling me a damned interfering busybody.' Toulac pointed her finger. 'And one day, my girl, I'm going to make you eat your words.'

Veldan made an obscene gesture. 'Eat some of this instead.' Pulling her sleeve down over her hand to protect it from the heat, she lifted the pan of bacon off the fire. Toulac hooked a slice out with her knife, juggling until it was cool enough to eat. 'I see you found the food, then,' she grinned.

'Kaz found it,' said Veldan with her mouth full. 'Then he roused me. He remembered you saying that there was food here somewhere, so he went to explore.' Her wan, scarred face lit up with a smile. 'Toulac, it's amazing! He said he found caves with enough provisions to feed a couple of small villages! Here—' She thrust a cup of strong black tea into Toulac's hand. 'This should please you.'

'I take it our big friend is in the upper caverns right now?' Toulac said drily.

'However did you guess?' Veldan chuckled. 'Taking his time picking out the best chunks of meat! He said everything is frozen up there – is that really true?'

Toulac nodded. 'That's why they keep it higher up. Those upper caves are above the snowline for most of the year, and they're always bloody cold. Very dry too. They keep the meat fresh for an amazingly long time.'

Veldan nodded. 'Kaz was muttering something about the first time he'd ever had to use his flame to thaw his dinner. Anyway, I told him to eat before he comes back in here. Firedrakes tend to be messy feeders.'

Toulac snagged another slice of bacon from the pan. 'Today he's not the only one.' She used her sleeve to wipe a drop of grease from her chin.

'How did you ever find this place?' Veldan asked.

The veteran shrugged. 'Oh, apart from the size of the Hierarch's prick, the tithe caves are the best-kept secret in Tiarond. I expect that's why Blade and the Hierarch and their bullies look so well fed, in comparison to the rest of us: the Sacred Precincts will be living on the contents of these caves while the rest of the city starves. Every year – apart from this year – all the farmers, hunters and fishers in Callisiora tithe to the Hierarch, and no one ever seems to wonder where all the foodstuffs go. I never used to think about it myself, but years ago, when I was about your age and in the Godswords, I was promoted on to the tithe cave guards. There aren't many of them, and they don't do anything else. The job is child's play, a real easy assignment, but they have to swear elaborate oaths of secrecy. If word of this place should ever get out, the guards are left in no doubt that they – and their families – will be losing various bits of their anatomy. This isn't the main entrance, by the way. A tunnel down from the lower caverns leads right into the back of the Temple itself, and that's the part that's mainly guarded. In the winter they don't bother to come up here much. The upper entrance is hidden, difficult to reach and, as you saw, it is barred with a bloody great iron gate. Only Blade and the Hierarch have keys.'

'So how did you get hold of one?'

Toulac shrugged. 'Well, I was a happy, loyal little Godsword soldier until that son of a bitch Blade took over the leadership, and decided, for some reason, to get rid of all the women. At that time I was the only female on the tithe cave guard, and I could see which way the wind was blowing. That bastard couldn't let a disgruntled ex-soldier bearing grievances go wandering off with such a vital secret, could he? I realised that I couldn't wait until the women guards were officially disbanded. Before that happened, I would just quietly "disappear" one day. So I "disappeared" through my own choice instead. I fled Tiarond, and spent years away as a mercenary among the hill clans . . .'

'But what about the key?' Veldan interrupted.

'What? Oh, that. I stole it from Blade before I left, had it copied by a blacksmith and put it back. He was never any the wiser. I always knew it would come in useful one day.'

'But however did you manage to steal it? He must have guarded something like that very carefully.'

Toulac glared at her. 'Well, if you *must* know, I disguised myself as one of the scrubbing women who clean the inside of the Citadel. It took days of snooping to find out where he kept the thing, and a lot longer than that before I could think of a way to steal it. Still, all that hard work and self-sacrifice has paid off this winter – and all these years I've had the pleasure of knowing that I put one over on the arrogant bastard.'

His knees knocking, Scall waited with the horses and an irritable, shivering donkey on the trail above the landslide. According to Elion – though Myrial only knew how he'd come by the information – two Godsword soldiers would be coming up the trail any moment now. He looked nervously behind him at the rigid body of the monstrous creature Elion and Tormon had dug partially out of the snow. A shiver went through his body that had nothing to do with the chill of the mountain air.

He *knew* it was dead of course, but it was so terrifyingly big, and why did it look as though it might move at any second?

It was almost a relief when the Godsword soldiers finally came riding into view around the bend in the trail. Scall took a deep breath. 'Help!' he screamed. *Oh Myrial – please don't let them ask me what I'm doing here!* 'Sirs – help. It's still alive! It isn't dead! I saw it breathing! Come quick and see!'

He saw the two Godswords exchange a swift glance. Their mouths had dropped open in astonishment, but they were also frowning – whether in concern, confusion or both, Scall had no idea. As one they leaped from their horses and came running.

'Quick, sirs – look! Look!' he shouted, pointing at the dragon. 'It blinked its eye!'

The two guards ran up to the boy. One bent to examine the rigid monster, which was all well and good, and according to plan, but the other grabbed Scall by the arm and jerked him around. 'Who the bloody blazes are you?' he demanded. 'Where did you come from? And what are you doing with Lord Blade's horses? Answer me, boy!'

'The stablemaster sent me—' Scall gasped.

A hard hand impacted with his ear. 'Don't lie to me, boy!' The guard raised his hand again but, before he could strike, a figure erupted from a pile of brushwood next to the track and, using a hefty branch as a cudgel, hit the guard on the back of the helmet with considerable force. The Godsword crumpled. On Scall's other side, the second soldier was receiving the same treatment from Elion. Tormon stooped over the fallen man, put his hands around his throat, and squeezed. After a short time the man thrashed, and then was still. The trader looked down on him dispassionately.

Scall stared at the corpse for a moment, then turned away hastily, only to see Elion meting out the same treatment to the other guard. He ran a little way up the track, and vomited profusely. After a moment, when the spasms were over, he felt a hand on his shoulder. Tormon stood there, offering him a cleanish cloth that had been damped with water. 'Here – wipe your face on that.'

Scall took the cloth from him, but could find nothing to say. His head was ringing from the guard's blow, but his empty stomach still felt as though it wanted to vomit.

The trader looked at him, and shrugged. 'No, lad – I don't know how I did it either. I never thought I would be able to kill a man like that, in cold blood. Annas and Kanella were almost enough of a reason, but there was still that little bit of hesitation, that shadow of doubt. When he hit you, though, for no reason at all – well, that finally tipped the balance. After that, it was a bit like squashing a wasp.'

Tormon patted Scall on the shoulder. 'I think I felt it so badly because that was me, last night. In the way he treated you, I saw myself. I'm sorry, son, deeply sorry. I wasn't in my right mind last night, and that's my only excuse. And if I can find a way to make it up to you, I promise that I will.'

'I – thank you.' Scall didn't know quite what to say. He remembered how afraid he had been of the tormented madman who had attacked him last night. He looked into Tormon's plain, lined, comfortingly ordinary face, and saw a good and honest man, who had strayed into matters that had raced out of his control – just like when the two black horses ran away with me, Scall thought. He remembered the feelings – the helplessness, the terror and the pain. Suddenly he realised that he and the trader were the same now. Both were caught up in a raging torrent of events; both of them, having already lost everything that was familiar and dear to them, were struggling just to keep afloat and to survive.

On impulse, Scall held out his hand to Tormon. 'I'll help you find your little girl,' he said. 'I'll help you in any way I can.'

Elion was wondering what had become of Shree. She had gone to find out what was happening at the sawmill, but that had been ages ago. In the meantime, he, Tormon and Scall had breakfasted on trail rations and cared for the animals, including Tormon's two huge Sefrians, who seemed to have weathered the night with nothing worse than a little stiffness in their gait and a ravenous hunger for the small amount of grain in Elion's saddlebags.

Shree had contacted him once, with her wild idea of ambushing the guards. After a lively argument over the matter, she had won her way and, much to his amazement, it had worked – so far. But here they were, he and Tormon, dressed up in mail shirts and helmets and long black cloaks. As he had expected, the breeches had not stood a chance of fitting, but as he and the trader were both wearing dark-coloured pants in any case, they stood a chance of getting away with it – if no one looked too closely. But when the Loremaster had attempted to contact the wind-sprite to tell her of her plan's success and ask her about the ambush that was still to come when Blade and the Hierarch headed down the mountain, he could get no answer, no matter how hard he tried. What was worse, he could feel no sense of her presence when he reached for her. It was as if she were dead – or had never existed.

With great reluctance, Elion decided to contact his fellow Loremaster. Maybe Veldan knew something he did not.

Veldan was having the most thorough wash that she could manage with a basin of warm water, while at the same time laughing helplessly at one of the veteran's more racy anecdotes.

Toulac never ceases to surprise me, she thought, as she towelled herself dry on an old blanket and put her clothes back on. If only she had been discovered when she was younger. What a wonderful member of the Shadowleague she would have made! Well, maybe it's not too late. Younger Loremasters would benefit from her experience and wisdom – and I intend to plague the life out of the Archimandrite until he finds her a place.

'Veldan? Have you lost your mind? You're actually planning to take this outsider – this doddering old *human* – back to Gendival with us?'

Veldan's chin came up. 'Shut up, Elion – who asked *you*? Though I may say, it's typical to find you eavesdropping on my private thoughts like the ill-mannered sneak that you are. I'll take all responsibility for this – not that it's any of your business. What's your problem with humans, suddenly? You're one – or you were last time I looked, and so was your partner—'

'Don't you dare drag Melnyth into this!'

'Then don't *you* malign my friends! Toulac *is* my friend, and there's nothing doddering about her, believe me. I'm right about her, I know it. She deserves to go back to Gendival. She's a listening telepath, at least, even if she hasn't learned to send yet, so she qualifies. She saved my life. On my oath, she can be trusted with our secrets. She's sensible and wise, and experienced in the ways of war. She knows the local situation far better than we do. She's helped and sheltered us; she doesn't deserve to be lied to. Besides, she's already *seen* Kaz. I think she's worked out by now that we aren't exactly from around here! We're safer if we include her – and besides, I owe her that much and more.'

'Veldan's right.' Kaz, who had come back from his feeding, filled the gap where the doorway once had been. 'The old battleaxe may be getting a bit long in the tooth, but she'd make a wonderful Loremaster. Better than some craven, snivelling streaks of misery that I know.' He growled, deep in his throat. 'When did *you* get here?'

'Just now. Just in time to catch Veldan thinking thoughts that were both unguarded and unwise.'

Veldan clenched her fists. 'I'll be the judge of that!' she snapped. 'What do you want, anyway?'

Elion dropped his mind-voice to a more conciliatory tone. 'Is Shree with you?'

'No – she said she was coming up here after she'd been to the sawmill, but she never did.'

'Will you try to contact her, you and Kaz? I can't seem to reach her, no matter what I do, and I'm getting worried.'

'Oh, I wouldn't worry about Shree. I mean, what could possibly happen to a wind-sprite? They must be just about indestructible. She's probably just preoccupied with something.'

'But we were supposed to be setting up an ambush for Blade—'

'You were *what?*' Veldan felt as though he had hit her with a shovel. 'An ambush? On the mountain trail? In other words, without me and Kaz?'

'Well – yes.' Elion suddenly sounded wary.

A sense of bitter betrayal flooded through Veldan, followed by the fireflash of anger. 'So you don't trust me any more, is that it?' she blazed. 'You think I'm no good, don't you? That I'll muck it up again! You bastard. How *dare* you! You just come prancing along, you take over my mission, then you start to plot to exclude me completely . . .'

'No, it's not that,' Elion said hastily. 'Have some sense, Veldan, you're on the wrong side of the bloody mountain! Blade and his prisoner will be leaving the sawmill soon – how could you possibly get here in time? This implies no failure on your part, I promise. There'll be other missions.'

'But Shree actually *told* me to stay here when she talked to me earlier!' Veldan cried. 'If she'd warned me then, there might have been a chance—'

'Come on, now, girlie,' Toulac interrupted, breaking verbally into the Loremaster's tirade of thoughts. Though she could not join in telepathically, she must have been listening to the exchange. 'He's right, you know. Even with Kaz's turn of speed, you'd have had an awful job getting all the way over there in time. And even if you'd managed it, you would both have been exhausted and in no fit state to fight. Maybe this Shree, whoever she is, was doing you a favour. Give yourself a chance, you blockhead! Only two days ago you were tangling with a landslide! Let somebody else do the bloody work for a change!'

Veldan took a slow, deep breath, and forced herself to calm down. Reluctant though she was to admit it, Toulac was right. Besides, this mission was in enough trouble without any more quarrels among the Loremasters. 'All right, Elion,' she said, 'I take your point – on the advice of the human outsider that you were maligning.'

'*What?* You mean she was listening to all that?'

'I told you she was a receiving telepath. You should be more careful about what you say behind people's backs.'

'She heard me call her an outsider, and a—'

'Doddering old human,' said Toulac grimly. 'Oh, yes, I heard *that* bit all right – and I won't forget it in a hurry, either, you can tell him. I can't wait until I finally get to meet this arrogant young pup. No wonder you hate his guts.'

'She heard you, Elion,' Veldan told him. 'I'll let you imagine for yourself how pleased she is.'

'Well, I apologise then, but never mind that now. Veldan, I'm sure there's something wrong. Thirishri shouldn't be out of communication like this.'

The Loremaster frowned. 'Well, I thought you were over-reacting at first, but on reflection, I believe you're right. This is not like Shree at all.'

'Well, what are we going to do? And what about Aethon? I can't manage this ambush on my own. I accomplished the first part of Shree's plan all right. She wanted us – Tormon and myself – to ambush the guards who were sent back up to find his body, and disguise ourselves in their uniforms so we could get close to Blade's troop without arousing suspicion. We're ready now, uniforms and all, but without word from Thirishri I don't even know when the Godswords are leaving the sawmill. They're probably gone by now. Besides, without Shree, we're far too badly outnumbered. I either need her help or yours – both you and Kaz – and now I don't have either.'

'May a doddering old human make a suggestion?' Toulac piped up in acid tones.

'Please do,' said Veldan. 'Just let me pass the word to Elion, then I'll send him the rest as you go along.'

Her fellow Loremaster was past making objections. 'At this point,' he said glumly, 'I'm so desperate I'll listen to anything.'

Toulac scowled. 'Myrial up a tree,' she muttered. 'I can't *wait* to meet this high-and-mighty young upstart. It's going to be a pleasure to teach him a few manners.'

Veldan grinned. 'You want me to repeat that?'

Toulac chuckled. 'No, you needn't bother. It'll be more fun if it comes as a surprise.' Then her face grew serious once more. 'Right – let's get on with this. This plan gives us more time than an ambush on the trail, but it'll take us longer to get into position, and we don't have all day.' She took a deep breath.

'Elion, at least your Godsword uniforms will come in handy after all. Veldan, do you remember me telling you that these lower tunnels actually came out in the back of the Temple? Well, here's my plan . . .'

Elion, sitting in his shelter for privacy, listened as Veldan passed on the details of Toulac's scheme. 'You must be insane!' he said at last. 'Both of you! Attempt a rescue from the middle of the enemy's stronghold? We'd be walking straight into a trap!'

'It wouldn't be a trap,' Veldan objected. 'We'd have the advantage of surprise. They would never expect to find an enemy coming out of the Temple! Then if you can create some kind of diversion to buy us just a minute or two, Kaz and I can take the Hierarch away up through the caves. You know how fast Kaz can move when he gets going—'

'Faster than a crossbow bolt?'

Ignoring him, Veldan ploughed ahead. 'I know he can only flame them once, but that'll teach them to stay back. Then, when we get out at the other end—'

'*If*, you mean!'

'*When* we get out at the other end, we can escape over the top of the mountain, where they can't follow, and make our way across the pass to Gendival.'

'Right. Which only leaves *me* at the mercy of the Godsword Commander, the new Hierarch and a howling mob. How nice of you to remember me. All I have to do is get out of the city without being discovered and put to the sword, make my way right up to the pass without anybody noticing, and I'll be home and dry. What about if I go over the mountain and *you* stay behind in the bloody city?'

'In your dreams, slime-bag,' growled Kazairl.

Elion could sense that Veldan was keeping her temper with

difficulty. 'Well, we're all waiting here with bated breath to hear your better suggestions,' she told him with poisonous sweetness.

Elion clenched his fists, ground his teeth, and swore. Why, if only he could get his hands on that scrawny bitch right now . . .

'I don't have any better suggestions,' he said at last. 'As well you know. All right – you win. I'll let Tormon know what's happening, and then we'll start heading slowly down. We don't want to run into Blade and his troops right now. Let me know at once if you hear anything from Thirishri, won't you? If she turns up, maybe she'll be able to find us a way out of this insanity.'

'Don't worry – I'm not exactly ecstatic about this plan myself, even though it *is* the best we can come up with . . . Elion?'

He wondered at her hesitation.

'Yes?' he answered warily.

'Toulac just asked me who Thirishri is. I'm going to tell her. I'm going to tell her everything.'

'*Veldan!* What in perdition are you *doing?*' Elion yelped. 'You can't do that! You know it's strictly against Shadowleague law . . .' His voice tailed away as he remembered the conversation, so similar, that he'd had with the wind-sprite the previous night, when he had wanted to rummage in Scall's unprotected mind. *Is this any worse?* prompted an inner voice. *Not really . . . On the contrary, in fact. It doesn't seem so bad.*

'Oh, very well then,' he said. 'Tell her everything, if you think it will help. I don't have time to argue with you all day. It's Cergorn's job to discipline you, not mine.'

'I'll talk him round somehow – I hope!' Veldan sounded relieved. 'In the meantime, it'll make things a whole lot easier, you'll see.'

'I'll talk to you later then, when we've made it down the

trail.' Elion couldn't wait to be rid of her. Before he could break the contact, however, he heard her beginning to talk to the old woman, rehearsing the words in her mind before she said them aloud.

'You see, Toulac, the boundaries of Callisiora – what we call the Curtain Walls – they aren't really the end of the world at all. Beyond this land there are other realms, a goodly number, inhabited by all kinds of strange beings,' Veldan continued. 'Some of them would make Kaz look very ordinary indeed. We believe that the world was created long ago by an ancient race who possessed tremendous knowledge and power far beyond our understanding . . .'

Unable to contain his disgust, Elion broke off contact quickly. How could she do this? Betray the Shadowleague's most precious secrets to a simple, gullible old crone from this accursed, benighted land of superstitious primitives! Unable to contain his disgust, he stood up abruptly, meaning to go outside, but a light touch on his mind stopped him in his tracks: Veldan's laughter. She was not bothering to shield her thoughts, and he could feel her delight at Toulac's reaction to the existence of the wind-sprite. All at once, he found himself grinding his teeth.

Veldan. I hate that woman. What right has she to sit there, laughing with a stranger? What right had she to survive something so terrible as that landslide? How did she do that? It's not fair! What right has she to be alive when Melnyth is dead? I hate her for being alive.

Elion sank back to the ground, shocked by the violence of his own feelings. For the first time since Melnyth's death he caught a glimpse of the savage, bitter, desperate creature he had become. Shaken by this revelation of the morass within his soul, he sat alone in the dark, with tears for his lost partner running down his face. After a time he crawled to the entrance of the shelter and knelt there, taking deep breaths of icy mountain air, as if hoping that his internal darkness could be flushed out by each clean, sharp inhalation. After a moment, when he felt calmer, he faced himself with resolution. *Are you truly sorry Veldan survived the landslide, after Melnyth perished in the labyrinth of the Ak'Zahar?* he asked himself. *Would it really make you feel any better if* both *of them were dead, instead of only one?*

No. In pity's name – of course not! Veldan has been damaged enough by what happened that dreadful day. We all have. Elion was surprised to discover that he did truly feel pity for her. Today had been the first time he had spoken to her for any length of time since Kaz had somehow brought them home from the caverns of the Ak'Zahar, a nightmare journey of which he had very little recollection. Today, he had sneaked a peek at her through the firedrake's eyes, and had been appalled by her pallid face and scarecrow body, not to mention the new abrasions and bruises she had received in the slide. Nevertheless, he understood now that his pity didn't change a thing.

If Veldan's death would bring Melnyth back to me – if somehow I could trade one for the other – I would take her life with my own two hands.

'Rest in peace, little Derla,' Rochalla whispered. 'If I could give my life to bring you back, you know I would, but maybe you're better off where you are. At least you aren't sick and cold and hungry any more . . .'

'I'm sorry, lassie, but it's the best I can do.' The gravedigger interrupted her thoughts. 'You can see how it is. We're too near the river here – the ground is waterlogged before we start . . .'

Rochalla turned away from the shallow grave, where the pristine snow was scarred with the gaping wound of muddy earth. The child's body, pitifully small in its wrapping of a ragged old blanket, weighed almost nothing in her arms. She clutched her little sister tightly, unable to bear the thought of her all alone in the cold, muddy water in the bottom of the hole. Unfortunately, she had no choice. 'It'll do,' she said dully, and took a deep breath to steady herself. Closing her eyes, she lowered the little body into the grave, flinching from the touch of the cold, dirty water. 'Goodbye, Derla,' she whispered.

Wiping her hands on her skirt, she turned back to the gravedigger and gave him a generous handful of coins, all the money that Presvel had given her the previous night. 'My thanks to you. I know you did your best, and it's better by far than those stinking pyres. I couldn't bear to think of her out there.'

The gravedigger nodded. 'Go well, lass,' he said softly.

Rochalla shook her head. 'Who can go well, these days?' With tears blurring her vision, she turned and walked away from the grave, refusing to look back.

The walk back from the burial ground seemed much longer when there was no one to share it with her. One by one, Rochalla had buried all her family in this desolate graveyard beyond the city. Now, for the first time in her life, she was alone indeed. I'm the last, she thought. When it's my turn, there'll be no one left to bury *me* . . . She tried to thrust the grim thought away – it had been a long time since there had been any room in her hard life for weakening self-pity – but as she trudged through the quagmire that was all that remained of the road to the city, a voice within her mind persisted, like a lost child crying in the darkness. *What shall I do now?*

Have faith, her mother would have said. Trust Myrial, He will provide. Well, Rochalla *had* trusted Him. Even if He had deserted *her* because she was a whore, surely He would never punish her innocent brothers and sisters? She had spent coppers she could ill afford on incense and sacrifices at the temple. She had prayed constantly, and with increasing fervour, throughout the children's illness – and much good it had done her, or them. Myrial had sent down the rain upon His people for months without end. Myrial had taken the last of her loved ones from her.

The worship of this so-called god was nothing more than a web of lies, hypocrisy and cruel deception. Rochalla knew that now. When her parents had died, she had been forced to sacrifice the innocence of childhood in order to survive. Today, however, she had lost something that cut much deeper – her faith.

Rochalla, worn by grief and hunger, weary from days spent nursing the young ones and nights spent wandering the wet and freezing streets, stumbled on in a haze of wretched misery – until, without warning, her foot sank into a deep pothole, hidden by the snow. She stumbled and pitched forward into the foul, clinging slush of the road – and her last thread of endurance snapped.

She levered herself to her feet, and scraped the freezing slime from her eyes and mouth. Deep inside, the anger that had been smouldering for so many days burst into flame at last.

Rochalla leaped to her feet and shook her fist at the sky, mud streaking down her face to mingle with the tears. 'I don't believe in you, Myrial,' she shrieked. 'No god so cruel could exist! I *won't* believe in you any longer! I'll curse your name for the rest of my life!' For a breathless, hopeful moment, she waited for the God to strike her down. 'Do you hear me, Myrial?' she cried again. 'I don't believe in you!'

'Ah – but maybe He believes in *you*.'

Rochalla blinked mud and tears from her eyes, to see a hand, elegant, manicured and clean, reaching out to take her work-worn, filthy paw. It was her customer of the previous night, whom she had driven away with cold words, and refused to see again. 'Sir?' She tried to keep the anger from her voice. She couldn't bear him to see her sunk so low. He's had my body, she thought furiously. Must he have my last shreds of pride and self-respect?

The man half smiled at her, tentative and nervous now, a far cry from the confident, rich client of the night before. 'My name is Presvel,' he said quietly. 'I work for Lady Seriema.'

Rochalla gasped. They never, *never* told her their names! Did this fool realise just how deeply he had put himself in her power? Right now, though, she could scarcely bring herself to care. 'What do you want?' she asked impatiently. 'I already told you last night that I've given up whoring. And I've just buried my baby sister, so I'm not in the mood—' She choked on sobs, unable to speak another word.

'I know, I know.' His hand was beneath her elbow, support-ive, undemanding and kind. A clean handkerchief, so pristine and finely embroidered that she hardly dared put it near her muddy face, was produced out of nowhere and placed in her hand. 'I wish I could tell you how deeply I regret your loss,' he told her, 'and I'm sorry I had to intrude at this time. But if you had not told me you were coming here this morning, I would never have been able to find you.'

'Why did you want to find me? How many times must I tell you I don't do that any more? Why can't you just leave me alone?'

'Because I can help you. No – don't say anything! Just hear me out, please?'

Rochalla shrugged. 'Whatever. I'm going home now.' She put the handkerchief back into his hand. 'You can walk with me if you must. I don't suppose I can stop you.'

Presvel's tentative smile returned. 'As long as you let me talk. Rochalla, I have an opportunity for you. Before I tell you what it is, I have to stress that it doesn't come with a price. I'm not in the market for a mistress, and as for a lover – well, if, sometime in the future you wanted to consider me, I wouldn't object, but for now, let's just try being friends, and see how we get along.'

'I thought you were talking about some kind of opportunity?' Rochalla interrupted, then shut her mouth quickly. She could have kicked herself for encouraging this lunatic.

'I am.' Suddenly, Presvel's confidence returned. 'After what you've just been through, I know it's hard to ask if you could bear to look after another little girl, but Lady Seriema has just adopted an heir, who desperately needs a nursemaid. It's a dreadful case – the poor child has just lost her parents, and saw her mother murdered in front of her eyes – though you didn't hear *that* from me or anyone else, and you'll never repeat it if you know what's good for you. The little mite is about four years old. After seeing her mother killed, the pitiful little thing won't even speak. She desperately needs someone loving and kind to care for her. Lady Seriema hasn't a clue about children, and doesn't particularly like them anyway.' Again, he took Rochalla's hand. 'Please – won't you help? You'd live in the biggest mansion in the Esplanade, and be warm and clothed and fed and safe. The child would be loved and cared for by a lass with a warm and tender heart, who was an expert with small children. Don't you see – everyone would win? Please,' he coaxed. 'Please say yes.'

Rochalla looked at him coldly. 'And you? Would *you* win?'

Presvel shook his head. 'No,' he said deliberately. 'In one way

I would lose, for I love you dearly, and wish you could be mine. But you must understand that I have a peculiar relationship with Lady Seriema. Though I'm only her assistant, and I've never been her lover – thank Myrial, she's never demanded *that* of me – she does demand my total dedication. She would kill me if she ever thought I had a lover, or throw me out on the streets at least. See the power you have over me? See the trust I'm placing in you? I'll introduce you as the daughter of an old family acquaintance, though obviously we'll have to get you some better clothing first, and wash away that mud. But we'll be colleagues, you and I – and I hope we will be friends. That's all.'

Rochalla frowned, still uncertain. 'You said in one way you would lose?'

Presvel grinned at her. 'In another, I would be triumphant. I already told you that I love you dearly. Most of all, I want you to be cared for and be safe, and to take away this burden of hard work from your shoulders. That's more important than any dream of mine. Please, Rochalla – don't let this chance go by.'

Somehow, despite her grief and weariness, Rochalla found her smiling back at him. 'All right,' she said. 'I'll try.' Then suddenly all her doubts and fears came rushing back. 'But to go from whore to nursemaid in one day – are you sure I *can?*'

Presvel squeezed her hand. 'I think you can do anything you put your mind to – but then again, I'm prejudiced that way.'

TWENTY-SIX

APPROACHING SUNSET

Elion had never been to Tiarond before. Though the city lay so close, geographically speaking, to Gendival, it had chanced that his missions with Melnyth had always taken him to the southern, seacoast area of Callisiora, or to other realms. The Loremaster, like most of his kind, loved to see and experience new places, and could barely contain his curiosity as he rode down the snowy track with Tormon and Scall, and rounded the spur of the mountain to drop down to the great plateau that stretched around the city's feet.

The Loremaster and his companions had followed the trail that cut down through the narrow valley, travelling on horseback, though Tormon had been understandably reluctant to take his precious beasts back into the city. They led the Sefrians and rode the horses of the troopers whose cloaks they wore, while Scall had graduated from the donkey to Elion's chestnut – not without some misgivings on the part of the Loremaster, who had been entertaining visions of picking the boy out of every snowdrift all the way down the trail. (He was even more chagrined, when they started on their way, to discover that the fiery little mare behaved like a perfect lamb for the boy.)

The story for the gate guards, when they eventually reached

the city, was to be the simple truth: Mistress Toulac was no longer there to train Lord Blade's new horses, so Scall was bringing them back to the stablemaster in the Sacred Precincts. Lord Blade had left two of his soldiers to follow behind as escorts for the precious beasts. Elion was hoping and praying that the Sefrians could be used as a diversion to deflect the guards' attention away from the fact that the two returning Godswords were not the same men who'd gone out the previous day.

The turbulent young river, swollen by brown floodwater, hurtled along on their right, while the steep, craggy spur of the mountain reared up on their left-hand side, its upper slopes shawled in layers of cloud. Beyond the spur the snowy plateau spread out across the broad lap of the mountain, bounded to the west by the river, with rising land on its opposite side that had been cleared and terraced. Above the fertile terraces loomed the tree-clad slopes of the adjacent peak. To the east, the plateau lapped the city's feet, before narrowing, according to Tormon, into an impenetrable maze of crags and canyons that formed the mountain's broken face to the north-east.

Elion looked around in faint disapproval at the desolate, windswept landscape. The plateau stretched, broad and fairly level, for about a league from the city walls, before dropping off abruptly as though the land had been sliced away by a gigantic axe. These townlands consisted of a scattering of farmsteads, stone-built and huddled low against the endless wind, surrounded by sparse, waterlogged fields, their thin, grudging soil now buried beneath a blanket of snow around the beleaguered dwellings.

The Loremaster shivered. 'You know, I could never understand why the Callisiorans put their capital in this forsaken spot. Surely it would have made more sense to build it in the central plains, or near the southern ocean, where there are many more resources, not to mention the maritime trade and easy travel along the coastline.' He pulled his cloak more tightly around his shoulders and shivered. 'The climate would be a damn sight better down in the lowlands, too. Why would the rulers of the realm choose to freeze their backsides off in the far side of beyond, in a place that's bleak, isolated and bloody inconvenient?'

Tormon shrugged. 'It beats me. But then I'm not religious, and most Callisiorans are. Because our ruler is also our High Priest, the capital must be located in the same place as the Holy City – and that's right here.'

There were few people abroad on the slushy road that morning. It was not surprising, Elion thought. There was nothing to harvest and nothing in the markets to sell or buy. What was the point in wasting energy and getting wet and chilled for nothing? Most people must be huddled in their homes, praying for better times to come. They sloshed along the road for about a mile as it ran alongside the swollen, muddy river, which was bridged by a three-arched span of stone about a bowshot from the city walls. About the same distance below the bridge, the river finally joined another, greater torrent that ran down the other side of the plateau from the eastern vale. The two waters formed a turbulent confluence to the south of Tiarond's great gates, before roaring off, as one vast river, towards the south.

Tormon, who planned to find his daughter when he reached the city, was tense with barely restrained excitement. Elion was concerned, lest something in the trader's jittery demeanour should betray them to the Godswords at the gate. 'Where does the river go?' he asked, to distract his companion from his thoughts.

'Across the plateau, and over the edge, eventually,' Tormon told him. 'You ought to see it sometime – it's one big bastard of a waterfall. The plateau ends in sheer cliffs that drop for a couple of thousand feet – it's just as though someone had chopped off the side of the mountain with a gigantic axe.'

'Then how in the name of all creation does anyone manage to get up here?' the Loremaster demanded. He was still slightly unsure of this dour, shrewd trader, and half suspected that he must be spinning him a tale.

'No, Elion, it's true, honestly.' Scall chipped in, greatly daring, to defend the older man. The Loremaster had noticed that ever since Tormon had killed the Godsword this morning, the boy had been clinging close to him, following his every word and move. This self-same man, who beat the living daylights out of him last night, has suddenly become his hero, Elion thought. Who can understand these people?

'There is a place,' Scall went on, 'some distance from the waterfall, where there's a winding trail in a fold in the face of the cliff. Sometimes it clings to the cliff face, and in some places it tunnels through the rock itself.'

'The boy's right,' Tormon added. 'It's a killer of a route, much harder than the roundabout way via the Snaketail Pass. It takes tremendous skill to drive a wagon in either direction, and a damn strong team to pull one. That's why traders who come up to Tiarond can charge such high prices.'

The Loremaster shook his head. 'As I said, it's a ridiculous location for a capital city.'

'You won't catch me arguing with that.' As they neared the bridge that led to the looming city, Tormon looked thoughtful. 'On the other hand, of course, it does make Tiarond absolutely impregnable – unless your troops could fly.' He chuckled, amused by the notion.

Elion remembered the Ak'Zahar, and suddenly turned cold.

The new dress, completed only days before, was a wonder of the dressmaker's art. Seriema, looking at herself in the long mirror, marvelled at the gown's fine cut, cunning stitchery and rich materials. Nothing of its like, she was sure, had ever been seen in Tiarond before.

And it's all wasted on me.

The vision of the gown wavered and blurred before her, as her eyes filled with tears. It's not fair! The secret voice of her inner self, that awkward, blundering girl Seriema had once been, rose up from deep in her mind, where she normally kept it locked away. It's not fair! it wailed again, the forlorn cry of the plain young girl, intelligent enough to know that boys drew straws and flipped coins to see which of them would have to dance with her at parties. She had always understood, too, that any clumsy advances from the pimply young merchants' sons had been instigated by the scions' avid parents, all itching to get their hands on her father's fortune. *It's not fair! Why couldn't I be pretty?*

What? arose the mocking voice of the older Seriema: Lady Seriema, the hard-headed, flint-hearted merchant, Lady Seriema, head of the Miners Consortium and the Mercantile Assembly: Seriema-in-control. What? You want pretty, too? It's not enough to be the richest woman Callisiora has ever known, that nobody in Tiarond dares cross or contradict you, and that you have every damn man in this city terrified to death of you?

All except one. All except him.

Oh, grow up, Seriema, she told herself, the Commander of the Godswords is no different from the others. He's just a man

– they're all the same. If you haven't learned that by now, there's no hope for you. He's only courting you because he's after something – and it's not your womanly charms, believe me. He probably wanted your support against the Hierarch for some devious scheme or other . . .

The reflection in the mirror grew very, very still. *That's not true. It can't be!*

Seriema paid no heed to the wailing voice. The events of recent months, suddenly freed from the jumble of tremulous, tentative emotions that had accompanied them, suddenly dropped into a stark new pattern. She saw with brutal clarity how Blade had led her, coaxed her, flattered and charmed her into doing his dirty work in instigating the Great Sacrifice of the Hierarch.

And I walked right into it.

Seriema clenched her fists so tightly that her nails, had they not been so bitten down and ugly, would have sliced into her palms. A vast and bitter anger rose within her, but even now it was directed at herself, her stupid, gullible lonely self, and not at its rightful target. Even now, pathetic, lovestruck idiot that she was, she couldn't bring herself to hate him.

Seriema looked back at the new dress, elaborately styled with its tight, boned bodice and its hooped and stiffened skirt. The fabric was a rich, gold brocade, oversewn with a webwork of real gold thread and glittering, thumbnail-sized rubies from her own mines. The dressmaker, she knew, had selected this style to try to give some shape to her washboard figure. The experiment had not worked. The gems, designed to distract the eye from the wearer's shortcomings, only drew attention to them instead. The blasted thing cost enough to feed a village for a year, Seriema thought bitterly, but on me it looks like a tawdry sack.

Her temper finally snapped. 'Marutha?' she bellowed. 'Marutha! Get in here!' She hauled on the bellpull with all the strength of her anger and frustration, yanking so hard that the tasselled cord came off in her hand.

'What *now*, for Myrial's sake?' The old woman stood panting in the doorway. Leaning against the doorframe, she clasped a hand dramatically over her heart. 'Near finished me off, you did. Making me run up them stairs at my age!'

Her scolding flow of words was suddenly checked. Seriema, crossing the room in three strides, slapped her so hard that it left an imprint – first white, then red – on her wrinkled cheek.

'If you're too old to manage the stairs,' Seriema snapped into the silence, 'you can pack your bags and get out of this house. And if you say one more insolent word to me, I will have you taken out into the yard and beaten in front of all the household. Do you understand?'

Marutha nodded, for the first time utterly silenced, her lower lip trembling as she pressed a hand to her injured face. Her brown eyes held a kicked-dog look that made Seriema seethe with guilt. She knew she would remember that sight and despise herself to the end of her days. Hurriedly she turned her back on the old housekeeper. 'Unfasten me and get me out of this damned, jewel-encrusted monstrosity – and fetch me my black wool dress.'

'*What?*' Marutha screeched. 'You're never going to the big ceremony in that old black thing?' True to form, the old woman had rallied well. 'It makes you look like the kitchen maid! And the rest of the household have gone up to the Precincts already, except Presvel,' she added with a flash of defiance, 'so you'll have your work cut out to beat me in front of them. The very idea . . .'

Seriema, however, noticed that all the time the old woman

was grumbling she was also obeying with unusual speed. Already she had unhooked the golden gown, and now, still muttering, she made her way to the big closet and started clattering the hangers along the rail with unnecessary force. Seriema tore the cursed dress from her shoulders and stepped out of it. She scrumpled the expensive fabric up into a ball, and hurled it into a corner of the room.

'Lady *Seriema*!' The scold came out of Marutha's mouth through sheer force of habit. 'That's no way to treat your good, expensive clothes. Oh, and by the way,' she added quickly, before her mistress could get in a quelling reply. 'I can't find your black wool dress. It's probably being washed.'

Seriema did not miss the flicker of cunning in the crafty old woman's eyes. Without saying a word, she walked out of the room and leaned over the rail of the landing. 'Presvel? Presvel!'

There was a hurried sound of scrambling feet overhead, then her assistant appeared – not down in the hall where she had expected him to be, but on the attic staircase that led down from the chambers of the maids.

'What on earth are you doing up there?' Seriema asked him in surprise.

'Oh – er – we've had a bit of pilfering from the kitchen lately. I thought I'd take the opportunity, and check the maids' rooms while they were out.'

On any other day, Seriema would have marvelled at his efficiency. Today, with the discovery that Blade had duped her raw and stinging in her mind, she looked on his excuses with a jaundiced eye. No, she thought wearily, I can't pursue this now. I daren't. If she caught him with one of the maids she'd have to dismiss them both, and she couldn't face the thought of life without him. Why, Presvel was her right hand!

'Lady?' His voice, courteous and helpful as always, brought her back to herself. 'Lady? Is there anything I can do for you?'

'Oh, yes.' Seriema took a deep breath, well aware of Marutha's eyes peeping curiously around the edge of the door frame. 'Run downstairs for me, Presvel, and fetch me the switch that the maid uses to punish the maidservants.'

'*What?*' Presvel's eyes nearly started from his head.

'Now don't start defending her,' Seriema told him firmly. 'I don't care how old Marutha is – she needs to be taught a lesson. I warned her what would happen if she continued to defy me.'

'Oh, you want to beat Marutha. Very well, my Lady, I'll go at once.' As he hurried off downstairs, Seriema stared at his retreating back with a puzzled frown. What had got into *him* today? He wasn't his normal, brisk, efficient self, somehow. Was everybody in this wretched house in some kind of conspiracy to plague her?

By the time Seriema had strolled back into the bedroom, she discovered that her ruse had worked. The black wool dress was laid out neatly on the bed.

'All right,' Marutha grumbled. 'You win. Please yourself. Go to the most important ceremony of the year dressed like a scarecrow – see if *I* care. But you can get that creepy-crawly Presvel to hook it up for you, for I'm sure I won't – not if you threaten to beat me till you're blue in the face.' With that, the old housekeeper went stamping out of the room, satisfied that, as always, she'd had the last word.

As Seriema was pulling the plain woollen dress down over her head, Presvel appeared in the doorway with the switch. 'Do you still want this, Lady?'

'No,' Seriema told him wryly. 'It served its purpose. Just leave it here for now. You can hook me into this gown,

Presvel, if you wouldn't mind, and then you can get back to whatever you were doing.' She scanned his face as she spoke, alert for a shifty glance or guilty flush, but he was as unruffled and urbane as always.

'Of course, Lady. It's always a pleasure to help you. By the way, I looked in on the child, and she's sleeping peacefully now, so you've nothing to worry about there.'

She felt that he had turned the tables, reproaching her for her lack of interest. 'Good, I'm glad to hear it.' Deliberately, she kept the irritation out of her voice. 'Have you done anything about a nursemaid yet?'

'I think I might have found someone, Lady. I didn't think you would want to be bothered on the day of the Great Sacrifice, so I arranged for you to interview her in the morning. She's the daughter of an old friend of the family – a little young for my taste, but she's looked after a stream of younger brothers and sisters, so she's had a great deal of experience. I think you'll like her, Lady. She's very shy and self-effacing, but she seems very capable.'

Seriema nodded calmly, though the word *young* had set a few alarm bells ringing. 'Very well. Thank you, Presvel. I'll see her first thing in the morning. It's important that we get someone as soon as possible.'

Already the streets of Tiarond had emptied. A few of the straggling populace were being rounded up in groups by Godsword soldiers, and shepherded up to the great Esplanade to await their turn to pass through the tunnel into the Precincts. The vast majority of the people, however, had hurried up there early, as soon as word spread that the Hierarch had returned. With such a crowd, it would be difficult to find a good spot, and they all wished to be first. Normally, the ceremony would be held up on top of the mountain. At the very crest of the flattened peak was a natural amphitheatre, the remains of an old volcanic crater. In its centre stood Myrial's High Altar, and around the sides were stony terraces where the crowds could stand or sit, and even the smallest child could see. Today, however, the storm had made the mountain inaccessible, and snow had filled the great bowl up to the brim. Hurried arrangements had been made to hold the Sacrifice in the Sacred Precincts, in the great courtyard before the Temple, and though there were many muttered complaints in the crowd, most folk were content to cram in somehow, and get the best view they could manage. No one really wanted to freeze to death on a mountain top waiting for a sunset which, if these last months of murk and cloud were anything to go by, would not even be seen.

Tormon, already tense with excitement and hope at the thought of finding his daughter again, was relieved to see the emptiness of the streets. The big Sefrians were accustomed to crowds – traders' horses were used to being surrounded by large groups of noisy people – but there was a mood of thinly concealed desperation and violence in this city that made the animals uneasy, unpredictable and unsafe. Clearly, Elion was even more relieved to have passed safely through the guardpost at the city gate. 'You know, I never really believed they'd fall for it.' His voice broke into Tormon's thoughts.

'I think they were all too excited about the Great Sacrifice,' the trader replied with profound disgust. 'It's absolutely barbaric, if you ask me, to take a man's life through superstition.'

Elion looked puzzled. 'But I thought you wanted to kill him yourself, for what he did to poor Kanella? Why, only last night you were saying you would like to carve out his heart while it still was beating!'

'Oh, I certainly do,' Tormon said bleakly, 'and I'm livid because they're going to sacrifice the bastard before I get the chance. But that's different. His death would be in payment for his evil deeds, not because some bunch of misguided, desperate idiots think that putting a man to death on a particular day is going to stop the rain.'

Elion shrugged. 'If you ask me, this entire realm is a sink-hole of barbarity and superstition.'

Tormon looked at him sharply. From time to time, the younger man had let slip a hint or two that he'd come from outside Callisiora. The trader had been all around the Curtain Walls in his yearly circuit, and it had always seemed impossible to him that they could truly mark the end of the whole world. He used the intriguing notion to distract himself from thoughts of Annas and Kanella. It was important that he appear to be the impassive, professional Godsword going about his duties. He must not let his grief or his excited hopes show in his demeanour or his face. So he listened carefully to Elion, alert for further clues to the other's origins, but the younger man was now back on the subject of the gate guards.

'They all seemed quite convinced, I thought,' he was saying. 'Except for that suspicious-looking skinny one. I wasn't sure of him at all.'

'Don't worry about Barsil,' Scall chipped in quietly from behind. 'He looked shifty, not suspicious, and he always looks like that. He was supposed to be escorting me up the mountain yesterday, but he sneaked off to play dice instead. He'll be too afraid I'll tell on him to give us any trouble.'

Elion looked startled to hear the boy speak with such certainty, but Tormon smiled a quiet smile. It was good to see the young lad finding a bit more confidence.

*   *   *

When they finally reached the Grand Esplanade, Elion was horrified to find the broad square choked with hundreds of people, all waiting, with varying degrees of patience, for their chance to enter the tunnel. 'Merciful providence!' Elion gasped. 'How are we ever going to get through?'

'What do you want to get through for?' Tormon looked surprised. 'That's Seriema's house over there.' He pointed to his left. 'The biggest one, with the high courtyard wall. We can go into the courtyard and take the horses round the back. She's probably gone by now, but if she is still there, I don't think she'll mind when I explain. Unlike most folk, I always got on pretty well with Seriema, and if she's looking after Annas for me, I don't suppose she was in cahoots with the Hierarch anyway. She always hated his guts, so that's another thing we've got in common now. We slip in, get my daughter, and slip out of Tiarond while they're sacrificing the Hierarch. Where's the problem?'

Elion opened his mouth – and shut it again. Only when Tormon spoke had he realised the misunderstanding that existed between himself and the other man, and the extent of his own mistaken assumptions. Of course, the trader knew absolutely nothing about the link between the dragon and the Hierarch. Elion had been very careful to represent himself as a simple storm-strayed traveller, and though he had talked of Melnyth as his partner who had met a tragic, early death, he had never let anything slip about the Shadowleague, Gendival or the current mission. Tormon had absolutely no clue as to the wind-sprite's existence, and unlike Toulac, who had been brought into this affair against Elion's better judgement and against his wishes, the trader had no idea why the Loremaster had made this dangerous trip into the city, for he had not been let into the plan.

By my life! He thinks I've come all this way just to help him save his daughter! Elion realised with horror. *What will he say when I have to tell him I've come to rescue the man who had his lifemate slain? And how can I explain that there'll be help from Veldan and that bloody firedrake?*

There was little time. Already, folk in the crowd were starting to look round curiously at the peculiar entourage of the two Godsword soldiers, the skinny boy and their collection of wildly varying horseflesh. Elion took a deep breath. 'Tormon, will you trust me? I have no right to ask you, because I've kept a whole lot of important information secret—'

Tormon's face had grown very still. 'I'd already guessed that,' he said.

Elion, startled by *that* revelation, floundered desperately for a moment. 'It wasn't by any choice of mine,' he lied. 'I'm under an oath not to give away my true identity, and a lot of other facts besides. But there are other matters afoot, greater matters—'

'From outside the Curtain Walls?' From the tone of voice, it was not really a question.

Damn! How the bloody blazes did he ever guess? 'Very well,' he said hastily. 'Yes, you're right – but please don't ask me any more just now. Anyway, there's no time. Listen – I can't let the Hierarch be sacrificed. The life of one of my companions depends on it.'

For the first time in the conversation, emotion showed on Tormon's face. 'You're telling me you're going to *save* that bastard?' he demanded angrily.

'I'm sorry, Tormon. I have no choice. Don't worry. It's not as crazy as it sounds. I have a plan, of sorts—'

'And you let me get all the way here thinking that you'd come with me through friendship, to help me get my daughter back.' The trader turned away from Elion. 'Well, if that's the way things are, I want nothing more to do with you and your accursed plans. I'm getting Annas, then we're leaving this place as fast as possible, and for good. I'm never setting foot in Tiarond again.' He started to urge his horse ahead, then suddenly turned back. 'There's one thing. At least I don't have to worry about you succeeding with this crazy scheme. But if you do come through the next few hours – and despite my disappointment in you, Elion, I wish you no real ill will – I'm warning you to beware Zavahl. The man's a venomous snake. It won't matter a single whit to him that you saved his miserable life. If he can, he'll use you, and when it suits him, he'll knife you in the back. Take care.'

'Wait!' Elion called. Again, Tormon pulled back on his reins. 'Will you take my horse for me, please? Just leave the trooper's mount – the boy can keep the chestnut if he wants. But a horse hidden out here may mean the difference between life and death for me.'

The trader shrugged. 'All right. Slide down and give the reins to Scall—' Suddenly he paused. 'What's going to happen to the boy?'

Elion shrugged. 'Please yourself. He certainly won't be coming with me.' With that, he slid down from the horse and slipped away into the crowd without a backward look. He couldn't face the expression of disgust that he knew he would see on Tormon's face. He wasn't very proud of himself right now. He certainly didn't need anybody else's opinion.

Zavahl dreamed. The Eye of Myrial was as cold and grey as a long-dead fire. The Voice maintained a brooding silence. In the profound darkness of the Holy of Holies, the vast circle of the Eye gleamed faintly, dull as lead, as though it had been cut out of the cloud-choked skies above Tiarond and placed in the Temple for the Hierarch's torment.

Zavahl, drowning in misery and despair, closed his eyes to shut out the wretched sight. 'Why won't you answer?' he cried, in a voice cracking with strain. 'I brought you word of tonight's Great Sacrifice planned for your glory. O Great Myrial, surely that must please you?'

He waited, but there was still no reply. The Hierarch clenched his fist, and hammered on the plinth in front of him. 'Is it me?' he cried. 'Have I failed in some way? Will nothing I do to appease you ever be enough?' Deep in his heart, he was afraid to hear an answer. If the sacrifice of the dragon was *not* sufficient to appease the God, it could only mean one thing: it was Zavahl's death that Myrial sought.

Was I mistaken after all? he thought. I *convinced* myself that the dragon was sent by Myrial, as a sign of His returning favour. What if I was wrong all the time, and the murder of the trader and his family was for no purpose? What if the sacrifice tonight is a failure, too?

The Hierarch took his other hand, with its ring that bore the crimson stone, from the niche in the plinth. At once, the pallid gleam of the great Eye's circle snuffed itself like a blown-out candle—

And Zavahl awoke to a different darkness.

The reality was even worse than the dream. Forlorn and hopeless, the Hierarch faced the bitter truths of the waking world. He was not in the Holy of Holies, but in a cell beneath the impenetrable fastness of the Citadel. Though they had unbound his limbs, he was locked into a guarded tomb of steel and stone. No one could help him now. No longer was there a dragon to be sacrificed. Instead, at sunset, he would take its place. Gilarra would don the Hierarch's jewelled robes, and preside at the great ceremony before the assembled city. As darkness fell, Gilarra would snuff out his life.

In a way, Zavahl couldn't blame her. He cared for Callisiora as a nation, with its peace and prosperity as his chief concern, but he knew that the Suffragan cared more about the people, all the individual sad, dull little lives of the faceless common toilers who made up this land. Due to the failure and short-comings of the Hierarch, there was starvation, suffering and disease throughout the land. And if he had failed so absolutely, it was Gilarra's right – her duty, even – to take his place, and carry out whatever action she deemed necessary.

Maybe Myrial will be better pleased with her, he thought. Maybe the Eye will waken once again, and speak to her. Maybe the rain and snow will cease, and the clouds will part, and the sun come out, and my death will have been worth something, after all. Maybe there *are* such things as miracles.

'*Maybe there are, Zavahl. And if you'll only listen to me, we may create a miracle of our own.*'

The Hierarch froze. It had been so long since he'd heard that inner voice, he'd almost convinced himself that it had been a product of his confused and tortured mind. Again, though, the reality had proved worse than his imagination. The Demon had come back.

All through the long, uncomfortable journey from the saw-mill, bound to the back of a bony animal with a jarring, jolting stride, Aethon had kept himself silent and apart from the Hier-arch. As desperate and despondent as his host, he had aban-doned himself, for some time, to black and deep despair. Only when they had reached the brooding Citadel, and Zavahl had fallen into a deep, exhausted slumber, had Aethon stretched himself at last, to investigate his own dark prison of the mind.

Hope, when it came, arrived from the most unexpected source. After a time, Zavahl began to dream – and in innocence and ignorance solved a mystery that had baffled the Shadowleague for many generations, far back into the distant past.

It was common knowledge to the Shadowleague that Myrial was not a natural place, but an artefact created by the Ancients, and divided by the Curtain Walls, so that all its gathered races should be kept apart. It was known that somewhere deep inside its heart lay the complex intelligence, inorganic and, again, created, that maintained and sustained this complex miracle of a world. It was also rumoured that there was a locus of entry, long forgotten and concealed, that permitted access to Myrial's very heart.

Aethon's heart soared with excitement. The place was here! All along it had been here, hidden right in this backwater of barbaric superstition. The dragon was both delighted and appalled. This idiotic priest called it the Eye of Myrial, and thought he was communing with his primitive god, whereas in reality, he'd had access all along to the first step on the road to halting the collapse of all the vital systems of this fragile world. The place that all the Shadowleague, for all of recorded history, had been desperately trying to find.

Then, as reality intruded, Aethon's spirits fell once more. There was no way he could share this knowledge, no telepathic reaching to a comrade who could pass on this vital news. Once more, with little hope, he began to reach out with his thoughts towards the Hierarch. Somehow, he had to make the fool listen! Unless he could find a way to get this wretched, hapless human out of here by sundown, the secret of Myrial's heart would die with them both.

TWENTY-SEVEN

The Slaughterman

Toulac and Veldan, with the firedrake behind them, had made their way down through the lower tithe caves into the tunnel beyond. The passage had been much longer and had sloped far more severely than the Loremaster had expected, though it took a meandering, zigzag path down through the mountain, which gentled out the worst of the steep gradients. Veldan was concerned about the kinks in the tunnel. 'These bends will slow Kaz down considerably,' she whispered to Toulac. 'They're going to be a hindrance to a quick escape.'

The veteran glanced at her sidelong, eyes twinkling. 'These bends are going to be a godsend when they start firing crossbows,' she replied. 'You've got to learn to think positive, girlie! There's almost always something you can use to your advantage in a battle. You've just got to learn to see it.'

They walked on in silence for a few more moments, going carefully by the faint light of Veldan's glim. The Loremaster felt a tightness in her belly, and a pressure in her throat as though she wanted to be sick. This would be the first time, since her wounding in the caverns of the Ak'Zahar, that she had faced a fight. She remembered the agony as the jagged sword ripped down the side of her face. She remembered screams –

her own voice, or that of Melnyth? – that seemed to come from far away.

'That was different, Boss,' Kaz said softly into her mind. 'This time we're only fighting humans. We could take on this lot between us in our sleep! Besides,' he added, with an approving glance at Toulac, 'this time you're with a human who has courage and good sense – someone you can count on.'

'Don't you think she's a bit long in the tooth for this kind of thing?' Screening their conversation carefully from the older woman, Veldan finally brought out the worry that had been nagging at her all the way down from the caves.

'I wouldn't fret about Toulac,' the firedrake told her. 'I suspect that she's forgotten more about fighting than we'll ever know.'

Their conversation was cut short as the veteran stopped Veldan with an upraised hand. 'This is the place,' she whispered. 'The lower guardroom is just around the corner there, down at the end of the passage. I'll just slip down and take a peek, then we'll get on with it, shall we?'

'Maybe I should go,' the Loremaster suggested.

Toulac shook her head. 'I know this place. I'll only be a minute – I just want to find out how many guards are there.' She made as if to go – and suddenly hesitated. 'Veldan? You know our escape plan?'

The Loremaster nodded, wondering at this sudden diffidence.

'Well, if we can manage it without putting ourselves at too much risk, would you mind going back to collect Mazal? Only if it's practical, though,' she added, a little too quickly. 'No daft heroics for a horse, I promise.'

Veldan smiled. She had forgotten about the big grey warhorse, but clearly, Toulac's old companion had never been far from her thoughts. 'Of course we will,' she told the veteran. 'In fact, we may need him. It's a long way for Kaz to carry all of us.'

Toulac's face broke into a delighted grin. 'Thanks, girlie. That means a lot to me.' Before Veldan could reply, she had stolen away, cat-footed, down the tunnel, and vanished round the corner.

The Loremaster barely had time to start to worry before Toulac was back at her side. 'Just four of them,' she whispered. 'No problems there. Now, listen, you two. You might think the other door, the one leading into the corridors behind the Temple, would be opposite the one we'll be using, but it's not – it's on the left-hand wall as you go in. The guardroom is about twice the size of the one we used, so we'll have more space to manoeuvre. Now remember, both of you, kill them quick and quiet. We don't want everybody in the Temple to know we've arrived. Kazairl, you go first, and I want you to go straight to the other doorway, preferably over the top of as many guards as you can manage.' Her seamed face split into a grin. 'Yours is the most important job – you've got to block that exit so that no one can get into the Temple and sound the alarm. Then the rest of the business should be easy. We'll just pick them off at our leisure. But you've got to remember, Kaz, no matter what else is happening in the room, you are not to move away from that door. Veldan and I will manage just fine between us.'

She turned to the Loremaster, and patted her on the arm. 'Don't worry, girlie. It's plain that somebody sliced you up real good not long ago, but don't worry. You just need to get back into your stride.'

Veldan's jaw dropped. How had Toulac *known*?

'I didn't need any mind-speech,' the veteran told her. 'I saw the scars – new scars – when you were at my house. I've taken some real bad wounds in my time, and I know how that kind of thing can affect your confidence. But take it from me, girl – you'll be fine. Think of all the fights you've been in and didn't get as much as a scratch. You get over this time, and your nerve'll come back to you, just in time for the *big* fight that we're going to have outside,' she added with a wry grin. 'Don't fret, now. I'll be watching your back.'

'Thanks, Toulac.' Veldan squeezed the older woman's hand.

'Good girl. Shall we do it, then? Everybody ready?' The veteran looked from the Loremaster to Kaz and back again. 'Let's go!'

The soldiers, playing dice before the guardroom fire, leaped to their feet, eyes goggling, as the firedrake erupted into the room. Kaz, as instructed, made straight for the exit, blocking the door with his long body. Veldan, following, narrowly missed being knocked down by his lashing tail, as he attempted to turn himself in the confined space. With the reflexes of long practice, she hurled herself aside into the corner just in time, and the tail clubbed down the first of the guards, who was making for the other door. As the firedrake dragged his tail out of the way, the Loremaster closed with the second soldier, in a rush that took the startled man back towards the fire. With their minds on the formidable monster, none of the Godswords had really considered the two women as true opposition. Though Veldan lacked a little of her former strength, at least it was not her sword arm that had been wounded last time, and she found that her former skills came back quickly in the heat of the affray. Her opponent, trying to keep the corner of one eye on Kaz, was barely concentrating, and there were holes in his defence big enough for a horse and cart. Veldan's sword slipped easily through an opening and between his ribs, making its way, with deadly accuracy, straight to his heart.

It was a quick, no-nonsense fight, over almost before Veldan realised it had begun. She looked around to see Toulac wiping her blade on the sleeve of a fallen man and Kaz licking blood from his chops with a long, red tongue.

The veteran thumped the Loremaster on the shoulder. 'There you are, girl, what did I tell you? No trouble at all. Now, if you and Kaz will pull these bodies out of the way so we aren't falling over them when we leave, I'll nip out into the back of the Temple and see what's happening.'

'Toulac, maybe I should do that,' Veldan began. 'Really, I'm not nervous anymore. I can still handle myself in a fight – I've proved that now. You don't have to keep nursemaiding me.'

'Nonsense. It's got nothing to do with that. I know the Temple, remember? I was on duty here for two years, just about. I know every hiding place and nook and cranny in the building. I could sneak around in there for days and they would never find me. So don't worry, and don't fret if you don't hear from me for a little while. I won't come back until there's something happening. Keep an eye on the door now, and stay out of sight whatever you do – especially our big friend there. You might be able to pass yourself off as some pilgrim who got lost – at least as long as they don't see the bodies – but you'd have your work cut out explaining Kaz. Now if anybody comes—'

Annoyance sparked in Veldan. 'Toulac, I *know* all this. I've got eight years' fighting experience under my belt, for goodness' sake. Now if you're going, go, instead of hanging around here wasting time and lecturing me as if I was some raw, wet-behind-the-ears recruit.'

Toulac shrugged. 'Fair enough. I can take a hint. Just you take care, that's all.' And she was gone.

Kaz exhaled, a long drawn-out sigh. 'Why is it that older people are obsessed with having the last word?'

Veldan shook her head. 'I don't know. Ask me when I'm older. If Toulac's anything to go by, you'll get more of an answer than you bargained for.'

Now that Cook had gone, it was safe for Marutha to enter the old dragon's jealously guarded domain. The two women had never seen eye to eye since the unfortunate incident of Marutha's grandmother's herbal brew, a vile-smelling green concoction that the housekeeper had decided would be the very thing to cure Seriema's cough.

'How was I to know they were her best pots and pans?' Marutha muttered, as she crept into Cook's spotless, tidy lair. 'And it wasn't true, neither, what she said about my grandma being an old witch. And I never stank the place out for a month! A day or two, maybe, but the old fool had no call to make all that much fuss . . .'

As she crossed the room Marutha had a shivery feeling of eyes upon her, but when she looked around, there was only the cook's old cat, watching from its accustomed place on the rug before the fire. 'You mind your own business, you stinking, mangy old fleabag,' she told it. 'You're that nosy – it's a good thing you can't talk.' She had been at war with the cat, as well as with the cook, ever since the equally unfortunate incident of the dead rat in Seriema's bed.

Her movements quiet and furtive, the old housekeeper hooked out a stool from under the table and took it into the pantry. She climbed up stiffly, hanging on to the shelving for support, and rummaged on the highest shelves, behind the crocks of bottled fruit and pickles hoarded from more abundant times, and rationed carefully now. As her hand closed around the slender shape of a bottle, she sighed with relief. Ah – there it was! Cook's secret brandy supply, used in puddings

The Heart of Myrial

and sauces, and, Marutha suspected, in the cook's hot posset every night. Clasping the bottle tightly, she climbed down with the greatest care. The lengths a respectable woman had to go to just to get a drink these days! Seriema had started to mark the decanters upstairs, following a series of very awkward questions (for Marutha), which had resulted in the dismissal of the parlourmaid. Since then, the housekeeper had been very careful – and very sober – but, by Myrial, she had to have a drink today!

Sitting down at the kitchen table with bottle and cup, Marutha poured a generous measure of brandy with shaky hands. She still could not believe that Seriema had actually raised a hand to her! 'Why, the ungrateful little snippet!' she muttered wrathfully, punctuating her angry words with swigs of the cheap, raw brandy. 'I was only taking care of her – and somebody needs to do it! That girl hasn't got the sense that Myrial gave a sparrow! It's that damned sneaky Presvel undermining me, that's what it is. Things have never been the same since *he* came – and he's probably in cahoots with that accursed cook! And threatening to beat me in front of the whole household! That's all the gratitude I get, for all those years of sacrifice and faithful service . . .'

Marutha's eyes filled with self-pitying, brandy-fuelled tears. I should just up and leave, she thought. That would show them! But wherever would I go? My whole life has been this family. I've looked after that wretched girl since the day that she was born. What would she ever do without me?

It was odd, but she still felt as if there were eyes on her. She looked around for the cat, but then remembered seeing it squeezing out of the partly open kitchen window a few minutes earlier, and jumping down into the yard outside. Maybe it was just a draught. She noticed that the door to the coal cellar was slightly ajar, but she couldn't be bothered to go and close it. Marutha shrugged, and poured herself another cup of brandy. The alcohol had made her reckless. If Cook and Seriema didn't like it, they could just go and do the other thing.

Ivar squinted through the narrow crack at the edge of the coal cellar door. Curse the old hag, he thought. Is she never going to go? He had counted on the house being clear by now. Surely this one must be the only one left by now – apart from the bitch, of course. *She* would be leaving by the front door, and he would hear her footsteps in the outer hall.

Ivar began to worry. Time was getting short. He had waited a good long time after the cook and maids had gone trooping out, dressed in their restday finery. Since that commotion a while ago, when the manservant had come down into the kitchen for the switch, he had heard no further noises from upstairs. If someone had been destined for a beating, the bitch must have changed her mind. Well, she wouldn't be hurting anybody else after today.

Ivar looked again at the old woman. The light from the chink in the cellar door gleamed in a silver streak on the honed edge of the great steel knife. 'No, my beauty,' Ivar breathed, as his fingers caressed the smooth bone handle. 'She won't have you.' The knives were only for Seriema. He wanted them sullied by no other blood – but something had to be done.

The old sot was well into her second cup of brandy now. Ivar could wait no longer. With sudden decision he turned and crept back down the stairs into the cellar where, by the dim grey light of the grating, he selected a nice, sturdy cudgel from the firewood pile. Hurrying back up the short flight of steep stone stairs, he opened the door a little further, and edged out.

The old woman was still sobbing and muttering over her

brandy cup. In two strides Ivar was across the room. He raised his arm – and hesitated. His hand, holding the cudgel, began to shake. *What am I doing?* he thought. *What's come over me, attacking this poor harmless old crone? I've always been a decent man, till now. I only came here for revenge on the bitch. After what her bullies did to poor Felyss, no fate is bad enough for her.*

Suddenly the old woman looked around, squinting at him narrowly through red-rimmed eyes. 'Who are you?' she snapped, then took a deep breath to scream for help.

Ivar felt the clutch of panic. His arm jerked. He brought the cudgel smashing down across the old woman's skull. She crumpled sideways from her chair and slid to the floor, with one hand clutching vainly at the rim of the table, then flopping down like the limb of a broken doll. An accusing finger of blood, darkly gleaming, oozed out from beneath her head and crawled across the stone-flagged floor.

Ivar stifled the guilt that stalked him, and the pity that threatened to throw him off his chosen course. *She served the bitch,* he told himself firmly. *She got what she deserved.* He looked at his cudgel. Its end was dark and sticky with blood and a wisp of stained grey hair, but it appeared to be undamaged. He decided to hold on to it, just in case anyone else was lingering in the house. He had never seen or heard the manservant leave, he reminded himself.

In his other hand the, big butchering knife still gleamed, pristine and unsullied, thirsting for the blood of the bitch. 'Not long now, my beauty,' Ivar told it. 'Not long now.' Turning aside from the crumpled body on the floor, he left the kitchen and made his way upstairs.

Seriema knew perfectly well that she was procrastinating, and despised herself for it. She ought to have been well on the way to the Temple by now. A way for her would be cleared through the rabble, of course – she expected no less – but who knew how long that might take? She knew that if she were to miss the Great Sacrifice, she would be setting herself up in enmity with both Lord Blade and the new Hierarch Gilarra by seeming to repudiate Zavahl's removal. Yet how could she face Blade now, knowing that she had been his dupe?

As always, when she was worried, Seriema drifted unthinkingly towards the window, and looked out at the dwindling crowds in the Esplanade below. It would not be long now. The afternoon shadows were already stretching far across the square. I really must get going, Seriema thought. What's wrong with me these days? If this is what men do for me, then I'd willingly consign the whole damn tribe of them to the blackest pits of perdition . . . Goodness! What in the world can that be?

While she'd been lost in thought, her eyes had tracked idly past the entrance tunnel to the Precincts and up the soaring palisades of stone that divided the Holy City from the town below. The clouds, which had lifted a little in the brief, merciful lull since the snow had ceased, were sinking again now. The temperature had risen throughout the day. The rain was drifting back in its inexorable, ceaseless drizzle, and already the snow was beginning to soften and disperse. Hazy tentacles of mist were threading the pinnacles of the high stone cliffs. Seriema squinted up into the murk. She could have sworn she'd seen something moving up there. Dark shapes with wings . . .

There was no warning. A rough hand, damp and reeking of sweat and blood, came over her shoulder and clamped down hard across her nose and mouth. An arm hooked around her ribs, hard and bruising, cutting off what little breath remained.

Seriema, struggling, suffocating, her mind one endless silent scream of terror, was dragged away from the window and hurled to the floor. As the hands loosed their hold she gasped a grateful breath and scrambled to her hands and knees, only to collapse again, in a flash of pain, the breath driven out of her once more as the unseen assailant kicked her in the side. Whimpering, she tried to curl up to protect herself, but hard hands seized her and flung her over on to her back. Someone knelt over her, straddling her and pinning her to the floor.

Seriema looked up into the broad face of a young man, aged by hardship, toil and privation, and swollen and contused by what looked to have been a savage beating. His simple, hard-wearing labourer's garb was stained with weather, dirt, and blood – streaks of dried, dark gore and, far more terrifyingly, a spatter of brightest crimson that glistened, fresh and new, on his jerkin and the sleeve of his coarse woollen shirt. His eyes were like those of a reptile, cold and flat with hate. All of this she noticed in passing. Her attention was fixed upon the broad, shining blade of the knife in her assailant's hand. With her eyes on it, she didn't see – until far too late – his other hand come up to strike her. There was a flicker of motion in the corner of her eye, then a starburst of agony from a stunning blow on the side of her face. The last thing she saw as the blackness crashed down was the cruel, gleaming knife.

In a half-conscious daze, Seriema heard the sharp rasp of ripping fabric. She fought to open her watering eyes, and succeeded just in time to see a wad of black cloth coming down towards her face. Dirty fingers pried into her mouth, trying to force it open, and Seriema bit down on them as hard as she could. With a howl of pain he snatched them back, and left Seriema gagging on the taste of warm blood. She only had time to get in one good, loud scream before he hit her again, but maybe it would be enough. This time the blood in her mouth was her own, and her teeth felt loose in her jaw. As he pushed the wadded gag back in her mouth, she felt one of them tear loose from its socket. Oh, if only someone would come in answer to her scream! Please, Presvel, she thought, please come. Then she remembered the fresh blood on her attacker's jerkin, and felt cold all over. Did it come from her assistant? Was Presvel lying dead somewhere?

It was as though the man had read her mind. 'That was a mistake,' he told her, as he bound the gag in place. 'You bought yourself nothing but trouble with that foolish scream. There's nobody to help you. Before I came in here I checked all these upstairs chambers, and your man has gone. Luckily for him, eh?'

Seriema tried to launch herself up at him, flailing with her fists, then froze, with the kiss of cold steel at her throat, as the knife seemed to leap back into his hand.

'That was another mistake,' the man said, 'but I'll not hold that against you. I left you untied for a reason, after all. I want you to struggle, as my lifemate did, and try to resist, as she did, and have the fight beaten out of you, as she had when your soldiers came.' He shrugged. 'It's a pity I'll have to do without your screams, but it can't be helped.'

He sat back on his heels, still poised over her with the knife at her throat, but looking down on her as though she were a cockroach that he was about to crush beneath his boot. 'Let me tell you, Lady Seriema, what happened yesterday to my lifemate, when your bully boys came to cast us out of our home. I want you to know every single detail of what she suffered, for then you'll know exactly what I'm going to do to you. You're going to suffer everything she suffered – the humiliation, and the terror, and the pain. You're going to feel everything she

elt – and more. Let me tell you how they beat her—' As he
poke, his hand smashed across her face, once, again, and then
a third time.

As the ringing in her ears subsided, Seriema heard his voice
again. 'They slit her clothes off with a knife . . .' The blade
moved away from her throat, and she felt the cold steel against
her skin as the blade began to slide into her bodice. 'I should
keep very still, if I were you,' he warned her. 'Felyss did. She
was terrified the knife would slip – as you should be. As you
might expect,' he went on as he worked, 'they raped her after
that. There were two of them though, and there's only one of
me, so I may have to think of one or two little extras, just to
even up the score.'

'Won't *she* be coming in search of you soon?' Rochalla asked.
She owed Presvel so very much that she didn't want to appear
ungrateful, but her life had undergone a tremendous alter-
ation. She was exhausted and depleted after burying the last
of her family, and she desperately needed time alone, in this
quiet, clean little garret that was hopefully to be her home, to
assimilate her sudden change in fortune.

Presvel was still hovering. 'No. I locked the attic door when
I came up. Besides, she'll think I've gone already, and so I
should have, really. You'll have the place all to yourself shortly,
once Lady Seriema has gone, and then you'll have a chance
to rest.'

Rochalla smoothed her fingers down the warm, thick fabric
of the brown dress, and thanked her stars that the dismissed
parlourmaid had been just about her size. 'But I won't be all
alone, really,' she reminded him. 'Who's staying behind to look
after the child?'

'The *child*? Gracious – I never thought of that!' Presvel's face was a picture of dismay. 'Lady Seriema put the whole matter in my hands, but I don't know anything about children. One of the maids has been looking in on her, but she's always fast asleep, or pretending to be. I thought it was the shock of losing her parents, and decided it better just to leave her to come out of it herself. She's such a quiet little thing, I had forgotten all about her.'

The corners of Rochalla's mouth drew down in disapproval. 'Dear Myrial, that's disgraceful! I pity the poor little mite, I do. For all Lady Seriema's fortune, there's no one in this household has a shred of common sense!' Suddenly alarmed by the realisation that she'd been scolding her new benefactor, she moderated her tone. 'Well, you don't have to worry now. Off you go to your ceremony, and I'll slip down every now and again to keep an eye on her. Don't worry, I'll listen carefully for anybody coming back, and retreat to my little nest up here.'

'My dear, you're a treasure!' Presvel stooped down to embrace her, and she could not stop herself from flinching back. Quickly he checked himself, and looked away. 'I'm sorry Rochalla. I promised I wouldn't do that.'

Rochalla floundered in the awkward moment, not knowing what to say – until the sound of a terrified, sharp scream from downstairs removed any need for a reply.

Rochalla, her reflexes cat-quick from her nights of prowling the Tiarondian streets, reacted first. When a woman screamed like that, the only reasons were murder, rape, or both. Without thinking, she snatched up the heavy brass candlestick from her bedside, and was halfway down the attic staircase before Presvel had time to take a breath. She turned the key in the door at the bottom, and slipped along the corridor on swift but silent feet. She wanted to see what was happening before she committed herself to any action. The silence that had followed the scream was ominous, and she had too much sense to run headlong into the hands of a killer. Behind her, she could hear Presvel's feet, clattering down the wooden stairs. Be quiet, you fool – oh, please, be quiet! she thought desperately. Surprise may be the only advantage that we have.

Earlier, when they had tiptoed past on their way up to the attic, Presvel had pointed out Lady Seriema's chamber. Now, as she neared the room, she saw that the door with the richly carved panels was slightly ajar. Coming from inside, she could hear the low, harsh murmur of a man's voice, followed by the sharp cracking impact of several blows, which made Rochalla flinch in sympathy.

A light touch on her shoulder sent a cold flash of shock right through her body.

'Shhh!' It was Presvel's voice. His face was bloodless and shiny with terror and his hands were trembling. 'Stay there – don't go in. I'm going downstairs for a weapon.'

'Hurry,' Rochalla whispered. For all Seriema's heartless reputation, she hated to think of another woman in such a plight.

It was hard to wait, and do nothing, and have no idea what was happening. Rochalla edged forward, barely breathing, and peered around the edge of the door. Though the intruder had his back to her, and was hiding her view of what was taking place, she could see what was happening reflected in the tall mirror on its pivoting stand across the room. Her stomach turned to ice as she saw the man kneeling over Seriema, saw that the woman had been gagged with black cloth torn from her own wool gown, saw the blade, catching starbursts of light as it trembled as if with eagerness, poised at her throat.

Without warning he moved the knife. In disbelief and horror Rochalla saw the blade slice down into the woman's breast.

Not rape then, but murder or mutilation! Without another thought she darted into the room and brought the heavy brass candlestick crashing down on the killer's head. With a groan he crumpled, and went sprawling over the writhing body of his victim.

But Rochalla was no Ivar, with a slaughterman's strength in the muscles of her arms. Though her blow half stunned her victim, it also jarred the candlestick from her hand. Suddenly he was slouching to his feet, his burning eyes all glazed and blood running in streams down his face from the wound across his scalp. With the roar of a maddened bull, he turned on her, his great blade flashing through the air from side to side. Seeing the blade clean and clear of blood, she realised her mistake – too late. It was rape he'd had in mind, initially, at least, and he'd been slicing cloth, not flesh. She could probably have waited for Presvel, and kept herself out of this mess.

Rochalla backed away from him, trying to remember the positions of the furnishings – the chair, the mirror and the bed – while always keeping her eyes on the weaving knife. She mustn't panic, she told herself, or scream, or try to run. That would only get her killed. She knew he would be gathering himself to rush her any time now, so she must be ready, and nimble, and fast on her feet to dodge—

He came at her, not in the mindless charge she had expected but in a great bound like an uncoiling spring, the heavy blade raised high above his head, arcing down with savage force in the momentum of his leap. Rochalla jerked her body sideways, bumping against the mirror. The knife flashed past her face, so close that she could feel the draught, and caught for an instant in her sleeve, tangling with the sturdy worsted cloth before she tore herself away. Through her terror, she was conscious of a ridiculous flash of anger that he'd ruined the first good new garment she'd had in years, and it was not until a heartbeat later that she felt the cold shock of savage pain, then a surge of hot blood down her arm.

The moment of frozen horror nearly killed her. Only the bright flash at the edge of her vision warned her. Feeling the mirror at her shoulder, she dodged around the side of it. With a splintering crack, the knife smashed down into the priceless silvered glass. The impact flipped the bottom of the mirror upwards. It cracked hard against his knees, and a howl of pain and rage burst from him.

Rochalla realised that he was beginning to corner her, forcing her further and further away from the door. If she didn't make a break now, while he was distracted, she never would. Summoning all her courage, she tried to slide and sidestep past him, but there was too little space, and he turned and lunged at her again. She hurled herself down, wincing as the weapon slashed the air above her head. She had almost forgotten her assailant now. The knife was her enemy. The heavy, coldly glittering blade had taken on a life and purpose of its own.

There was no more room to move. Rochalla found herself trapped in the corner, the knife above her, ready to strike, the face of her attacker, wild-eyed and covered in blood, glaring down at her with a savage animal rage for her attempt to thwart his plans. His eyes burned into her – then suddenly his expression altered, changing swiftly from a grimace of agony to a vacant, slack surprise. The knife fell from his hand and clattered to the boards a hair's breadth from Rochalla's outstretched hand. She retained just enough presence of mind to scuttle from the corner before he crumpled down on top of her.

She looked up to see a sword sticking out of the assailant's back, and Presvel, shaking from head to foot, looking down at the body as if he couldn't tear his eyes away. Then, with a cry, he reached down to Rochalla, helped her to her feet and hugged her tightly. This time – shaken, grateful, and desperate for comfort – she did not flinch away.

A voice broke through their tableau. 'Presvel?' Though the slurring word was thickened by split and swollen lips, the tone was sharp with venom. Lady Seriema stood there, swaying like a willow in the wind, but on her feet, clasping the remains of her bodice around her like the tatters of her dignity. Her face, a mass of bruises, was like a thunder sky, and her eyes flashed like lightning between their swollen lids. 'How *dare* you!' she snarled. 'Get that slut out of my house.'

Presvel's mouth fell open. 'But Lady . . .' he began to protest.

Great Myrial, woman, I just saved your blasted life! Rochalla thought. *Of all the damned ingratitude!* The fear that was still scouring through her veins began to curdle into anger – but her furious response was drowned by the clatter of feet on the stairs.

Everybody flinched. The anger seemed to fall away from Seriema like a cloak, and she ran to huddle behind Presvel, who reached down for the sword.

'Hello?' A voice called. 'Is anybody here?'

At least he didn't sound *like a mad knifeman, Rochalla* thought, relaxing a little.

Suddenly a head came round the door – that of a dark-haired man with a worried expression. He seemed not to notice the state of Lady Seriema, or the upturned furniture and broken mirror, or the corpse upon the floor. 'Please,' he asked, 'is my daughter here?'

Presvel's mouth fell open. 'In the room at the end of this corridor,' he answered faintly.

The man's face lit up like sunrise. 'Thank you – oh, thank you!' Then he was gone.

Twenty-eight

Out of the Fire

His heart racing, Tormon ran into the pink-flowered bedroom. The only sign of his little girl was her neatly folded clothing lying on a chair, a small hump beneath a pile of quilts, and a fan of dark hair on the pillow. 'Annas,' he cried. 'Annas!'

No sound came from the canopied bed. There was not the slightest stirring in the mounded bedclothes. Cold fear stabbed the trader's heart. He ran across the room and pulled back the quilts, dreading what he might find, but she seemed to be only sleeping, her colour good, if a little flushed, and her breathing slow but even. So why hadn't she heard him shouting? Why had she not woken?

'Annas?' he called, shaking her gently by the shoulder. 'Annas, love – it's me – it's Dad. Everything's going to be all right now. I've come to get you.'

For a moment there was no response, then the child's dark eyes sprang open. With a whimper, she threw her arms around his neck and began to sob.

Scall was waiting nervously, with the horses, in the courtyard behind the kitchen. He was anxious not to let Tormon down, but he knew he had no right to be here, and he was

483

overawed by the magnificence of the mansion, its solid, high, intimidating bulk. The multitude of windows seemed to look down on him like so many accusing eyes, and at any moment, he was sure, the back door would open and angry housefolk would come bursting out to send him on his way.

Scall also felt uneasy because the day was fading, and the corners of the high-walled yard were sinking into deep, dim pools of shadow. Though the rain had started again, it was not the discomfort of the drizzle that bothered him, but something else – a weird, uneasy sensation like an unplaceable itch between his shoulders. A feeling that he was not alone. The horses, not to mention the snap-tempered little donkey, seemed even less happy about this place than he did, and there was a lot of snorting, foot-stamping, head-tossing, eye-rolling and shifting about.

Scall was becoming really worried now. Seriema kept her horses up in the stables of the Precincts, so there were no stalls here in which he could pen the animals. He had hitched them to the rings in the wall provided for that purpose, but even so he had his work cut out to keep his charges quiet and under control. There were too many of them, with the two troopers' horses, the donkey, the pair of Sefrians and the neat-footed little chestnut he was already beginning to look upon as his own. If they snapped their tethers and there was a general stampede, he wouldn't be able to do a thing.

Nervously, the boy scanned the yard. There was little to be seen: a washing line, two drooping shrubs in pots outside the kitchen door, a pump with a long, curved handle, and the narrow iron gate that led, Scall had discovered on investigation, to a small, sunken garden with a fountain in its midst. 'There you are,' he told himself. 'Nothing amiss.' So why were the horses spooking?

A slight noise from above sent him spinning back towards the house, but again there was nothing to be seen. Just a big, imposing house, quiet in the fading light, with the low clouds drifting trails of mist around the gargoyle on the roof.

Scall screamed as the gargoyle flexed its wings, and launched itself into the air.

Tormon rocked his sobbing daughter, his own face wet with tears. Dear Myrial, he prayed, after what she's been through, let her be all right. Please help her to forgive me for leaving her and her poor mother to be killed. Even now, Kanella's face hung before his tear-blurred vision like an accusing ghost. No matter how hard he tried, he couldn't bring himself to believe that she was really gone, and that he alone would be responsible for bringing up their child. The thought reminded him that he should be moving. He had already decided to use the safe time, when everyone was attending the Great Sacrifice, to get out of Tiarond. And, as he had told Elion, he was never coming back. Maybe he could find some provisions in Seriema's kitchen. Since she had been kind enough to shelter his child, he was sure she wouldn't begrudge Annas a little food . . .

All at once, the scene he had witnessed in the other chamber finally registered in Tormon's mind. Seriema, her face all bruised, her dress half torn from her body, that assistant fellow and a strange girl with blood running all down her arm, a corpse on the floor with a sword in its back . . . 'What the blazes . . . ?' Tormon muttered. Gently he unclasped his daughter's arms from round his neck. 'Come on, lovey. Let's get you dressed—' At that moment, there was a thunder of feet on the stairs, and Scall's voice shrieking for help.

Annas, frightened by the screams, clutched her father

tighter, burying her face into his jerkin. The trader ran to
the door and saw Scall running along the passage from the
landing. 'Tormon,' he gasped, half sobbing with terror. 'Things
– horrible creatures – everywhere!'

Shifting the child to one arm, Tormon shook the boy
roughly by the shoulder. 'Stop this nonsense now!' he roared.
'You're scaring Annas!'

Scall shook his head, pointing back into the room. 'Go and
look – please! Look out of the window!'

With a shrug, the trader went back into the room, crossed
to the window, and parted the flowered curtains. The room
was at the front of the house, looking out on to the Grand
Esplanade and the soaring pinnacles of the palisade cliffs that
enclosed the Sacred Precincts. Up there . . . Tormon's breath
caught in his throat. Above the canyon of the Holy City, a
host of dark, winged creatures circled. Already he could see
them dropping down, in ones and twos, into the bowl below
– and even as he listened, the screams began. Tormon's
blood turned to ice. Those things were attacking the folk
in the Precincts! 'Dear Myrial,' he shouted. 'Come on, Scall,
let's get away from here!'

Scall was at the door, holding up a blanket and a bulging
pillowcase. 'I've got the little one's clothes,' he shouted, and
Tormon blessed the lad for his presence of mind. He snatched
the blanket as he went past, and wrapped it round Annas
even as he pelted down the corridor, with Scall following close
behind.

There was no time now to work out what had happened
in Seriema's chamber. Tormon saw her assistant – Presvel,
he remembered – struggling to haul the body out of the room
single-handed, and Seriema sitting on the bed, her ruined
gown replaced by a fresh garment, having her bruised face

bathed by the little blonde lass, who was talking to her in a calm and soothing voice. The trader broke the tableau. 'Quick,' he roared. 'We've got to get out!'

Instead of obeying, they all jumped up and flocked round him, demanding explanations and scaring Annas with their gabble. I've no time for this, he thought. I have to save my daughter. 'Look outside then, damn you,' he yelled. He strode across to the window – and leaped back in alarm. One of the strange winged creatures he'd seen above the cliffs was flying past the house in the direction of the Precincts. Close up, it was a hideous mockery of the human form, the pallid colour of a corpse, its flesh stretched tight across its bony frame. His injudicious movement in the window had caught its eye. Abruptly it turned in the air, heading straight for Tormon, and flew through the window in a burst of splintered glass.

The emotion of the crowd, concentrated by their need, their sheer numbers and the echoing bowl of the Sacred Precincts, hit Gilarra with redoubled force as she stepped out of the Basilica doorway. Her garb of office – the long rich robes of amethyst silk and the heavy, sleeveless, wide-shouldered over-robe, thickly embroidered with thread of purest silver and encrusted with gems – pulled at her shoulders like the burden of power itself. Its weight, together with the elaborate, jewelled silver headdress, was almost enough to pull the little Suffragan to the ground.

On either side of her she could feel the presence of her cohorts as they stepped up to flank her. For the Great Sacrifice, only one priest of Myrial was permitted to officiate – the Suffragan, or Hierarch-Elect. The others were not asked to participate in the slaying of their leader. Instead Gilarra was accompanied by Godswords: to her left, Galveron, doubtful and disapproving; to her right, the sardonic, ever watchful presence of Lord Blade. Gilarra had no eyes for them. Before her was the pyre, a vast pile of wood the height of a tall man and twice as wide. It encompassed her entire world. Set securely into the top was the stake, to which the former Hierarch, in the long white robe of the Great Sacrifice, had been bound.

The priests and Godswords had built a platform between the pyre and the temple doors, so that the Suffragan could appear high above the crowd, where the huge bonfire would not dwarf or hide her. Gilarra, about to climb up the rickety steps, found herself hesitating, shaking with nerves. She tried to swallow, but her throat was parched and closed tight as a fist. Impatiently she gestured Galveron to her side. 'Wine,' she whispered. The young officer handed a flask to the Hierarch-Elect, who took a generous gulp, and felt fortified spirits like liquid lightning blast a path down her clogging throat. Wordlessly she returned the flask, then composed herself to take the first irrevocable step up the rickety wooden stairs that led to the top of the platform.

Suddenly Blade put out a hand to forestall her. 'Here,' he said. 'I almost forgot.' He held out the Hierarch's ring with the great red stone. 'I took it off Zavahl,' he said. 'You should be wearing it now.'

'Thank you,' Gilarra said. She pushed the ring on to her finger, where it slipped round loosely, far too big for her smaller hand. Still, she could have it altered later. Summoning all her courage, she nodded to the Godsword Commander, picked up the trailing skirts of the jewelled robes, and set off up the steps.

When she made her appearance on the flimsy wooden stage, Gilarra been bracing herself for an intense reaction from the crowd – a roar, of approval, or hostility, or even derision. She was unnerved, therefore, by the utter silence that met her appearance. The atmosphere within the constricted arena of the Sacred Precincts was a haze of suppressed emotion so intense as to be almost visible, like a wraith of marsh breath hovering above the crowd. And like the noxious exhalations of the eastern marshes, it would only take a single spark to send the whole of Tiarond up in a fireball. The mood of the crowd mirrored the brooding presence of another approaching storm, palpable in the still, heavy, prickling air, and the bank of solid cloud, the deep purple-black of bruised flesh, piling itself in higher and higher ranges over the Basilica and the mountain peak beyond.

The tight-packed Tiarondians were clustered – almost too close for safety – around the Hierarch's pyre. At the very forefront, a cluster of seats had been placed for the most important citizens – merchants, mostly – all muffled up against the weather and all of them, it seemed, wearing expressions both hostile and self-righteous. In the midst of them the Suffragan noticed an empty chair, and wondered what in perdition Lady Seriema was up to, that she had elected not to attend, in defiance of the Temple's edict.

Then Gilarra looked across at Zavahl, and all thoughts of Seriema were scattered. He was as still, pale and emotionless as a block of marble, his gaze blank and uncomprehending as though he was completely unaware of what was about to happen to him – or he had managed, in some way, to blot out the reality of his plight. At the sight of him, a shudder passed through Gilarra. If things don't start to improve soon, that could easily be me this time next year, she thought.

She wished she could know exactly when the sun would sink. Already the pale, upturned faces of the crowd were blurred and obscured by shadows, and Gilarra began to worry. *I waited for sundown – did I wait too long? Am I already too late?*

Below the Hierarch, a susurrus of restless whispering could be heard from the crowd. Blade's elbow nudged her hard in the ribs, rousing her from her reverie. 'For Myrial's sake, get *on* with it,' he muttered through clenched teeth, as he handed her the flaming brand to start the conflagration.

Gilarra took a deep breath. 'O Great Myrial – hear our prayer!' she cried, and felt the congregation's own indrawn breath as she lifted the torch aloft. In a Temple-trained voice pitched to carry right to the back of the crowd, she began to intone her heartfelt plea for the mercy of the God:

'*O Great Myrial, who formed our world from your body, blood and bone.*

'*O Great Myrial, return to us.*

'*We are your children, your chattels and your harvest. You seed our souls throughout the world, and reap them in your time and at your will.*

'*O Great Myrial, return to us.*

'*Great Myrial, protect us.*

'*Great Myrial, forgive our sins and our shortcomings. Accept our atonement and our sacrifice.*

'*Great Myrial, turn your face to us once more.*

'*Great Myrial, succour and comfort us. Bathe us in the radiance of your love.*'

Gilarra's voice rose to a crescendo, winging its way over the heads of the assembled congregation. '*Great Myrial – hear our prayer!*'

As the Tiarondians echoed her words in an earthshaking roar, the Suffragan plunged her torch into the centre of the pyre. Nothing happened. The sweet oils that soaked the wood flared up a little, but the sappy, rain-soaked boughs were slow to burn. After a moment, the flames died down. As the damp wood sizzled, a vast white cloud rolled up into the heavy sky – mostly steam, not smoke. Panic spurred Gilarra's heart into a gallop. *It's going out! Oh, Myrial, no!* She lifted her eyes to the grey skies in supplication – and became aware of strange, winged creatures, circling round the palisades. What in the name of all creation were *they*?

Suddenly, from behind her, came the earth-shattering roar of an enormous creature. Gilarra felt herself falling as the fragile platform collapsed beneath her. She hit the ground hard, and something sharp struck her across the forehead, laying open the skin. She clawed at her eyes frantically, blinded by blood from the open wound and by the ceremonial headdress that kept falling across her eyes. She pushed it up hastily and rubbed her eyes back to blurry sight – just in time to see the sacrificial pyre burst into brilliant golden flame.

By the time the creature hit the window, Tormon was already halfway across the room. The others, when they saw what was in their midst, were right behind him – save for Scall, who stood frozen, his face stark white, staring at the corpse of Seriema's assailant. Tormon spared an arm from his daughter to drag the boy behind until, with a jerk, he got his legs moving and began to run again on his own. Presvel, last out, snatched the key from the inner keyhole, slammed the heavy door and locked it from outside. They heard a harsh shriek of rage and then the guttural sound of snarling, and the scrape of thick, strong claws tearing gouges from the wood.

'Come on!' Tormon yelled again, running downstairs, with Annas in his arms and Scall still sticking to his heels. 'Dear Myrial!' he shouted to the boy. 'I hope those damned things didn't get the horses!'

With the others following him, he raced down the back corridors and through the kitchen. He was far too bent on escape to pay attention to the body on the floor until Seriema let out a heartbroken wail. 'Marutha! Oh, Marutha!' Out of the corner of his eye he saw Presvel pulling her away, and paid the matter no more heed. All that mattered to him now was getting Annas away from this accursed city.

To Tormon's profound relief, the horses, though sweating and terrified, were still tied up in the yard. He was trying to keep one eye on the grey sky above, but so far, the hideous creatures seemed all to be within the Precincts. After a moment's confusion, Scall, with the donkey's lead rope in his hand, was beside his chestnut and Presvel and Rochalla, who clearly had never been on a horse in her life, were mounted double on one of the Godsword beasts. That left the Sefrians and the other trooper's horse for Seriema and himself – but he had promised to leave the extra beast for Elion . . .

Seriema looked at him. 'I'm a superb rider,' she said, with neither modesty nor conceit. Before he could say another word, she had taken the halter of the great black gelding from his hand, knotted the end of the rope to the other side of the headstall to make a rein, and had used the mounting block to boost herself up, with a little struggle, on to Avrio's broad and shining back.

'Here.' Suddenly Scall was at Tormon's other side. 'You mount, and I'll lift her up to you.'

The trader, making the lead rope into a rein as Seriema had done, scrambled up on to the Sefrian stallion and took Annas in front of him. 'All right – let's go!' With many nervous glances at the darkening sky above, the little cavalcade clattered out of Seriema's yard.

The Grand Esplanade was a scene from darkest nightmare.

People were streaming out of the Precincts' tunnel, running, screaming, slipping and falling on the slushy ground. A few winged shadows swooped and killed, but it looked to Tormon as though most of the creatures preferred the easier pickings in the packed bowl of the Holy City. *The whole of Tiarond is in there,* he thought with a shudder. *So many people . . .* A pang of fresh concern for Annas made him drive the stallion forward, urging it with his knees and heels to a faster pace. The other horses followed, going as fast as they dared down the slippery, slushy streets. Behind them, the screams of a dying city began to recede.

As soon as the Suffragan and Lord Blade left the Temple to begin the Great Sacrifice, Veldan, Toulac and Kazairl crept up into the shadows of the open doorway. 'Elion?' the Loremaster sent out a call. 'Are you there?'

'I'm in position,' came his reply. 'Near the foot of the pyre, disguised as one of the Godsword troops. I'll be ready to step in if anything should go wrong. I'll meet you later, over the other side of the pass, depending on when I can slip away.'

Veldan's mouth was dry with apprehension, though Kaz seemed like his usual, cocky self. 'Do you remember the plan?' she asked him for the hundredth time. 'Are you sure?'

'Don't worry, Boss. I'll take care of it. Look – it's time.'

They saw Gilarra lift the torch to the pyre. With a roar Kaz burst out of the shadows and charged through the Temple doorway, leaping up on to the platform, which splintered beneath his weight, spilling Lord Blade, the new Hierarch and the other bystanders to the ground in a burst of broken timber. The torch flew up into the air and blew out as it came arcing down.

'Let me,' Veldan heard Kaz say in mind-speech.

'Kaz — no!' she cried, but it was too late. The firedrake exhaled mightily, his sides heaving, and a jet of flame shot forth to ignite the pyre, adding to the confusion and fear. In the Temple courtyard, people were screaming. Already folk were being crushed and trampled as the crowd shrank back from this demonic monster of the flame.

Though the firedrake's flame was hot enough to ignite the damp wood, a cloud of thick grey smoke began to pour out of the centre of the pyre. It billowed across the courtyard in the swirling wind, confounding the aim of the Godsword archers stationed to either side. The Sacrifice screamed as flames began to flare, leaping up around the stake and round his feet. Impervious to his own fire, Kaz stretched his long neck up to the top of the pyre and plucked the stake, with Zavahl still securely attached, from the top of the burning pile. With a quick, sideways flick of his head he snatched the former Hierarch through the flames, and dragging the stake by its end, turned tail and bolted back through the Temple doors — but not before a flicking sideswipe of his tail had scattered the sacrificial pyre, sending a firestorm of burning brands across the square.

As the firedrake hurtled into the Temple, the two women moved smoothly out of the shadows behind him and closed the massive, delicately balanced doors of bronze. Immediately Kaz backed up broadside and put his heavy body against them to wedge them shut. Already angry cries and blows could be heard on the other side, interspersed with screams of panic from the crowd. Rapidly Veldan and Toulac cut Zavahl free from the stake and beat out the odd smouldering patch on his smudged and tattered sacrificial robe. The Loremaster was a little troubled to see that he'd lost consciousness, but her companion was less concerned. 'Fainted, I think, at the sight of Kaz,' she said tersely. 'He's breathing all right. Just a bit singed here and there, but nothing at all bad.' She shot a glare up at the firedrake. 'No thanks to you, you silly great bugger. Fire was never in our plan!'

'It was a good diversion, though, wasn't it?' Kaz replied with innocent glee.

'Come on, the pair of you!' Veldan urged. 'Let's get out of here!'

Between them they hoisted and hauled Zavahl up on to the firedrake's back, and then scrambled up themselves, with Toulac remembering to haul up the sacks of food she had brought from the upper caves. Kaz grunted a little with the weight of an extra passenger. 'It's a good thing none of you has been eating much lately,' he muttered. 'Hold on tight, girls – here we go!'

With a bound he sprang away from the doors, and they fled into the shadowy recesses of the Temple with a hail of arrows clattering at their heels as the Godswords burst through into the building. 'Bloody good thing it's so dark back here,' Toulac muttered. 'They can't see to shoot.' In the open stretches of the building's broad back corridors, the speed of the firedrake easily outdistanced the men on foot. To Veldan's relief, they were through the lower guardroom in a flash, and out into the tunnel above.

Blade was on his back, trapped beneath a solid length of timber. One of the supports of the platform lay right across his body and was wedged tightly in position by other broken bits of the fallen structure. Helplessly he watched as the firedrake burst through the wreckage and plucked Zavahl from the pyre. Blade cried out in rage to be cheated of his prey. Since returning to the Citadel with his captive, he had questioned Zavahl repeatedly concerning the other presence in his mind, but neither Hierarch nor dragon had given him any kind of answer that made sense – and now they were escaping! Curse that interfering woman and her firedrake!

Frantically the Godsword Commander fought to free himself. Though the support had not been heavy enough to inflict much damage, it was wedged so tightly that he could not move it. Still dragging the stake, the firedrake vanished back inside the Temple, and the great bronze doors swung shut behind it. The Godsword soldiers were beginning to collect themselves now. Some were already hammering at the doors, which apparently would not budge. Blade, almost wild with frustration, hammered on the restraining timber with his clenched fist. 'Somebody get this thing off me!' he bawled.

Galveron, with some half dozen guards, detached themselves from the group at the door and ran to Blade's assistance. They were halfway to him, when they stopped, their eyes on the darkening shy, their faces distorted in a rictus of horror. Before Blade could turn his head to see what they were looking at, the screams began. A horde of black-winged demons were swooping down on the crowded Precincts. Already folk were falling, bleeding, dying, as the creatures fastened on their prey, tearing at soft flesh with teeth and claws.

'Don't just stand there, damn it!' Blade roared. 'Get me free!'

Galveron came to himself, and superintended his men in freeing the jammed timber. From the corner of his eye, Blade saw the Temple doors opening, and a squad of his guards running inside. He discounted that line of pursuit. To get in behind the Temple, they must have come through the tithe caves. Rather than try to race the firedrake up the mountain, it would be better to mount another pursuit on swift horses, and go up the trail to try to overtake them at the Snaketail Pass.

Even as his mind was racing through these possibilities, the timber came free at last, and Blade scrambled to his feet. Galveron caught at his arm. 'What *are* those things?' he yelled.

'I don't know.' The Commander did know, however, that it would be impossible to defeat such numbers of a fearsome, airborne foe. Down in the Precincts there was already carnage, with blood and bodies on the ground, folk screaming, the crowd surging this way and that like a flock of terrified sheep as they tried to flee their hunters.

'Start getting folk into the Temple,' Blade ordered his second-in-command. 'Barricade yourselves inside. Where's Gilarra?' He looked around, and saw her sprawling near by, looking dazed and trying, ineffectually, to mop at the blood streaming down into her eyes. 'Help her—' he began, and then a sparkle, in the light of the still-burning pyre, caught his eye. The ring – the Hierarch's ring – had fallen from her finger and lay on the ground near by. Blade cursed. This very day he had switched the rings back, at least for the time being, so that Gilarra would be able to operate the Eye of Myrial. That was the original – the precious, true and irreplaceable ring which lay there glinting blood-red in the firelight.

Blade darted forward to pick it up, but at that moment there came a shadow above him, a concussion of wind that knocked him off his feet and a thunder-roll of wings. A hideous winged creature swooped down upon the ring with its glittering red stone, snatched it up, and bore it away. Blade gave a cry of despair and anger. The ring had gone!

Within an instant, the creature had been lost in a host of others, circling round the great bowl. There was nothing to be done, Blade knew, no way to rectify the disaster. Cursing foully he turned away, to round up a squad of men to go after the accursed firedrake and its mysterious human companion.

As Galveron looked on, furious and disbelieving, Blade and his troop of riders left the Sacred Precincts in pursuit of the Hierarch, abandoning the Callisiorans to their fate. There was no time to ponder such blatant desertion, however. The black-winged abominations dropping from the skies put paid to that. Within moments the Sacred Precincts had turned into a slaughterhouse. The ghastly creatures seemed to be everywhere, hurtling down from the cliffs around the bowl, or plummeting like hawks from the overcast skies. More and more of them were arriving by the moment, in endless numbers.

Gilarra was looking around wildly, her brain numbed with shock, barely able to comprehend that her people were being slaughtered before her eyes. Her pose of rigid horror was shattered by Galveron, who fought his way through the remains of the shattered platform and grabbed her arm. 'Hierarch!' he yelled, straining to make himself heard above the shrieks and screams of the panicking crowd. 'The people need shelter! We've got to get them into the Temple—'

Suddenly Gilarra was thinking again. 'I'll help you!' she shouted. 'Where's Blade?'

'Gone after Zavahl.' Galveron flung the words over his shoulder as he ran off to organise the remainder of his Godsword troops.

Already folk were surging up the low steps in front of the Temple door, unstoppable as the advancing tide, guided and ushered by Galveron's men, whose chief task was to prevent the panic-stricken mob from pressing forward all at once and crushing those at the front. Other Godsword soldiers were firing crossbows at the skyborne foe, but night was falling, and the light was too bad for accurate shooting. The bolts, arcing back down into the frantic crowd, were probably doing more harm than good.

While Gilarra and four Godswords kept the crowd moving forward steadily through the bottleneck at the Temple doors, Galveron managed to edge his way out into the Precincts once more, trying to help those poor souls under attack from the vile monstrosities, though for many Tiarondians, it was too late. So many bodies lay there, their throats ripped open and their guts torn out. His boots slipped and slithered on cobblestones awash with blood and entrails. The attackers were indiscriminate, taking men or women, young or old alike.

Galveron was overtaken by a killing rage. Sword in hand, he sought the invaders, slaying them as they fastened on their prey. One by one they fell to his blade, their blood, stinking, black and steaming, mingling with that of their slaughtered prey. All too soon, though, he began to find himself outnumbered as more of the enemy came teeming down from the sky, and was forced to retreat. The droves of terror-stricken people were dwindling in number now. Many had found sanctuary in the Temple, but more had fallen to the fierce winged creatures. Gathering a handful of his men, Galveron fought a rearguard action, protecting the vulnerable edges of the crowd as the stragglers made their way to safety.

Suddenly the young officer recognised Agella's voice, calm and authoritative, loud and clear above the weeping and the screams. 'You there, stop shoving! It won't get you in any faster, you idiot. Can't you see that folk are jammed up tight in front? Keep together, everyone – it's the stragglers they're taking now . . .'

MAGGIE FUREY

Galveron craned above the heads and shoulders of the crowd, and saw the smith near by, a sword in her hand, shepherding the laggards as she came. With her, to Galveron's surprise, were the family he'd rescued from Seriema's bullies the day before. Why hadn't they left the city as they had said? Belatedly, he remembered that the woman was Agella's sister. In defiance of the law, they must have come to her after all – once they had given his Godsword the slip. They were right at the back of the retreating mob, hampered by their daughter who was paralysed with terror. The parents were supporting her, doing their best to drag her along, while Agella guarded their backs with clumsy but powerful swipes of her sword.

Yet another abomination launched itself at Galveron with its fangs bared and dripping blood, and its long talons extended. It lashed out in a blur of speed, and he cried out in pain as the claws ripped the skin above his cheekbone, an inch from his eyes. He ran it through and looked for the next assailant. By Myrial, but these things were fast! His arms, face and shoulders were badly scratched and scored where the accursed creatures had penetrated his guard. The shallow wounds burned as though hot brands had been laid across his skin, and he was beginning to suspect that the claws of his foe carried some kind of venom.

The malevolent entities were still attacking, their targets those poor unfortunates on the edges of the crowd. Galveron was reminded of a wolf pack harrying a herd of deer and taking the most vulnerable – but where wolves hunted only what they needed to eat, and culled the weakest, these creatures indulged in indiscriminate slaughter which grew even more frenzied as they saw the last of their victims vanishing into the safety of the Temple.

Everyone had reached the broad sweep of the Temple steps

now. Only a handful of survivors remained outside the door when Galveron heard the smith's cry for help. Dispatching his own assailant, he ran to her assistance. He came too late. Agella's sister lay dead and bleeding at the bottom of the steps, and the smith was fighting to save the girl and her father from the clutches of the winged invaders. Seeing his lifemate already dead, the man gave a despairing cry and thrust his daughter into Agella's arms. Before the young officer could intervene, he had thrown himself forward into the creature's clutches, sacrificing himself to save the others.

Galveron grabbed the girl and, pushing the smith in front of him, raced towards the Temple. Everyone was inside now, save themselves. The great bronze doors were closing. The Godsword warrior felt claws tear at his shoulders as he threw himself through the narrowing gap, almost into the arms of Gilarra, who waited with Bevron and their terrified son.

With a hollow boom, the great doors closed. The survivors – all that remained of the citizens of Tiarond – were besieged.

Here, in the narrow zigzag corridors, Kaz's size offset his speed. He could not manoeuvre so quickly round the cramped turns, and was forced to scuttle at an awkward half-crouch so as not to smear his passengers against the ceiling. After a time Veldan could hear the sounds of pursuit catching up with them again. 'How much further?' she asked Toulac.

'Not too far – I hope!' the veteran replied. Veldan, with Zavahl slung over the firedrake's neck in front of her, heard him beginning to mutter and moan. She pressed the back of his neck to keep his head down. 'Not now,' she prayed. 'Please don't wake up now.'

Suddenly, Veldan heard Elion's voice in her mind. 'Veldan

– they're here! They're attacking the crowd in the Precinct! *The Ak'Zahar are here!'*

A cold spear of terror rammed through Veldan's guts. Here? The vampires here? 'Elion? Are you all right? What's happening?'

'I'll be all right. Blade has worked out that he can't follow you across the mountain. He's decided to take a troop of men and ride around to the pass, so don't dawdle. I'm joining them, I'll give them the slip later.' For all his reassuring words, Elion sounded as terrified as she felt. 'Oh, perdition! This is terrible! They're hunting the crowd in the Precincts. Easy prey. Poor bastards are packed in so tight they can't escape. There'll be dreadful carnage in here.'

Kaz had reached the vast open spaces of the lower storage cavern. They streaked across, gaining a precious minute or two. Even so, before they reached the far side they heard the zing and slap of crossbow bolts, though none came near enough to reach them. The last stretch of corridor was fairly straight, and Kaz could make much better time.

'We're out of the Precincts now, and heading down into the town.' Elion's voice sounded once again in the Loremaster's mind. 'We should get clear, I hope – the Ak'Zahar are concentrating all their attentions on the Precincts.' He was having trouble, as always, managing his horse, Veldan realised, and his voice tailed away as he concentrated on keeping his seat.

'Take care, Elion,' she called to him.

There was a moment's hesitation, then he spoke. 'Thanks, Veldan. You too.'

The Loremaster turned her mind back to her own escape.

They were back to the upper reaches now, and in minutes they had passed the entrance to the upper guardrooms – and were out.

'Get round the corner of the ledge,' Toulac shouted. 'Out of bowshot.' Without warning, she slipped down from Kaz's back.

'What are you *doing*?' Veldan yelled.

'Locking the door, you ass! Now *move*! I'll be there in a minute!'

Veldan and Kaz, safe around the corner, heard shouts, the sound of bowshots, then a curse. Then silence. Veldan and Kazairl looked at one another, the firedrake angling his head back on his sinuous neck. 'I'm going back,' said Veldan firmly.

'In your dreams, sweetie,' snapped the firedrake, and lumbered into motion. 'I'm not having both of you killed.'

'Damn it, Kaz – we can't just leave her . . .'

'Hey – wait for me, you idiots!' The voice, very much out of breath, stopped their quarrel dead. Veldan looked back to see Toulac hurrying behind them, slipping and slithering along the ledge. A crossbow quarrel was sticking through the sleeve of her sheepskin coat, and though there was a small patch of blood soaking through the soft hide, it was clear that the weapon had barely caught her. She was swearing as she came, with viciousness, venom and great originality.

Laughing with relief, Veldan reached down to help her friend scramble up. Toulac may have been gasping, but from somewhere, she could still find breath to complain. 'Look at that! Just look at it! My best coat! Those bloody bastards! Had that coat for years, I have . . .'

Veldan and Kaz exchanged another look. Despite pursuit, peril and hardship, they dissolved into laughter. After a moment, Toulac joined in, and the sound of their mirth echoed across the stony slopes as they made their way back up through the high, safe reaches of the mountain.

TWENTY-NINE

The Archimandrite

The Archimandrite got up before sunrise, as he had done each morning since Shree had gone away. As the rising sun set the grass aglitter around the Tower of Tidings, he paced the stretch of green turf between tower and lake, and worried. What was happening to his Loremasters in Callisiora? Why hadn't Shree reported? What had gone wrong? As he walked, his imagination offered one scenario after another, each one more alarming and more dreadful than the last.

Cergorn was at the far end of his paced-out track, on the shores of the Upper Lake, when a call from the tower brought him speeding back at the gallop. Veldan had made contact at last! Her telepathic voice, boosted by the listeners in the tower, sounded stronger and more positive than it had done in months, though, as she sketched the brief details of recent events, he wondered why. His own heart plummeted towards his hooves with every word of her account. The dragon dead? His mind – the mind of Aethon the Seer, whose vast store of lore and wisdom was so badly needed – trapped in the body of an unwilling and terrified human? Kaz revealed to the whole of Tiarond, the Sacred Precincts in an uproar, and the Loremasters pursued by Godswords? Cergorn dropped his face into his hands and groaned — but worse was to come. The news that Thirishri was missing pierced him like a sword through his heart.

With great determination, the Archimandrite put aside the pain and fear as an indulgence he could not afford just yet. 'Come home,' he told her. 'Elion, too. Give the Godswords the slip as fast as you can, and get back here. Once you're all safe in Gendival, we'll find some way to deal with this mess.'

'All right,' said Veldan. 'I'll see you soon — with company. I've found you a new Loremaster.'

'*What?*'

'We'll be back as soon as we can,' the Loremaster interrupted quickly. 'We'll be on our way shortly. We just have to rescue a horse first.'

'A *horse?*' Cergorn couldn't believe what he was hearing. 'What the blazes do you think you're playing at, girl? You get back here at once. Veldan? Veldan!'

There was no reply. With a swift glance round to make sure no one was watching, the Archimandrite kicked the base of the tower, and swore.